THE HISTORY

OF THE

TEMPLE OF JERUSALEM

TRANSLATED FROM

THE ARABIC MS. OF THE IMÁM

JALAL-ADDÍN AL SÍÚTÍ

WITH NOTES AND DISSERTATIONS

BY THE REV. JAMES REYNOLDS

Elibron Classics
www.elibron.com

Elibron Classics series.

ISBN 1-4021-3253-0 (paperback)
ISBN 1-4021-2664-6 (hardcover)

This Elibron Classics Replica Edition is an unabridged facsimile of the edition published in 1836 by A. J. Valpy, London.

THE HISTORY

OF THE

TEMPLE OF JERUSALEM.

كتاب اتحاف الاخصا بفضايل المسجد الاقصي

تاليف الشيخ الامام (مولانا) العلامه (العامل)

العالم العلم الشيخ ابرهيم* السيوطي

رحمه الله (تعالي) ورضي عنه وارضه

(امين)

The words within a parenthesis are peculiar to the (probably) more recent MS.

* One MS. gives محمد for ابرهيم

THE HISTORY

OF THE

TEMPLE OF JERUSALEM:

TRANSLATED FROM

THE ARABIC MS. OF THE IMÁM JALAL-ADDÍN AL SÍÚTÍ.

WITH NOTES AND DISSERTATIONS.

BY THE REV. JAMES REYNOLDS, B.A.

LATE SCHOLAR OF CATHARINE HALL, CAMBRIDGE.

JUVAT IRE JUGIS, QUA NULLA PRIORUM
CASTALIAM MOLLI DIVERTITUR ORBITA CLIVO.
VIRGIL.

PUBLISHED UNDER THE AUSPICES OF
The Oriental Translation Fund of Great Britain and Ireland.

LONDON:

A. J. VALPY, M.A.

PUBLISHER TO THE ORIENTAL TRANSLATION FUND, &c.

RED LION COURT, FLEET STREET.

M.DCCC.XXXVI.

A. J. VALPY, M. A.
PRINTER TO THE ORIENTAL TRANSLATION FUND,
RED LION COURT, FLEET STREET.

TO

THE RIGHT HONOURABLE

GEORGE

EARL OF MUNSTER,

VISCOUNT FITZCLARENCE,

BARON TEWKESBURY,

&c. &c.

THE FOLLOWING TRANSLATION

IS VERY GRATEFULLY AND RESPECTFULLY

INSCRIBED.

TRANSLATOR'S PREFACE.

THE following work, entitled 'Choice Gifts existing in the advantages of the Masjidu-l-Aksá,' * includes an account of the history and antiquities of that renowned Muhammadan basilica, as well as of the adjoining Al Sakhrá: it contains also historical and traditional notices of the Holy City of Jerusalem, wherein these places of worship are situated, and of Palestine and Syria, the scene of early Muhammadan success.

The two MSS. of this work, to which the Translator has had access, are deposited in the British Museum, and belong to Rich's Collection. They are of different ages: the more recent MS. is the most legibly written; but the

* The word فَضْل seems to denote "*superabundant merit,*" and hence "privileges," "meritoriousness," "works or gifts of supererogation."

earlier possesses a more accurate text, and is that which the Translator has generally found it convenient to abide by. There are many various readings throughout; and the arrangement of the introductory matter is different in the two different copies. But the only important discrepancy between them appears to consist in a variation in the author's name: the older designates him as Ibráhím, the more recent as Muhammad; not that such a variation is so important in an Oriental MS. as it would be in a European one, the uniform practice of *surnames* adding a greater degree of precision than before existed; but still the substitution of so differently formed a word as *Muhammad*, for *Ibráhim*, can scarcely be attributed to oversight, especially in a title-page. It is therefore probable that one MS. was derived from some ultimate copy, varying from that whence the other was transcribed. The two MSS. coincide in designating the author as a Moolla and a Shaikh,—a divine, that is, and a teacher, or public professor, or a man of rank and respectability. They both give him the gentile appellation Al-Siútí, denoting, in a general sense, a native of Siút, in Upper Egypt. One adds the title of Amil, signifying either an intendant of the finances, a collector of the revenue, who is at the same time invested with some magisterial authority, (an officer somewhat resembling the ancient quæstor,) or simply 'the Author:' the other substitutes for this last, the word Imám, which is a word of widely various signification, but which, with the majority of orthodox Musalmáns in the early centuries, and universally, perhaps, in modern times, expresses *a priest*, one who leads the public prayers. Both MSS. coincide in determining the age in which the author lived (which, Ockley asserts with regret, can so seldom be done as regards Oriental writers):—"I said, to pass my time in the venerable house of God, is better than a return to Cairo, in the beginning of the year 848 from the prophetical Hijra," (*Introduction,*) which date corresponds with April, A. D. 1444.

The appellation Al-Síútí, or Al-Usíútí, coupled with the date, would seem to afford us some clue to the author. There would appear but little doubt, that the copyist who wrote the title-page of one MS. and perhaps of both MSS. designed thereby to attribute the work to the celebrated

Jalál-Addín-Abdurrahmán-Al-Síútí, a very learned commentator upon the Korán, and a most voluminous writer. But there was another Jalál-Addín, also a commentator upon the Korán, one of whose names is Muhammad. The latter does not bear the gentile cognomen of Síútí, his name at length being جلال الدين محمد بن احمد المحلي Jalál-Addín-Muhammad-Ibn-Ahmad-Al-Mahallí. (Pococke, Specimen, Notes, p. 368, &c.) This Jalál-Addín illustrated the Korán with certain short scholia and notes, but, dying before he had fully completed his labours, the remainder was accomplished by Jalál-Addín-Al-Síútí, who seems to have considerably enlarged upon the comments of his predecessor and namesake. There is but little doubt, that the greater part of the following work must be attributed to this last Jalál-Addín, being compiled with some variations and additions from his commentary. To him may also be assigned the ninth chapter, and the more historical passages interspersed in different parts. We know that Jalál-Addín-Al-Síútí was an eminent historian. His book entitled 'The Lyre, or Harp,' or 'The Flowery Meadow,' (Mizhar) is quoted with approbation by the very learned

Pocock; and we might readily conclude that an author who was at once an eminent historian and divine, and who had drawn from his stores of information upon the latter topic the greater portion of the subject-matter of those chapters which relate to Muhammadan theology, would not, in arranging the historical parts of his work, fail to recur to his own historical knowledge. But, in truth, Ockley (Hist. Sar., vol. i.) expressly quotes a MS. history of Jerusalem by Jalál-Addín-Al-Síúti, and appeals to its authority in support of the fact of a difference of opinion between Alí and Othmán respecting the expediency of the Khalíf Omar-Ibn-Al-Khattáb's visit to Jerusalem, to receive its submission. This story is found in the ninth chapter of the following translation, the original of which is, in all probability, the work alluded to by Ockley.

Unless, however, the two MSS. consulted by the translator are extremely incorrect, the introductory portion of this work cannot be the production of Jalál-Addín-Al-Síúti: that author was born in the year of the Hijra 849, and completed his commentary upon the Korán A. H. 871; whereas the writer of the Introduction remained at Mecca (as stated above) after the departure of the other pilgrims in the year of the Hijra 848. This is the difficulty; and it seems to have constituted the difficulty which perplexed the copyists. The Introduction purports to be written before Al-Síútí was born: the mass of the work is evidently to be ascribed to Al-Síútí. Possibly it was with a view of evading this difficulty, that one copy gives Muhammad as the author's name, thus ascribing the whole book to the elder Jalál-Addín, and that both omit the prænomen (Jalál-Addín), which would have fixed the authorship too decisively. The names Ibráhim and Muhammad are indeed neither of them inconsistent with that of Abdurrahmán; the latter being the epithet superadded to the original name: but it is not probable that a Muhammadan would bear both names, as he generally assumes one simple name, preceded and followed by epithets or surnames; thus, for example, in the name

ابو عبد الله محمد بن ابي الحسن اسمعيل البخاري

which signifies, the Father of God's servant *(Muhammad)*, son of the Father of Hassan *(Ismaël)*—(of *Bokhara)*, where Ismaël or Muhammad would appear to be the real first-imposed name. The distinguishing name may be sometimes omitted where the individual is well known; but a change in this argues a change in the personal identity, and entitles us to look for some motive which could lead a copyist to the alteration. The name Ibráhim might, or might not, be the name of Jalál-Addín-Al-Síútí, the later author; but Muhammad was the appellation of the older; and the inscription of that name upon the title-page might reasonably induce us to conclude, that the apparent anachronism (in making Al-Síútí write a book before his birth) led one confused copyist into an error of the same kind, and brought him to ascribe to the elder Jalál-Addín a book written long after his death, whilst, with a half-consciousness of some lurking error, he admits the name Al-Síútí, which did not belong to the elder Jalál-Addín. The other copyist, giving the name of the reputed author, makes no attempt to reconcile the discrepancy.

It will be profitless to enlarge upon a subject, in discussing which our data are so scanty. Jalál-Addín-Al-Síútí may be considered the responsible compiler and composer of the work; and with regard to the difficulty of reconciling the date of the Introduction with the date of Al-Siútí's birth, we may hazard a reasonable and probable conjecture. May not Al-Síútí, who inherited the unfinished work of his namesake Jalál-Addín upon the Korán,—who so considerably enlarged, and who completed it,—have undertaken in like manner to recompile and augment a work upon the Masjidu-l-Aksá at Jerusalem, originally composed by the elder Jalál-Addín in a less diffuse manner, and prefaced by a personal narrative which he did not think proper to disturb? There are difficulties which this conjecture will not entirely solve, because the author speaks of himself in the ninth chapter as well as in the Introduction; and since Al-Síútí is the author of the former, some confusion would seem to be caused if he were not the same individual as the person who introduces himself in the latter. These difficulties are of no great moment. Accuracy was not always regarded by ancient authors in matters not affecting the grand design, nor do they often attempt to obviate possible objections. Al-Síútí may have thought it unnecessary to intimate that the individual who began the work was not the same as the writer of the ninth chapter; for this chapter contains no marks of individual character, but merely mentions the authorities and books to which the writer recurred. Upon the whole, the above conjecture may, under the circumstances, fairly obtain. Some conjecture of the kind must be made, unless we are inclined to imagine either that the dates of the Introduction in both MSS. are erroneous,—which is highly improbable; or that Pococke was mistaken in the date of Al-Síútí's birth, which is equally so. We will then assume our hypothesis to be true; and, knowing from other sources of intelligence that Al-Síútí is accountable for the mass and bulk of the work, we will regard him as the author, and leave the difficulty of explaining the discrepancy between the Introduction and the remainder of the book, to be resolved by future research.

Jalál-Addín-Abdurrahmán-Al-Síútí was probably born, and certainly flourished in Egypt. That remarkable country had long been the prey of civil convulsions, subjected to the rule of strangers, and often deprived of the advantages of political independence: but it was favoured in other respects: Egypt was a sort of debateable land, wherein the contending zealots of Muhammadan sects met upon more common ground. The *soi-disant* Fátemite Khalífs, whilst they naturally professed considerable respect for Alí, endeavoured to connect this reverence with a degree of acquiescence in those opinions which the Muhammadans of the Sunna regarded as orthodox. Of the ever-varying and trifling shades of sentiment which divided the doctors, one occasionally prevailed over the others, if espoused and maintained by the reigning Khalíf; but, in general, both under the Khalífs, and the dynasties that succeeded them, many points were left open for discussion, which elsewhere it would not be suffered to question. This degree of liberty of conscience, and freedom of deliberation, may possibly have had the effect of enlarging the mind and expanding the thoughts of the Egyptians. Certain it is, that to them we owe some of the most interesting, eminent, and intelligent of the Arabic writers. Our author lived under the dynasty of the Circassian Mamlúk Sultáns of Egypt. He is said by Casiri, in his 'Escurial Catalogue,' to have written singly more works than others perhaps have read. It is probable, however, that many of these works are erroneously ascribed to him; and many others he merely compiled. If we could rely upon Casiri's authority, Jalál-Addín-Al-Síútí was indeed a most prolific author, who might be entitled a Muhammadan *Bede.** Grammar, rhetoric, dogmatical and practical theology, history, criticism, and medicine, including anatomy, comprise some of the subjects upon which he wrote. His medical works are doubtless of no great value: they probably include the maxims of the school of Salernum (who in fact borrowed their theory and practice from the Arabians). But it would be interesting to examine, whether his knowledge of anatomy enabled him to avoid in any degree the errors of his age. His criticism and system of logic were probably modelled after the rules of the schoolmen, and consisted of mere quibbling evasions, substitutions of expressions for ideas, and subtle argumentations, in which men then persuaded

* He composed a comment upon the Ajrúmía. This fact would imply that he was not the first expounder of the principles of Arabic grammar; for the Ajrúmía is a kind of *corpus grammaticorum*, an elegant and concise digest of the many subtle rules and canons upon the subject. It would be strange for an author to expound himself.

themselves that they solved a knotty point by a neat definition or an apt word. His theological writings are probably more valuable, as proceeding from a very skilful compiler of many of the ancient traditions and customs of the Terah-ite branch of the grand Semitic races, and as illustrating the history of the most important of all the heretical impostures that have ever prevailed in the world. But his historical compositions must possess high value. Upon the Mizhar, the accurate Edward Pococke passes what Casiri calls his "locuples commendatio," and from this professes to have derived great part of the matter of his Notes to the 'Specimen Historiæ Arabum.' Our author wrote also a history of Egypt, entitled 'The Beautiful History,' and a 'Critical History of Traditions.' Perhaps his 'History of Jerusalem' (which we have assumed to be that, of which the Translation is before us) may have been compiled from his General History, and the last-named 'History of Traditions.'

We may well imagine that these works possess much interest. Eastern history sometimes perplexes the mind, which experiences difficulty in following the rapid vicissitudes it presents:

yet there is something extremely winning and delightful in those lively records of brilliant exploits and ever-varying changes,—dynasties planted and uprooted, vast conquests and fast-following ruin, battle, bravery, grandeur, pride, caprice, fanaticism, degradation, and misery. Much of the curious annals of the various Muhammadan dynasties founded in different regions of the world, remains yet to be presented to the public, and it is surprising that it should so remain. On Oriental poetry a variation of opinion will prevail. Scarcely understood, injudiciously translated, the poetical productions of the East have met with admirers, who have hastily challenged for them a reputation which was indignantly denied as undue: thus claiming more than they deserved, the Eastern poets were awarded a rank below their true merits. But Oriental history may justly claim the suffrages of all. The Eastern historians are not always chargeable with turgid and exaggerated diction: they will often be found to relate the remarkable facts they record with considerable simplicity and clearness: they are annalists, who, relating facts sincerely and correctly, reserve their rhetorical flourishes to adorn their own reflections and digressions. Saladin's secretary, Omad, indulges in some far-fetched redundancies, expressed in difficult idiom; yet in narrating events he is as plain as Makrizi. From these historians we could expect no philosophical disquisitions. In countries where no public discussion is permitted, where deliberations are carried on and resolutions taken in the midst of secrecy and intrigue, it is impossible to obtain much insight into the hidden springs which effectuated great results,—an insight often pretended by European writers without much foundation. It is in the wonderful and important exploits, and revolutions, and reigns, recorded by the Eastern historians, that their charm and their usefulness consists; and it is on this account that they well deserve our careful perusal and study.

In grammatical science Jalál-Addín was eminently versed, and is reported by Casiri to have been the first promulgator of that system of Arabic grammar now generally adopted. If it were possible to believe this, he must have possessed a most superior degree of ingenuity and acumen, as well as a consummate knowledge of all the subtleties and metaphysical niceties of general grammar. The assertion is, however, hardly credible to its full extent. Grammarians certainly flourished long before our author, and the Jewish writers had long before applied in explanation of the Hebrew principles of grammar borrowed from the kindred Arabic. Elias Levita was contemporary with Jalál-Addín; but Hebrew grammar had been treated of long before that author. Jalál-Addín may possibly have simplified and arranged a concise system of grammatical instruction.

Among Muhammadans, however, the fame of our author is chiefly founded upon his work on the Korán: it seems to be a sort of running comment and paraphrase, wherein the ceaseless incoherencies are connected, the difficulties explained away, and the contradictions reconciled by the convenient but strange postulatum of abrogation, whereby some verses are said to be abrogated, or annulled by others,—sometimes immediately following, sometimes preceding, it being not always sure, which is the abrogated, and which the obligatory passage; strange traditions are interspersed, and acute arguments upon the absurd scruples and questions of Muhammadan theology.

Some of the works attributed to Jalál-Addín must, judging from their titles alone, be curious and interesting:—'A Confutation of the Millenarians,' or those who asserted that the world was to be at an end in the 1000th year of the Hijra, shows that the Millenarian delusion was borrowed by the Musalmán divines from the Christians. 'A Dissertation upon Muhammad's Parents,' in which they are said to have been raised up from the dead, converted to the Muhammadan faith, and received into heaven, being contradictory to several passages of the Korán, was perhaps a fable derived from the corrupt notions promulgated by the Latins respecting the parents of the Virgin Mary. A work entitled 'The Tortures of the Tomb,' and said by Casiri to be 'De Purgatorii Pœnis,' is probably not correctly so designated, for the Muhammadans do not seem to hold the Romish opinions on that subject. The work in question, in all probability, treats of the famous and long-disputed point—the eternity, or non-eternity, of the future punishment of true believers. 'Ten Dissertations upon the duty of not avoiding the plague' would seem to imply that the author held the extreme opinions of the Jabarians, or Absolute Predestinarians. 'A small Collection of Traditions,' and a 'Critical History of Traditions,' as well as 'A Life of Muhammad,' would probably throw some interesting light upon Muhammadan superstitions and metaphysics. A Manual of Prayers for the morning and evening are inscribed سِهامُ الاَصابَةُ 'unerring darts.'*

The above is all that the Translator can find upon the subject of the author. His public life indeed consists in his published works, and to deductions from these but little can be added. He lived at a period when the Ottoman power had attained the zenith of prosperity; and the latter part of his life was contemporary with the early part of that of Peter Bembo, one of the great revivers of European learning. The work upon the Masjidu-l-Aksá appears to be made up

* سِهامُ الاَصابَةُ The above title is appropriate and becoming; but a work mentioned by Casiri, upon Muhammad's wives, is strangely entitled 'Columbæ;' a name which these ladies scarcely deserved. Aísha, at least, was a very wrathful dove.

of selections from various authors and authorities, sometimes minutely and tediously enumerated. The Moslem writers are mostly faithful and sincere narrators; breach of faith in any way is generally avoided. But the exact mention of various authorities would scarcely appear to guaranty perfect correctness, (which Ockley thinks,) since the authorities themselves may often possess little or no value; and when the authority alleged, ascending step by step, terminates at last in "a Shaikh of the noble house of Shaddad," "a certain man of the province of Khorasán," it is plain that the chain of testimony, if not broken, is materially weakened. We know also that many of the Muhammadan traditions are, as the doctors themselves acknowledge, entirely forged; and although this fact does not discredit assertions unconnected with their religious belief, yet it shows that we must guard against the error of confounding particularity, in tracing up authorities to their source, with the purity of the source when found. Al-Síútí appears to have made his selection with much judgment. Even his legendary matter, although absurd, is amusing, and his historical and geographical notices display much information and erudition.

The book contains seventeen chapters. After an Introduction, in which the author describes the motives that induced him not only to visit Mecca, but also to remain there, and subsequently to proceed to Medína, and (after some interval) to Jerusalem,—concluding by a very intelligible appeal to the liberality of Musalmáns, to reward his zeal in accomplishing such excellent pilgrimages,—the first chapter relates the various names given to the Holy City at different eras, and a slight sketch of its history. Although the whole work is inscribed 'A History of the Masjidu-l-Aksá,' yet the contents of this first chapter would justify us in entitling it 'A History of Jerusalem' generally; nor do the subsequent chapters so exclusively relate to this mosque as to lead us to a different conclusion, although it be certainly a very prominent object of the author's regard. In the following chapters he proceeds to describe the Glorious Rock, the Temple of Solomon, the Mosque of Omar founded upon its site, the various saints and martyrs who have consecrated

Jerusalem by their presence, the different sacred spots now objects of veneration, the conquest of Jerusalem by Nebuchadnezzar, (which in another place seems to be confounded with the sacking of the city by the Persians in the beginning of the seventh century, as well as with its demolition by Titus,) the surrender of the Holy Abode by the Patriarch Sophronius to the victorious Abu-Ubaidah, lieutenant of the second Khalíf Omar-Ibn-Al-Khattáb, its capture by the Crusaders under Godfrey, its recovery by Al Salah-Addín, its partial restoration to the Christians under the Emperor Frederic Barbarossa, and its final subjection to Muhammadan sway: the different spots of peculiar sanctity to be found in Palestine and Syria are described; the traditionary sayings of Muhammad, miracles, legends, visions, are introduced; the sacred cities of Damascus, Acre, Tyre, Antioch, &c. are mentioned; many traditions relating to the Patriarchs are brought forward; the peculiar privileges of the Holy City, (especially the Masjidu-l-Aksá and Al Sakhra,) and of Syria and Palestine generally, are very earnestly urged; and in the concluding chapter the geographical limits of the latter countries are pointed out. Throughout the work many quotations from the Korán are introduced, as well as some from the Hebrew Scriptures; the latter generally corrupted. Glosses upon the Korán are frequent; and there are also some specimens of Muhammadan theological discussion, sufficiently grave and absurd. The object of the writer appears to be, to exalt the merits of Jerusalem as a place of prayer and pilgrimage; in pursuing which, he is sometimes obliged to evade and reconcile the superior claims of the Prophet's own cities: he does this with some dexterity, and seems to have good reason for his preference. To establish the meritorious efficacy of gifts, offerings, and alms, in the Holy Abode, (more especially, as he hints, to readers and copiers of the Korán, pious men, and constant adorers in the sacred precincts,) he heaps up authorities with ludicrous accuracy. Not only are prayers herein offered multiplied many thousand times, and sure of acceptance, but the petitioner, by an especial privilege, receives the double of whatsoever he asks. Moreover, these prayers can be offered by deputy; and since the inhabitants of the Holy City are nearer to Heaven than any of the rest of men, they are obviously the proper persons who ought to be selected by absent wealthy Musalmáns for that purpose. All this is amusing, but perhaps not entirely selfish. From many causes, much poverty and wretchedness exist in Eastern countries, and it is by a merciful counteraction that superstitious error should in any way alleviate the misery it creates.

The veneration paid to saints, relics, and holy spots, appears to have been superadded to the Muhammadan religion. The respect offered to the Kaaba was of a different nature, and appears to have been rather a perversion of that sacred and peculiar principle, which enjoined the Israëlites to pay due regard to the place which the Deity "had chosen to put his *Name* there." The corruptions of Christianity enter but very slightly into the original composition of the religion of Muhammad. Dr. C. Buchanan mentions a translation of the New Testament into Hebrew, by a Jew of Malabar, for the purpose of confuting Christianity, in which he denominates Christians "The Epicureans." This expression displays the leading idea of early Muhammadanism. To eat of things common or unclean; to go in unto the uncircumcised, and also to eat with them; to destroy the distinction of meats; to violate the τὰ νομιζόμενα, appeared to the Arabians an unaccountable and perverse outrage against the barriers of pride, self-denial, and due propriety and dignity. It was by dexterously laying hold on this feeling at an opportune conjuncture, that Muhammad succeeded; and it was partially thus that the flattering nature of his pretensions absorbed the just incredulity of his countrymen. We must not imagine, however, that our author contents himself with a mere detail of uninteresting superstitions, traditions, and legends: he introduces many geographical and historical remarks, and curious anecdotes, bearing upon the subject of the Holy Land. This subject he appears, according to Muhammadan notions, to exhaust; and we may in short agree with him in his declaration, that he who reads this book will need no other (*Muhammadan*) guide in matters relating to the peculiarities of Syria and Palestine.

Many of the author's strange tales resemble the Talmudic legends, and were probably borrowed from a common source. Notices of various Khalífs, and other princes, of different dynasties, abound; several descriptions of renowned buildings are given; and there are a few poetical passages. Style, in a compilation of this description, cannot easily be traced. The author appears, however, to write more easily and fluently when he treats of some of the nice points of theological discussion, which require a dexterous use of apt and neat phraseology.

If the Translator may be permitted to express an opinion as to the value of the original work, he would be inclined to regard it as consisting in the two following particulars:—*First*, as containing many hints, which may ultimately become the germs of much interesting thought and discussion on Syro-Arabic antiquities and history; and consequently on the history, errors, divisions, and fortunes of the Jewish and Christian religions, of which Syria-Palestina was the cradle; on the early corruptions of Christianity in the East; on the brilliant exploits of the Crusaders, the extraordinary conquests of the Saracens, the rise of the Turkish power, and all the various vicissitudes affecting a region which has been the scene of events interesting to all mankind: and, *secondly*, as displaying in a peculiar form most of the leading tenets and peculiar feelings of practical Muhammadanism. This is a subject which merits our attention. Islám, like Judaism and Christianity, possesses a definite founder and originator, not lost in cloudy traditional antiquity, but clearly presented in the full light of history, as claiming to be the authorised promulgator of a divine law. Probably one of the designs of Providence in permitting this arch-heresy to spring up and overwhelm the greater portion of the known world, was to confirm the truth by bringing falsehood into such a juxtaposition with it, as to enable us the more readily to contrast them. There is no truth, to which the mind assents, and in which it acquiesces with fuller satisfaction, than the conviction of the imposture of the Pseudo-prophet; and yet we are willing to receive the history of himself, and the statement of his doctrines, from his followers. Surely then the same principles which we rely upon, in proving that the one religion is false, may be equally relied upon if they should lead us to the conclusion that the other is true.* There is no

* Ὥσπερ τὸν χρυσὸν τὸν ἀκήρατον, αὐτὸν μὲν ἐπ' ἑωϋτοῦ

such analogy between Buddhism, or the system of the Hindoos, or of Confucius, and Christianity, as exists between the latter and Muhammadanism. Both the latter produce well-authenticated founders, exhibit intelligible doctrines, and claim our assent upon certain grounds; and the consequence has been, that sceptical writers commend the moral code of ancient sages as almost divine, but with much unwillingness decide on the falsehood of Muhammad's pretensions. The clear evidence has enforced determination.

Gibbon, indeed, remarks, and Mill copies him, that had not the progress of the Saracens been checked by their defeat near Tours, by Charles Martel, they would in all probability have soon possessed themselves of Great Britain; in which event, he says, the schools and colleges of Oxford might be now resounding with evidences and demonstrations of the truth of Muhammadanism. No observation was ever more uncandid and sophistical. If the establishment of Islám in our country was accompanied by its usual ignorance and obtusity of intellect, then the demon-

οὐ διαγινώσκομεν· ἐπεὰν δὲ παρατρίψωμεν ἄλλῳ χρυσῷ, διαγινώσκομεν τὸν ἀμείνω.—Herod. lib. ii.

strations of Musalmán Oxford would avail not more than those of Damascus the Begirt. But if it were possible to imagine that this religion could exist in connexion with that erudition, civilization, enlargement of mind, and power of argument, now to be found among our seats of learning, then we may be assured that it would have been rejected. No one could produce any demonstration or proof upon the subject which could at all weigh with acute and well-informed minds, even were they with sincere industry to apply the utmost force and vigour of intellect, combined with the most extensive learning, to the task. The Musalmáns possessed Spain, where they flourished for centuries, and cultivated literature and science with success. *They* also produced some apologetical treatises upon the subject of their religion, which only demonstrate the weakness of the cause. The truth is, that nothing is taken less upon trust than Christianity: both as it regards masses and individuals, it is carefully and zealously canvassed and examined; and nothing but the completeness of its evidence and moral power could obtain for it a footing in a country of learning, virtue, and freedom.

Some acquaintance with Islám may be of use therefore in enabling us to contrast it with Christianity. But, in pursuing this subject, many are deterred by the tediousness and dulness of the Korán. Few celebrated compositions exhibit more unimaginative prolixity and redundance than "The Forkán." The 55th chapter, imitated from the Psalms, and the adjurations which commence the 52nd and some of the latter chapters, seem to compose a principal portion of the spirit and beauty to be found in this remarkable book. The Korán also is not the sole depository of Muhammadan faith: *Tradition* is an essential part of Islám, both as regards opinions and practice; and the doctrine of *abrogation* renders it absolutely indispensable in the interpretation of the sacred signs,—so little are they entitled to the appellation of *Perspicuous*, bestowed upon them by their inventor. A book therefore which contains most of those portions of the Korán which are the chief foundations of Muhammadanism, combined with the principal authoritative traditions which illustrate and explain it, united and exhibited in an abridged, popular form, may be of service to the theological enquirer; and, of the many books of this kind current in the East, the following may, for many reasons, be regarded as a fair specimen. In it will be found most of the texts of the Korán upon which the Musalmán system is constructed, (which a reference to Sale's Preliminary Discourse and Notes will sufficiently explain,) and also many of the principal traditions: from these we may obtain a just notion of the religious sentiments of the Muhammadans. Nor are such enquiries to be regarded merely as theological: the religion of the merchant and warrior Prophet is now again fast losing its hold upon men's minds, wasting and languishing to decay: it has no such moral power over the intellect and affections, as would enable it to rekindle exhausted fanaticism: there is now also no reason to dread that Islám will again be re-inforced and re-animated by the accession of barbarian hordes of converts and conquerors; yet, when the waning crescent shall set, (to yield, we trust, to a pure sun, which warms and enlightens too,) she will leave imperishable memorials of her ascendency. The habits which Islám has engrafted; the institutions it has established; the laws it has deeply enrooted; the noble language it has consecrated; will still connect the system of Muhammadanism with the most important and interesting subjects of human research, and deserve the study and investigation of men, long beyond the period when the fanaticism and the crimes of that system shall be despised or abhorred:—

"Mentibus hæret
Pænè recens, adeò sanctum est vetus omne."

HISTORY

OF

THE TEMPLE OF JERUSALEM.

INTRODUCTION.

In the name of God, the merciful, the compassionate; He it is who can aid us; Of Him is succour to be sought. Praise be to God! whose favours are supremely great; Mighty is the wise Ordainer. His Names are too high to be computed, to be defined, to be comprehended. His wisdom shines gloriously, and His compassion is pre-eminent. That is a blessed place which He hath chosen to be His own, Because that therein He hath communicated favours to all men. This hath he chosen as his peculiar mansion, wherein to manifest his majesty. Now this place is the Venerable and Peculiar Temple (this shares his favour), together with the Glorious Pilgrimage, the accomplishment of the divine precept of the sacred journey, and the performance of all those devout services thereon dependent, according to His injunction; This is the place wherein His Glorious might is displayed, the place sanctified by the prayers of the perpetually-succeeding adorers. This is the place set apart among the temples of Islám. For as to this place, I will magnify it by prayer and holy customs, says God Mighty and Glorious. Praise be to Ḥim who by night brought His servant from Baitu-l-Harám to Masjidu-l-Aksá. Him will I praise, and to him will I return thanksgivings for that he hath granted the accomplishment of my proposed journey, the completion of my wish respecting my pilgrimage to the Venerable House of God, and the tomb of the prophet Muhammad, (on whom be God's supremest blessing and peace!) and the Consecrated Rock, and all those resting-places of Martyrs and Confessors which are within the precincts of these Temples. (These places, renowned as spots wherein prayers are favourably heard, and services liberally rewarded.) For, by God, this is what I had wished to effect before the attack of death. And do ye also hope from the generosity of the mighty and glorious God, to accomplish this excellent journey, thus to put a joyful seal to your life, and to die in the profession of Islám, please God!—Now I bear witness that there is no God but The God. He has no partner. His favours are communicated and widely distributed to the far and the nea. . also are his beneficent gifts liberally imparted, and he allows his blessings to fall both upon the obedient and the rebellious. Again, I testify also that our lord Muhammad is his servant and his apostle who is one of his most perfect creatures; For God hath made him superexcellent. I witness also the Pilgrimage which his Night of Ascent to heaven hath rendered glorious, when he was transported by night from the Baitu-l-Harám to the Mosque Al Aksá, to the highest heaven, upon the back of Al Borák, on the early watch of the "night of the journey,"* when he alighted in front of all the prophets, and prayed among them on that night in the Chapel of Al Sakhrátu of the Consecrated House. I here witness also to Gabriel, God's Muezzin and servant, who was adorned with blazing beams of light, and who enjoined upon him that which he revealed, and brought him back to his chamber in Mecca. And the dark clouds of that night removing and dispersing, he informed his wife in the morning of that which had been revealed unto him. Upon him may the peace and the blessing of God remain! also upon his noble lineage, and upon those his comrades who believed in him and supported him, and aided him, and followed the light which he

* See Note.

brought down from heaven, and engaged their hands to establish his great ordinances; Who lifted up his standard on high, who manifested forth that Faith which he enjoined, Who fought for God the due warfare, Who, after his decease, ceased not from the faithful observation of his precept, until that the minarets of the meeting-houses of Islám were erected and frequented, and until that the stairs of the pulpits of the preaching of Islám, wherein the Unity is clearly asserted, were mounted (by the preachers). Blessings be also upon his wives, the mothers of the faithful, and upon his offspring, and upon the whole company of his household,—the good, the pure, the followers (of truth)! Also upon all who follow them in holiness! Blessings be upon them until the day of judgment, and much peace!—Now, therefore, when the broad road (to Mecca) raised my admiration in description, and the shade of the clouds (of misfortune) had quickly become clear, my hitherto quiescent inclination was pressed by an urgent desire to visit the most noble of places; I said thus therefore, It is a matter of absolute necessity to hasten towards the performance of the indispensable precept of the Sacred Pilgrimage: On the whole, I resolved upon the sacred warfare, by all means; I mounted therefore the beast of burden (to carry me on my proposed journey)—the swift she-camel I desired: and I said when I firmly seated myself upon her, May God prosper her voyage, and bring her safely to anchor! Now the driver (i. e. the absolute Disposer) of all favours, who far exceeds description, drove me to the glorious Mecca. And I entered this place upon the second of the month Rabía, the beginning of the year 848. Having performed the sacrifice of the sacred Visit, I took up my abode in that venerable city,—an abode which the greatest kings of the earth might desire, if that by any means an habitation might therein be adjudged to them. I continued also (praised be God!) for the rest of this year in this glorious abode, in adoration, in sacred processions, in a happy condition. When, however, we had passed through the usual period assigned for pilgrimage, and had accomplished the sacred precepts, by performing all which is incumbent upon every pilgrim, both as regards whispered words and meditated meanings, (i. e. both inwardly and outwardly, esoterically and exoterically,) and when the whole number of days had been duly observed by us, there fell into the mind some backwardness respecting hastening to set off on our route back to the Egyptian land, whether we should set off in company. I made up my mind then to remain (in the performance of religious duties in the Temple of Mecca). I said, To remain within the venerable House of God is better than to return to Al Káhira; And in the beginning of the year 849 from the prophetical Hijra, took place my journey and my expedition to the Glorious and Elect Medína, for the purpose of visiting our prophet Muhammad, lord of the first and the last prophets. Upon him may the peace and blessing of God remain! Upon his father Adam also, and upon all the prophets and apostles who lived between the two, Peace, grandeur, generosity, and glory be upon them all! Now this blessed journey (I mean my second journey) was undertaken on account of the advantages I hoped to obtain therein (in obtaining information) from those who knew wonderful things, and were subtle expounders of significations (meanings); as also on account of (the advantage of) *his* (Muhammad's) intercession, absolutely ratified to whosoever shall perform a pilgrimage to his tomb; On account also (of the promise made to such a person that) he shall be enrolled under the banner set up on the day of judgment as a direction-point upon Muhammad's abiding-place; On account too of the blessedness of him to whom God shall grant an entrance among this assemblage, and allow to perform the salutation of the Glorious, and Elect, and Prophetical beings, lip to lip: These things therefore urged on his mind, (i. e. the author's mind,)

Also (he was induced by the merits of) the sacred procession between his tomb and his glorious pulpit; For the pilgrim thereby gathers for the second time the fruits of adoration in the garden of friendship, thus systematically arranged by the glorious God (The Garden), situated in those clouded lights, which appear amongst those (brighter) lights where his Holiness is (more especially) present; This distinguishing mark of God's favourable satisfaction is granted however to him alone who consents (to all His commands), to none other; This blessed journey therefore was accomplished in this year by the aid of God, by his prospering and forwarding mercy. I then returned to the glorious Mecca, going for the second time over the Pilgrim's route,—a route which no one of a zealous soul would consent to change for any other. Thus, then, I concluded the pilgrimage, and designed to return to the place whence I came; Yet my soul refused her consent to that which I desired: and when I saw that the matter could not be avoided or evaded, I entreated the propitious aid of God, who hath never ruined those who beg for his good help, nor caused any to repent who invoke his protection. I took up my abode therefore in a fixed place of residence near Mecca, together with my household and my children; In the country of the faithful God, in perfect confidence, earnestly entreating necessary support from Him who doth support us from the time He creates us until we die. He is the Almighty Guardian. It is the Word of the mighty and glorious God which hath unfolded mercy for man ; which mercy He will not withhold. He is the truest of speakers; and whatever you spend, he shall supply to you ; He is the best of providers ; He is the end of all good ; the Pearl (*spring*, or *primum mobile*) of all sustenance. He, remaining hidden in the depository of all subtle secrets, unfolds to us some of the obscure mysteries. That which is with you shall perish ; that with God, shall be exalted.—Now sufficient support was obtained for us, and for our household, and for all with us,—a support continually augmenting, and the clothing of abundance, and an abode in peace, and prayer every day in the Ancient Temple. I thus obtained from the venerable and noble chiefs of Mecca and Medina (upon which two glorious cities may the supremacy of prayer and peace be ever invoked!) numerous benefits; and from those who are devoted to the pursuit of adoration, I obtained many advantages, which this is not the place to recount. But this was the beginning of those events, which at length drove my mind to resolve absolutely upon a narration of the Good Journey along the Path of Adoration.—When then nine years had elapsed, in the beginning of the year 857, I returned to Al Káhira the Begirt. (May God render it an abode for Islám unto the day of judgment!) Thus, therefore, when I had returned from the glorious Hejáz, and when my late journey, thus concluded, had obtained for me those advantages which the blessed land affords, then my heart dwelt upon the accounts of the Baitu-l-Mukaddas, and longed to accomplish all my wish by visiting it; Yet when I arrived in Egypt, certain impediments (of business) which I met with in that part (of the world) impeded this design, and several accidental circumstances threw obstacles in my way, and some events caused by Divine Providence erected barriers between me and my object. It happened (however) that the person in whose service I was, drew near to the stage (or post, or resting-place) of Aleppo. Then I said, Praise be to God! the Route of Pilgrims will be undertaken, and we shall enter upon the desired Pilgrimage, and (if God will) thou shalt accomplish the visitation of the Masjidu-l-Aksá, and the Rock of the Holy One, and all the abodes of Martyrs and Confessors within their precincts, which the Supremacy of Intelligence hath founded for the pious with whom he is satisfied. Yet, on the road, certain occurrences hindered him; and he who was going to this consecrated station began to make excuses, under pretence that his suite would not be (sufficiently) becoming to him. Then I, for my part, reverted to my Asylum, my Fortress, and seized a firm hold of this last (verse) by the rope of the first (verse), (i. e. resolved to accomplish this visit, as I had accomplished the other two, by trusting in God.) And I said, Surely the Lord of that house to which God hath given a consenting ear, that therein his name may be loudly adored, surely he will give me a favouring ear, and prosper his long-desired performance of the heavenly precept. Nevertheless, the commander shall ordain it; the Disposer shall end it. Then I seized for the second time the bridle of determination, to journey on the Pilgrimage, and stirred up hope, and firmly attached myself to (my resolution respecting) prayer in the shrine of favourable audience, and, fully resolving to say that the matter is now absolutely pledged, I determined to put myself under that Guardianship (i. e. the guardianship of prayer), and to leave all the accidents of destiny and providence to Him who can protect (us) from them. Now the extended space of this journey, and the great distance between the kingdom of Syria and the Egyptian country, greatly afflicted me; and design was changed after design, resolution after resolution, desire after desire; So I thought in my soul, that there would be some bar, some repelling power, some prohibitory force; and I feared that I should die, and never accomplish the pilgrimage in full, and that my time would come to an end. Then I said, If I die, surely events and power belong to God Almighty and Supreme, who will never change any thing of his plighted covenant. (Relying) upon the (supporting) bough of this opinion, I trusted in God's aid, until I should enter the Baitu-l-Mukaddas, and accomplish my eager wish to visit it; and until I should arrive, together with the other pilgrims, at the last terminating object, and acquire a footing in the broad road of the Way (of truth), and thus also be enabled to arrange all the remarkable matters of the Temple, and all its marvels, and all those ancient descriptions and portraitures therein comprised, the beautiful narratives of which I might meet with, in an harmonious, digested order: and this, on the whole, would constitute a very clever compilation; a work for which I might cull among the native and the exotic, and in which might be found the most ingenious information regarding the matters relating to the Baitu-l-Mukaddas, which is the most important of the abodes (of the divinity), one of the three mosques, —to arrive at which is to perform to the uttermost the divine commandment of the Pilgrimage, and wherein are to be found in great abundance philosophers skilled in marvels. I also felt inclined (to describe) all the venerable places—great, blessed, eminent, noble—hoping that I might find for this work (in itself of no account) some recompence from that Sovereign, God, who thereby might double the merits of his servant, and forgive him his sins. For this is the perfect Pilgrimage incapable of any addition; and God is the Lord ever to be praised. Thus, therefore, on the third of Shaban, in which lights begin to be dispersed (or divided), I set off from Syria the Begirt, to the low-lying country; and, for the sake of refreshment, I went to visit Moaz-Ibn-Jabil, Bishrahil-Ibn-Hassan, and Abu-Ubaidah-Ibn-Aljirah, *i. e. to visit their sepulchres,* (may God rest satisfied with them, and make them well satisfied!) and so it was, that I set out upon my determined expedition, (truly wise is the prosperous Guardian, and mighty is thy Lord in all things); For so it came to pass, by the decree of God, he who arranges no events for good but according to his own disposing power, nor strings event after event, both on earth and in heaven, but as the pen of destiny runs;—that destiny which reduces to a just compass my power of free-will, and binds us with fetters in a narrow-bounded orbit of prohibition, or the foresight of every free-agent, (i. e. circumscribes the extent of free-agency.) Thus therefore did I enter the glorious and holy city, encompassed with glorious rarities and rare glories, upon the day of the blessed Sabbath, the 28th of the month Ramadán, great in power and veneration, the year 874 of the prophetical Hijra; and in the very first place, for the ten remaining days of Ramadán, I obtained those benefits which all good people (if God please) obtain, abundant favours, and liberal kindnesses; and I was present all that blessed feast, in that meeting-house which is unique in its desk for preaching and its pulpit, and where the Happy one of all Happy ones displays his prospering favour upon his sacred tower, and hath here founded his broad extent of space, or firmament, and hath spread from hence the greatness of his mighty kingdom, unto the utmost point of the horizon. Here it is that he hath decked out (as it were) his visible form, and here constituted the key-stone of the supporting columns of his external glory. Here arises the chapel of the Holy Rock, near to Soha, and the dawning light of the morning brightens in the heaven of its holiness. But the Rock stands by itself; for that God raised it up who supporteth the Heavens and the sun's course (path) without columns. (Verse.) "The goal towards which I have bent my steps hath been attained, and my heart receives from you the terminating object of desire. Oh, by your benefactions make my condition a contented state; For this is the eagerly-longing aim of my wishes; For this have I taken up my abiding-place in your land, to refresh myself under your shade, to beseech you to rain upon me from the clouds (of your abundance). O may the big clouds (of your favours) pour upon me reiterated streams! O may the showers (of your beneficence) gently soothe me! the showers of your comforts and your magnificence, the showers of your valuable gifts, renowned for their splendour."—Then I said, Now hath my journey been attained, my request is perfected (I am now at leisure from the business in hand); nor is there any thing more as respects my pilgrimage to be sought, or to cause hesitation (perplexity). From this time, therefore, I hastened to fulfil the engagement into which I had previously entered. I therefore looked into such books already published (or those writers still existing) as suited the design in which I was occupied; For then the Shaikh, the very learned

Star of the Faith, Abu-Mahmúd, Ahmad-Ibn-Muhammad-Ibn-Ibrahim-Ibn-Hallál, Ibn-Tamina-Ibn-Sarúr-Almukaddisí, a Sháfí, author of the book entitled Al-Muthir-Alfarán ('The Minute Text-sifter'), was engaged in a pilgrimage to the holy place and to Syria, (may God have mercy upon him for the excellent compositions, all proceeding upon the wide right road (of truth) which he hath compiled, arranged, and been delivered of in great abundance !) As also the Shaikh, the very learned man, the Ocean of the Ocean of Intelligence, the noble lord, the very centre of the knot of those whose illustrious genealogy is referred to Ibn-Aled-Manah-Shaikh-ul-Islám, the very learned man, the doctor, Crown of faith, Abu-Nassar, Al-Wahâb-Al-Hussain, a Sháfí of Damascus, (may God illustrate his existence by the outpouring of his beneficence, and make the star of his prosperity to glitter in the loftiest horizon !) author of the 'Gardens of Exercise,' upon the Marvels of the Baitu-l-Mukaddas,' (I referred to these,) together with every one who had arrived at the real facts (in their works), and plucked the fruits (of knowledge), and ascended to the source of things, and searched into the marrow of matters, and probed causes, and weighed examples, and fixed proper bounds, and followed the good path in their volumes. I reduced to a just arrangement all those component descriptions not contained in one place. Hither were transferred all that had been originally transferred by preceding writers. Here were melted and fashioned (as trinkets), from beginning to end, all the traditionary stories of the Marvels of the Baitu-l-Mukaddas. (This was done) by himself (i. e. myself) under the shadow of God, who alone can adorn or exalt me; For my guiding bridle consists in those benefits which he hath conferred (in bringing me from poverty unto the enjoyment of all that people of the first rank enjoy). In addition to consulting these authors, I betook myself to such converse as would produce to me the most entire beneficial results: For thus some generous and skilful writers informed me of the opening parts of every book in a summary way. Thus they caused me to consider 'Virtues of the Baitu-l-Mukaddas,' by the Shaikh, the Imám Abu-Al-Faraj-Abdurrahmán-Ibn-Al-Jauzi, (may God Almighty have mercy upon him!) who is a most (acute) historian. Thus also I met with (the information) which is to be found in the 'Diligent Collections upon the Virtues of the Masjid-ul-Aksá,' by the Imám, the historian, Shaikh-ul-Islám, Abu-'l-Kasim, Alí-Ibn-ul-Hussain, Ibn-Abdallah-Ibn-Isákir, that is to say, the middle volume (or roll) and certain divisions thereof, especially those following the 16th and 17th sections. Now, the above-named volume, relied upon by the compiler, consisted of several parts; one having twelve, and the last fifteen chapters (or series of disquisitions): the title-page of one part of which work is dated the 19th of Ramadán, the year 596, in the Mosque Al Aksá; and of the other, the 7th of Rabia the 1st, of the year 578. There are other parts by another author; viz. the Shaikh, the learned Imám-Taki-Addín-Abu-Mahmood-Ismaël, who names in his work the Imám the historian, the learned Taj-Addín-Abdurrahmán-Ibn-Hanja-Al-Kaza, and the Imám-Abu-Zakia-Yahyá-Amúr. Thus, again, I met with information in the first volume, first part, and the latter portion of the tenth part of 'The Book of Social Converse, on the wonders of the Baitu-l-Mukaddas, by the son of the uncle of the historian above-mentioned; viz. the Kádí-Imám-Al-Alam-Al-Thakat-Amín-Addín-Ahmad-Ibn-Muhammad-Ibn-Hassan-Ibn-Hebat-Allah, the Sháfí. Now, the above-mentioned volume is dated the fifth day, 15th of Shawwal, the year 603, in the mosque (or college) of Damascus. The compiler also relied upon others. In one of these works, then, says the Kádí-Amín-Addín-Ahmad above-mentioned, "Now, I have composed this book; and in this book I have taken, as my authority, the work of (my uncle's son) Al Hafiz (one who knew the Koran by heart) Mahmud-Al-Kásim-Ibn-Al-Hafiz Abn-Al-Kasim; (may God Almighty compassionate him!)" The just-named author hath been very useful in his 'Diligent Collections on the Marvels of the Masjidu-l-Aksá.' From him I gained certain verses and narratives, (by alleging which as my authority, I will sufficiently satisfy him). This author's historical works I would class, on account of the diligence and singular care he has expended upon them, with any ancients before him; for he displays therein most singular acuteness and memory. He is also superior to the whole of them in loftiness of expression, and most beautiful in the didactic style, in any branch of literature, on which, in the course of his work, he must dilate. Again, that said author of the 'Gardens of Exercise on the Virtues of the Baitu-l-Mukaddas' observes, "I met with a book called 'The Stirring up of Souls to the Pilgrimage to the Holy Place,' by the Shaikh Birhán-Addín-Al-Kazarí, who asserts in his Preface that for the Wonders of the Holy House he selected chiefly from the work called 'The Lucid Book,' by the historian Bihá-Addín-Ibn-Asákir, and a small portion from the book of Ibn-Al-Muáled-Al-Mushrat-Ibn-Al-Mirjá-Al-Mukaddisí." Part of his work was transferred from this author; but the remainder from 'The Lucid Book.' He also says, "When, in completing my work, I arrived at a subject of which these authors also treated, I retrenched all their introduced quotations, taking only the original portions." The same Said observes again, "I met also with a book, 'Directions for the Adorer, in his judgment of Mosques,' by the Shaikh Badr-Addín-Al-Zarkashí, who says, "I met with a book, 'A Smoothing of the Road, for the Visitors of the Mosques,' by the Shaikh Shaháb-Addín-Ahmad-Ibn-Al-Omad-Al-Ifkahsí, a Sháfí, who says, "I met with a most shrewd extract, on the Wonders of Syria and Damascus, by the Shaikh Abu-l-Hassan-Ali-Ibn-Mahmúd-Ibn Shajaz-Al-Rebi-Al-Malíkí." This extract is dated at Damascus, in the mosque of the Jámi, (or *cathedral*,) the year 35. It was abridged by the Shaikh Birháin-Addín-Al-Thazari, by cutting off the references, and carefully considering which were the absolute facts. He named it 'Directions to the Virtues of Syria.'" The Said again remarks, "In the mosque of Abraham (prayer be upon his abiding-place, and peace upon his person—an asylum from those who compel us to seek it!) I met with a work ascribed to Ishak-Ibn-Ibrahim-Ibn-Ahmad-Ibn-Muhammad-Ibn-Kámil-Al-Tadmeri, preacher and Imám in the reposing-place of Abraham (peace be upon him!). This work is named 'The Minute Text-sifter,' upon the pilgrimage to the tomb of Abraham (peace be upon him!). He introduces into this book useful information, reported by two Shaikhs; viz., Al Isnúí, and Al Balakiní; for he says, in different passages, 'Thus said our Shaikh Abdurrahmán-Al-Isnúí, and spoke most usefully; or, thus said our Shaikh Sirás-Addín-Al-Balakiní, and spoke most instructively.'"

These, then, are the works with which the said Taj-Addín-Al-Mashár met; and on references from which he chiefly supported the foundations of his work, 'The Gardens of Exercise.' With this work the pilgrim can have no need of examining any of the books of Wonders; and oh! may God perpetuate the profitable effects (of this pilgrimage)! —may he perpetuate a confident knowledge of the traditions of the sacred journey, all those transferred histories, all those (accounts) which I resolved to collect for the completion of this work! —a work which I have commenced, set about, and arranged in the manner I desired, and which I contrived so as to contain seventeen chapters.

HISTORY, &c.

CHAPTER I.

Upon the Names of the Masjidu-l-Aksá, and its Marvels, and the supreme merit of visiting it.

KNOW that there are many names, all expressive of the Glory of the place in question. Thus, to use the words of the author of the 'Descriptive Characters of the Mosques,' for forming a judgment upon mosques—" I have collected *seventeen names* of this Temple, all bearing upon the precious privileges (and pre-eminence) attached to the Masjidu-l-Aksá. It is called Al Aksá, because it is the most *distant* mosque towards which pilgrimage is directed. It is said that beyond it there is no place for adoration, and nothing after it but filth and impurity. It is reported that Abdallah Ibn Salam said to the prophet of God, (upon him be the peace and blessing of God !) when his discourse appeared in the course of conversation to bear upon the mosque Al Aksá, and the reason why it was called Al

Aksá; 'It is, because it is the middle of the world: it is beyond the centre neither on this side nor on that.' Upon which Muhammad said, 'Thou hast truly spoken.' It is also named 'the Mosque of Elya,' (or Elia,) spelt with *hamza*, having *kasra* for its vowel; then a quiescent *ya*, then a *lam* with *kasra*, then another *moveable ya*, then long *alif;* as, for example, *karazyá* (carraway-seed). It is also reported that the dawn of morning and evening meet in it; which means that the Baitu-l-Mukaddas is in the *midst* of all wonderful and excellent things. The author of the book 'The Derivations of the Three Languages,' says, it is spelt with *gesma*, and *lam*, and *medda;* also in the Sunna of Abu-Yalí-Al-Musallí, it is said (from Ibn Abbás) that the word is Ilya, with *alif* and *lam*, and that its signification is foreign. It is called also the Holy House (Baitu-l-Mukaddisu), with a *fatha* over the *mim*, and a *gesma* over the *kaf*, meaning a place purified from pollution, and derived from the word Kadds, or Kads, which means purified, blessed, or holy. The noun or root has the sense of purification or sanctification. Thus we say the Holy Spirit Gabriel, (peace be upon him!) because he is a spirit who causes or effects holiness and purity; for of him (it has been said), 'We will sanctify for thee one by whom thou mayest flee from those things which become thee not.' He is called the Vessel of Sanctification, because in him is purification found.

"Thus, therefore, the meaning of the Holy or Consecrated House is, *a place whereby we may obtain purification from sin.* It is also called the Upraised Place, uncontaminated by Paganism: moreover, it is called the *Consecrated House,* (Baitu-l-Mukaddas,) with a *damma* over the *mim,* and a *fatha* over the *dal,* which has *teshdid,* signifying a pure place, sacred from idols. It is called also Bait-Al-Mukdus, with *damma* over the *dal,* and *sukin* (*gesma*) over the two syllables. It is also called Salem, on account of the abundance of mercy of the angels therein, as says Ibn Bari. Also it is called Shallam; the initial letter being *shin,* with the diacritical marks: this *shin* is foreign: (in Arabic it is *sin*:) the *lam* following this *shin* has *teshdid.* It is a synonyme of the Holy House. It is also said to be written without the diacritical points, and with a *kasra* under the *lam* (*Sallam*). This is Arabic; and in Arabic its meaning is, The Holy House. Again, it is called Ushalim, with a *damma* over the *hamza,* a *fatha* over the *shin,* and the short *kasra* under the *lam.* But we are told by Abu Obeidah, in addressing himself to Omar-Ibn-Al-Umthari, that many spell the word with a *fatha* over both the *shin* and the *lam.* It is still further named Kùrat Elya (i. e. Civitas Elia) and Salem, and Bait Ayyil, and Sion, and Kashboth and Kasrùt, with *sad* plain, and *tha* with the three points; also Baboosh, or Babús, being *shin*, or *sin ;* also Kúr Shalah, or Kúr Shallum, and Ariel and Salim, or Salúz. From the Muther Alfaram we learn, that the words Baitu-l-Mukaddas (بيت المقدس) may be spelt either with long or short vowels, and the last word may have a *gesma*, or be moved. It is also called the Holy Land, and the Mosque Al Akúr, and Ilya and Elia, and Shallum with *teshdid*, and Oor Shalem, or The Lord's House, and Sihym, the *sad* having a *kasra* beneath it. The Consecrated House is surnamed 'The Place of Olives,' but is not called 'The Venerable.'"

Now, with respect to its marvels:—truly, they can never be computed nor defined, nor attained to by human intelligence. First, we will mention these circumstances, bearing upon its pre-eminent Dignity, which are to be found in the book of God. This is his word: "Praise be to him, who brought his servant by night from the Baitu-l-Harám Masjidu-l-Aksá; which place we have blessed to all succeeding generations by our signs!" (verses of the Koran.) Truly, God is the all-hearing and all-seeing; and if the Temple was remarkable for nothing besides these verses, it would be supremely eminent, and be most highly blessed,—on account also of the visit of Burák to its precincts. Thus it hath a double blessing; for God, when he wished to raise up his prophet Muhammad (upon whom be God's peace and blessing!) to heaven, brought him by this glorious road, in order to glorify this city, and in order that the glory and dignity of both cities might centre in him; and associated the journey from Mecca to heaven in equal honour with the journey from Jerusalem to heaven. Also it is said, "Praised then be God, who preserved him safe from evil!" i. e. Praise God by saying the word Praise! Also, "There are two mosques, the Venerable mosque and the mosque Al Aksá; and in these two fell down the perspicuity of the glorious Signs; and we have blessed its precincts. God shall cause rivers to flow around the Baitu-l-Mukaddas, and cause fruits there to ripen, and display its blessedness, and display also most blessed companies of persons: there shall gently walk the firm in the right" (firm of purpose). The meaning of this is, that God shall bless the constant in good from his own bounty and by his own treasures.

Thus may this house be said to be exalted and holy in dignity and grandeur for all future time and all eternity. Thus again we hear from Khálid Ibn Házím as follows: Al Zoheiri was standing in the Holy House, whilst I was performing a procession in that place and praying therein. I said therefore to him, Is there no Shaikh here, who will recite from the Hidden Book the verses upon the Holy Place, which exist in chap. 12? Who said, Akibah-Ibn-Abu-Zainah will do so, if we sit down by him. Then he began to narrate the Virtues of the Holy House; which having related in great abundance, Al Zoheiri said to him, O thou Shaikh! thou hast not yet arrived at that which I will impart to thee—the mighty word, "Praise to him who brought his servant by night from the Venerable Mosque to the Mosque Al Aksá, whose precincts we have blessed!" as also that word revealed unto the children of Israel, "Enter into these well-watered meadows, and eat when ye desire of all good things:" and again, "Enter ye the gate with praise, and say Remission," for your sins shall be pardoned you, and the hand of the good-doers shall he protect. Now God hath appropriated to no other mosque a gift equal to the privilege granted to this, in engaging to pardon the sins of those who worship there. It is above all others; for no others have so supremely excellent a privilege set apart for them. Again, I will mention the word which was revealed to Abraham and to Lot, (peace be upon them both!) "We will bring him and Lot to a land wherein all the universe shall be blessed, and wherein shall the Holy House be sought:" also another word revealed, "We will give them a home on high ground, full of cool streams and rivulets."

We will now quote from some of the expoundersof

questions respecting this Temple (from them we learn) a word revealed to the sons of Israel: "Enter ye the Holy Land which God hath decreed to grant you: do not turn your backs, lest your hearts be wounded, whilst straying from the way:" and God named this passage, 'The Blessed and Holy Passage.' Also another word revealed, "Thus they departed from their abode in haste, in order to erect a place to sacrifice the Passover," upon the Rock, they say, of the Baitu-l-Mukaddas. And again another word revealed, "We have allotted in return to the children of Israël a sure place of rest: their abode is called Syria, and the Consecrated House; and that Holy House shall be called 'the Peculiar.'" And again, another word, revealed on the day when he manifested the mysteries of his will in the "place of near access," which is said to be the Rock of the Holy House. Also another word, revealed when they were in the untrodden ground (the desert) and the borders of the Consecrated House. And another word revealed "The figs and the Olives." Now Akibah-Ibn-Omar observed that the figs signified Damascus, and the olives the Consecrated Abode. Also another word revealed, "God hath fixed among you a wall, within which is mercy, and on its external front is punishment." This is the wall of the Baitu-l-Mukaddas, within which are the Gates of Mercy, and without, the

Valley of Hinnom (Gehenna). We may further quote those passages bearing upon the supreme eminence of this Temple, from the Sunna of the traditions of Abu Huraira (may the satisfaction of God be perfected in him!): "The fixed abiding-place of the Deity shall be in three mosques alone, the mosque Masjidu-l-Harám, the mosque Al Aksá, and this mosque (i. e. Medina)." Also a passage found among the traditions of Abu-Soad-Al-Hadhari (may the satisfaction of God be with him!): "The prophet of God (upon whom be the peace and blessing of God!) said, 'There shall be no fixed residence except in three mosques—those of Mecca, Jerusalem, and Medina. Neither shall there be any fasting upon two days—the day of the dawn (i. e. the solemn sacrifice offered at Mecca) and the day of the fast-breaking; neither shall there be prayer at two moments of time, viz. from the prayer before the dawn until sunrise, and from the evening prayer until sun-set; nor shalt thou journey with a woman more than two bareed, (i. e. 24 miles) unless with your wife or nearest relations.'" Thus also in the traditions of Abu Tharir (may the satisfaction of God rest with him!) we have the following: "I said, O Apostle of God, which mosque hath been placed first upon the earth? Who said, in reply, The mosque of the Kaaba. I said, And then? He said, The mosque

Al Aksá. Then I said, How muc. 'ime between them? He said, Forty years: also he sa. In these two mosques divided prayers concentre; a. this (i. e. Medina) is also a mosque."

Also, to quote from Omra-Ibn-Hussain: "I said, O Apostle of God, which is the most beautiful city? Who said, How, if I say that I think the Consecrated House to be the most beautiful? Then I said, That therefore is the most beautiful. Thereupon he said, How then may there not be some place of second rank, besides that, possessing an increase of honour, which may be visited by pilgrims, and to which the winds may point? (But the wind of the Baitu-l-Mukaddas is directed only towards God.) Truly Medina is most noble. Truly to me its savour is sweet; for herein I live, and herein will I die: and if this had not been so, I would not have fled hither from Mecca: also I have never seen a more beautiful moon than that here."

Again, to quote from Kaab-Al-Habbar, "The hour is fixed (by divine decree) when the Masjidu-l-Harám shall visit the Baitu-l-Mukaddas; and they shall both be conducted to Paradise together; and all their inhabitants within them: also, the last judgment, and the final reckoning shall be in the Baitu-l-Mukaddas." Again, from the same Kaab, "God brought down the sons of Israël to the Consecrated or Holy Land: and David and Solomon, (peace be upon them both!) being of the number of prophets, were kings of the land: also God Almighty named this migration 'The Blessed Passage, and The Holy Passage.'" Again, another word written to us in the Psalms, among certain traditions, that "the land which the sincere worshippers shall tread, shall be called the land of Paradise: they shall tread it who have performed (true) obedience to God."

Now, it is said that the word 'land' here means 'the world,' and 'the sincere' means the people of Muhammad, (on him may the blessing and the salutation of God remain!) It is also said that this word applies to the sons of Israël. Moreover, this land is said to be that in which the souls of the faithful will assemble together; which means, that the resurrection of the dead will take place therein, and it shall be called the Holy Land, because it shall be trodden by Muhammad, (upon whom be the blessing of God! and whom I salute).

Again, another word revealed, "They act unjustly, who repulse us from the mosques of God, nor suffer his name to be mentioned therein, and by their superior strength persist in desolating these places, so that (the Moslem) cannot enter them but with fear and trembling. Truly in this world they shall have their reward, and in the next a grievous punishment; which punishment shall come down upon them when the Moslems drive the Greeks from the Holy House. God shall trample upon them; God shall repay them; nor shall one of them enter that land for ever, but with dread. They shall put on the robe of shame, and contempt, and livid paleness." Again, a tradition delivered by Abdallah-Ibn-Omar (may God's satisfaction rest upon him!) is as follows: that "the holy of holies in the seventh heaven is a counterpart (type, or measure) of the most venerable places on the earth, and that the Baitu-l-Mukaddas in the seventh heaven is a measure of that in the earth." Also, that "in heaven, one of the gates of Paradise is always open, whence every morning descend (streams) of affection and compassion upon the Baitu-l-Mukaddas at a certain moment." Also, that "the Holy Land, compared with other lands, holds a rank in God's esteem, to which no resemblance can be found, but that of a man who hath great wealth, and a coffer of treasures amongst his other riches which he loves best of all, and who every morning thinks of no other thing before his wealth; so also is this the chief treasure of the Lord of the universe. Every morning he thinks of no other land before this. He pours down abundantly upon it the showers of his love and mercy, and then afterwards does the same upon all lands."

Again, we are informed that "the abode of spirits yearns with affection towards the Holy Abode, and that in the mansion of spirits the Holy House is Firdús (Paradise is properly so called); which Firdús is the flower, the most exquisitely beautiful of gardens, said to be the most splendid." This Firdús is said also to be a rising ground in the abode of angels, and is the very midst of that abode, the highest point, the most supremely glorious. Again, "Whosoever cometh unto the Baitu-l-Harám shall be forgiven, and be advanced up eight degrees (steps) (of beatitude): whosoever cometh into the mosque of the Apostle of God (the blessing and peace of God be with him!) shall be forgiven, and be advanced six degrees; whosoever cometh unto the Baitu-l-Mukaddas shall be forgiven, and advanced four degrees." Again, "Whosoever shall pray for pardon to be granted to all faithful men and women, standing within the Holy House, every day, five-and-twenty times, God shall preserve to him the communion of the holy ones, and cause him to enter among the ever-succeeding adorers." Yet again, from Khalid-Ibn-Moad: "Unto the house is joined a gate from heaven, by which God despatches down every day seventy thousand angels, to remit the sins of all who chaunt and pray therein." Again, from another: "The inhabitants of the Holy Abode are God's neighbours, and there is a claim of right upon God, that he shall not punish his neighbours. Again, That moment shall not tarry in coming, when God shall drive, as a flock of camels, his good servants unto the Baitu-l-Mukaddas; and therein shall God cause them to dwell. Again, In this Holy Land abides the redolence of the prophets, (peace be upon them!) the marks of their residence are therein, neither is there a handbreadth's space therein, in which some angel hath not prayed and stood. Again, One said to Naaman-Ibn-Ata, What sayest thou of the Baitu-l-Mukaddas? Who replied, There is not a place therein, where some prophet or angel is not praying; and if, perchance, I should hit you a blow upon the forehead, it would light upon the forehead of some prophet or angel: moreover, there is a tradition, that every night seventy thousand angels descend upon the Mosque of the Holy Abode, to sing Hallelujahs to God, to magnify, repeat thanksgivings, to praise, to ascribe holiness to, to glorify and to magnify him; nor will they return until the day of judgment. Again, it is told of Moáz, that he came to the Holy House, and remained there three days and three nights, fasting and praying. Then, when he came forth, his head was turned upwards, looking on high; when, therefore, he came in front of his companions, he said, Your sins have departed from you, and God hath pardoned you: see therefore that ye conciliate his favour in all your actions that yet remain to be done.

Let me now mention various other traditions, such as this; viz. That the rock of this Temple is the middle of the world; and if a servant were to say unto his master, Let us set off unto the Holy Land, then God would say, O my angels, be witnesses that I now pardon those two persons, before they set out, provided they persist not in sins. He says also, Whosoever shall dwell in the Holy Land, God will answer for his sufficient support, if his property fail him. If any one die here, his state at the resurrection is computed and settled, as if he died in Heaven; and if any one die in the precincts of the Temple, then (his reward is computed) as if he had died within the Holy House; and the Holy Land is the first land which receives God's blessing; and the glorious Lord shall take up his glorious stand on the day of judgment on the soil of the Baitu-l-Mukaddas, and shall make it clearly visible to all lands: also, this is that sacred land which God mentions in the great Korán, and says, This is the land whereby we will bless all the universe (or all generations), namely, the land of the Consecrated Abode. Also, said the Mighty One to Moses, (peace be with him!) Depart into the Holy Land, for therein is my fire, and my light and my illumination; which signifies, my burning thick mass, (i. e. of bushes, hair, &c. &c.) And God spake to Moses in the Baitu-l-Mukaddas, and displayed his Majesty on the mountain, in the consecrated land; and Moses (peace be with him!) beheld the fiercely-burning light of the Lord when he displayed his Majesty in the land of the Baitu-l-Mukaddas. Moses also beheld the rocks of this Temple, which was in the very middle of all the land: also, if a man shall say unto his master, Let us set off for the Baitu-l-Mukaddas, and if they do so, God says, Happy is he who spake, and he who heard; he shall stand on high before me.

Al Makatil observes, In the land of the Baitu-l-Mukaddas did God call David and Solomon (peace be with both!) unto repentance. In the Baitu-l-Mukaddas God sent his angel to Solomon; in the Baitu-l-Mukaddas God announced joyful tidings to Zacharias and to John; in the Baitu-l-Mukaddas the angels showed a descriptive painting of the Tower to David; in the Baitu-l-Mukaddas God put all that walked the earth, or flew in the air, under subjection to David; in the Baitu-l-Mukaddas, the prophets (God's peace and blessing be with them!) offered sacrifice; upon the Baitu-l-Mukaddas the angels (peace be with them!) descend every night; in the Baitu-l-Mukaddas, unto

Maria, (peace be with her!) were winter fruits made to come in summer, and summer fruits in winter; in the Baitu-l-Mukaddas did God cause the palm-tree to bud forth (or bear fruit) for her; in the Baitu-l-Mukaddas did Jesus (peace be with him!) speak, whilst a boy in the cradle; in the Baitu-l-Mukaddas was born Jesus (peace be with him!); and from the Baitu-l-Mukaddas did God raise him up unto Heaven. Unto the land of the Baitu-l-Mukaddas shall he descend from Heaven. In the land of the Baitu-l-Mukaddas did the Strengthener descend unto him. Yajúj and Majúj shall conquer all the earth, except the Baitu-l-Mukaddas; and in the Baitu-l-Mukaddas shall God destroy them: also, God thinks every morning for good upon the Baitu-l-Mukaddas: God also gave unto the Prophet (the peace and blessing of God be with him!) the Camel Al Burák, who carried him to the Baitu-l-Mukaddas: God also revealed unto Abraham and Isaac, (peace be with them!) that when they died they should be interred in the soil of Baitu-l-Mukaddas: God also revealed unto Adam, (peace be with him!) when he died in the land of Eden, that he should be interred in the Baitu-l-Mukaddas: Maria also (peace be with her!) died in the Baitu-l-Mukaddas. Unto this holy land did Abraham (peace and blessing be with him!) fly from Kútha.

In the last times there shall be a general flight unto the Baitu-l-Mukaddas, and the ark and the gracious presence (Shechinah) (of God) shall be lifted up on high in this Temple. Also the Prophet (the peace and blessing of God be with him!) prayed here, for some time. Here shall be the general gathering of all men, the general resurrection: unto the Holy Abode shall God come, in the darkness of thick clouds, amidst his angels; and all creatures shall burst through their graves without difficulty, and all (the inhabitants) of Paradise shall come down with pomp on the day of judgment unto this Temple. Hereunto shall all men assemble for the reckoning of the day of judgment. Here shall the bridge Al Sirát divide between Gehenna and Paradise. On the day of judgment, here shall the balances be placed, and hither shall all the orders of angels come; and on the day of judgment shall the Seraphin blow the trumpet on the wall of the Temple, and proclaim those great and terrific words, "O flesh torn from the bones! O bones gnawed and cut! come forth unto your reckoning, and let your breath breathe forth again, and receive the recompense of your deeds." Here did Zacharias bring up Maria, (peace be with her!): here did God grant to Solomon to comprehend the articulate language of birds: here Solomon preferred his request of a kingdom, with which no subsequent kingdom could compare; and here that request was granted. Here was that fish-pond which, being upon the surface of the earth, had its source from the East, its end in the West, and its middle beneath the Baitu-l-Mukaddas. Here was granted unto Solomon the secret, whereby to walk in one of the gardens of Paradise, and to find out the Sakhrá of the Baitu-l-Mukaddas. In this place God confirmed the kingdom unto him, and softened iron for him: here God revealed his gracious will respecting the wife of Imram, that she should devote herself to God: here God forgave to David his crime; and here did God confirm Jesus (peace be with him!) by the Sacred Spirit. In the Holy House did God cause the revelation of his will to come unto John whilst a child: in the Holy Abode did Jesus (peace be with him!) resuscitate the dead, and work miracles. Whosoever shall pray herein, his prayer shall be brought as near (to God) as if he prayed in Heaven. The whole earth shall be destroyed; but the Baitu-l-Mukaddas shall still be inhabited and still uninjured. Here did the palm hasten the ripening of its sour fruit to be gathered by Maria, (peace be with her!) Unto this Temple, affirmed the prophet, there shall be flight after flight of all good people. Whosoever prayeth here, after having performed his ablutions and perfected that ablution by offering four *rakas,* shall be forgiven all that hath passed before this.

So far the prophet himself. In the traditions it is said, Whosoever prayeth herein shall come forth as clear from sins as he was on the day his mother bore him; and on the day of judgment there shall be, on every hair of his body, a hundred lights from God. His performance of the pious pilgrimage shall be graciously accepted; and God shall grant to him a thanksgiving heart and a confessing tongue, and shall place him in the midst among the damsels (i. e. the houries of the Mahommedan Paradise), and God shall associate him with the assembled prophets. Whosoever also shall wait patiently a year in the Baitu-l-Mukaddas, occupied in divine things, and suffering the extremity of want for that purpose, God shall bring down an abundant sufficiency for subsistence; before him, and behind him, on his right hand and on his left, below him and above him, he shall eat of overflowing and supremely good things, and shall enter into Paradise, please God!

Also, the very first corner that was founded (created) of the whole earth, was the spot of the rock of the Baitu-l-Mukaddas. Also, in the other world, the fountain of Moses in the Baitu-l-Mukaddas shall be clearly visible. Here did

God reveal to Maria the joyful tidings of Jesus, (peace be upon them both!); and God repulsed her enemy Dajjál from entering the Baitu-l-Mukaddas, who shall conquer all the earth, except Jerusalem, Mecca, and Medina. Among all his lands, this is God's especial chosen: here is the middle point of the earth; here the commencement of the spiral of Creation. Again, every morning God reflects upon peace and rest for the Baitu-l-Mukaddas, and rains abundantly upon it the streams of his mercy and longing affection: then he does the same to all other worlds. Again, the dew which descends upon the Holy Abode is a cure for every disease, since it is the dew of the tender mercies of Heaven. Also, thus saith the Mighty One, He who is buried in this Temple is among those who lie all around my house, the cloisters of heaven; a house to which none shall come; in which none shall be seen but he who is munificent and gentle. Also, said the prophet of God unto Abu-Ubaidah-Al-Jirah, Hope of all hope shall rest upon this Temple, when the time of temptation and tumult shall appear. Who said, O Apostle of God! what if I cannot reach that holy place? Who replied, Then I will be thy substitute; and I will take care to insure thy vicinity thereunto. Again, the place in Syria most beloved by God is the Baitu-l-Mukaddas; and the most beloved of all mountains is that whereon stands the Sakhrá. This also is the last country that shall be destroyed (in later times), by forty years. Again, This is one of the gardens of Paradise. Again, God says unto the Sakhrá of Baitu-l-Mukaddas, Thou art my strength; upon thee will I assuredly fix my friendship, that my people may assemble together upon thee. Surely the rivers that flow within thee shall be rivers of milk and rivers of honey and rivers of wine; for I this day am their Lord, who doth most surely love them.

Again, Al Mushrah told me, that Abul Pharaj assured him, that Ahmad-Ibn-Khalif-Al-Hamad asserted as follows: Abu-Mahomed-Abdallah-Ibn-Mohamed-Al-Herzi, who was one of the monks, told me, I saw, as one sees when asleep, on the tenth day of the month Muharram, the year 335, just as one sees when asleep, whilst I was in the inner dome of the Masjid of the Baitu-l-Mukaddas, and was standing in front of that chapel wherein is the Sakhrá, when, lo! the chapel became magnified with glowing beams of light from above; and upon the summit was a great pearl: upon this I entered the chapel, in order to look upon the Sakhrá, when, lo! I found it to be of jacinth-stone, whence a brilliant light proceeded. Upon this I said, Praise be to God who hath made this stone visible to mortals, and shown that it is of jacinth.

Then it was said to me, Go to meet the people with an account of this appearance of the rock. After this, I prayed upon the black pavement, when, lo! a light was diffused from the western side, and four rivers began to flow from beneath the rock. I said then, What are these streams? Then it was said unto me, These are from Paradise. Then I departed from the chapel, and, lo! there were trees of flame, extending from the gate of the Sakhrá as far as unto the gate of Misfortune, in front of the Tower of David. Then said I, What are these trees? And it was said unto me, This is the road for the believers in God to walk by unto Paradise. I said therefore, How will it be distinguished by them. It was replied, Look at the path; it is *black*. Then I asked about the prophet of God, (the peace and blessing of God be with him!) about the night of his journey to heaven, and the footmarks of the road he walked. It was said then unto me, Look upon the ground; which I did; when I beheld a bright light whiter than the white of snow, which he had trodden with his feet, (may the peace and blessing of God be with him!) And in like manner appeared his entire path. Then I looked upon the chapel of the Prophet, (the peace and blessing of God be with him!) when it was said unto me, That is the spot whereon he prayed, in the midst of prophets and angels. Then I said,

The Chapel of the Chain, what is that? and where is the chain? And it was said unto me, This is the spot wherein is the chain, and this is the light; but not one of the children of Adam shall ever see that chain.

Then I asked respecting the Gate of Remission; when it was replied, Whosoever shall enter that gate, or descend towards it, shall come forth free from all his sins, as completely as upon the day when his mother bore him, according to the word of God, "Enter ye the gate with adoration, and say 'Remission,' for we have forgiven your sins." Then I asked about the place of the nativity of Jesus, (peace be with him!) Upon this it was said unto me, Whosoever shall pray therein shall enter Paradise: whosoever shall enter therein shall receive the same benefits as if he were looking upon Jesus the son of Maria, (peace be upon them both!) In like manner also with respect to the Tower of Zacharias. Then I asked about the Gate of Compassion, when, lo! the gate appeared to be of fire on the side nearest the mosque, but of iron on the side nearest the valley (of Jehosaphat). Then it was said unto me, Every prophet of the prophets (the blessings of God be with them!) receives, as his allotted share, six cubits square; and the like quantity is allotted to each believer. Then I entered the mosque, nearly where the first row of columns begins; and it was said unto me, Look! and, lo! there were certain beings swallowed up in the earth, with their heads protruding above the ground: I asked, therefore, who are these? and it was replied, These are some of the hated-ones of past ages. Then four (beings) began to address me; whom I asked, who were the princes of the angels? They replied, Gabriel, and Michael, and Seraphiel; and the fourth I know not. Then they informed me of the blessed greeting which Muhammad received; for all the holy ones met him before the mosque: and it was said to him, Preach that discourse which thou didst deliver before God; and thus did each one to him: and when he had concluded this, we prepared for him a throne of light in Paradise, that he might be exalted thereupon, and raised up above all other men.

To the same purpose are the traditions directed of Abu-Bekr-Ibn-Alamah, and Abu-Mahmood-Ibn-Abdarrahmán of Cesarea, who all persist in the same story. To proceed: At this time there are seven pillars of the earth, who are seven Musalmáns, in the Baitu-l-Mukaddas: herein also the portion of the believers in God. Upon this I said, Where then is the portion of the heretics (or innovators)? And it was said unto me, In the valley of Gehenna. Then I looked down from above upon the valley;

for I eagerly desired to behold; and, lo! there was Hell: there the wicked were shot at with burning coals, like palm-trees, and horribly cut with saws, (or with thrashing-fans, winnowing-fans.) O may God bring me safe therefrom, of his grace and bounty!

CHAPTER II.

Upon the original Foundation of the Temple, and upon its Construction by David (peace with him!); also of the Buildings of Solomon, in a form that was one of the world. Also, the account of his Prayer, which he prayed when he had finished it, on behalf of every one who should enter it, and the place of his Prayer.

Now we are told by Ibn Almubarak, from Othman, When God commanded David (with whom be peace!) to build this Temple, he said, O Lord, where shall I build it? Who said, Where thou shalt see the angel with a drawn sword. David then did see the angel in that place. David therefore fixed the corner-stones of its foundation, and raised the walls; but when the walls were raised, they were pulled down again. David then said, O Lord, thou didst command me to build a house for thee; and now that I have raised the walls, thou dost pull them down. Then he said, O David, it is because I have not appointed thee my vicegerent among created beings; nor must thou alienate the place from its possessor without a price. As to that building, a man of thy sons shall construct it. Again, it has been said that the meaning of the building being pulled down after it had been raised, was, that the place belonged to the whole community of the children of Israël, every one of whom had a right in it. David therefore requested them to give up the land, to which part of them assented *viva voce*, and part of them in silence. David then understood of those who were silent, some were well content, but others were not content, within their hearts. David therefore brought the whole matter into open discussion, and the affair of his intended building also.

Then came one of the possessors of the common right unto the sons of Israël, and said unto them, Do ye wish to build upon my rightful portion? Now, I am a poor man; and that is a place to my hand, whence I can gather my food; and I am greatly benefited by its productions, which I can carry home, on account of its proximity to my dwelling: consider therefore my circumstances. Thereupon said unto him every one of the sons of Israël, Are either your right or yourself to be avariciously kept back from serving a good purpose? If thou wilt give up obediently, it is well;

but if not, we will take it, whether thou wilt or not. Then he said, Expect the judgment of David in this matter. Then he departed, and complained of them unto the king, who entreated them, and said unto them, Would ye build this Temple unjustly? I will not see you do so, O sons of Israël. Submit yourselves therefore unto God; for I do not think but that in this matter ye have acted tyrannically. Then David said unto him, Make thy own demand for thy right, and we will follow thy decision: who replied, What wilt thou give me for it? Then he said, If thou wilt, I will fill it for thee with sheep, or, if thou wilt, with oxen, or, if thou wilt, with camels. Then he said, O prophet of God, make an advance for me; for thou art buying for God; therefore be not avaricious with me. Then David said unto him, Demand thy utmost; for thou canst not ask a thing but I will give thee. Then he said, Build for me a caldron upon it, capable of containing twelve feet solid measure; then fill it with gold for me. And David (peace be with him!) replied, Yes; this is but little for God.

Then came this man unto the children of Israël, and said, Truly God is the Unchangeable, the Faithful, the Saving. Then he said, O ye men of Israël, God hath appropriated this place to me as a means of obtaining an obliterating pardon of my sins: this gift is the privilege I love far beyond the filling of the land with gold. How therefore did these imagine that I should act niggardly in a matter from which I hope for the obliterating forgiveness of my sins, and of their sins? Now therefore I give it up to you, in return for mercy displayed to you, for compassion towards you; for I had already devoted it to God. Engage earnestly, then, in the work of the Holy Abode. Then David took the matter in hand himself, and began to collect stores for greater dispatch, and to place them in their proper places (to be used); in which the Scribes of the sons of Israël concurred with him.

There is also another reason for the building of this Temple by David (peace be with him!) found in a tradition of Ibn Ishále, viz. that God revealed unto David (peace be with him!) when the children of Israël had become exceedingly impious and immeasurably wicked, as follows:—"I have sworn by my might that I will afflict you with a drought of three years; or I will cause your enemies to obtain complete conquest over you for three months; or I will send a divine pestilence for three days." Therefore David assembled the children of Israël, and proposed these three things to their acceptance, desiring them to choose one of the three. But they said unto him, Thou art our prophet; and thou art more acute than ourselves: choose, therefore, for us. So he said, As for the famine, that is a stunning evil, which no one can endure. As for enemies and death, I should be inclined to propose for your acceptance, to be subject to the unresisted power of your foes: but, at any rate, the effects of that choice await you under any circumstances; for death is in God's hand. You will die at the appointed season, even in your own abodes. Refer this, then, entirely to the good pleasure of God; for he will be merciful unto you. Then he made his option for them, and chose the Pestilence from above, and commanded them to prepare and dress themselves in their grave-clothes (shrouds), and bring forth their wives and their slaves and their children, in front of them, and themselves behind, and thus to stand upon the Rock, and the soil whereupon the Temple was afterwards built, which was then bare ground, on a level with the Sakhrá. So therefore they did. Then David loudly exclaimed, O Lord! thou hast commanded us to follow faithfulness; and thou lovest those who stand faithfully to their word. Oh, be faithful to us, as regards this compassion! Thou hast commanded us to give freedom to our collar-bound (slaves). We beseech thee, of thy compassion, that thou wouldst give freedom to us this day. Thou hast commanded us never to repulse the suppliant who standeth at our gates; and thou lovest him who doth not refuse him that asketh. We even have now come to thee beseeching: turn us not away!

Thus they continued praying from the rising of the dawn: and from that moment, until the sun declined from his meridian height, did God cause the plague to rage among them. Then he relieved them from it: then was it revealed unto David (peace be with him!) that they might lift up their heads; for I have heard thy intercession for them. Then they raised their heads. And there had already died of them one hundred and seventy thousand, struck by the heavenly pestilence whilst prostrate in prayer. Then they beheld angels walking among them with great cimeters in their hands. David (peace be with him!) thus received support, and mounted the Rock, raising his hands, and prostrating himself to God in thanksgiving. After this, he assembled the sons of Israel, and said unto them, God, the ever adorable and great, hath had compassion upon you, and hath forgiven you. Render therefore to God a thank-offering, in proportion to the good thing which he hath done unto you. So they said unto him, What wouldest thou? He replied, I know nothing which can display more fully your thanks, than to build a place of worship, wherein

God may be adored, and wherein you, and those after you, may sanctify him. Then they said, So will we do. David therefore asked his Lord, who gave ear unto him. Then they zealously engaged in the building.

All this happened when he had reigned eleven years: but he died before he had accomplished the building, and enjoined his son Solomon (peace be with him!) to build it; which he did, and built it in nine years: and when he had finished it, the children of Israël feasted therein upon twelve thousand oxen. It is again said, that the cause of this was, that David (peace be with him!) saw angels, with flaming swords, ascending by a golden ladder from the Rock unto heaven. Then said David, This is a place whereon it is fitting that a Mosque should be built to God Almighty. Thus therefore he built it; but, dying before it was completed, he enjoined Solomon to build it; who built it, and finished it.

Now, with regard to all the transactions of Solomon in building this, we are told as follows:—When God revealed unto Solomon that he should build him a Temple, Solomon assembled all the wisest men, genii, and Afrites of the earth, and the mightiest of the devils, and appointed one division of them to build, another to cut blocks and columns from the marble mines, and another to dive into the ocean-deeps, and fetch therefrom pearls and coral. Now, some of these pearls were like ostrich's or hen's eggs. So he began to build the Temple: but the building was found not to be firm; therefore he ordered it to be pulled down. Then he dug down into the earth until he came to the water. Then he began to found it upon the water: and they cast great stones into the water, which the water cast out again. Then Solomon called for the very best of his wise men, at the head of whom was Asaph, son of Barachias, and said, Give me your advice. Then they said, We think that thou shouldst take a pitcher of brass; then fill it with stones; then write upon it the writing which is upon thy signet-ring; then cast the pitcher into the water. Thus, then, they did; and the pitcher fixed the foundation. Then they cast earth and stones thereupon, and built until the building attained some height. Then were the devils distributed by him into different sorts of labour; who were constantly engaged in the work. And he appointed one section of them to cut the quarries of jacinth and emerald. Thus they brought various kinds of precious stones. Also, the devils made highly-polished cemented blocks of marble, for the walls of the Mosque: and whenever they cut from the quarry a block, or a column, the first of them threw it from him, and the nearest to him did the same, and so, one after the other, until it at last arrived at the Mosque. He also appointed a division of them to cut white marble; some of which was in the quarry, as white as milk, of that kind which is called adamant; but this was not like the adamant which is now to be seen in cities, in the hands of men, and is so named. This was from an adamantine quarry belonging to an Afrite of the devils; which mine was in one of the islands of the ocean-deeps. Now these men were subject unto Solomon: therefore he sent unto this Afrite a letter, sealed with a signet-ring of iron; for his signet-ring was composed of brass and iron: with the brass he sealed his commands to the genii, and with iron to the devils. Now, this signet-ring had come down unto him from heaven: its exterior setting was white; but the part wherewith he impressed the seal was like blinding lightning: no one could long bear to look upon it. Now, therefore, when this mandate came to the Afrite, and he had come to Solomon, Solomon said unto him, Have you no device whereby to cut stones? for I hate the sound of iron in this our Mosque. Then said the Afrite unto him, I know not in the heavens a bird stronger than the eagle, nor one more acute in expedients. So he set out to examine this eagle, and found a nest, wherein were some young eagles. Then they covered this nest over with a thick iron case. Then the eagle, coming unto her nest, and finding the iron case, began to strike on it, from above, with her feet, in order to push it away, or to break it: but not succeeding in this, she whirled and soared aloft into the sky, and, having delayed a day and a night, returned with a piece of adamant. Then the devils frightened her away, and, taking it from her, brought it unto Solomon; and by this adamant were the great stones cut. Moreover, we learn as follows, from Wahab:—When Solomon wished to build the Consecrated House, he said unto the devils, God hath commanded me to build him a house, wherein there shall not be one stone cut by iron. Therefore they said, No one has power in this matter, except a certain devil, who dwells in the ocean-deeps, and who has a certain fountain, whither he comes to drink. They repaired, then, to this drinking-place, and, emptying all the water, put wine in its place. Thus did they: so, when this devil came to drink, he found out the smell, and said, Shall I drink, or shall I not drink? But however, being vehemently urged by thirst, he drank, and was captured. Now, whilst they were on the road, they met with a man buying garlic for onions; on which the devil laughed: then they passed by a woman telling fortunes by art magic to the people; upon which the devil laughed again. When, therefore, they brought him to Solomon, they informed the latter of the devil's laughter; and he demanding the cause, he replied, I passed a man who was buying the disease with the remedy; and I passed a woman telling fortunes, whilst beneath her was a treasure, of which she knew nothing. He informed this devil, therefore, of the business of the building, who thereupon ordered a caldron of brass to be brought, which none had ever breathed upon; which they having brought, he said, Cast it over the young of a vulture. This they did. When, therefore, the vulture came to her young, and could not approach them, she soared up, and went aloft into the breezes of heaven; then she descended, bringing a tortoise in her beak, which she placed upon the caldron, and thus broke it. They, therefore, making up to this tortoise, took it, and cut the stones therewith. Now, the number of men who co-operated with Solomon in building the Sacred Abode was thirty thousand: ten thousand of these were occupied in cutting wood. Those also who worked in stone were in number seventy thousand men: of these, three hundred were clerks of the works. All these, in addition to the genii and the devils, pressed for the work. Solomon moreover raised pillars therein, which no one can describe, and at the number of which no one can arrive: these he adorned with gold and silver, and pearls, and jacinth, and coral, and various precious stones. In like manner he adorned the roofs, and the pavement, the gates, the skirting-boards, and the cornices; so that nothing was ever beheld like unto it. He placed herein also one hundred bolts of gold; each bolt (or lock) weighing ten pounds. Herein also he hid the ark of Moses and Aaron.

Again, we learn that when Solomon had finished building this Temple, God caused two trees to bud forth, and bear fruit, at the Gate of Mercy, for Solomon. One tree produced gold, and the other silver: from each tree he gathered, every day, one hundred pounds of gold and silver. Also, the floor of the Mosque was paved with a pavement of gold and silver. Again, there is a tradition from the prophet, that Solomon, son of David, whilst he was building the Temple, asked of God three wise men to be his friends, whose wisdom should be unrivalled; and God granted them to him. Also, he prayed for a kingdom which should be of unapproachable splendour: this also God gave him. And when he had finished the building of the Mosque, he asked that no one should come to pray in that Mosque, but should depart as free from sin as he was the day his mother bare him.

To proceed—When therefore Solomon (peace be with him!) stayed his hand from the work, having accomplished the building, and having provided for its permanent security, he assembled a public meeting, and informed them that this was a Temple for God, which he had commanded to be constructed, and that every thing therein belonged to God, which if any one diminished, in any way, he was a traitor to God. After this, Solomon began to prepare a great feast, and assembled all the people together. Never was such an assembly, or so great a feast seen before. Then he gave orders about the offerings to be offered to God: and he carried this oblation of sacrifices into effect, in the great area of the Mosque: selecting two bulls, he placed them near the Rock: then, standing upon the Rock, he directed an introductory prayer to be offered before he began his commemorative sacrificial prayer, which he did by adding to the first prayer the following additional words:—O God! thou gavest to me this kingdom as a gracious gift, long to remain with me: thou hadst already given it to him who was before me: thou hast granted both to me and to him the first-fruits of thy grace and bounty: thou didst make him supreme judge between thy servants and the creatures of thy land; and thou hast appointed me his heir after him, and the successor to his dignity: thou also art he who didst set me apart for the supreme government of this Mosque; for thine is the superabundant (majesty); and thou didst appoint me to receive thy bounty before thou didst create me. Praise be to thee for this! Thine is the benevolent bounty; thine the perpetuity. O God! I now beseech of thee, on behalf of all who enter the House of Adoration, five pledges of thy mercy:—That no sinner shall enter this Mosque, relying upon its efficiency, and beseeching repentance, but thou shalt receive him graciously, and grant him repentance, and forgive him:—That no one, suffering from drought, shall enter and lean upon this column, entreating a copious shower of rain, but thou shalt send rain upon his land:—That no one, dreading injury, shall enter this Mosque, in full reliance, and entreat safety, but thou shall grant him full relief from all his fear, and pardon him:—That thou shalt never turn away thy sight from any who shall enter it, until he departs therefrom:-- And, O God! that thou shalt love my prayer, and give me my request:—And, to crown all, that thou should graciously accept my sacrifice, and receive with favour my oblation. It is also traditionally said that the heads of the people made the same supplications as were mentioned in Solomon's prayer. There is also an account that the prophet of God, Solomon, when he had concluded the building, sacrificed three thousand cows and seven thousand sheep; and then was formed that place, on the lowest part of the Mosque, near the gate of Sabát, which is called the Throne of Solomon (peace be with him!). Also we have another story:—Solomon said, O God! if any one, possessed by sin, come here, pardon him, or, afflicted with injury, relieve him of his affliction. And this is the place known by the name of Solomon's Throne; being one of the places especially endowed with the gift of a favourable hearing of prayer, when prayed therein. Again, by another tradition, Solomon, when he had built the Consecrated House, and finished it, closed up the gates, and fastened them, lest they should open: nor were they ever opened until he said, after the words of the prayer of his father David, "Open ye the gates! let the gates be opened!" Also, Solomon constituted ten thousand companies of Readers of the children of Israël; five thousand for the day, and five thousand for the night; that there might not be one moment, by night or by day, wherein God was not adored.

By a tradition we learn, that, with respect to opening the gate of the Consecrated House, there was not one of Solomon's attendants who could trust himself to do it. Then came the Spirits of the night to do it; but it was too hard a matter for them. Then he called in the aid of men; but it was too hard for them. Then he asked aid of the genii; but it was too hard for them. Then he sat down in grief, thinking that his Lord had forbidden him to open it: and when he was in this mood, there presented himself before him an old man, leaning upon a staff, and mumbling with his teeth. He was one of the counsellors of David, and he said, O prophet of God! I perceive that you are sad. So he said, I resolved to open this gate; but it was too difficult for me. Then I summoned the assistance of men and of genii, but neither can open it. Then said the old man, Shall I then inform you of the words which thy father David used when he suffered despondency, when also God relieved him of his sorrow? He answered, Yes. Then said the old man, "Say, O God! in thy light will I go the right road; and in thy superabundance will I be contented (will I be satisfied). To thee in the morning, to thee in the evening, will I come. My sins are before thee. Of thee will I ask pardon; and will turn in repentance unto thee, O tenderly merciful! O bounteously gracious!" So, when he said these words, the gate opened. Also from Al Mashrah, who thinks it good that pilgrims should pray the same prayer when they enter the gate of the Sakhrá, as when they enter the gate of the Mosque. Also as follows, When the building of the Temple was completed, ten years had elapsed of the reign of Solomon (peace be with him!) and 546 years from the decease of Moses (peace be with him!), and from the descent of Adam (upon earth) to the period when Solomon began the building of the Consecrated Abode, 4470 years: nor did the Mosque Al Aksá cease to remain in the wonderful condition in which it was until Nebuchadnezzar destroyed it, with seventy thousand standards;—for he entered the Holy Abode with his army, and utterly subdued Syria, and slew the children of Israël until he had utterly destroyed them, and beat down the Holy Abode, carrying from thence ninety waggon-loads of gold and silver, and sent it to Greece, and commanded his army to fill the earth with every man who could bear a shield, and stone them in the Holy Abode.

Now this expedition took place after the murder of Isaiah, and in the time of Jeremiah. And after the death of Nebuchadnezzar, Azir returned to Syria; and the Law was restored to the sons of Israël, from memory, and taken by them (and committed to writing). Also, from the beginning of the building by David, unto the destruction by Nebuchadnezzar, and the overthrow of the dynasty of the sons of Israël, elapsed 454 years. Again, from Abu Abdallah Almubarek, the Temple remained in ruins until it was built by a Persian king, named Kúshak; for Al Baghooee says Kooshan-Ibn-Kúshak-Ibn-Achúndash, built it seventy years after its demolition by Nebuchadnezzar. Then certain weak kings conquered Syria; the kings of Rome giving them the government thereof. These kings caused Syria to embrace their Christianity, until God brought Islam. Among these kings was Jabil-Ibn-Al-Ayham. And God gave the Moslem an entrance into Syria, at the time of Omar-Ibn-Al-Khattáb, (God rest content with him!). Then the Temple was surrendered to Omar by capitulation, and continued in the hands of the Moslem from the Omarian conquest until the Franks seized upon it, and wrested it from the hands of the Moslem, and ruled over it, under the dynasty of the Fathemites, until God again opened Syria to the hand of the Sultan of Islam and of believers, Saláh-ud-dín, (God show mercy to him!) according to the victories and the great events which will be accurately embodied (please God!) in a chapter of this book, which is to follow.

CHAPTER III.

Upon the Virtues of the glorious Sakhrá, and the description of its form in the age of Solomon, and the account of the splendid Chapel erected upon it at that time. Also the account of the river from Paradise; and how the Rock on the day of judgment will change its form, and be white coral; and also the meaning of this.

Now, we are informed by Ibn-Mansoor that the Rock of the Baitu-l-Mukaddas, in the days of Solomon, was of the height of twelve thousand cubits; each cubit, at that time, being the full cubit, viz. one modern cubit, one span, and one hand-breadth. Upon it also was a Chapel, formed of aloës (or sandal) wood, in height twelve miles: also, above this was a net-work of gold, between two eyelet-beads of pearl and ruby, netted by the women of Balka in the night; which net was to serve for three days: also, the people of Emmaus were under the shadow of the chapel when the sun rose, and the people of Bait-Rahmat when it set; and even others of the valleys were under its shadow: also, upon it was a jacinth (or ruby) which shone in the night like the light of the sun; but when the light began to dawn, its brilliancy was obscured; nor did all these cease until Nebuchadnezzar laid all waste, and seized whatever he found there, and carried it into Greece. Again, by a tradition we learn that the Sakhrá of Baitu-l-Mukaddas was raised aloft into the sky, to the height of twelve miles; and the space between it and heaven was no more than twelve miles. All this remained in the same state until Greece (or Rome) obtained the mastery over it, subsequent to its devastation by Nebuchadnezzar. But when the Greeks obtained possession of it, they said, Let us build thereupon a building far excelling that which was there before. Therefore they built upon it a building as broad at the base as it was high in the sky, and gilded it with gold, and silvered it with silver. Then, entering therein, they began to practise their associating Paganism; upon which it turned upside down over them, so that not one of them came out. Therefore, when the Grecian (king) saw this, he summoned the Patriarch and his ministers (deacons), and the chiefs of Greece, and said, What think ye? Who replied, We are of opinion that our idol-gods are not well pleased, and therefore will not receive us favourably. Hereupon he commanded a second Temple to be built; which they did, spending a great sum thereon: and having finished the second building, seventy thousand entered it, as they had entered the first. But it happened to them as it had happened to the first: when they began their Paganism, it turned over upon them. Now their king was not with them. Therefore, when he saw this, he assembled them a third time, and said unto them, What think ye? Who said, We think that our Lord is not well pleased with us, because we have not offered unto him abundantly; therefore he has destroyed what we have done: therefore we should greatly wish to build a third. They then built a third, until they thought they had carried it to the greatest possible height; which having done, he assembled the Christians, and said unto them, Do ye observe any defect? Who said, None, except that we must surround it with crosses of gold and silver. Then all the people entered it, to read and cite (sacred things). Having bathed and perfumed themselves, and having entered it, they began to practise their associating Paganism, as the others had done before them; whereupon, down fell the third building upon them. Hereupon the king again summoned them together, and asked their counsel about what he should do. But their dread was very great; and, whilst they were deliberating, there came up to them a very old man, in a white robe and a black turban: his back was bent double, and he was leaning upon a staff. So he said, O Christian people, listen to me! listen to me! for I am the oldest of any of you in years, and have now come forth from among the retired votaries of religion, in order to inform you that, with respect to this place, all its possessors are accursed, and all holiness hath departed from it, and hath been transferred to this (other) place. I will therefore point out *this* as the place wherein to build the Church of the Resurrection. I will show you the spot; but you will never see me after this day, for ever. Do therefore with a good will that which I shall tell you. Thus he cheated them, and augmented their accursed state, and commanded them to cut up the Rock, and to build with its stones upon the place which he commanded them. So, whilst he was talking with them, he became concealed; and they saw him no more. Thereupon they increased in their infidelity, and said, This is the Great Word. Then they demolished the Mosques, and carried away the columns and the stones, and all the rest, and built therewith the Church of the Resurrection, and the Church which is in the valley of Hinnom. Moreover, this cursed old man commanded them, "When ye have finished their building upon this place, then take that place whose owners are accursed, and whence all holiness hath departed, to be a common sewer to receive your dung." By this they gratified their Lord. Also, they did this, as follows:—At certain seasons, all the filth and excrement was sent in vessels from Constantinople, and was at a certain time all thrown upon the Rock, until God awoke our prophet Muhammad (the peace and blessing of God be with him!), and brought him by night thereunto: which he did, on account of its peculiar consecration, and on account of the greatness of its superexcellence. We learn also, that God, on the day of judgment, will change the Sakhrá into white coral, enlarging it to extend over heaven and earth: then shall men go from that Rock to heaven or hell, according to that great word, "There shall be a time when this earth shall change into another earth, and the heaven shall turn white; the soil shall be of silver; no pollution shall ever dwell thereon." Now from Aísh, (may the satisfying favour of God rest upon him!) I said, O apostle of God, on that day when this earth shall become another earth, and this sky shall change, where shall men be on that day? He replied, Upon the bridge Al Sirát. Again, a certain divine says, That, in the Law, God says to the Rock of the Holy Abode, Thou art my seat; thou art near to me: from thy foundation have I raised up the heavens, and from beneath thee have

I stretched forth the earth; and all the distant inaccessible mountains are beneath thee. Who dies within thee, is as if he died within the world of Heaven; and who dies around thee, is as if he died within thee. Days and nights shall not cease to succeed, until I send down upon thee a Light of heaven, which shall obliterate all the (traces) of the Infidels of the sons of Adam, and all their footsteps. Also, I will send upon thee the hierarchy of angels and prophets; and I will wash thee until I leave thee like milk; and I will fix upon thee a wall, twelve miles above the thick-gathering clouds of earth, and also a hedge of light. By my hand will I insure to thee thy support and thy virtue: upon thee will I cause to descend my spirits and my angels, to worship within thee; nor shall any one of the sons of Adam enter within thee until the day of judgment. And whosoever shall look upon this Chapel from afar, shall say, Blessed be the face of him who devoutly worships and adores in thee! Upon thee will I place walls of light, and a hedge of thick clouds—five walls of ruby and pearl. Also, from the Book of Psalms, "Great and glorious art thou, thou threshing-floor! Unto thee shall be the general assemblage: from thee shall all men rise from death." Moreover, from the same author, God says to the Rock of the Holy Abode, Who loveth thee, him will I love; who loveth thee, loveth me; who hateth thee, him will I hate. From year to year my eyes are upon thee; nor will I forget thee until I forget my eyes. Whoso prayeth within thee two Rakás, him will I cause to cast off all his sins, and to be as guiltless as I brought him from his mother's womb, unless he return to his sins—beginning them afresh. This is also a tradition of old standing:—I solemnly engage and promise to every one who dwells therein, that, all the days of his life, the bread of corn and olive-oil never shall fail him; nor shall the days and the nights fail to bring that time, when, out of the supremacy of my bounty, I will cause to descend upon thee the assemblage of man for judgment—the whole company of risen mortals. There is a tradition, that Mukátil Ibn Sulaiman came to this Temple, to pray, and sat by the gate looking towards the Rock: and we had assembled there in great numbers: he was reading, and we were listening. Then came forward Ali Ibn Bedawwee, stamping terribly with his slippers upon the pavement. This greatly afflicted him; and he said to those around him, Make an opening for me. Then the people opened on each side; and he made a threatening motion with his hand, to warn him, and prevent this stamping; saying, Tread more gently! That place, at which Mukátil is pointing with his hand, and on which thou art stamping, is the very place redolent of Heaven's breezes ; and there is not a spot all around it—not a spot within its precincts a hand's-breadth square —wherein some commissioned prophet, some near angel, hath not prayed. Now, from the mother of Abdallah, daughter of Khaled, from her mother, the moment is surely fixed, when the Kaaba shall be led as a bride to the Sakhrá, and shall hang upon her all her pilgrimage-merits, and become her turban. Also, it is said that the Sakhrá is the middle of the Mosque : it is cut off from every touching substance, on all sides. No one supports it but he who supports and holds up the sky ; so that nothing falls thence but by his good permission : also upon the upper part of the west side stood the prophet (the blessing and peace of God be with him !) on the night when he rode Al Burák. This side began to shake about, from veneration of him ; and upon the other side are the marks of the angel's fingers, who held it up when it shook : beneath it is a deep hole cut out on each side, over which is the gate opened to men for prayer and devotion. I resolved (says a certain author) one day to enter it, in great fear, lest it should fall upon me, on account of the sins I had contracted : then, however, I looked, and saw its darkness, and some holy pilgrims entering it, at the darkest part, who came forth therefrom quite free from sin. Then I began to reflect upon entering. Then I said, Perhaps they entered very slowly and leisurely, and I was too much in a hurry ; a little delay may facilitate the matter : so I made up my mind to enter, and, entering, I saw the Wonder of Wonders, the Rock supported in its position, or course, on every side ; for I saw it separated from the earth, so that no point of the earth touched it. Some of the sides were separated by a wider interval than others ; also, the mark of the glorious Foot is at present in a stone divided from the Rock, right over against it, on the other side, west of the Kiblah : it is upon a pillar. Also, the Rock is now almost abutting upon the side of the Crypt ; only divided from it by that space which allows room for the gate of the Crypt, on the side of the Kiblah. This gate, also, is disjoined from the base of the Kiblah : it is between the two : below the gate of the Crypt is a stone staircase, whereby one may descend into the Crypt. In the midst of this Crypt is a dark brown leather carpet, upon which pilgrims stand when they visit the foundation of the Rock : it is upon the eastern side. There are also columns of marble abutting on the lower side upon the path of the rows of trees upon the side of the Kiblah, and on the other side forming buttresses to the extremity of the Rock : these are to hinder it from shaking on the side of the Kiblah. There are buildings besides these. There is a building in the Chapel of the Rock. Beneath the Chapel, the spot marked by the angel's fingers is in the Rock, on the western side, divided from the print of the glorious Foot above-mentioned, very near to it, over against the western gate, at the end.

CHAPTER IV.

Upon the surpassing efficacy of prayer in Baitu-l-Mukaddas, and how it becomes double. Also upon the New Moon of Reduplication, when by prayer, the Sacred Precept, and the merits of Works of Supererogation may be diffused to the public. Also the New Moon of Reduplication, when blessings and cursings may be communicated. Also the marvellous effect of pious donations, and fastings, and listening to preaching therein. Also the New Moons of the Sacred Pilgrimage, and the Sacred Visitation. Also the marvellous efficacy of supplying Oil for the Lamps; and how by this the rank and merit of Pilgrimage may be made to exist for those who are unable to undertake the journey.

First, from Kaab-Al-Ahbár, who says as follows:—The Temple complained unto its Lord of its demolition. Then God revealed unto it the words following:—The prayer-intercepting veil shall not long be upon thee. Soon shall men sew again thy beautiful torn garment to its strings, and brood over thee with tender affection, as the turtle-dove broods over her eggs. Upon this, a man said unto Kaab—O Kaab! reverence God! Has the Holy House a tongue? Then Kaab said, Certainly; and a heart too, like any of yours. Also, the Baitu-l-Mukaddas complained to its Lord. (Then a man of the people of Syria said, Why, Kaab! has the house a tongue? Certainly, said Kaab, and ears too.) Then said God unto it, Long shall they use thy clefts for prayer: they shall reserve thy torn beautiful veil to its strings; they shall brood over thee as a turtle-dove over her eggs. Also, from Aní-Ibn-Mẩlik; who says, The apostle of God said, Whoever shall purposely visit the Temple, God shall grant him the reward of one thousand martyrs. Also, whosoever shall honourably visit a learned man, shall be considered as visiting this Temple: and whosoever deliberately (lit. counting the cost) visit this Temple, God shall keep his flesh and body safe from hell. Again, we are told, that if any company set out, desiring to reach the Holy House, ten thousand angels shall bear them company, entreating God's pardon for them, and praying for them. These angels shall act as their agents and managers; and when they arrive at the Holy House, seventy angels shall every day offer prayer for them. Also, whosoever shall enter the Holy House, being pure, and crying out, Allah Akbar! Allah Akbar! God shall meet him with one hundred mercies, beyond the mercies which by an oath he has sworn to grant in abundance to all creatures. Again, the prophet said, There are three angels. One angel is the deputed guardian of the Kaaba; one angel of my Mosque; and one angel of the Mosque Al Aksá. Now the angel, deputy guardian of the Kaaba, cries aloud every day, Whoso leaveth the divine precepts of God, shall be cast forth from the peace and pardon of God. Also the angel, deputy guardian of my Mosque, cries aloud every day, Whoso leaveth the Sunna of Muhammad, shall not be able to avoid the fish-pond, nor obtain the mediation of Muhammad. Also the angel, deputy guardian of the Mosque Al Aksá, cries aloud every day, Whoso eateth any forbidden food, acts as if he were to give his guardian-angel-provider a blow upon the face. Again, the apostle of God said, Whosoever shall pray in this Temple five prayers, adding to those prayers, over and above, as a supererogatory work of merit beyond the prescribed precept, four Rakás, reading at the same time the verse, "Say, God is one God," then his soul shall be purchased and redeemed of God: hell shall have no power over him. Now from Abu Zaharah Jarír-Ibn-Karíb: I came unto the Temple for the purpose of praying; and, my eyes being unaccustomed to the place, I lost my way out; so that the candles and lights were extinguished. I lost all my companions; and the gates were shut. Now, whilst I was in this condition, lo! I heard a gentle whisper, as of two responsive bands, which were coming forward, and who began to say, Praise be unto the Eternal Self-subsisting! Praise to the Self-subsisting Eternal! Praise to the Highest of the High, and the Almighty! Praise to the Ever-living, the Disposer! Praise to the King of Saints, the Lord of angels and spirits! Praise and exaltation to the great God! Then another whisper began, responsive to the first, repeating the same words. Then they began to sing alternately a gentle chant, chant following chant, until the whole Mosque was filled with the strains. Then, behold! some of them approached me, and said, Art thou one of the race of Adam? I replied, Yes. Then said one, Do not fear; these are the angels of God. So I said, I ask thee, in the name of God, who is that mighty one among you, whom I see in the foremost rank? He said, Gabriel. Then said I, And who is that next to him? He said, Michael. Then I said, who those that follow them? He said, They are angels. So I said, I ask thee, in God's name, who hath exalted you? as I see, what is the greatest of rewards, next to yours? He said, His who shall say the Sunna once a day. He shall not die until he sees his seat in Paradise, or have it exhibited unto him. Then said Abu Al Zaharat, I said to myself, the Sunna is long to get through: I shall not live. However, I said it every day, for the whole number of the days of the year; that is, three hundred and seventy. Then I saw my seat in Paradise.

Now, with respect to the Reduplication of Prayer in the Baitu-l-Mukaddas: —First, from the traditions of Katádat, from Abádat, Ibn Al Samát (God rest content with him!) from Abu Dhirr, I said, O apostle of God! is prayer in this holy Mosque more meritorious than prayer in the Baitu-l-Mukaddas? Then said he, One prayer in this my Mosque is more meritorious than four prayers in the Baitu-l-Mukaddas. But let the prayer-offerer know that this land (of the Holy Abode) is the place where the risen shall all assemble; for the appointed time shall arrive to men; and at the distance of a bow-shot from hence shall be seen the Baitu-l-Mukaddas. Truly it is good and right entirely the most beloved of all the lands of the world. Now, with respect to the Reduplication of good and evil things, we will quote from a tradition; which affirms, that Kaab set out from Emessa, desiring to pray within the Baitu-l-Mukaddas—the mosque of Elia: and when he arrived within a mile's distance from Elia, he immediately ceased from words, and was silent, except chanting from the Book of God, and proclaiming the sacred titles. Then he entered by the gate Al Sabát, in order to come right in front of the Holy Place. Then he repeats all the prayers at once in the Mosque, and, changing the behaviour he had observed for one mile, he began to speak, and said, Praise! Then they said unto him, O Abu Ishák, what hath induced thee to do thus? Then he said, I have read in a certain book, that good words, things, or blessings are doubled in this Mosque; and bad words, things, or blessings are doubled in like manner. So he said, or spoke, words to that effect; adding also as follows: Therefore I was greatly desirous that nothing but good words should proceed from me until I should depart. Now, from Dhamarat Ibn Al Layth, Ibn Soad, Ibn Náfa, who says, Ibn Omar said to me, whilst we were in the Holy Abode, O Náfa! I will depart from the Holy House; for evil words are doubled therein; as also are good words: therefore I feel a dread. Then he departed from the Holy House. Now, from Soám, Ibn Omar, Ibn Sharíh, Ibn Obaid, who says that Kaab said, Prayer in the Holy House is worth a thousand prayers, and sin in the Holy House is worth a thousand sins elsewhere. Now from Al Mughírat. He said, Abadat told us, from his father, thus: Whoso cometh into the Holy Abode, let him not buy or sell any thing; for a sin therein is as a thousand sins, and a good word is augmented in an equal proportion.

Now for the marvellous efficacy of pious donations in this Temple, and of fasting, and articulate praises, (or listening to preaching) herein. Whosoever, saith a divine, giveth pious donations in the Temple, to the amount of ten thousand dirhems, shall thereby obtain a safe covert from hell; and whosoever shall give in alms common scraps, shall be considered as giving their weight in gold: also, whosoever shall give in the Holy Abode a pious donation of ten thousand dirhems, shall thereby redeem his soul from hell; and whosoever shall give in alms the meanest scraps, shall be regarded as giving mountains of the earth, all of gold. Also, from the same author, from Al Saray, Aliyas (Elias), and Phinehas (St. George), fasted during the month Rhamadán in the Holy Abode, and accomplished the sacred pilgrimage to Mecca every year.

Now from Jairám:—A man said to Muhammad, O apostle of God! what created beings are to be found on first entering Paradise? He replied, The prophets. Then said the man, And who then? He said, The martyrs. Who then? They who pronounce the *viva voce* chant in the Baitu-l-Mukaddas. Who then? They who do the same in the Kaaba. Who then? They who do the same in my Mosque. Who then? They who desire and set forward to pronounce the chant in the Baitu-l-Mukaddas. Who then? All who pronounce that chant. Now from Ibn-

Harún:—"He said, I have heard that the company of Martyrs heard the *viva voce* chant of the Muezzins of this Temple, at the time of the early morning prayer, on the day of assembly (Friday)." Now from Kaab:—"There is not a man who ever suffers martyrdom for piety and devotion to God's cause, but he from the parts of the earth listens to the chant of the Muezzins in this Temple: for truly that chant is heard in heaven." Now from a certain Muezzin in this Temple:—"He was pronouncing the chant for Morning Prayer, when he suddenly changed the chant, and said, There is no God but God. Now, there is not a martyr upon the face of the earth but hears my chant. Then he proceeded, and called aloud the other prayers."

There is, however, some difference of opinion about the Reduplication. The author of the Muthír Alfarám says, in the first chapter of the aforesaid book, that not only is there a reduplication of *prayer* in the Mosque Al Aksá, but a reduplication of *every good* we seek. No distinction is made between the two. Some, moreover, of the sect of Shafís, and followers of Málik, say, that the reduplication in the three mosques is not restricted to prayers of obligations, but common to all prayers of supererogation. There are also those who hope in the bounty of God, that *every* work of piety shall, in like manner, obtain this crowning blessing, by the accomplishment of his word. Now from that great saint, the Imám Nuwwí, (God be merciful unto him!): he says, "Prayer receives a double reward if offered at Mecca; and, in like manner, all kinds of obedient services and duties which are here performed with prayer." And in like manner shall the same be the case here at Jerusalem, please God! Again, Al Muhibb Al Tibraní relates from Ibn-Abbás, (the satisfying favour of God be with him!) "Every good deed in the Kaaba is magnified one hundred thousand times." Then he said, I will mention an existing circumstance, confirmed by the kadi of kadies, Azuddín, Ibn-Jamá, who was a very great saint. Then he mentioned all the supreme efficacy of fasting, in the words of Ibn-Abbás. These, however, are still further confirmed by the authority of thirteen saints after him. Then he said, The word of Ibn-Abbás is the most ancient: There is a privilege that good deeds herein shall be augmented one hundred thousand fold.

Many persons will feel a distaste to the rules laid down in this chapter; for therein there is no space for the exercise of acumen; and they have not been given by the prophet over and above necessary acts of devotion. It has not been propounded by him, that good deeds receive a hundred thousand fold, freely granted. Nevertheless, with respect to prayer in the Kaaba, it appears to be confirmed and established as a consummate privilege that such is the case: the definitive conclusion appears to be, that all this does not here take place *without* prayer. The following is the observation of the author of the Muthír Alfarám: "The sect of the Shafís say, that reduplication in the three Mosques is not peculiar to the prayer of necessary obligation, but is common to the prayer of Supererogation;" as Al-Nuwwí said in his 'High Road to Islamism,' viz. That the true orthodox opinion and tradition is, that the prayer of a man in his house is the smallest in value; that the written assertions do not agree with previous traditions respecting the reduplication. So it may be concluded, that works of supererogation are redoubled in the three Mosques; that they are the most glorious of Temples; and that in one of the three Mosques must the thus privileged prayer be offered.

Now, from the tradition of Tálík, the Kadi Abul-Taib. He appears to throw some doubt upon that which hath been unfolded with respect to prayer in the Mosque: for he thinks that to do supererogatory *works* therein is more meritorious. The tradition is free and open to discussion: the arena of the schools, for the most part, feels averse to it: however, as to the observations of Záhir about the traditionary explication of all this, they appear to be founded upon a scarcity of manifest facts respecting those matters which his eloquence would penetrate.

Know also, that those works of supererogation, so meritoriously performed in the Baitu-l-Mukaddas, which are of necessity required, by no means supersede the Rakás of the Sacred Procession round the Kaaba. To perform these last in the Masjidu-l-Harám is the most meritorious; and to perform the supererogatory prayers on the day of assembly, before all the congregation, is most meritorious. Now from a certain whirling-devotee of the Shafís, one of our authors. He differs from some about the Evening Prayer: he says, unfolding the argumentative reasons herein, that such prayer is more meritorious within the house (privately); and that this is the most authorized tradition; for that *He* (upon whom be God's blessing and peace!) began the great chapel, at Mecca, in Rhamadam, and prayed in the night; and the men of his companions began to pray too: which discovering, he began to sit up; and, going out to them, said, I have remarked what I see you doing, O men! Pray within your houses; for more meritorious is a prayer said quietly in your dwelling, than any thing, unless it be a portion of

Scripture purchased, or perhaps the Rakás in the Masjidu-l-Harám. Again, in the visit to the Garden, it is said, Our authors say, that among the means of preservation from sin, is that Mosque wherein prayer is favourably heard. With respect to the reduplication of good and bad things, and the necessary means of procuring the reduplication of evil things, our proof is the tradition of Kaab-Al-Sábik (the ancient), how that, coming from Emessa, he wished to pray in the back part of the Mosque of Elia; and also said, I was unwilling that any but good words should proceed from me until I departed. Know also, that the historian Abul-Kásim has the following passage, viz.—" Next follows his *i. e.* Kaab's) remark, and also the remark of others besides him, asserting that sins herein committed are multiplied one thousand fold, and so on. His meaning is, that whosoever is convicted of sin in the Mosque of Jerusalem, or in the Mosque of Mecca or Medina, deserves a greater punishment than he who commits the same sin anywhere else; and this on account of their glory and pre-eminence. He also remarks, that one sin committed in either of these, is greater than all sins together, committed in other places; and the reward of one sin here committed shall be precisely equal to the reward of all sins elsewhere perpetrated. As to the word Reduplication, the meaning is, that the *punishment* will be greater—a meaning expressed in harsh words. Not that a man shall be *made* to work sin. Moreover, it is written, God says, Whosoever cometh with good, he shall have ten times; whoso cometh with evil, shall be repaid the like: for the holy doctors have greatly augmented the price of blood, which he must pay who committeth murder in the forbidden place, or who killeth any near relation entitled to enter the Haram;—their appointed fine is greater than that of others. Also, God hath said, Whoso here committeth a wicked action, in the dark, shall quickly leap into a painful and torturing punishment, more than he shall endure whom thou *beholdest* doing wrong. And if thou seest any one doing wrong in this Mosque, he is a greater sinner than he who does the same offence in any other Mosque. The reproach of the man so doing in the Mosque will soon arrive, even if the two parties were companions in guilt, equally obnoxious in other respects." Another author remarks, that sinful actions here committed are greatly augmented in filthiness and baseness. For a dereliction of duty committed at times, or in places which are more sacred and glorious than at other times and places, shows that the offender possesses the utmost degree of audacity, and as little as possible of the fear of God.

Now, with respect to the marvellous merit of the observance of the New Moons of the Sacred Pilgrimage, and the Sacred Visitation in this Temple. First, from the traditions of the Prophet, He said, Whoso shall sing the Hallelujah, and observe the New Moon of the Sacred Visitation, in the Baitu-l-Mukaddas, shall be pardoned. Now, from another tradition: "Whosoever shall perform the dread and sacred procession round the Baitu-l-Mukaddas, with the due mortifications, shall receive pardon from God. This awful procession was executed by Omar-Ibn-Al-Khattáb, in the course of his religious journey from Mecca to the Holy Land; when he said, Truly I love to come unto the Baitu-l-Mukaddas." Also, Abú-Davad said, Wakí performed the awful procession in the Baitu-l-Mukaddas (having passed thereto from the far distant places, and obtained the benefits of its wonderful efficacy,) without one of his comrades (the satisfaction of God be with them!); for all were unwilling then to undertake it, and Omar-Ibn-Al-Khattáb (God's satisfaction be with him!) had prohibited Imrám-Ibn-Al-Hussain from undertaking the sacred circuit, from Basra, which Al-Hassan and Atá-Ibn-Ríah, and Málik, also felt averse to. Therefore, said Imran, I praise the face of him who performs the rites of the due seasons. Then said one of them, More honourable is the face of him who detests that one should think of opposing the Muharran, or of violating that sacred month.

Now, with respect to the marvellous effects of supplying oil for the candles upon those who cannot contrive to come to the Holy House, and how there is established a place of prayer for them. First, from a tradition of Maimúma, one of the prophet's wives, how she said, Apostle of God! give us an opinion upon the virtue and eminence of the Baitu-l-Mukaddas. Who replied, That is the land wherein the risen will assemble. Go ye thither and pray, for one prayer there is equal to a thousand. Then one said, O apostle of God! suppose a man is unable to depart thereunto. He said, Whosoever cannot go thereunto, let him present some of the (olive) oil, to supply the candles: for if that oil be given by him, it is just the same as if he went there; or, (to use, according to some, the precise words of both,) she said, I see that you do not clearly express yourself, whether we must set off for this Holy House, and actually come there. Then he said, Let the oil be presented by you—the oil that supplies light for the lamps; for, to present this oil, is the same as if one prayed there. Whosoever shall supply light for one lamp within the Holy Abode, for the forgiveness of his sins, the angels shall never cease to pray whilst the smallest stick or stone of the Mosque remains. Praise be to God, the Almighty and Omniscient!

CHAPTER V.

An account of the Water which flows from the foot of the Rock which is over one of the Rivers of Paradise, and is completely cut off, and remains in the midst of the Mosque, not coming into contact with any of the surrounding parts. Also, the due and approved way of entering within the Rock, with the proper ceremonies, and the great eligibility of praying therein; and from what side he who desires to enter must enter, and the prayer outside it, which is unacceptable. Also, an account of the Chain, and the cause of its removal (from sight). Also, an account of the black marble pavement over the Gate of Paradise, and the great eligibility of prayer thereon, and supplication in a form set apart for that purpose.

First, from Abu-Horaira, from the prophet of God. He said, That the sweet waters and the fertilizing breezes proceed from beneath the rock of the Baitu-l-Mukaddas; also from the Abu-Ibn-Kaab, who mentions the glorious verse (of the Korán), "We have brought him, and Lot, in safety unto a land in which we will bless all the world." This verse alludes to Syria, and to the sweet water which flows from beneath the Sakhrá of the Baitu-l-Mukaddas. Another writer says, From below the rock of the Holy Abode flow four rivers of Paradise—Seehan, and Geehan, and Al Níl, and Al Furát. Now, Seehan is the river of Balkh—the Oxus, in Khorassán; Geehan is the river Tigris; Al Níl is the Egyptian Nile; and Al Furát is Euphrates—the river of Kúfa: also, all the water which the sons of men drink, is derived from these four rivers, which flow from beneath the Sakhrá (rock). Again, from Ibn Abbas (God's satisfaction be with him!): God hath sent down *five* rivers from Paradise unto the earth:—Seehan, which is the river of India; and Yihún, which is the river of Balkh; and Al Furát and Al Dijlat, which are the rivers of Irak; and Al Níl, which is the Nile of Egypt. These all flow from one fountain, which is itself one of the fountains of Paradise. They were brought from the remotest depths of Paradise upon the wings of Gabriel. They were set down upon the mountains by him; and God made them to flow upon the earth, and gave them for the service and advantage of men in all the various purposes of life. To this purpose is the great verse (of the Korán), "By our power have we sent down water from heaven upon the earth; and, behold! when Majúj and Yajúj come forth, God shall send down Gabriel, who shall carry away from the earth the Korán and the true knowledge, and the corner-stone of the Temple, and the spot where Abraham stood (peace be with him !), and the ark of Moses (peace be with him !), and all that is therein." And these five rivers shall all be carried away to Heaven : for this is the divine word :—" I am he who can cause the mighty to come ; and, lo ! I will carry away these things from the earth, upon which the Faith, and mankind, now dwell."

Now, with regard to the Chain, which is among the miracles of the exterior surface of the glorious Rock in the Baitu-l-Mukaddas, Ibn-Abbas tells us that the Prophet said, That, with regard to the Rock of this Temple, the children of Israël had an immense hole, in which was a chain ; and this hole was bored in the Rock : also from this hole they suspended their chain, which was in the middle of the hole. Then they approached with their offerings ; and whatever was graciously received, was taken up ; but whatever was not accepted, remained attached and adhering to the ground. In like manner were their fastings and sackcloth clothings accepted or rejected. Now, from Ali-Ibn-Abu-Tálib (God's contentment be with him !)—He said, Men never more needed the chain to be among them (than) this day. So they said, What chain ? Who replied, The chain which God gave unto David (peace be with him !).

By this chain, assertions were judged: for there came two men, in order to claim justice: one of these, having gone to a distance, had committed to the care of the other man a pearl, or some gold, (I do not know which, said Ali). Then the last man took a stick, and, boring a hole within it, placed the pearl therein, or melted the gold and placed it therein. Then he denied to its owner that he had ever received it. This last came to David (peace be with him!), who said, Go ye unto the chain. Then the man who owned the property said, O God! thou knowest that I gave him the pearl (or the gold); but he denies it: I pray thee therefore that I may make the chain shake. Then the chain shook. Then said the other man, Hold my stick, whilst I take the oath. So he gave him the stick, in which was the entrusted property, and then said, O God! thou knowest that I have given him his deposited property again. I ask thee that I may make the chain shake. Then the chain shook. Then said David (peace be with him!), O Lord! what is this? The injurer and the injured party both make the chain shake (in assent). Upon this God revealed unto him that the property was within the stick which the one had given to the other. From this time the chain was removed (from sight). Also, it is said, that this chain was one of the signs of David (peace be with him!): for he was judging between two of the sons of Israël by God's law, and said, O God! would that thou wouldst give me to behold some clear evidence whereby to know the just from the unjust, and the true from the false. Then God sent down unto him from heaven a chain of light, suspended over the spot now on the Rock, between heaven and earth; and whenever he proceeded to give judgment, he sent the men to the spot wherein was the chain. Whoever, then, was true in his saying respecting the matters in dispute, towards him the chain gently moved; but whosoever was a liar, unto him it moved not. Until that fraud and deception fell among men, and their inward minds became depraved, then the chain was removed, for this time. This chain was one of the miracles; and was suspended from heaven to earth, east of the Rock, on the spot where now exists the Chain Chapel, built by Abdul-Málik-Ibn-Marwán. Upon this subject, a certain poet says (verse), "The Scripture hath gone; nobility is dead; generosity is carried away with the chain."

This is the place for examining a different story, told by the author of the Muthír Alfaram. He says, There were two Jewish men; one of whom confided to the other one hundred deenars; which sum he reclaimed; but the other denied that he had it; which affair caused the removal of the chain: for the one, a Jew, in his fraud, and wickedness, and craftiness, had melted down the deenars, and, hollowing out a stick, placed them therein. When, therefore, he came to the spot where the chain was, he gave the stick to the owner of the deenars, and laid hold of the chain, swearing by God that he had restored them. Then the owner of the deenars gave the stick back, and, going forward, took hold of the chain, swore that he had never received them, and the chain touched both of them: upon which, the people were surprised beyond measure. From that day, the chain was removed. Before this, whoever spoke the truth, could touch the chain, but whoever spoke folly, saw it rise up, and could not reach it.

Now, for the eligibility of praying at the entrance of the Sakhrá, and the proper and commendable rites and ceremonies to be observed upon entering: also, upon the proper seasons when any one, desiring so to do, may enter it. First, from the traditions of Abu-Al-Muálí, in his sayings, and the opinion he expressed regarding the supplication to be used in preference by any one entering the Rock of the Baitu-l-Mukaddas: "It is best," he says, "for any one entering the Sakhrá, to do so on the right hand; so that he may have his back towards the sacred processioners around the Temple of the Kaaba: then let him go on towards the spot where the public pray, and place his hands thereon (falling prostrate), and by no means move them onward: then let him pray what he will. It is rather preferable that he pray the Prayer of Solomon (peace be with him!), which he prayed when he completed the building of the Temple, and was offering his sacrifices. This is the prayer: "O God! if any sinner enter herein, pardon his sins; if any suffer evil, remove his sufferings" (this is a very ancient piece of traditionary scripture): then let him supplicate whatever he will, relating to the accomplishing of all good and advantageous things, both relating to this world and the next. If he earnestly desire to descend below the Rock, let him do so: let him perform his designs; and he will seal his repentance by a sincere adoration and recurrence to God. Let him be diligent in prayer; and, when he descends, let him descend with the commendable ceremonies, the humiliation, and the prayer which occurs to him. For, if he will but use diligence in prayer beneath the Rock, to that prayer a favourable hearing is certainly assured; please God! However, the author of 'The Book of Social Converse,' and 'The Book of the Resurrection of Spirits,' says, That prayer which is here offered, is by no means peculiarly acceptable in this place; for that, if men undertake prayer, a favourable answer is promised in his Word. Your Lord hath said, "Pray to me; I will favourably hear, and I will send my servants (to aid you): for I am near, and favour the prayer of him who prays, when he prays unto me." Also, an indispensable part of prayer consists in extracts from the glorious Sunna of the Prophet. Now, from Abdallah-Ibn-Yazíd, from his father: That the Apostle of God (the peace and blessing of God be with him!) saw a man praying thus:—"O God! I beseech thee, because thou art one God; the Lord to whom we must have recourse. Thou never didst beget; thou art not begotten; there is no one thy compeer." Then said the Apostle of God, (the peace and blessing of God be with him!) That man hath prayed to God in his great name; therefore his petitions shall be granted, and his prayer favourably received. Now, from Ali-Ibn-Arút—from one who informed him—That Omaz-Ibn-Yásir was praying among the people, who however made light of his prayer. Then he said, By God! I will not depart until I have prayed to God the prayer which the Prophet (the peace and blessing of God be with him!) prayed, and asserted that every angel nearest to God's throne, and every commissioned prophet, and every true and faithful servant, prayed no other prayer than this:—"O God! in thy works there is mystery, and mystery in the fated power over the creation. Grant that I may live in the enjoyment of all those pleasures which are profitable for me, and die, when thou dost appoint me, a death good for me. I beseech thee, grant me thy guardian shield in doubt, and testimony and the word of truth in wrath, and content and right direction in poverty and in competency. I beseech thee, grant me the good that shall never fade away, and large domestic enjoyments which shall never be cut off, and the refreshment of a joyful life after death. I beseech thee that I may be made to behold thy face, and be urged by a vehement desire to meet thee (come before thee), without suffering any utterly ruinous sorrow, or falling into any temptation which may lead me astray. O God! adorn me with the ornament of the faith, and lead me in the straight and right road."

Now, also, from Al-Hassan-Ibn-Al-Hassan, who says, I think it was Ibn-Masúd who narrated and said, The prophet Idrís (peace be with him!) prayed a prayer, and commanded that they should not give their minds to silly trifling; but pray it. And this was the prayer:—"O thou majestic and bounteous One! O thou Eternal One! there is no God but thee. Thou art the helper of all who take refuge in thee; the guardian of all that seek thy aid; the assurer of all who fear. O God! if in the book of thy decrees it is laid down that I must suffer misery, and straitened circumstances, and a scanty supply of needful things; then, O God! obliterate therefrom my misery, my wants, my deficiency of necessary things; and assure to me (happily, in the right way, most adapted for the attainment of good,—the way by which thou revealest the means of obtaining sufficient supply), assure to me that competence which may supply my needs: for thou hast said it. Thy true and faithful word is in thy book, which thou didst send down to thy apostolized Prophet, viz. 'God wipes out whatsoever he willeth, and confirms whatsoever he willeth; for with him is the source and origin of all the decrees of the book.'" Also, observes the same author, he will obtain in the end abundance of good, and receive an overflowing fortune; being abundantly presented with rewards and recompenses. Moreover, many good and worthy people go to the Temple, and, whilst entering the glorious Rock, use the words which a certain old Shaikh, who had been one of David's comrades, (may peace be with him!) taught to his son Solomon (peace be with him!) when he found it a difficult matter to open the gate; viz. "O God, thou shalt lead me by thy light, in the true path, for the time to come, as we have been told thou didst in time past." It is very much to be preferred that thou shouldst pray this prayer when the Rock is entered. Let him that entereth place his hands upon it, but not kiss it, as we have enjoined; although I have seen one who saluted all the points of the Rock, and kissed more especially its lower part, near the Gate of Compassion. For this there is no authority or quoted opinion.

Now, for the unfavourable acceptation of the praising prayer upon the surface of the Rock, we find, from the author of 'The Resurrection of Spirits,' and the 'Keys of all matters thereon dependent,' and from a part of his 'Sunna,' derived from Abu-Al-Huraira, the Kadi, that thanksgiving prayer is unacceptable in the seven chapels on the area of the Kaaba, and upon the surface of the Rock of the Baitu-l-Mukaddas, and Mount Sinai and the Mount of Olives, and Al Safá, and Marút, and Mount Arafat. Nevertheless, he says, in his 'Keys:' Our companions insist upon the necessary excellence of prayer upon the broad part of the Kaaba, where the building is kissed, upon a space of three cubits square. They are led by a tradition, that the Prophet (the peace and blessing of God be with him!) prayed within the Kaaba, whilst several of his neighbours were there. But other traditions have it, that no one must pray upon the surface of the Temple of the Kaaba, and that this exterior is forbidden ground. We must confide in practices of long standing and universally followed, and not depart therefrom. And if we ascend upon the surface of the Baitu-l-Mukaddas, let us not be inactive or inattentive in repeating with the utmost care the Magnifying Words!

Ibn-Abbás says that the surpassingly valuable jewel, and the horn of Abraham's ram, and the tiara of Cyrus, were suspended upon the chain which was hanging in the midst of the chapel over the Rock, and were subsequently transported to Mecca.

Now, with regard to the Black Stone, and the supplication and accompanying prayer to be performed thereon. First, from the traditions of certain divines; viz. "We were informed by Nahíla, who was incessantly occupied with, and constantly remaining within, the Rock of the Baitu-l-Mukaddas, as follows:—There entered one day, by the Syrian Gate, a man in glittering array, whilst I was talking (*i. e.* praying) to Al Khidr (peace be with him!); then he prayed two Rakás, or four Rakás. Then he went out, and hung his garment upon the rails. Then said I, O thou wretch! I have seen what thou hast done, and know not wherefore thou hast done it!

Then he said, I am a man of Yaman ; and I came forth in quest of the Baitu-l-Mukaddas. And, meeting Wahab-Ibn-Umbah, (God's satisfaction be with him !) he said, What seekest thou ? Then I said, The Baitu-l-Mukaddas. Then he said, When thou hast entered the Mosque, enter the Sakhrá by the Syrian Gate ; then go forward towards the Kiblah, until you see pillars in the middle, on your right hand and on your left, standing in parallel rows. Look then between these pillars that stand in the midst, and thou shalt see a black stone, which is one of the gates of Paradise : pray thereon, and offer supplications to God ; for prayer thereon is highly to be preferred." This said stone is green, but its exterior surface is now changed into black. The green becomes visible beneath the black. It is what they call black *surfaced* colour ; which is such as the dark-green of some trees and plants."

My author goes on to say, "It is highly preferable to pray hereon three or four Rakás, or as many as you like ; then the supplication of the Prophet (the praise and blessing of God be with him !) mentioned in the 'Social Converse,' that, when he prayed with his companions, he stood before them, and said, O God ! be thou my refuge, and save me from a state of dependence, which may make me contemptible. O God ! be thou my refuge, and save me from riches, which may make me proud and overbearing. O God! be thou my refuge, and save me from a superior, who may tread me down. O God! be thou my refuge, and save me from power, which may make me careless. O God! be thou my refuge, and save me from poverty, which may make me forgetful!"

CHAPTER VI.

Narrative of the Night-Journey of the Prophet (the peace and blessing of God be with him!) unto the Baitu-l-Mukaddas; and his ascent, by gradual stages, thence to Heaven. Also, the Account of the Divine precept of the Five Prayers; and the Chapel, wherein is the spot where the Ladder of Ascent began. Also, of Prayer therein. Also, the spot where stood the Prophet (the peace and blessing of God be with him!). Also, the marvellous virtue of that Chapel, and of his Prayer; and how, on the night of this Ascent, he prayed among Angels and Prophets, and offered thanksgivings. Also, respecting the Chapel of the two memorable and glorious Kiblahs. Also, the benefits of prayer therein; and of diligently using a supplication especially appropriated for that purpose. Also, the merits of prostrations upon the place where the ladder was placed, as well as the merits of so doing upon the standing-place of the Prophet. Also, a Prayer designed for this especial purpose. The words, also, of the Prayer before the two Kiblahs; and all the traditions and reports therewith connected.

First, from the tradition of Al Balaki, found in his book, 'Prophetical Evidences,' taken from the reports of Hadís-Khanís-Ibn-Sharíf. He said,

We said unto the Apostle of God, (the peace, &c.) How didst thou ascend by night? He replied, I was among my companions in Mecca, praying the twilight prayer, standing upright, when Gabriel brought to me a white beast, which was an ass above and a mule below. Then said he unto me, Mount! But however, I feeling some reluctance in obeying, being at a loss to account for this, he took me up, and placed me upon the beast. Off then he went, soaring aloft with me, and dropping his (winged) legs in alighting, when arriving at a place of his destination; thus on, till we arrived at a land full of palm-trees. There he caused me to alight, and said unto me, Pray here. So I prayed. Then he said, Knowest thou where thou hast prayed? I said, God knoweth. He replied, Thou hast prayed in Yathrib; thou hast prayed in Taihat (Medina). After this, we again alighted, and I again prayed. When I had remounted, he repeated his question, and I again saying, I know not the place, he said, Thou hast prayed in the city of Salat, under the tree of Moses. Then we arrived at a place where towers and buildings appeared to be in a desert. Here I prayed as be fore; and, again professing my ignorance, he told me that I had prayed in Bethlehem, where Jesus, son of Maria, was born. After this, we entered the city at the right-hand gate, and came in front of the Mosque. Then fastening up the beast of burden, we entered the Mosque by the gate wherein the sun and moon set. There having prayed, I was seized with extreme thirst, the severest I ever suffered. Upon this, he brought me to two springs, one containing milk, and the other honey. I hesitated a long time between the two, thus being together, and thought them nearly of equal value. God, however, led the right way: so I chose the milk, and drank until I had sufficiently quenched my thirst. (In the traditions the fountains are said to have been of *wine* and milk; and it is added, Then there appeared before me an old man leaning upon a stick, who said, Begin to magnify thy Lord, because he hath led thee in the right way.) After this, we were brought to the valley of Hinnom—the valley near the city, which appeared, when displayed, to contain small holes, (upon this one present said unto me, Apostle of God! how didst thou find them to the feet? I replied, Like furiously boiling fountains of hot water). After this, we passed by many camels of the Koraish tribe, in a place just like this, which were straying about; and certain persons were wandering with the flock, whom I saluted. Then one of them said, This is Muhammad's voice. After this, I came to my companions in Mecca, before the dawn of day; and Abu-Bekr came to me, saying, O Apostle! where hast thou been the night? for, truly, I sought thee, but could not find thee in thy usual place. Then I said, I have been to the Baitu-l-Mukaddas. He replied, How can that be? for that is a month's journey; therefore describe the route to me. Then he said, The whole road was openly shown to me, and perfectly known by me; nor can any one ask me any one circumstance relating thereto, but I will describe it unto him. Then said Abu-Bekr, I bear witness that thou art the Apostle of God. Nevertheless, the Pagans said, Look at Ibn-Abu-Kabshah! *he* pretended that he went unto Jerusalem by night. Upon which the Prophet said, As a proof, I tell you that I passed by your camels—the camels of your tribe, wandering about in such or such a place (describing it). At that time you were dwelling in such a place; and on such a day there came to you, and came in front of you, a brownish red camel, with black streaks, and two bright white spots, and black legs: at that time the people were on the high ground, looking down; and it passed them no nearer than the middle of the river, going on, and leaving them behind. This, then, was the camel which the Apostle of God described. Moreover, it was put forth by Abu-Hussain-Ali-Ibn-Shabr, in the second of his 'Useful Compilations from the Consolidated Traditions,' and in another portion of his 'Faithful and reconciled Parts of the Traditions of Abu-Haraira,' (God's contentment be with him!) that the Prophet (the blessing, &c.!) said, The angel made me visible among the prophets, and the time of prayer was near, and I approached them; and, when I had finished my prayer, one said, O Muhammad! this is the angel, the master of Hell; therefore salute him. Upon this I turned round, and addressed a word of salutation unto him. That night we entered the Holy Abode: we found all the prophets were assembled; and Gabriel pushed me forward until I came near them. Then we ascended by steps unto the heavenly world.

From other traditions we learn that the Prophet was desired to alight, and perform two Rakás at two places; one being (said Gabriel) the tomb of thy father Abraham, and the other the birthplace of thy brother Jesus (peace be with him!). After this, he came to the Rock (Sakhrá), and, having prayed thereon, ascended thence to heaven. From other traditions we are informed, that Gabriel remained in front of the Prophet until they arrived at the Syrian Gate of the Rock;—that Gabriel cried out with a loud voice; and that some angels came down from heaven, and God assembled all the commissioned ones;—that Gabriel prescribed a prayer, and the Prophet prayed among the angels and commissioned ones;—that he then went on towards the right of the Rock; and Gabriel placed for him a ladder of gold and steps of silver, which constituted the means of the sacred ascent;—that then they went up to heaven;—that Gabriel demanded admission. Upon this, it was said unto him, Who art thou? He replied, Gabriel. And who is with thee? Muhammad. Wast thou sent unto him? Certainly, I was sent unto him; open therefore to us. Then said the Prophet, Adam came near, and welcomed me, and spoke good words to me. Then we mounted up to the second heaven; where, the same ceremonies taking place, we were admitted by the Prophet's cousin, Jesus son of Maria, and John son of Zacharias. In the third heaven we in like manner saw Joseph, who gave me one half of his beauty. At the fourth heaven we saw Idreus (Enoch), who welcomed us, and said, God is great, and hath exalted us to a lofty place of reward. At the fifth heaven we saw in like manner Aaron. At the sixth in like manner we saw Moses. At the seventh, with the same ceremonies, we saw Abraham, his back resting against the re-established House of God; whereunto, every day, seventy thousand angels descend, who shall not return until the day of judgment. Then he conducted me to the lotus-tree—the utmost boundary of heaven, whose leaves possessed an articulate voice, like the voice of an elephant, and whose fruit was like immense water-buckets. This tree, by the command of God, of all God's creatures, is raised to the very highest splendour and perfect beauty that creatures can possibly possess. There God revealed to me what he revealed, and issued the divine injunction of fifty prayers, every day. After this I came down to Moses, (peace be with him!) who said, What hath thy Lord enjoined upon thy followers? I replied, Fifty prayers. Upon this he said, Return unto thy Lord, and beseech him to lighten this burden, for thy people cannot endure this; for I myself have tried the sons of Israel, and I know them by experience. Therefore I returned unto my Lord, and said, O Lord! lighten this imposed burden upon my people! Then he abated me five. I then returned to Moses, who sent me back again, saying as before. Thus I went on, going between my blessed Lord and Moses, until he said, O Muhammad! I finally fix upon five prayers every day, and every night—ten in all; and these shall be accounted as fifty prayers. Also, Whosoever designs to do a good deed, and effects it not, I engage to give him that good deed's reward. Whosoever effects it, I engage to give him tenfold. Whosoever meditates an evil work, and effects it not, I promise to give him nothing at all. Whosoever effects it, I promise to inflict upon him but one single punishment for that one single ill deed. After this, I came down again to Moses, who desired me to return again: but I said, I have gone back unto my Lord until I am quite ashamed.

Again, a tradition says, Whosoever shall designedly come unto this chapel, and be enduring any want or deficiency, either relating to this world, and shall therein pray three or four Rakás to him, is assured a speedy performance of his request; and he shall know the blessedness of that spot wherein the Prophet prayed. This chapel is called the Chapel of the Prophet; viz. the chapel east of the Rock. At this time the Chapel of the Chain is neglected—the chapel built by Abdul-Malik-Ibn-Marwán. There is an old tradition about this last chapel,—That herein the Prophet met with the bright black-eyed ones, on the night of his ascent to heaven. The tradition is derived from Abdurrahmán-Ibn-Yazíd, and is as follows: Muhammad never saw the bright black-eyed ones until the night of his journey to Jerusalem. Then, whilst he was walking about the underground vaults of the Mosque, Gabriel met him, and said unto him, Would you like to see the bright black-eyed? Upon his saying, Certainly; Gabriel said, Then enter the Rock.

Muhammad, upon this, advanced towards the chapel, and came upon them; for, behold! certain women sitting. He saluted them. Upon which they said, We salute thee also. The peace and compassion and blessing of God be with thee! He then said, Who are ye? God's mercy be with ye! They replied, We are the good and beautiful wives of the people who follow piety. They shall be strong, and never weak; they shall be youthful, and never old; they shall endure, and never depart. Then another tradition asserts, that Gabriel said to Muhammad, Enter this gate, and look towards the right, and thou shalt see their curtain: which he did, and saw the women sitting; who replied to his interrogatories, We are the good and beautiful wives of good and pious men, who shall behold our bright and merry eyes.

This, then, is the great privilege of which this glorious Mosque can boast. It can boast of the numerous assemblage, the unanimous confluence of every one of the prophets and apostles and angels; and also it can boast of the especial virtues of prayer offered therein by those who believe in, and are bound by covenant to, the Elect One, to Adam, and to all the prophets from Adam downwards. Nevertheless, all the world do not agree; and learned men have some difference of opinion about the prayer offered up by Muhammad among the prophets that night. One of these says, The prayer was the commonly used prayer, *totidem verbis;* viz., the Supplication, and the commemorative Expressions of God's name: for he says, These are the most eminent and noble prayers; these the soundest and safest words. Especially, new forms of expression impose a burden upon divinely-sanctioned duty. There is another tradition, that when Muhammad rode upon the black one to Heaven, he prayed among the prophets the noontide prayer, the afternoon prayer, the twilight prayer, and the night-shadowing prayer, before he went up to Heaven. In another tradition it is said, that several learned men, and those orthodox, assert that Muhammad prayed merely the essential part of the prayer, as of necessity prescribed in the divine law, without pronouncing the summons aloud, and without any standing upright.

We are told also that the Prophet stood and prayed in the night; and having prayed two Rakás before dawn, he said, O God! I beseech thee for thy mercy, whereby my heart may be led in the right way, and all that is scattered abroad may be brought together, and all dispersed bands may be assembled in one, and whereby agreement with me may return again, and my grand points of doctrine be committed to memory, and my testimony be openly proclaimed, and my deeds be remembered, and my face be made white, and my right and true way be breathed in upon men, and I myself preserved from every ill. O God! grant that I may follow the true faith, the true opinion; nor be of the number of the infidels. Oh! of thy mercy, grant to thy people an exaltation in this world conjointly with glory in the next. O God! grant me salvation in thy judgments; and grant me the reposing-place of martyrs, a blessed existence, and the companionship of prophets, and victory over my enemies. Aid me, O God! in my need, when my design cannot be effected, or my work is weakened (whenever I am frustrated in my plans, or weak in effecting them): for I deliver myself as a poor pensioner upon thy bounty. Thus, then, I beseech thee, O efficient Orderer of events! O thou that healest heart-cares, as thou knockest down and prostratest the deeps! save and deliver me from the wrath that inflames, from wishes that destroy, from the temptations that bury us. O God! let not thy design be frustrated, or thy work be weakened; and let not any one of those who believe thee entertain at the last any doubt respecting thee, the sole Saviour and giver of all good things that render life happy; or doubt respecting the emolument (among the saints) of one of thy servants, or of his happy condition; for thou givest to all thy creatures. Thee, therefore, I herein supplicate; and this do I beseech of thee, O Lord of the universe. O God! lead us in the right way, with those who pursue the true road; not with those who stay therefrom, and hold back, evading war with thy enemies. Peace to those men whom we may love with thy love; but foes will we be unto thy foes—those of thy creatures who rebel. O God! this is my supplication: with thee is favour and consent. This is our earnest endeavour; but we commit ourselves to thy supreme efficiency. There is neither device nor power but in God. O God! thou originator of irresistible cause and righteous effect! I beseech of thee to grant me peace on the day of thy threatenings, and Paradise on the day of eternity, among those martyrs who approach thee nearly; there to bow the head and adore with those who fulfil to the utmost thy covenant. Thou art the compassionate, the tender-loving; thou hast done what thou wilt. Praise be unto him who putteth on might as a cloak! Praise be unto him who is clothed with the robe of majesty and glory! Praise be unto him unto whom alone praise is due! Praise to the still-surpassing one! the ever-propitious one! Praise to the mighty and bounteous one! Praise to him whose force of intellect in his works exceedeth every thing. O God! grant unto me light in my heart, and light in my ears, and light in my eyes, light in my hair, light in my skin, light in my flesh, light in my blood, light in my bones, light before me, light behind me, light on my right hand, light on my left, light above me, and light beneath me. O God! give me light, and augment my light, and make me all light!

Now, it is very desirable that a pilgrim should advance right up to Muhammad's Chapel, behind the Chapel of the Sacred Ladder, and pray there, and be earnest in supplication; using, if he will, the supplication which God taught to Muhammad, when he said unto him, that the highest angels would contend and quarrel for it; and afterwards any supplication he will, provided it be one of the authorized traditionary ones. I would, moreover, observe that, at present, there are only two chapels in the Mosque of Aksá behind the Chapel of the Ladder; one a small one, at the farthest extremity of the Sakhrá, on the western side, to the right of the northern staircase, just by the western portion of the exposed part of the Rock.

I am of opinion that several servants of the Mosque, from whom much useful information could be obtained, are now dead; nor is there now any tradition in Jerusalem that this was a chapel of the Prophet. The other chapel is by the other gate of the Mosque, on the north, near the Gate of David: this chapel is now called

Solomon's Chapel; not Solomon the prophet, but possibly Solomon-Ibn-Abdul-Málik-Ibn-Marwán. The Chapel of the Ladder is outside, in the roof or outward exposed part of the Rock. It is celebrated for being approached by pilgrims, and perhaps it is the curiosity chiefly valued in noble sayings and by eminent authors. The author of the 'Social Converse,' and the author of the 'Resurrection of Souls,' speaking of Muhammad's Chapel, and the Chapel of the Chain, built by Marwán, and now still existing, and the chapel on the spot where Muhammad prayed amidst the prophets and apostles, say, That upon the side of the Chapel of the Ladder, on the exposed part of the Rock, was a delicately-carved chapel, and when the area of the Temple was paved, the position of this chapel was distinctly marked out, and upon it was constructed an exquisitely wrought tower, upon the ground, beautifully engraved and sculptured in red marble, rising up in a spiral form, perpendicular to the pavement. This place was called the Tower of the spot where Muhammad prayed. If you go behind this, you will find the spot where there was placed before Muhammad stairs of gold and silver. This is the place of the Sacred Ascent.

With respect to the advantages of praying in this chapel, various well-confirmed traditions assert as follows:—Let the suppliant, having sat down, not rise from his seat until he has prayed the Sessional Supplication, in the words attributed to the Prophet, and said to have been offered by him whilst sitting. These are the words of the prayer:—"O God! grant us such a portion of thy fear as may cause our trials to depart. Give us such a measure of thy salvation, and obedience to thee, as may cause us to meet at last with Paradise. Grant us that sure confidence of opinion, which may make us indifferent to all the accidents that may happen in this world and the next. O God! grant us to enjoy our hearing, our sight, our vigour for ever. Grant this unto us whilst we live, and to our heirs after us. Grant us boldness against those who oppress us, and give us victory over our foes. Let no ills afflict us in this world; nor let the world be too much in our thoughts, nor the fulfilment of our engagements occupy us too much. Let not our path be the path that leads to hell, and let not those sins tyrannize over us, which fear not thee, and have no compassion upon us."

Various authors of traditions confirm this: one of whom says, Two men disputed with us; one of whom was, I think, a native of Jerusalem. One said that no prophet ever made that his Kiblah or praying point, except Muhammad: the other was of opinion that all the prophets did so; but Muhammad only made his Kiblah towards the Kaaba. The matter was referred to certain eloquent and orthodox arguers; and the whole argument being clearly stated, they said (God be merciful unto them!)—There can be no doubt but that both disputants entertain a corrupt opinion.

The following was the argument:—The first said, The Kaaba is the Kiblah of all the prophets: I quote from Abu-Al-Alíat. Said the other, I quote from Zabarí. From the time that God sent Adam, he hath sent down no prophet into the world, but he hath appointed the Rock of the Baitu-l-Mukaddas to be the Kiblah of that prophet. Now it is notorious that these two assertions are at issue with each other. Learned men, therefore, have especially directed their attention to this path, this theological argument. They have determined to walk along the path of explication, whereby the public may be profited, and that the reins of these coursers, who were running the road of schismatical variableness of discordant opinions, might be pulled in by the final sentence and decree of a judge who held the ends. Moreover, besides these, two several other learned men came forward to embrace their argument. I, therefore, please God! will lay down before thee their arguments, according to the verity of evidence, and will produce to thee (the quotations of authors) in chronological order, according to the series of years.

First, for the reconcilement of the first opinion. The first whom God set apart, to adorn with the glory of prophecy and the marrow of constancy, was the Elect One, our father Adam (peace be with him !). Now it is not known, whether, during his life, there existed any foundation of the Baitu-l-Mukaddas, except in the foreknowledge of God. The proof of this is to be found in the 'Derived Traditions' of the historian Abu-Muhammad-Al-Kasíni-Ibn-Isákir, in his choice book upon the marvels of the Mosque Al Aksá. He refers to Kaab, who says, The ancient foundation of the Baitu-l-Mukaddas was that laid by Shem, the son of Noah: upon this foundation David and Solomon built. It is also established, as a certain truth, that, between Adam and Noah, ten ages elapsed.

This, then, is the most ancient of all quoted testimony respecting the foundation of the Baitu-l-Mukaddas. Now, with regard to the narrative of Al Kartubay, he says, that it is a matter of indifference, whether we believe that some of Adam's sons laid the foundation, or whether the angels again did so subsequently to the building of the Kaaba. It is a *sine qua non*, however, that this opinion must not be considered as absolutely rejecting all that is opposed to itself. With respect to the fact of its foundation, nothing can discredit this. As to the Baitu-l-Harám, although it existed in external form, yet it was not made an object of pilgrimage and visitation (long may peace be with it!), nor did any one go in pilgrimage thereto, or perform the sacred circuit around it; yet, in the book of our Imam-ál-Shafí, (God's satisfaction be with him!) we find, that Adam, whilst performing the Sacred Pilgrimage to the Baitu-l-Mukaddas, met with angels, who said, O Adam! you act a pious part in performing the pilgrimage. We have performed the pilgrimage to this house two thousand years before thee. In the 'Chronicle' also of Ibn-Jarír, in his 'Derivations from Ibn-Abbás,' it is said, From this time Adam went on pilgrimage to the Holy Abode, on foot, forty pilgrimages. In the 'Chronicle' of Al-Izrak, that he dwelt in Mecca until he died, and made the sacred procession around the Temple, using seven prayers of praise every night, and five every day. These traditions will not be rejected by any, except those who think that the Kaaba was not in being before Abraham, and that he himself was the person who sought it out; and that it was created from a previous state of non-existence. This last opinion, however, is the free-will assumption of some later writers. Nevertheless, most people are opposed to this; and I would say, Was not the form of prayer divinely enjoined in the time of Adam? Yes, we all say; the world never was left void of a divine institution respecting prayer. Another tradition asserts that Adam, when it had happened to him to desire the grapes of the vineyards of Paradise, then made use of traditionary prayers, which he made use of until he took his noontide repose in the other world. Then they washed him, and embalmed him, and put him in a coffin, and Gabriel prayed over him; so they buried him. Others say that angels carried him to the gate of the Kaaba, where Gabriel prayed over him. Others assert that Muhammad said, that Gabriel pronounced over Adam the exclamation "God is great!" four times. Others say that Seth said unto Gabriel, Pray over Adam. But Gabriel said, Thou art the higher in rank: pray, therefore, over thy father, and pronounce the prayer "God is great" thirty times. Five of these were the ordinary prayers, and five-and-twenty supererogatory prayers in honour of Adam. This tradition seems to aim at the authorization of the Burial Prayer, as of divine injunction, and as being established long before any similar prayer was ordained. By another author it is said, that the morning-dawn prayer was Adam's prayer; the noontide prayer, David's; the afternoon prayer, Solomon's; the twilight prayer, Jacob's; and the night-overshadowing prayer, Joseph's. Now, herein are found many unconnected yet faithful traditions. Yet, to this time, not one of these establishes an argument that can give even the least smoke or sign whereby positively to point out the place of their Kiblah. There is therefore good ground for supposing that they used the Kaaba for their Kiblah; for God says, "(This house is) for all religions: this is the chief." Another quotes the verse as follows: "This house is for all people,"—all the people of the faith, and for every nation. There is no doubt that Adam was the first who entered it in these cycles of time; and that he had a peculiar and visible Kiblah, that is, the Kaaba: for is not this the great place whereunto pilgrimage tends? the pilgrimage whose evident origin, the origin of its establishment, must be referred to God. Have we not received of old the injunction respecting going on pilgrimage thereunto, and making procession around it? Then it is by no means so far from probability, that he should have prayed towards that place.

With regard to the prophets who succeeded Adam and his sons until the time of Abraham, the Friend, (prayer and peace be with him!) we have arrived at no information as to their Kiblah. It is notorious, however, that they greatly honoured the Kaaba; performing the pilgrimage, the procession, the prayers and supplications there. We may also refer to the traditions about Noah, and Hud, and Saleh, and Shírib; and the story of Ad, about sending some one to draw water from the venerable well, is well known. Also, the assertion of the sons of Halik, about some of them coming to Mecca, and remaining there to adore God until their death, and how that their tombs are all around the house. So that we may finally arrive at the conclusion, that it is not unlikely that they prayed there. Abu-Al-Alíat tells us, that he saw the Mosque of Sáleh, which was full of carving, and that the Kiblah was towards the Masjidu-l-Harám. In like manner was the Kiblah of Daniel placed: who said, I assert that although this house now exists, yet shall its precincts be devastated and demolished, and its divine sanction cease. Another prophet also said, The spot of the Kaaba shall be hidden, and it shall be obliterated by being overwhelmed: its site shall become a dismal desert of red sand. No paths shall there be trodden, except by those who know the site of the House, where it stood. The unjust tyrant shall come thereunto from the utmost parts of the earth, and shall demand that it be ploughed up, which shall be granted him. Now this agrees with a tradition from Harík, that this House shall be removed, and between Noah and Abraham none should perform pilgrimage thereunto. Yet further, with regard to our father Abraham, how he was sent by God to Nimrod, who was in the land of Babel, and in what condition he there was brought. God hath described all this in his Book. How also he saved him and delivered him from Nimrod's hatred and Nimrod's fetters, and how he fled thence unto Syria; and there they remained in the Holy Land, all solitary in their worship of God, after their arrival. The people of the Book are of opinion that he founded the eastern chapel of the House. During this period also, Hagar became pregnant, and brought forth Ishmaël. Her adventures with Sarah are well known. Abraham then transported her to the wilderness behind Mecca, (may God glorify her!) and visited them from time to time, mounted upon Al Burák, subsequently returning unto the Holy Land. What Kiblah he used at this period, hath not reached us; nevertheless, when God commanded the Kaaba to be built, he built it; and his sons after him used that as a Kiblah until the time of Moses (peace be with him!). I am not aware of any difference of opinion among the Musalmáns upon this point; nevertheless, there is some difference of opinion among the Jews: for it is commonly reported that they possessed a jealous desire of singularity, upon the authority of Ibn-Abbás, in expounding the following verses:

"God hath not removed from you the Kiblah which you possessed before: for your Kiblah was hidden in mystery. You have now returned to the practice of Abraham, and Ishmaël, and Isaac, and Jacob, and Sabat." For they pretended, says Abbás, that Abraham's Kiblah was the Baitu-l-Mukaddas, which was the principal cause of their lies and bragging. Upon the verses, "We have placed on high for you a Kiblah, of good acceptance," several commentators remark, This was Abraham's Kiblah. An opponent might here remark, If Abraham and his sons really used the Kaaba as their Kiblah, surely they would have been buried therein; but thou seest where are the fabrics of their sepulchres—a manifest proof that they placed their Kiblahs upon the Rock. But to this it may be replied, It is evident that the spot where their tombs were placed is a mere matter of chance. They placed their tombs just where their fixed habitation happened to be, on any side (therefore not towards any particular Kiblah). And it has been said, that a certain individual, possessed of great strength and courage, ascended the steep rock wherein was the cave, and arrived at last as far as the sepulchres, and found our Lord, the Friend, (the peace and blessing of God be with him!) lying in his coffin, on his back.

Respecting Moses, I have met with *three* confident assertions. One, that he prayed towards the Rock. The argument for this is the observation of Kaab to the Khálif Omar, when the latter requested his advice on the proper position of the Mosque. Place it, said Kaab, *behind* the Rock, and construct two Kiblahs—the Kiblah of Moses, and the Kiblah of Muhammad. Upon this Omar said, Thou wouldst make it quite Jewish. The second opinion is, that Moses used the Kaaba as his Kiblah. Upon this we will quote from Abu-Alíat, in his book called 'A Looking-glass for certain Jews.' A Jew, he says, was using the Rock as his Kiblah; but I was praying towards the venerable Mosque: hereupon certain schismatical people began to quote from the Korán several of those passages which we do not think decisive, repeating them in a clear and distinct manner. We did the same, and thus divided the people into two parties (just as you disputants are). The words which mostly weighed with me, are those which asserted that Moses magnified the two places in question in equal proportion. He magnified the Kaaba, because the Sacred Pilgrimage was appropriated thereto; and he magnified the Baitu-l-Mukaddas, because he prayed at his death to be brought near thereunto, and was shot thither at one shot, like a stone. The third opinion is, that Moses made his Kiblah of the *Ark*, called the Ark of the Covenant, which God had commanded to be constructed of cedar-wood, and to be adorned with fine linen, gold and silver. And when he departed, he commissioned his young man, Joshua, the son of Nun, and gave into his hand the sure possession of the Holy Land. The ark in question then was founded upon Al Sakhrá, and towards this all the sons of Israël prayed. This went on from generation to generation; and when it had perished, from lapse of time, they prayed towards the spot where it had stood, *i. e.* the Rock. It is evident that all this was pursuant to God's revealed will, and would have still remained if our lord Muhammad had not refused consent. So it passed away; but it had been the Kiblah of all the prophets who had inhabited the Holy Land. Withal, they magnified the Kaaba also, and performed the pilgrimage, according to the word of Al Abbás. Since Abraham, God sent no prophet who did not perform pilgrimage unto the house. From many traditions, this fact is positively brought home to Moses, and Jesus, and Jonas (peace be with them!). Some of these traditions are derived from eloquent expounders of orthodox truth.

It is said also, that Muhammad re-united the two Kiblahs, which had been separated. Much controversy has arisen upon the question of the possibility of this. A certain Imám says, that whilst Muhammad was in Mecca, he used the Kaaba as his Kiblah; but whilst in Medina, he used the Holy House as his Kiblah, and then also made a general change; so that one period was abrogated by another. In a certain exposition it is said, that he first prayed in Mecca towards the Kaaba, and then changed to the Baitu-l-Mukaddas, which also his followers did at Medina, for three pilgrimages, or even sacred processions; that after his flight they did the same; but that afterwards the Kiblah was altered to the Kaaba. That is an orthodox opinion, in which the greater number agree, that in Mecca he prayed towards the Baitu-l-Mukaddas; but that he prayed between the right-hand corner and the black stone, viz. the Kaaba. Now, the Kaaba was before him; and, in looking at him from behind, it seemed as if he prayed towards it; and that he did this, either because it was the Kiblah of our father Abraham, or to gratify the Koraish: but that in Medina, he joined the two Kiblahs, praying towards the Baitu-l-Mukaddas; a thing, however, which he reproached the Jews for doing; and, seeing them, forbade them, lest they should pretend that any change or transference was made with regard to Mecca. Those who discourse of this subject differ; yet the most part agree that their Kiblah is the Baitu-l-Mukaddas, when in *Medina*. Many also say that when he came to Medina, God gave him his option between the two Kiblahs (or, as some say, the two sides), to go towards which he pleased; when he chose the Baitu-l-Mukaddas, and then afterwards chose the Kaaba. To this the following verses bear testimony:—"To God appertaineth the east and the west, and all the borders thereof." After this, God altered the custom, and now binds the universal profession of Islám to use the Kaaba as their Kiblah, except whilst in grievous terror, or whilst performing any meritorious deeds which are over and above the precise rules of the volume of necessary duties. This is now settled in the arguments of Theologians, who have collected that the verses alluding to the alteration are the following: "We have thought fit that the verses should cause thy face to turn to the sky." There is some dissent as to the days of this descent (of the verses); some saying it took place in Rajab, others in Shabán, in the 3rd year. By reason of this, some doubt hath arisen respecting the length of time during which he made use of the Baitu-l-Mukaddas as his Kiblah, whether it were sixteen months, or seventeen months. A commentator observes, this doubt consists of several divisions and modifications: one says sixteen months, beyond all doubt. And Sháfií also lays this down as an indisputable point of doctrine, in his final opinions on the Korán. Another says seventeen months and three days; and that the change took place on the *middle* day of the month Shabán. Another says the *third* day, as the time of the descent of the verses. Some say that the verses which prescribed the change descended between the two prayers; so that the *Evening* prayer was offered before the Kaaba. Others say that they came down before noon; so that the noontide prayer was the first offered towards the Kaaba. A third opinion is that they descended whilst Muhammad was praying the noontide Rakás in the Mosque of the sons of Salmah, who were then going the sacred circuit, when the precept of the prayer drew near to them; therefore that was named the Mosque of the two Kiblahs. The same commentator observes, When I came to this passage, it struck me that Muhammad, when he prayed with the whole company of prophets on the night of his journey to Heaven, prayed towards the Baitu-l-Mukaddas. But then this does not admit of the meaning which Zabarí would attribute to it; for all the prophets assembled and associated themselves to Muhammad on that night, he being their Imám and leader; and this took place before the Hijra, and consequently before the alteration.

To which conclusion arrive the arguments of Ibn-Jamáh, who mentions the reasons that oppose the first opinion, and verify the accurate interval between the first of the altered Kiblahs.

A tradition asserts that Al-Bára-Ibn-Azib said, We prayed behind Muhammad, in Medina, *towards* the Baitu-l-Mukaddas for sixteen months. God, however, made it known that he chose rather that Muhammad should turn his face towards the Kaaba; which he doing, all the people turned their faces with him. After this, several people who were of the number of the aiders came to Medina, who began to make the Rakás towards the Holy Abode. Upon this the above Bára-Ibn-Azib said, whilst they were performing the Raká, I testify that the Apostle of God turned his face towards the Kaaba. Upon this they wheeled round, still going on with the Raká, and made the Kaaba their Kiblah. Another tradition from the same person asserts, that the first prayer after the change was the twilight prayer: also, that the Jews and the people of the Book (Christians) were much surprised whence he prayed before the Baitu-l-Mukaddas; but that when he turned his face towards the House (Mecca) they refused, and opposed him; but that he died, still using the latter Kiblah, before he had prevailed upon the people to do the same; therefore they began to fight; but we possess no great abundance of their different arguments. Then God sent down some verses:—"God hath not designed the verses to overthrow your faith." All the learned men, therefore, agreed that Muhammad first, whilst at Medina, used the Baitu-l-Mukaddas as his Kiblah, but afterwards altered it to the Kaaba. To these facts most first-rate authorities assent; one almost contemporary with Muhammad. Nay, others besides say, that after the Hijra he prayed towards Jerusalem sixteen months, but, wishing to change and turn towards the Kaaba, he said unto Gabriel, I wish exceedingly that God would alter the turning of my face from the Jewish Kiblah. Gabriel however said, I am but a servant; but I will pray to thy Lord, and beseech him. When, then, the Prophet was praying towards the Holy Abode, it happened that he lifted his head towards Heaven; upon which a voice came down: We have seen that you have turned your face away; we have seen it in Heaven. It is a verse—"Turn thy face towards the Kaaba." Then he commanded them to turn the faces towards the Baitu-l-Harám: they wheeled round it, and the people of the Moslems went round with him, towards the Kaaba, towards the Aqueduct. He then said, The angels are praying before me. The same commentator says, Did not Muhammad visit the mother of Bashr-Ibn-Al-Baruah, a nobleman of the sons of Salmah, who prepared meat for him; but that, the noontide prayer drawing nigh, he prayed the Rakás among his companions. Then he commanded them to turn their faces towards the Kaaba, and made the Aqueduct his Kiblah. Therefore the Mosque is called the Mosque of the two Kiblahs. A certain commentator, in his work upon 'Changes and Abrogated Laws,' quotes the mighty word of these verses :—" Foolish men will say, Wherefore hath he removed the Kiblah, which they had?" Ibn-Abbás says, moreover, The first abrogation made in the Korán was the change of the Kiblah. On the night of Muhammad's journey, God gave him the divine precept of the three prayers. He then prayed towards the Kaaba, but with his face turning towards the Baitu-l-Mukaddas, (i. e. *in front of the Kaaba, but inclining a little.*) After this in Medina, when his face had been changed, and turned towards the Kaaba, two more prayers were superadded, pursuant to his wish. Muhammad (he again says) and his companions first prayed towards the Baitu-l-Mukaddas, and did so in Mecca one year. But after the Hijra he felt a zealous wish to pray in front of the Kaaba, inasmuch as it was the Kiblah of his father Abraham and Ismaël. Yet he continued to pray towards the Holy Abode for sixteen months; and whilst praying he lifted up his head to Heaven, expecting perhaps that the Kiblah would be altered, and said to Gabriel, I desire very much that thou shouldst beseech God to transfer my Kiblah to the Kaaba. Gabriel, however, said, It is impossible that I should originate any matter before God; for he is the governor of every request. And it happened that whilst Muhammad was praying, he turned his face to Heaven, and saw Gabriel coming down to him. He was then praying the noontide prayer, towards the Baitu-l-Mukaddas, with the Raká; but God then transferred the Kiblah to the Kaaba. Some dissension arose upon this; and the hypocrites said, Why hath he turned them from the Kiblah, which they before had? Many believers also said, What becomes of all our prayers, prayed towards Jerusalem? What becomes of those of our brethren who have died, praying towards Jerusalem? Hath God reversed their hope and ours? So said obedient Musalmáns. But the Jews said, Muhammad longs after the land of his father, and wishes to satisfy the people thereof: he would resolve to embrace our Kiblah, if he could make us hope that he was the prophet for whom we look, that he shall come. The Pagans of the Koraish said, Muhammad is ashamed of his religion, and only made your Kiblah his own Kiblah, that he might keep you quiet; pacifying you by patting you with the hand, like an infant. He will soon embrace your religion. Upon this, God sent down to each party a verse, to reconcile their objections. To the hypocrites came the verse, "Say, To God appertaineth the east and the west. He leadeth those whom he willeth to the broad and fixed and strait road of Islám." To the believers, "Know ye not that the Apostle followeth that which his ancestors did before him? Let it be said then, Surely we will try it; for truly the Kiblah that was sent down to you was the Kaaba." To the believers again, who obeyed, came the verse, "God will not overthrow the covenants if ye be obedient in this matter." Then said he to the Apostle, "We grant thee the Kiblah thou longest for and thinkest most acceptable to thyself; for long hast thou cast one eye upon the Kaaba." To the Jews came the following verses:—"Truly deceit hath come upon you respecting those who come to the book, and search every verse. They follow not your Kiblah. You are deceived in every verse sent down by God, in the latter times, respecting the Kiblah. That Kiblah is the Kaaba. God hath sent down to the people of the Book that which he hath caused to come unto them; the Book which they know, as their fathers knew. Also, (God did so) that he might make a division among them; that some might know the hidden mystery of the truth, and know that this is the truth from thy Lord, and not be of the number of those who turn aside and doubt." Then came down to the Koraish the following verses:—" No sure evidence can be imparted to men, but they will act unjustly with regard to it." Also, " Fear ye not their calumnies:" which means, " Fear ye not but that I shall confirm your faith (the Moslem faith), and fulfil my favour towards you, and exalt your faith above all faiths." Another commentator says, The disputants were whirled about like chaff. Upon which came down three signs respecting turning the face to the Kaaba, because many rebelled against transferring the Kiblah from the Holy Abode to the Kaaba. These were of three kinds: the Jews, who wish no abrogation in the principal point of their method of worship; the doubters and hypocrites, who were the more vehement in their stiff rebellion, because this was the first abrogation that descended; and the infidel Koraish, who said Muhammad repents of altering our faith. These then began to bring forward arguments, saying, Muhammad pretends to invite us to the religion of Abraham and Ismaël, and now he transfers the Kiblah of Abraham to Ismaël, and substitutes another Kiblah. Upon this God said, Never shall a credible message be brought down and testified, but some men will act unjustly towards it. They will not return: they will not be led by the right way. Also, there is a heresy among them, to conceal the truth; for they know that they now conceal what they before alleged—that the Kaaba was the Kiblah of the prophets. Abu-David, the author, tells a story from Ibn-Shaháb, that Sulaimán-Abu-l-Malik did not make so much of Elía as the people of the House did. "I," said Ibn-Shaháb, "went with him, when he was heir presumptive, the time that Khálid-Ibn-Yazíd-Ibn-Muáwwiyah was with him. Sulaimán then said, whilst sitting there, By God, I deny that here is the Kiblah, before which the faithful people of the Book may more acceptably pray. Khalíd said then, By God, I find, when I read the Korán, that command respecting the Kiblah which thou knowest. And as to the Jews, they may not become restive, and resist that which their own books assert—how that the Ark of the Shechinah was placed upon the Rock;—but that when God was wrath with the sons of Israël, it was removed; and that they prayed towards the Rock, as the place where counsel may be sought. Abu-David also relates that the Jews quarrelled with Abu-l-Alíak about the Kiblah. Then said the latter, Moses prayed just by the Rock, but used the Baitu-l-Harám as his Kiblah: the Kaaba was his Kiblah, and the Rock before him. Then said a Jew, Between me and between thee, then, is the Mosque of the prophet Sáleh. Upon this, said Abu-l-Alíak, I pray in the Mosque of Sáleh, and turn towards the Kaaba as my Kiblah; and I pray in the Mosque of the Two-Horned (Alexander the Great), and use the Kaaba as my Kiblah. Thus ends the matter.—But God knows.

CHAPTER VII.

Account of the Wall which encircles the Mosque Al Aksá, and all those haunts of Confessors and Martyrs therein to be seen. Also, the Towers most chiefly frequented for the purpose of Pilgrimage and Prayer; such as the Tower of David, the Tower of Zacharias, the Tower of Maria (peace be with her!), the Tower of Omar-Ibn-Al-Khattáb, and the Tower of Muáwwiyah. Also, all that has been asserted publicly about the Gates, their number and their names. Account also of the Stones which are near the lower gate of the Mosque. Account also of its length and breadth in cubits. Account of the Traditions of the Leaves and the Valley of Hinnom, which is without the Wall on the eastern side. Also, the residence of Al Khidr and Elias, (peace be with them both!) which are both in this abiding-place and precinct.

Know that the origin of the foundation of the wall of the Mosque Al Aksá, which encircles it on all sides, has already been defined and laid down before, in the account of the commencement of the Temple. It is said, David first built the foundations and corner-stones of the house, and then the wall; all which fell down; and then God said, that they must be *purchased* of the owners: that one of these owners claimed a quantity of gold, filling a solid square, whose side was equal to its height; which was granted. When the matter fell into Solomon's hands, the man asked for an additional sum, requesting a bull-hide full—a talent of gold. Solomon said then unto him, Thou hast already effected a complete sale of this land. Then said the owner, That good thing is the mother of the other. Solomon said, But that was a good thing itself. He said, Yes; for it was the beginning of others. Then said Solomon, But didst thou not completely effect a sale? He replied, Very true; but when we are bargaining for good things, it is a pity to separate them. (This, our author says, gave rise to that saying at merry meetings, "Good things shall not be divided.") Also, the man said, I will ask no more. But so he went on demanding more, until he obtained seven talents of gold, or nine, as some say. Solomon then built the House, and encircled it with a wall, as described in Chapter II. Another commentator, among several other things, says, that David prevailed with all but one man to grant him the land; also, that it was a divine precept, that when a thing was once dedicated to sacred uses, it never could return to secular uses. Therefore David built the wall as a boundary. Also, that he built the Gate of Mercy within, and the Gate of Punishment without. A Muezzin of the Baitu-l-Mukaddas observes, from the Korán, that the Valley of Hinnom was also beyond the precincts. Several other commentators say that Ábadat-Ibn-Al-Samat once stood leaning his breast upon the eastern wall of the Mosque, looking down into the Valley of Hinnom, and weeping. Being asked the reason, he said that the Prophet once told him that he saw Hell there, and an angel cutting the heart (of the condemned), by throwing stones, as thick as grapes fall at the vintage. Another of the Prophet's followers, being found weeping in the same spot, replied to those who questioned him, that he was thinking of what the Prophet had told him about the wall encircling the vicinity of the Baitu-l-Mukaddas; how that it was the wall that cut off and separated the House from that valley. Over this valley is the bridge of Sirát. The Prophet himself also says, Hell is an inclosed precinct in the world; inclosed on all sides, and Paradise behind it. The bridge Al Sirát, over Gehenna, forms the path to Paradise.

Now with respect to the remarkable towers.—*The Tower of David.* There is some dispute about this tower, whether it be the tower by the eastern wall, or the tower near the pulpit. One says that the Tower of David is in the citadel of the Baitu-l-Mukaddas upon its site, and that his residence was in the citadel, devoted to pious uses; and that to this the Korán alludes: the verses, "Ascend ye the tower!" Also that the tower where he prayed is in the citadel, in the place where he adored God; that the greater tower within the Mosque was the spot where he offered thanksgivings when he entered the Mosque; and that, when Omar-Ibn-Al-Khattáb came hither, he directed his steps first towards this place, and there prayed. It is called, therefore, the Tower of Omar; because Omar was the first who prayed there, on the day the city yielded. This Mosque abuts upon the place where Omar effected the sacred duty of warring against and vexing the infidels. Here it was, that, contrary to the advice of Kaab, who wished the Mosque to be placed *behind*, near the Rock, Omar described and delineated a Mosque upon that tower which marked the place where David prostrated himself upon entering the Mosque. For this opinion of Omar, and this place, whereon his care was exercised, both point out this spot as being that which David selected of old, and chose as his oratory.—*The Tower of Zacharias* is, by most, said to be the tower just by the entrance of the Mosque, in the cloister near the eastern gate.—*The Tower of Maria* (peace be with her!) marks the spot where she adored, and is now known by the name of the Tower of Jesus (peace be with him!). It is notorious that prayer, herein offered, is granted. It will be assuredly accomplished to whomsoever shall pray in this oratory, and read the Súrat of Maria—so much of it as relates to her—and shall then prostrate himself, just as Omar did, in the Tower of David, who, whilst praying therein, read the Súrat *Sád*, wherein David is commemorated, and prostrated himself. In this Mosque it was that the prayer of Maria was followed by her justification. The best prayer, and the most meritorious to be here offered, is the prayer of Jesus, which he prayed when God raised him up unto himself from the Mount of Olives.

As to the Tower of Omar-Ibn-Al-Khattáb, men differ about it. Some say it is the great tower, just by the columns of the glorious pulpit, right in front of the great gate by which we enter the Mosque Al Aksá. Others say that it is the tower in the eastern portico, or cloister, close adjoining the wall of the Mosque Al Aksá. Those who incline to this latter opinion allege, in support of it, that this cloister, and all the area it incloses, is commonly called the Meeting-House of Omar, and that this was the place he chiefly distinguished, and to which he went with his comrades (with whom may God be satisfied!) at the time when it was full of filth, which they swept away, and prayed therein; that for this cause it was named Omar's Meeting-House. The majority, however, apply this name to the Tower near the Pulpit, and to the space between its pillars. All this shall be described in that chapter of this prosperous book, which narrates the surrender of the Holy House, and the entrance of Omar on the day it surrendered, please God!

The Tower of Al Muáwwiyah is said to be that light and elegantly-carved tower which now is within the Preaching Chancel, between that and (partly) between the tower of the glorious Pulpit. It is thus *within* and *without* the Mosque Al Aksá, and is one of those greater towers which jut out beyond the wall. It was placed here to be a point of boundary between the different divisions and portions; a mark where one class of sacred observances ends, and another begins. Here, traditions say, the Prophet of prophets, and Chief of chiefs, prayed. The whole is an excellent place wherein to adore during pilgrimage. Here is the spot which marks the cleft made by Gabriel when he bound Al Burák outside the House, by the Gate of Muhammad. It is a place of great and obligatory sacredness; which is verified by the concordant assent of the Sacred Verses and Martyrs, which relate to the potency and acceptability of this site. Behind this Tower are the stones, in the hinder part of the Mosque, near the Gate of the Tribes. In it is the place called Solomon's Throne, where he prayed after the completion of the Temple. All these Towers and glorious spots are highly to be venerated by pilgrims, being noted for causing favourable answers to prayer, and for the liberal gifts of all desirable things to those who pray therein.

Now, for all that is publicly believed about the Gates.—The Gate of *Mercy* is by the Eastern Wall. It is mentioned in the Korán, "The gate within the wall is the Gate of Mercy; without, the Gate of Punishment." This gate is within the precinct, very near the Mosque. The other gate mentioned in the Korán, near to the Valley of Hinnom, is closed, and will not be opened until God proclaims aloud that it shall be opened. The Gate of Mercy is an admirable point, towards which pilgrims should direct their prayers and supplications. All will be accomplished for those who, in addition to other observances, here pray to God to grant them Paradise, and beseech him to save them from Hell, and repeat a multitude of prayers to this effect. For Muhammad himself said, O

God! whosoever shall beseech thee three times, to grant him Paradise, let him enter therein. Whoso shall three times have recourse to thy guardian succour to save him from Hell, deliver him thence. For the most becoming requests we can address to God are, to obtain Paradise, and to be protected from Hell. Which of the two sides of this gate is more efficient in obtaining these blessings is matter of opinion. Let us, however, hope, from the bounty, the goodness, the surpassing majesty, and faithful truth of God, that he will grant to us to be of the people of Paradise—of those who therein obtain salvation, and enter therein in peace, received under God's safeguard, please God!

This gate is on the hinder part near the wall and the Tower of David. As to the Gate of Repentance, it is joined in one with the Gate of Mercy. Neither of them in these times is opened. Hard by the Gate of Repentance, between the Gate of Mercy and the Gate of the Tribes, is the dwelling of Al Khidr and Elias, (peace be with them!) as chroniclers say. As to the Gate of Al Khidr, I do not find it mentioned in the Muthír Alfáràm. His dwelling-place is mentioned in certain commentators and interpreters. From them we learn that Al Khidr prayed every Friday in five Mosques—Mecca, Medína, Jerusalem, and the Mosque of Kissa (near Larissa), and the

Mosque of Tyre, every Friday night; also, every Friday he ate nothing except two mouthfuls of turnips and garlic, and drank once from Zimzim, and once from the Well of Solomon, in Jerusalem, called the Well of the Leaves, and washed in the fountain of Siloam. Again, we learn that Elias and St. George kept the month of Rhamadán every year in Jerusalem, and fasted, and performed the feast-observances of Mecca. The historian Abul-Kásim relates, that Abú-Tálib said, whilst performing the procession around the Kaaba, I saw a man leaning close by the curtain of the Kaaba, and saying, "O Thou, whose ear is never pre-occupied, nor incapable of hearing! O Thou, whose thoughts never wander, and who never overlookest the suppliants! O Thou, who art never wearied with the ceaseless urgency of suitors! give to me my pressing, my indispensable need—thy forgiveness, the sweetness of thy compassion." Tálib hereupon said, Repeat these words, O servant of God! Who said, Didst thou hear them? He said, Certainly. He then said, These words were breathed by St. George* into his hand, i. e. secretly; who also asserted, that there was no one who should adore, repeating the words thus written, but should be forgiven, although his sins were in number like the grains of sand, or

* See Note.

the froth of the sea, or the leaves of the trees. A tradition says also, that the Prophet asserted, that St. George received the name Al Khidr because that he sat down one day upon a seat covered with white skins, which were changed into *green*. Al Bukharí also is reported to have said, I one day entered the Holy House before the twilight had become full light, in order to pray therein, when, lo! I heard a voice, speaking in very low tone for a time, and for a time speaking clearly and distinctly. Thus it spake, "O Lord! I am poor, and I am fearful. I flee to thee for succour. O my Lord! cease not to hear me; change not my hearing; alter not my body; enforce my trials." Upon this I went out in confusion, and passing by some who were at the gate of the Mosque, they said unto me, What is the matter with thee, O servant of God? Then I told them. Upon which they said, It is no trifling adventure you have met with. This is the Green One, St. George; and this is his hour of prayer. Another commentator says, that the stones called *Al-Bakh-bakh* point out where St. George prayed; which is a very propitious spot for prayer. Other commentators assert that St. George was a prophet, and a most eminent Imám of Cordova (in Spain); which opinion is the received one of the most truth-telling Shaikhs. The belief of some is, that he is a Patron Saint; of others, that he is still alive: one asserts that a certain person asked St. George where he prayed; who said, The morning-prayer in a corner of Yaman; the noontide prayer in Medína; the evening-prayer in the Holy House: after each prayer I perform that arduous duty which God hath imposed and enjoined upon me. Another commentator observes, that the cause of St. George's preservation in life is, that he drank of the Fountain of Life: for he observes, in addition to the concourse of the waters of the deep, there is a fountain, called the Fountain of Life. The water of this spring, if it comes in contact with any thing, causes it to live. Others, however, say that he is dead; which the most observant theologians declare definitively.

A certain historian also, Shemseddín-Muhammad-Ibn-Amín, who had travelled to the West, and, long dwelling there, had obtained from learned eyes of Spain and elsewhere much information, and who died in the glorious and prophetical Medína, in a most super-excellent condition of prayer and peace, in the year 739, declares in his book 'The Gardens of Supreme Consolation,' as follows:—I one day entered the Vault, and lost my way; when, behold! I met St. George, (peace be with him!) who said, Where I am now walking is the utmost limit and boundary. Then I walked with him; and, seeing one with him, I said, What is thy name? And he said, Abú-Abbás. Seeing also another, I said, What is thy name? He said, Elias. So I said, The mercy of God be with you! have you seen Muhammad? They replied, Certainly. Then I said, By the might and strength of God, I adjure you tell me something that I may narrate upon your authority. So they said, We heard Muhammad say, "Whatever believer shall say, The peace of God be upon Muhammad!" God's brightness and beauty shall remain upon his heart. Also they said, There was among the sons of Israël a man named Samuel, to whom God bountifully granted victory over his enemies. Now he marched out with his army; and they (the enemy) had said, This enchanter (Samuel) will bewitch our eyes and destroy our army. Let us therefore assemble by the sea-shore, and we shall rout them. Then they marched out in divisions of forty men, and pitched by the sea-shore. Then said the comrades of Samuel, How shall we act? Who replied, Make the attack, saying, "Praise be unto Muhammad!" and charge: which they did; and, attacking their enemies by the sea-shore, broke them all, and routed them.

Whilst thus present with us, St. George and Elias said, Whosoever shall say, Peace be upon Muhammad! shall be completely purified from hypocrisy, as a thing is purified in water. These two also said, A man of Syria came unto the Prophet, and said, O Apostle of God! my father is a very old Shaikh, who desires to see you. Then Muhammad said, Bring him to me. But the man said, He has lost his sight. Then he said, Let him say, for seven weeks, "The peace of God be upon Muhammad!" and he shall see me in a dream, and shall relate a tradition from me. Which the old man did, and saw Muhammad in a dream, and related a tradition from him. Also they said, We heard Muhammad say, When ye sit down to a feast, say, In the name of God the Merciful and Compassionate, the blessing of God be upon Muhammad! for if ye say these words, God shall cause his angels to eat with you, and ward off all backbitings and calumnies from you, as long as you yourselves abstain from scandalizing others. Having concluded these traditions, they said, Accept these admirable traditions of the Prophet; regard them as an especially fortunate gift; make much of them!—So much for the choice and secret treasures of the Spanish writer!

The Gate of Remission is so called because it is said that the children of Israël were directed to enter their Mosque, prostrating themselves, and creeping on hands and knees, and saying, "Remission!" that their sins might be forgiven. They also used the word in their Psalms. A commentator on the Korán says, When the people entered a village, journeying towards Jerusalem, they were allowed to eat whatever was good or necessary for them; and they entered the gate of such a village, prostrating themselves, and saying *Hittatun*, which means, There is no God but the God. This expression *remits* sins. (See Korán, chap. 2.) Those who were wicked changed the word, saying *Hinnat*,—a Hebrew word, signifying a brownish grain, or buckwheat. God, however, rained down fevers, as a punishment for the rebellious. Also, whosoever shall repeat two Rakás before the Gate of Remission, shall be put in the place which they vacated, who, when desired to enter the promised land, refused to do so. Another commentator remarks, The brazen gate in the Mosque, in the middle, called the Ram's Gate, is that brought by Cyrus as a gift. The brazen gate over the gate of the Mosque of David's Gate, is the gate whence David went forth unto Solomon's Market, from Sion. The gate called the Gate of Remission is that which was formerly in Jericho. The word *Remission* was appointed by God to be used by the children of Israël when they carped at Moses about entering the Holy Land, in which were giants. God wishing to forgive them, ordained this word. Here, it is said, the quarrelsome rebels were ordered to bow the head, which they refused. Another commentator remarks, Whenever one of the children of Israël was guilty of any sin, he wrote upon his door, "Thus and thus have I offended:" upon which they all repulsed and excommunicated him. After this, he came to the Gate of Penitence, which gate is hard by the Tower of Maria, and where was a common-sewer, and wept, and stood awhile. Then, if God granted him repentance, the children of Israël caused him to approach near; but if God did not grant him repentance, then they excommunicated and repulsed him.

The Gate of the Glorious Prophets is now called the Gate Al Dawídári (the Gate of the Templars): it is on the western side, but itself is in a northern direction. The Gate of the Sheep is west of the Gate of the Guard, on the front side of the Mosque. This gate is called the Antechapel of Abraham. The Gate of the Conqueror is said to be the same as the Gate of the Jealousy-search: it is now called Angel's Gate, because Gabriel is said to have bound Al Burák there.*

Now, with regard to the *length* and *breadth* of the Mosque in cubits, one historian says, The length of the Mosque Al Aksá is 755 cubits, using the royal cubit, and its breadth 465 cubits, taking

* See Note.

the royal cubit. Another says, Looking directly in front of the northern boundary wall, just above the gate called the Templar's Gate, and within the wall of the marble pavement, and thence estimating the length and breadth of the Mosque, the length will be 784 cubits, and the breadth 455 cubits. This is the variation existing between the two accounts. A person observed to the last, that though he had thus described the size of the Mosque in cubits, yet that he wished to know whether these were royal cubits or not, and that perhaps this caused the different accounts of writers. Upon this they measured on the spot with ropes, when the *length* of the Mosque from the eastern side was 733 cubits, not taking into account the thickness of the walls. Thus ends this matter.

Now for the *Leaves*. The following tale is told: Muhammad had said, that a divine revelation had asserted as follows, "Truly, there shall be a man of your people who shall assuredly enter into Paradise, although he be walking upon his two feet, and be still alive." Now, says an old worthy, I was standing before the congregation in the Holy Abode, who were engaged in prayer, with the people of Omar-Ibn-Al-Khattáb, when there arrived a certain Tamímite, named Sharík-Ibn-Habásh. He was drawing water for his comrades, when his bucket, or pitcher, fell into the well. Descending to bring it up, he found a gate in the well, opening to the Angel-land, by which he walked into the said land, and took some leaves of the trees thereof. This took place after the summons to prayer. He then returned to the well and climbed up. This story being told to the governor of the Baitu-l-Mukaddas, he sent for the man, and with several others went down himself into the well; but they found no gate, nor any angels or genii. This being communicated to Omar, he replied that this was the verification of Muhammad's assertion. He also desired them to remark the leaves. If they dried up and changed, they were not the leaves of Paradise, which wither not. It is said that they neither dried up nor changed. Some say that the man was in the *mountain* of the Holy Abode, and that, having descended into the well, to bring up his bucket, a personage appeared unto him, and said, Come along with me. So, taking him by the hand, he brought him into Paradise, whence Sharík having plucked the leaves, he replaced him on the same spot where he had before stood. A certain Imám and Muezzin of Solma, in Canaan, asserts positively, that having heard that the man was still living, he caused him to be brought before him; who informed him of his visit unto Paradise, and of the leaves he brought thence. He said that he had reserved only one leaf for himself, which he did not greatly regard. The Muezzin begging to see it, he called for a certain large volume, and took it from between two leaves. It was still green. He took it up, and presented it to the said Muezzin, who restoring it unto him, he first placed it between his eyes, and thence removing it, put it between the two leaves of the volume. Also, when he died, he desired that it should be placed between his bosom and his shroud. I was subsequently assured, says the Muezzin, that this was done. Some one asked this Muezzin, Did they describe it? What was it like? He replied, It was like the leaf of the Durrákin (Persian apple), about a hand's length, sharp at the top. Another story says, That there was a certain Temamite; named Abul-Mushin. This man was very strong; and men would speak of his personal advantages. One day, they lost him; and, after long search, hearing nothing of him, they began to despair, and to think he had been suddenly cut off, or carried away; but whilst they were sitting, he suddenly appeared amongst them, holding two leaves, of most surpassing size, surprising fragrance, and brilliant green. His companions asking him whence he came, He said that he had fallen down the well, and, walking along, had arrived at a great abode, such as my eyes, said he, never beheld, nor any other mortal eyes, I think. Here I dwelt many days in a most blessed state, which no other blessedness can resemble, amidst sights and scents of surpassing splendour and fragrance. Whilst in this state, a certain Spirit took me by the hands and brought me back to you. I had however plucked these two leaves from the tree—the lotus-tree—under which I was sitting, which remained in my hands. Then the men came forward, and, taking the leaves, found them to be of surpassing fragrance and sweetness. Another account states, that the leaves are preserved in the Khalif's Treasury, and that the man, being sent to Omar, was by him placed among other men, and, all turning away their faces, he was immediately pointed out by Kaab as the man described by Muhammad, who should enter Paradise. This Well of the Leaves is situated at the entrance of the Mosque Al Aksá, or the left of the Gate of the Court-yard of the Towers.

CHAPTER VIII.

Account of the fountain of Siloam, and the fountain hard by, and the fountain which can be traced to the time of our lord Job. Account also of the blessings and miracles which have taken place in the Baitu-l-Mukaddas, and all that happened upon occasion of the murder of the Imám Ali-Ibn-Abú-Tálib, and his son Al-Hussain, (the satisfying favour of God be with them!) Also, the character of the inhabitants of the Holy Abode. Also, the account of the Talisman of the Serpent. Also, the account of the Mount of Olives, and the scene of the General Judgment thereon. Also, the Holy Mountains, and the account of Sion, and its especial blessing.

FIRST, a tradition from Muhammad, as follows:—God hath chosen *four* capital cities—*Mecca*, capital of his own province; *Medína*, the Palm city; *the Holy City*, which is the Olive city; and *Damascus*, which is the Fig city: also four border-towns, *Alexandria* in Egypt; *Kaswín* in Khorassán; *Abádán* in Irak; and *Ascalon* in Syria: also four fountains, according to the sentence of the Korán, "There shall be fountains, which shall leap up abundantly and flow together." These fountains are Bísán and Siloam (which two communicate together), the fountain of Akka, and the fountain of Zimzim. Also he hath chosen four rivers—Sihon and Gihon, the Nile and the Euphrates. Another tradition says, Whoso shall pray in the Tower of David, praise God by the fountain of Siloam (which is from Paradise), never enter a church, never buy and never sell in Jerusalem, shall do well; for good and bad is there multiplied.

Again, another tradition says, In the time of the children of Israël, there was a fountain, hard by the Well of Siloam, in the Holy City. When a woman was accused of adultery, they brought her thither, and she drank thereof. If she was innocent, it hurt her not; but if she were guilty, she became accursed, and died. Also, when Maria (upon whom be peace!) was with child, they brought her hither. Now, they brought her upon a mule, which stumbled with her. Upon this she prayed God that the she mule might ever be barren; and so she is, unto this day. When Maria arrived at the fountain, she drank of it, and found nothing but good effects therefrom. Then she prayed God that no believing woman should henceforth be exposed to shame by this fountain; which fountain, from that day, was united to the fountain of Siloam. Another, speaking of the well attributed to our Lord Job, (peace be upon him!) said, I have read, that water being very scarce in the Holy City, men had recourse to this well: they sank it to the depth of eighty cubits; and the size of its head or spring was ten cubits; four of which were blocked up by great stones; every stone being five cubits long, and from one to two in length and breadth; so that they wondered how these stones could have been brought down to such a place. Amidst these stones sprang up the fountain, spouting up briskly and cool. For many years they supplied themselves with water from this well, eighty cubits in depth. In winter the water of this spring overflowed, and inundated the surface in the lower parts of valleys, so that mills were turned by it, whereby flour was ground. Whenever they needed this fountain, or the fountain of Siloam, they went down to the lower part of the well, where the water remained at a certain height, and brought with them great dams and pieces of wood, to block up the holes whereby the water effected its egress. Then they saw the water rushing up from the stones, to the height of two cubits, to all appearance. Here also was a cave, whose entrance was three cubits by one, from the midst of which rushed a wind of intense coldness. Then they brought a light there, and saw the cave blocked up with immense masses of stone; and, entering more nearly, the light could not be kept in, by reason of the force of the wind proceeding thence. This fountain is in the very heart of a valley, and this cave in the very midst of the fountain, on one side. It is surrounded by mountains of immense altitude, which no one can scale or ascend but by extreme labour. And this is according to God's word revealed unto his prophet Job, (peace be with him!) viz. "Move thy feet quickly to this bathing-place; this cool and swift water, fit for drinking." So much for this matter. Now, to despatch all that is to be said of subterraneous caverns, narrow at the orifice and wide at the extremity, and holes in the earth, a commentator observes, that Kaab said, Go ye not unto the Church of Maria in the Holy House, or to the Church of the Body of Christ, or to the Two Pillars, in the church of Mount Olivet; for these are all of them idolatrous. Whosoever cometh thereunto shall be disappointed in his desire. Others say, that Kaab met two men, whom he asked, Whither bound? They said, To Elia. Then said Kaab, Say not Elia, but say Baitu-l-Mukaddas, or God's Holy Abode. Neither go to Maria's Church, nor to the Two Pillars; for they are idols. Whosoever goeth there shall be disappointed and frustrated in his prayer until that he turn back from those Christians who say that God was killed. All is inefficacious which they have built, except the church in the Valley of Gehenna. Another says, that the Tomb of Maria is in the church called the Church of the Body. So it is now said; but no revelation has ever asserted that her tomb is beneath the crypt of that church. The above churches and places cannot be approached by Musalmáns without permission; a wall is built to keep them off. A commentator observes, that a Musalmán pilgrim may approach the shrines and oratories of these churches, under *four* conditions: First, that on entering any one of them, a person should be chanting the Korán, provided it be a church in which the Christian books are read, just as he chants the Korán in entering his own house: but if it be not a church wherein books are read, and such as the churches of Egypt, then he may enter without this chant. Here is an obvious and necessary distinction, which cannot be dispensed with. Secondly, provided there be no paintings or figures therein; for if there be paintings and figures on the walls, this forms an insuperable and overpowering objection to the permission of entrance. Let not any one stand or take up his abode within a house wherein are any paintings, for if there be paintings no dispensation can possibly be permitted; and, truly, that commentator is very wide of the mark, who says that this prohibition is repealed. Thirdly, that no corrupt opinion result from thus entering, such as making any account of their stocks and stones, or exalting and embellishing the beauty of their hymns, or suffering any suspicion or idea to enter the mind respecting the truth and soundness of their mode of worship, nor any heightening commendation of the objects of their adoration. Fourthly, provided there be no impurity therein; for if there be, it cannot be sound, or orthodox, for us to do any thing else than walk around it; entrance is absolutely prohibited. (In my opinion this condition is here needlessly introduced; for purification is a prescribed duty in all places.) Entrance into a church, and prayer there, is, says a commentator, forbidden, if there be pictures therein, under pain of God's indignation coming down upon the offender; so that, upon the whole, we conclude that we may not enter the church at Bethlehem, because there is imagery therein.

Now, for the Fish-ponds and Pools of the Holy House, and the places consecrated by the murder of Alí and Hussain, and the guardian Places of Refuge, the Sanctuaries and Talismans which belong to its inhabitants, or pertain to the neighbourhood of Jerusalem. First, it is said, that one of the kings of the sons of Israël, named *Khaskíl* (Hezekiah), provided in the Holy City six ponds; three in the city—the Pool of the sons of Israël, the Pool of Solomon, and the Pool of Eyád (Gad); and three without the city. These he made to be reservoirs of water for the sons of Israël. With respect to the murder of Alí and Hussain, it is said, that the Christians asserted, that when Alí was murdered, and on the night that Hussain was slain, there fell down at Jerusalem stones, on the under side of which was streaming blood. Not a stone of Jerusalem could be picked up, which did not stain the fingers with blood. A certain woman asserted that darkness came over her when Hussain was slain, and that no one dressed in yellow or dark colour passed by, but shone brightly, and their faces appeared all in a blaze.

A commentator says again, The Holy House is like a lion's den. Whosoever entereth therein, he will either eat him up, or become a friend to him. Whosoever entereth therein will either find safety or utter ruin and destruction (as another says). Also another says, The Lion will either eat you, or you will find an asylum which will preserve you, among the interweaving and luxuriant branches of trees. Again, Sulaiman-Ibn-Kaisán said, I met in Egypt with Abu-Izzá of Khorassán, and said, Do you dislike then the Holy City? Who replied, I dislike not the Holy City, but I cannot endure the people of the Holy City. Another commentator has said, It is written in the Law of Moses, The Holy City is a goblet of gold filled with scorpions. The meaning of this word "scorpions," observes a commentator, must be the children of Israël, who rebelled against God until he grieved them with trials. The word cannot allude to the people (of Muhammad), for the expression "scorpions" evidently points to rebellious people, not to obedient people.

Now for the unexampled Miracles which took place in the Holy City. These were wrought by Al-Dhahák-Ibn-Kais. People of science and intelligence assert, that when Alexander the Great was marching on towards the Holy Abode, having received the submission of the people of the country, the princes of the Holy Abode invited him to consider the miracles wrought by Dhahák in former times. How that he produced a blazing light of fire, and whosoever was not obedient to God was that night burnt by the light. How that, when the Holy City was shot at by arrows, he made them to return against the enemy. How that he placed a wooden dog at the gate of the

Holy House. Whosoever endued with the power of enchantment came near, and commanded the dog to move off, at him the dog began to bark; and when he barked, the person in question forgot all his witchcraft. How that he set up a Gate, by which gate if any Jewish or Christian evil-doer entered, this gate shut upon him, and held him fast until he confessed his offence. How that he placed a staff in the Tower of the Holy Abode, on which staff no one could lay hands unless he were one of the descendants of the Prophet (peace be with him!): as to any one else, his hand was burnt. How that the princes and others of the royal family being imprisoned in the Tower of the Holy City, lo! one morning the fingers of their hands were smeared and covered with gold. To this was conjoined, the miracles wrought by Solomon. How he made (a pond) below the ground, and therein constructed upon the surface of the water a flat pavement, of sufficient space to allow a seat for a great man; of which seat the stuffing would burst open. Then, whosoever was a worker of vanity, falling into the water, was drowned; but whosoever was a follower of truth, was not drowned. When, then, Alexander the Great arrived at the Holy City, and saw the wonders which Al Dhahák had effected, he declared to him, Thou art a dead man: thy last hour hath now arrived. Also, a great serpent arrived at the Holy City and would have destroyed it, but for the supreme goodness of God unto his servants. In the Mosque which overlooks the road which Omar-Al-Khattáb took, in marching from the Church of the Resurrection, are two columns of stone, on the top of which stands an image of a serpent, said to be a talisman. If any man, stung by a serpent, runs up to this serpent, he receives no injury; but if he departs from the territory of the Holy Abode, by the least space, he dies upon the spot.

Now from Awf-Ibn-Málik. He says, I went to see the Prophet, who was in an upper chamber. I saluted him; when he said, Is that Awf-Ibn-Málik? I replied, Certainly. Then he said, Enter. Sir, I said, shall I come quite in, or only partly? He replied, Come quite within. Then he said, O Awf-Ibn-Málik! count upon your fingers; number the spaces between your fingers, waiting a moment between each; for after that will be my death. Then I began to utter lamentations; but he silenced me. Then he said unto me, Say *One*, (then pausing a moment) *Two*—The Holy House shall be captured.—Say *Two*. Now *Three*—Great slaughter and deaths shall happen amongst my people, which shall seize them as a death-striking lion seizes upon the sheep, or a deadly disease strikes them down upon the spot. Say *Three*; (which I did). Now *Four*—Temptations, trials, and strifes shall come amongst my people, and greatly distress them;—Say *Four*. Now, *Five*—Money and wealth shall be so abundant amongst you, that if one hundred dínars be presented to a man, he shall feel indignant contempt at so small a gift.—Say *Five*. Now *Six*—There shall be a broad road between you and the yellow-haired sons: they shall pass over and march upon you under eighty standards, each standard comprising twelve thousand men. At that day the metropolis of the Moslem shall be in the land called Al Fútat, (the well-watered,) in the city called Damascus. (Another commentator makes him add, Another village of Islám shall go to war with this city.) Another commentator makes Muhammad say, Between the great slaughter and the capture of Constantinople shall intervene *six* years. In the seventh, the Messiah, the Antichrist, Dijjal shall come forth. Others put months for years. Also, according to tradition, he said, The black standards shall be advanced from before Khorassán, but shall not be beheld until they be lifted up on high in Elia.

Now, for all that is said about the Prophet's Fish-pond.—I shall have (said Muhammad) a pond, or lake, extending in length from the Kaaba to the Holy City, whiter than the milk of vessels, more numerous than the stars of heaven. Every Prophet shall also stir up and summon his followers, and every prophet shall have a pond. Out of these prophets, unto some shall come plebeians; unto some, noblemen; unto some shall come a great crowd; unto some, two men; unto some, one man; unto some, no one at all; then, at last, I will come, and will add or augment the honour and number of no prophet but he who has some follower. He moreover said, My people shall have none of the earth remaining, except a space as large as the sun, wherein to pray the afternoon prayer; and my pond shall be full of believers, as bright and numerous as the stars of heaven, or as goblets of gold and silver.

Now for the Mount of Olives, and the scene of the General Judgment, how it is to take place in the Holy Abode. Thus said Abú Horaira:—Thy Lord shall apportion, and shall judge, and shall swear (his irrevocable oath), upon the Figs and the Olives. Now, the olives mean Mount Olivet. Again, Thy Lord hath set apart four mountains,—the Olives and the Figs, and the Mounts of Sinai (this means the Faithful Land; for the word Figs alludes to the Mosque of Damascus, and the word Olives to Mount Olivet, the Mosque of the Holy City, and the Mount Sinai, where God spake with Moses) (peace be with him!), and the Faithful Land, Mecca. Also, Sophia, the wife of Muhammad, came to the Holy Abode, and ascended the Mount of Olives, and stood (as another commentator adds) upon the table-land at the summit of the mount, and said, Here, on the day of judgment, shall God separate men, and distribute them into Heaven and Hell. Two ancients remark, That they were one day sitting by Muhammad, when he said, Men shall be summoned unto judgment—a mingled, confused, hurrying, tumultuous multitude. They shall be brought unto The Place Appointed, which is in the coasts of the Holy City. There shall men stand over a widely-expanded space; and there shall they be judged by the spoken voice of God Almighty. This is said to be the great plain by the side of Mount Olivet, near the oratory of Omar, and known by the name of "The Appointed Spot,"—"The Sleepless Place." For (observes an author) we must make a distinction in the meaning of the word Sahara. It may signify, *a desert,—the surface of land,—a widely-extended plain*; but in Arabic it also signifies, *a land which causes sleeplessness to the night-traveller*, who journeys in its neighbourhood; so that people cannot sleep, but remain awake there. It is said that the surface of this place is of white earth, but good within the marrow of the soil. Also, whatever (a commentator thus expounds) we cut off from the earth, shall be added to Palestine; and whatsoever is cut off from Palestine, shall be added into the Baitu-l-Mukaddas.

As for Places of Pilgrimage here, there is the Tomb, a square Tomb, of the daughter of Samuël, mistress of a noble family, in ancient times. Of her it is said, That during her secret converse with God, all about her heart would seem to blaze with fire, splendidly radiating with light. And when we screamed out loudly, What shall we do? she seemed to have no idea of ill or harm, but said, Think not of that which is outside my robe; regard not that. She came to the Holy City, and died there, and her tomb is without the city, upon Mount Olivet: it is a place of pilgrimage. She departed (God be compassionate unto her!) in the year 135.

It is said by several authors also (and among them Abul Pharagius, in his book, 'The Virtues of the Holy City,') that Jesus son of Maria ascended up to Heaven from Mount Olivet. He came down from Heaven upon the Mount of Figs, in Damascus. When he was taken up to Heaven he was thirty-three years old. Another ancient says, There are four mountains:—Abraham's Mountain, Lebanon, Mount Olivet, and Arafát, which, on the day of judgment, shall all become of resplendent white, shining like the bright sky. All the earth shall be collected and brought together unto the Holy Abode, whilst the reports are collected. Here shall the throne be fixed, whilst the final distribution is made between Heaven and Hell. The angels shall traverse, with naked feet, the sacred precincts of the Shrine of Mecca, and praise their Lord, Muhammad, who shall judge between them with truth, and say, Praise be to God, Lord of the universe! Again, The close-pressing assemblage shall take place on *five* mountains,—Lebanon, the Mount of Olives, Sinai, and Ararat, (and Mecca). These shall all be bound into one grand hall. Thus also said God unto the mountain Kasyún:—"If thy shadow and thy blessedness hath departed, and gone to rest upon the mountain of the Holy Abode, be it so: nevertheless, thus will I do—I will build for myself a house within the midst of thee;" (now this house is the Mosque of Damascus, wherein God will be adored for forty years after the destruction of the world;) "neither shall day or night cease and depart before I restore to thee my overshadowing protection, and thy blessedness." (This, then, came down from God.) May the believer, the weak, the humble suppliant, obtain its accomplishment!

CHAPTER IX.

Narrative of the Capture of the Holy City by the Commander of the Faithful, Omar-Ibn-Al-Khattáb (may God crown him with contentment!), and how he cleansed the dirt and filth from the glorious Sakhrá. Narration of the Edifice erected by Abdul-Málik-Ibn-Marwán, and of the Ceremonies transacted therein. Account of the unrivalled Jewel, which was in the centre of the Chapel of the Sakhrá, with the Horn of Abraham's Ram, and the Diadem of Kosroës; which were subsequently removed to the glorious Kaaba, when the Khiláfat passed to the sons of Hisham. History of the victorious seizure of the Holy City by the Franks, from the Moslems, subsequently to Omar's conquest. The length of time it remained in their hands. The victory of the Sultán Málik-Al-Násir-Saláh-Adeen, Yúsuf-Ibn-Ayyúh (upon whom be God's mercy!). The wresting thereof from the hands of the Franks, and the demolition of all memorials of their rule. Restoration of the Masjidu-l-Aksá, and Al Sakhrá, the glorious, unto their former state. Their continuance in this state until now (and unto the day of judgment, if God please!).

Know that the capture of the Holy City by Omar-Ibn-Al-Khattáb (may God crown him with contentment!) occurs in the writing of 'Rare Events deserving of credit, and narrated in numerous ways and by various relaters,' which I delighted to collect from the different chapters, and adduce each with expressions of applause, in arranging the history of this splendid conquest, which fell to the lot of those dynasties of Commanders of the Faithful, when righteous Khalífs ruled; under whom God magnified the faith, and whose just government restored blessings to the Moslems. Among these reciters, the author of the Muthír Alfárám introduces Al Walíd, saying as follows:—A Shaikh of the noble tribe of Shaddád informed me, and said, After the conclusion of the battle of Yarmúk (Hieromax), the whole army of the Moslems marched into the territory of Palestine and the Jordan. Here we closely besieged the Holy City. The conquest thereof was, however, attended with difficulty, until the arrival of Omar with four thousand horse. He came down upon the Holy City on the eastern side—the Mount of Olives—which, in our siege, we were closely encircling. When, therefore, these comrades of Omar joined us, men who could fight so vigorously, their friendship and the arrival of Omar stirred up to energy and activity our hopes of victory. Long time did we fight with them, until, at last, a party came on the walls to ask for a truce during a parley. Having agreed to this, they then said, What army is this which hath now arrived? That is the army (we replied) of the Commander of the Faithful. Also, Omar sent unto us, to command us to cease fighting; saying, The Apostle of God informed me that we should obtain possession of this place without violence. And the Patriarch demanded a safe conduct for a messenger to convey a letter unto Omar. This we permitted, and the envoy came without hinderance; who said, We will give unto thy excellency that which we will grant unto no one except thee. He proceeded to request Omar to make peace, to accept tribute, and to grant safety unto their lives, property, and wives; to which Omar consented. The envoy, upon this, demanded a safe conduct for his master, the Patriarch, in order that he might preside over the preliminaries of peace, and the writing of the treaty. Upon Omar's assent, the Patriarch, with his attendants, came forth unto us. With him the Khalíf made peace; of which we were witnesses.

Al Walíd also said, A Shaikh of the army of the volunteers of Khorassán told me, that when the Moslems came unto the Holy City, the chiefs thereof said, We have here met to make peace with you; and since you acknowledge the dignity of this Holy Habitation, and allow it to be that Masjidu-l-Aksá, whereunto your Prophet was brought by night, we prefer that your prince should (first) himself make his entry within it. Now, the Khalíf then was Omar-Ibn-Al-Khattáb. Unto him the Musalmáns sent an express; to the Grecians at the same time sending an envoy with the Moslems unto Medína. Arriving here, the Moslems began to inquire for the Commander of the Faithful. For whom are they asking? said the Grecian envoy to his interpreter. For the Commander of the Faithful, he replied. The Grecians hereupon were much surprised, and said, Here is a man who hath conquered the Grecian and the Persian, and won the treasures of Cyrus and of Cæsar; yet hath this conqueror of nations no ensigns nor place of honour whereby he may be distinguished and known! After this, they found him asleep upon the spot where he had thrown himself down among his attendants, which increased their wonder. Having read the letter of Abú-Ubaidah, he ordered us to continue the truce until he should arrive at the Holy City.

Within this city there were 12,000 Greeks and 50,000 natives. Omar therefore made peace upon these conditions:—viz., That the Grecians should depart; for which three days were assigned; the safe conduct and truce being null and void with respect to any one who should remain after the expiration of that term. Unto the natives Omar granted quarter, enjoining upon them the payment of a tribute. Five dínárs were imposed upon the richest class; four upon the next; three upon the next. Very old men, or very young children, paid nothing. After this, Omar proceeded to the Tower of David (upon whom be peace!), and read a *Súrat* of the Korán.

And they relate further, that Abú-Ubaidah (with whom may God rest satisfied!) came to the Jordan, and closely besieged it, and sent a messenger to the people of Elia and her inhabitants, and wrote to them as follows:—"In the name of God, merciful and gracious! from Abú-Ubaidah son of Jirah, to the Christians of the people of Elia, health! to all who follow the way (*i. e.* the *right* way) and believe in God and in his Prophet! To come to the point—For my part I beg of you to bear witness that there is no God but God, and Muhammad is the Apostle of God, and that the moment of judgment will come, beyond all doubt, and that God will resuscitate men from the dead. And if you will persist in this, your blood is sacred unto us, as well as your property, and your children, and you shall be to us as a brotherhood; but if you refuse, I will bring down upon you a people, who are more earnest in their love of death than you are in the drinking of wine and eating of hogs'-flesh; nor will I ever pass away from you, please God! until I have killed your warriors and made captives of your children." Further he said, Then Abú-Ubaidah waited for the people of Elia; but they declined coming, or entering into a capitulation with him; so he proceeded to advance upon them, until he came down upon them with hostilities, and besieged them very closely, and reduced them to extremity. Therefore they made a sally upon him, and the Musalmáns fought. Then the Musalmáns prevailed against them on every side, and fought until they forced them to enter the citadel; and the commander on that day's engagement was Khálid-Ibn-ul-Walíd (with whom may God rest satisfied!), and Yazíd-Ibn-Sufyán; each of these two on a side.

Moreover, they have said, These tidings came unto Said the son of Zaid, who was with the people of Damascus. So he wrote to Abú-Ubaidah,—"In the name of God, the merciful and compassionate! to Abú-Ubaidah-Ibn-Jirah, from Said son of Zaid, health to thee! With regard to myself, I praise God on thy account—He who is the only God;—there is no God but *the* God. To come to the point:—I never in my life was more effeminate than thee or thy comrades in the sacred warfare, both as regards my person and those things which have become my portion by the mercy of my Lord. Now, when this my letter comes to thee, I will stir up, to the business which thou hast in hand, him, than whom few are more eager therein, you may be assured. Therefore I am coming to thee quickly, please God Almighty! So peace be on thee! and the mercy and blessing of God!" Then said Abú-Ubaidah, when the letter came, Let him support the cause by coming afterwards. Upon this he asked for Yazíd, and he said to him, Be my deputy at Damascus. So said Yazíd, I will be thy deputy therein, please God! And he went there, and took the government thereof for him. Moreover, it is said, when Abú-Ubaidah had closely besieged the people of Elia, and they saw that he was unremitting against them, and found no strength in battle, then they said, We will capitulate to thee; but we refuse to treat with you. Send therefore thy Khalíf Omar, and it shall be he who shall give us this treaty, and write for us the truce. Abú-Ubaidah thought fit to agree with them (to write), and Abú-Ubaidah (with whom God rest satisfied!) had already sent Moaz to the Jordan; who had not gone far, when Moaz said to Abú-Ubaidah (suppose), that thou dost write to the Commander of the Faithful, and dost inform him of the determination (of the people), and perhaps he will come: then these people will refuse the capitulation: thus his coming then will be superfluous and humiliating. Therefore do not write to him until they have entered into a firm engagement, and previously taken an oath under a heavy penalty, on their faith, and firmly agreed that if thou dost write to the Khalíf, and he does come to thee, and grant them security for their lives and for their property; and if he shall write them this in writing; then they shall accept it, and be willing to allow the tribute, and contribute according to that which the people of Syria have contributed. Therefore Abú-Ubaidah sent this proposal to them; to which they agreed. So when they had done this, Abú-Ubaidah wrote to Omar, Commander of the Faithful (with whom may God rest satisfied!),—" In the name of God, the merciful and compassionate! To the servant of God, Omar, the Commander of the Faithful, from Abú-Ubaidah-Ibn-Al-Jirah, health be upon thee! I praise God for thee. He who is the only God! To come to the point: We have stood firm against the people of Elia, and they thought that in their procrastination there would be relief, but God never withdrew from them weakness and loss, and leanness and misery. Therefore, when they saw this, they asked that the Commander of the

Faithful should come to them, and that he should ratify the security for them, and be the writer of the treaty of peace; but we fear that if the Commander of the Faithful should come, and the people should excuse themselves, and go back from their word, then thy arrival (may God keep thee in safety!) would be superfluous and humiliating. So we have exacted from them a firm promise, secured under a great penalty by oath, that they will assuredly assent, and agree to the tribute, and pay according to that which the people of Syria have paid, and those people who have been received into capitulation, which they have also done. Therefore, if thou thinkest fit to come, then do so; and may there be in thy coming advantage and security. So may God conduct thee, lead thee in the right way, and prosper thy affairs! and peace be upon thee, and the mercy and blessing of God!"

Now, when this letter came to Omar, (with whom may God rest satisfied!) he summoned the chiefs of the Moslems, and read to them the letter of Abú-Ubaidah, (with whom may God rest contented!) and asked their advice regarding the affair which he had mentioned in his letter: thereupon Othmán (with whom God rest contented!) said, if God has thus lowered them, and made them vile, and reduced them to difficulty; and if he is every day augmenting their weakness, and their leanness, and their loss, and their terror; then, if thou remainest and dost not go down to them, they will see that thou makest the affair light and cheap, not regarding them of great moment; then they will delay but a little while until they give up their determination, and pay the tribute of slaves. Then said Omar, (with whom may God be content!) Are there none of you that hold an opinion besides this? Upon this said Alí-Ibn-Abú-Talib, (God be content with him!) Yes, I have a different view. He said, What is that? So he said, They have made proposals wherein is humiliation and degradation to them, but to the Musalmáns victory; for it is a part of their engagement to yield up the city to us now, immediately, in peace. Between you, then, and between them, there is now nothing, but that you should go down to them; and to thee, in thus going to them, there is a reward for all your thirst and hunger, and for every valley, and for every expense, until thou come unto them. If thou goest to them now, there is peace, and security, and safety, and victory; but there is no security, if they despair of thy granting peace to them, that they will not keep fast their citadels; and their power will be multiplied and their condition be ameliorated; their misfortunes will accrue to the Musalmáns, and the siege will be prolonged and the Musalmáns be reduced to difficulties from the hard labour, and famine will ensue; and perhaps the Musalmáns may be worsted by sallies from the strongholds, and the enemy may shoot at them with arrows, and cast at them with javelins; and it may happen that some of the Moslems may die. If (therefore) you prevent the slaughter of one Musalmán by your entrance into the frontiers of the land, then the Moslems will be in a happy condition among their brethren, (*i. e. if the city yield without the loss of one man, the whole brotherhood of Moslems will rejoice*). Upon this said Omar, (with whom may God rest satisfied!) "Othmán's advice is the best with regard to military tactics against an enemy; but Alí's is best with regard to the advantage of Islám. Go in the name of God Almighty! I am also going."

So he marched out, and encamped out of Medína, and published among men his place of encampment and his expedition. Therefore Abbas-Ibn-Al-Mútallib collected an army from among the companions of the Prophet, (upon whom be the blessing of God and peace!) and the chiefs of the Koraish, and of the aiders (of Muhammad), (with whom may God rest satisfied!) and of the Arabians, until, when the full complement of his men was complete, he went to Medína, to seek after Alí-Ibn-Abú-Talib (with whom may God be content!). Thus they went; and Alí, with his chiefs, met the Musalmáns, and said, "Praise to God! who hath exalted us by Islám, and honoured us by the faith, and hath displayed his mercy towards us by his Prophet Muhammad, (upon whom be the blessing and peace of God!). Moreover, he conducted us from error, and reconciled us after that we had been at variance, and united our hearts, and hath thereby given us the victory over every one of our enemies, and established us in the country, and made us kindly-affectioned brethren. Therefore, O ye servants of God! praise God for this benefit, and entreat of him an increase thereof, and thanksgivings thereon, and the accomplishment of that which ye proceed to undertake to-morrow! since God adds augmentation to those who seek, and fills with his favours those who render him thanksgivings." So said they; nor did they lay aside this word every dawn and every day. And when the army drew near to Syria, he halted the soldiers until the number of those soldiers who were coming up should be complete. When, therefore, the standards upon the spears, and the soldiers upon the horses, already drew near, the Syrian army went out to meet Omar-Ibn-Al-Khattáb, (with whom may God rest content!) and he was the first, seated on a small saddle, conspicuous among the men. Then it was called out, Is there any one among you who knows the Commander of the Believers? And they were silent, and passed on. Proceeding onwards, they met others, who saluted us, and then asked, Respecting the Commander of the Believers, have any of you any knowledge of him? Upon this it was said to us, Inform the people as to your master. Then we said, This is the Commander of the Believers. Therefore they proceeded to cast themselves from their horses; and Omar called out to them to cause to return the others who had passed by. Then they returned with us, and the Musalmáns came forward, forming their horses, and brandishing their spears in the path of Omar, until Abú-Ubaidah appeared among the chiefs. Now he was upon a (young) she-camel, covered with goats'-hair trappings, and her bridle of hair, armed in full panoply (with bow, quiver, lance and sword), with his bow over his shoulder. When, therefore, he beheld Omar, he caused his camel to kneel, and Omar caused his camel (a poor beast) to kneel. Then Abú-Ubaidah dismounted. Thus, when Abú-Ubaidah came near, Abu-Ubaidah stretched out his hand to clasp Omar's hand. Then Omar stretched out his hand. Then Abu-Ubaidah took it, and Omar wished to (pre-occupy) him in taking it. Upon this said Abú-Ubaidah, Do not, O Commander of Believers! And Omar said, Do not, O Abú-Ubaidah! Then the two Shaikhs embraced, and they remounted to proceed, the men going in front of them; and some of the Syrian people thought fit to offer Omar a charger and white robes; and they earnestly desired him to mount the charger, that the enemy might behold him, and he be reverenced among them thereby, and that he should clothe himself in the robes, and throw away his garment of skins from him; but he refused. Then they vehemently urged him; therefore he mounted the charger in his skin robe, and his garments. Then the chargers went slowly on with them, and the bridle of his camel was after him, (held) in his hand. Then he descended and mounted the camel, and said, *This* troubled me, whilst I feared lest you should consider yourselves great, and become proud, since, O people of the Moslems! it is Moderation (Temperance) which hath made you great. Go on therefore in that way whereby God, the great and glorious, hath exalted you."

Moreover, we have a tradition in the chapter of Ibn-Shabáh, to the following effect:—When Omar (with whom may God rest content!) was coming from Syria, a ford (of a river) fell in his way.

Then he dismounted from his camel, and drew off the sandals, or lower soles, of his greaves, and, holding them in his hand, thus forded the water, and his beast with him. Upon this said Abú-Ubaidah to him, Thou hast done a great deed in the sight of the people of the land. But Omar struck his breast, and said, "You are not great in that word,* Abú-Ubaidah; for ye were the most despicable of people and the vilest of men, and the fewest in number of men; yet God hath exalted you with Islám. And he who seeks to be great without God, him shall God abase." Moreover, there is a tradition from Yúsuf, who had it from his father Hatim, on the authority of Othmán, who had it from Khalíd and his servants, as follows:—Omar-Ibn-Al-Khattáb (with whom may God rest satisfied!) concluded articles of capitulation with the people of Elia, in the village Jabít. This treaty of capitulation is a model for capitulation of every city besides the people of Elia. "In the name of God, the merciful and compassionate! The following are the terms of capitulation, which I, Omar, the servant of God, the Commander of the Faithful, grant to the people of Elia. I grant them security for their lives, their possessions, and their children, their churches, their crosses, and all that appertains to them in

* *i. e.* Your remark is not worthy of you—is vain.

their integrity, and their lands, and to all of their religion. Their churches therein shall not be impoverished, nor destroyed, nor injured from among them; neither their endowments, nor their dignity; and not a thing of their property; neither shall the inhabitants of Jerusalem be exposed to violence in following their religion; nor shall one of them be injured; nor shall one of the Jews be impoverished in Elia. And (it is stipulated) with the people of Elia, that they pay a tribute, according to the tribute paid by the people of the cities, (i. e. by the inhabitants of other capitulated cities). Moreover, it is incumbent on them that the Greeks and robbers depart therefrom. And whosoever departeth therefrom, he also is secure as regards his life and his property, or until whilst they bring out what is in their houses. And whosoever remaineth, to him there is security in like manner as to the people of Elia, and security for their goods, whilst they are conveying that which is in their houses. And whosoever there be of the people of the land, who wish to reside therein, upon him is the same tribute as upon the people of Elia. And whosoever wisheth to go with the Greeks, or to return to his land, from him there shall not be taken a thing which his repositories (warehouses, magazines) produce. And of all this may God be Ratifier! and be this the Covenant of his Apostle (upon whom be the blessing and peace of God !) and the covenant of the orthodox Khalífs, if they yield possession. Witness to this, Khalíd-Ibn-Al-Walíd, and Abú-Urrahmán-Ibn-Uf, and Múash-Ibn-Jabil, and Muáwwiyah-Ibn-Abú-Sufián."

Again, Khalíd-Ibn-Abi-Málik relates traditionally in his account derived from his father. When the Musalmáns came down upon the Holy City, and had remained besieging it, and their stay thereon was prolonged, they sent to them to open the city to us, for that we would give them security for their blood and for their possessions. Then they sent word to them, We will not confide in a capitulation from you, until your Khalíf Omar-Ibn-Al-Khattáb shall come ; for we have been informed of his superexcellence, and goodness, and probity. Therefore, if he come, then will we surrender, and trust in his capitulation, and open the city to you. Upon this they wrote to Omar, informing him of this. Then Omar rode from Medína, until he came to them. Now they had taken possession of places of which they had not taken possession before, and had seized a vineyard that day, which was in their power, belonging to a man who had been received into the protection of the Musalmáns, in which were grapes ; and they began to eat them. So the client (*i. e. the man received into protection*) went to Omar-Ibn-Al-

Khattáb, (with whom may God rest content!) and said, O Commander of the Faithful! my vineyard was in their power, and they did not eat of it, nor approach it; and I am a man under safe conduct with the Musalmáns; but when the Mussalmáns took possession of it, they fell upon it. Then Omar asked for a charger, and mounted, and rode forward in haste. Thus he came at a quick trot towards the neighbourhood of the Musalmáns; and the first who met him was Abú-Huraira, carrying grapes upon his head. Then he said, And thou too, O Abú-Huraira! Then (the latter) said, O Commander of the Faithful! a great hunger fell upon us; and it was more just that we should eat of his property than fight with his men. And Omar rode on to the vineyard, and looked, and, lo! there were men hurrying about in it. Then Omar asked for the client, and said unto him, What didst thou expect from the produce of this vineyard? And he replied, So much, or so much; and augmented it a little. To this said Omar, Then let it go free. And Omar took out the exorbitant price which the man had said, and gave it to him, who therefore gave up the vineyard as common property to the Musalmáns.

Moreover, we learn from Abdurrahmán-Ibn-Tamím as follows:—The people of Syria wrote thus to Omar, when they capitulated with the conquerors:—"In the name of God, the merciful and compassionate! This is the writing from the Christians of such and such a city, to Omar-Ibn-Al-Khattáb, the Commander of the Faithful. When you came down upon us, we asked of you a capitulation for ourselves, and our possessions, and our children, and the people of our religion; and we have stipulated with you, that we shall not be polluted by interruption in our places of worship, or whatever chapels, or churches, or cells, or monasteries of monks, may be therein; and that no one shall live therein who may have the impress of Musalmáns (by long residence), and that we will not prohibit the Musalmáns from entering them, by night or by day; and that we will open the gates wide to passengers and to travellers; and if any Musalmán, passing by, shall take up his lodging with us three nights, we shall give him food; and not entertain in our churches a spy, nor conceal him unknown to the Musalmáns; and not teach our children the Korán; and not publicly exhibit the Associating or Christian Religion, and not beg any one to embrace it; and not hinder any one of our relations from entering the Musalmán religion, if he will; and that we should honour the Musalmáns and make much of them, and place them in our assemblies, if any one of them will; and give them the chief seats, and not imitate them in our dress, neither in girdles, nor in the turban, nor the slippers, nor the parting of the hair, and never write in their language, nor call ourselves by their surnames; and that we should never ride upon great saddles, nor suspend our swords by belts, and never accept arms (the bow, sword, and club), nor carry them with us; and that we should never engrave upon our signet-rings in the Arabic language; and that we should not sell wine, and that we should shave the front of our heads, and tie up our dress, wherever we may be, and not wear wide girdles at our waist; and that we should never publicly exhibit the cross upon our churches, nor expose our crosses, nor ever inscribe them in the path of the Musalmáns, nor in their market-places, and never strike our bells the (quick) stroke, nor raise our voices over the dead, nor publicly expose the lights, or any thing else, in the roads and markets of the Moslems, and never come near them with our dead, and never receive any slave who has drawn upon himself familiarity with Moslems, and never look upon them in their houses."

We learn, moreover, from the same authority, as follows:—When Omar ratified the treaty, he added thereto,—"And that we will not strike any one of the Moslems. We stipulate this with you for ourselves and the people of our religion; and we accept these terms of capitulation: and if we subsequently violate a point of that which we have stipulated, upon our lives be it, and let there be no faith with us, and may it be allowed you to do to us whatever is lawful against rebellious and revolting subjects." We are, moreover, informed by the Imám-Al-Bíkhí, and by others (but the first has a beautiful passage by Abdurrahmán-Abú-Tamím), the Kádi, Abú-Muhammad-Ibn-Razin, requested a final decision on this at the foot of the assembly; and the chiefs of Islám confirmed this treaty; and the orthodox Khalífs acted upon it.

Moreover, we have a tradition from Ibn-Omar, on the authority of Náfá, from Islám, that Omar commanded the capitulated inhabitants to shave off their front locks of hair, and that they should ride upon small (pack) saddles on one side, and not ride as the Moslems ride; and that they should fasten the clasps of their girdles. It is also traditionally reported from Shadad-Ibn-Awís, that he accompanied Omar when he entered the Mosque of the Holy City, on the day when God, the great and glorious, opened the gate the second time by surrender. Now he entered by the Gate of Muhammad (upon whom be the peace and blessing of God!), creeping on hands and knees, he, and those with him, until he came to its underground drain (or sewer). Then he looked on the right and left. Then he said, God is great! Then he said, Yes, by God! this (unless I speak at random, or am beside myself) is the Mosque (or place of worship) of David (on him be peace!), of which the Apostle of God (upon whom be the peace and blessing of God!) informed us, when he said, "He hath brought me to come to him by night, and raised me up before him to a station before him, among the nearest of uncreated beings." Then Omar said, Let us take here a Mosque.

Moreover, there is a tradition from Al-Walíd-Ibn-Muslim, on the authority of a Shaikh of the sons of Shaddad-Ibn-Awís, from his father, from his grandfather,—That Omar, when he had concluded a treaty of peace between himself and between the people of the Holy House, said to the Patriarch thereof, Conduct me to the Mosque of David. He said, Yes. Then Omar went forth, belted with his sword, amidst four thousand of his comrades, who went forward with him, belted with swords; and all of us who were therein had no arms but swords; and the Patriarch was at a short distance from Omar, with his companions; and we went after Omar when we entered the city of the Baitu-l-Mukaddas.

Thus we entered the church which is called the Church of the Resurrection: and the Patriarch said, This is the Mosque of David. Whereupon Omar considered attentively, and said to him, Thou hast spoken falsely; for the Apostle of God (upon whom be the blessing and peace of God!) described to me the Mosque of David—a description which answers not to this. Then he proceeded with him to the church called Sion, and said, This is the Mosque of David. Upon this Omar said, Thou hast spoken falsely. So he went on with him to the Mosques of the Holy City until he came, at last, near unto a gate called the Gate of Muhammad; and he drew down all the filth (dung) that was on the declivity of the steps of the gate, until he came to a narrow passage; and he went down a number of steps, until he almost hung upon the top of the interior or upper surface. Then said the Patriarch to him, Thou canst go no farther, except creeping on hands and knees. Then said Omar, And I will go, even creeping on hands and knees. So Omar went upon his hands, and we went upon hands and knees after him, until we came to the central sewer. And we stood here upright. Then Omar looked and contemplated a long time. Then he said, By Him in whose hand is my life, this is that which the Apostle of God (upon whom be the peace and blessing of God!) described to us.

Moreover, there is an account in the traditionary history in another chapter, by Hishám-Ibn-Omar, from Al-Haitem-Ibn-Omar, that Al-Abbás said, I heard my grandfather, Abd-Ullah-Ibn-Abí-Alid-Ullah, say, When Omar-Ibn-Al-Khattáb possessed the government, he visited the people of Syria. Then he took up his abode in Al Jabít, and sent two men of the noblest of his faith to the Holy City. Then he obtained an entrance thereunto by capitulation. Afterwards Omar-Ibn-Al-Khattáb (with whom may God be satisfied!) arrived with Kaab; to whom Omar said, O Abú Ishák! make me to know the place of the Sakhrá (the Rock). Then he said, Measure out one cubit on each side of the wall which is nearest to the Valley of Hinnom; then dig, and thou shalt find it. Thus said he. And that place was at that time a public cess-pool. Then he dug, and the Sakhrá became manifest. Omar therefore said to Al Kaab, Where thinkest thou that we should place the Mosque? the lofty palms of the Kiblah? Then he said, Place it behind the Sakhrá, and then join together the two Kiblahs—the Kiblah of Moses and the Kiblah of Muhammad (upon whom be the blessing and peace of God!). Upon this Omar said to him, Thou wouldst imitate the Jewish (mode), O Abú Ishák! (but) the Mosque is best in front of it;—and he built the Mosque in front.

It is moreover traditionally reported, in 'The Collection of Histories upon extraneous authority,' *(accounts believed to be true, but of which the authors are not verified)*, in other supplementary chapters to ancient traditions, by Ibrahim-Ibn-Abú-Ablah-Al-Mukaddísí, upon the authority of his father, as follows:—Omar-Ibn-Al-Khattáb (with whom may God be content!) came to the Holy City, and encamped upon the Mount of Olives. Then he descended the declivity, and entered the Mosque by the Gate of the Prophet (upon whom be the mercy and peace of God!). So, when he had stood upright awhile therein, he gazed to the right and left. Then he said, By Him who is the only God! this, this is the Mosque of Solomon son of David, respecting which the Apostle of God (upon whom be the peace and mercy of God!) has informed us, that he was carried thither by night. Then came Omar to the Mosque (or oratory), and said, We will place a Mosque (a place of worship) for the Moslems here—a place of prayer, wherein they may pray. Again, we learn from Saad-Ibn-Abdul-Azíz,—When Ibn-Al-Khattáb (with whom may God rest satisfied!) took possession of the Holy City, he found fault with the quantity of dung which the Greeks had thrown there, in insult towards the sons of Israël. Wherefore Omar (with whom may God be content!) stretched out his mantle, and began to sweep up this dung; and the Musalmáns began to sweep with him. We are also informed by Al Walíd, that Saad-Ibn-Abdul-Azíz said, A letter (an epistle) of the Prophet of God (upon whom be the mercy and peace of God!) came to Al Kais; and this it is—"In the Baitu-l-Mukaddas, and upon the Sakhrá of the Baitu-l-Mukaddas, there shall be a great sewer, whereby the Tower of David (on whom be salutation!) is spoiled by the injurious abuse of the lying Christians, in order to hurt the Jews, until those changing times shall come that the cities be stirred up to wrest the precinct from Greece. Then shall the Sakhrá be met with. Therefore said Al Kais, when he read this epistle of the Prophet of God (upon whom be the mercy and compassion of God!), For ye, O people of Greece! a time is coming, when ye shall be slain upon this sewer, upon the place wherein ye have violated the sanctity of this Mosque, just as the sons of Israel slew John the son of Zacharias." Then he commanded it to be cleared; and they began so to do. Then the Moslems came to Syria, and they did not clear it more than a third part. But when Omar-Ibn-Al-Khattáb came to the Holy City, and obtained possession of it, and saw the great quantity of dung thereon, he commanded it to be cleared, and pressed into that service the Nabathæi of Palestine.

Again, we have it from Kais-Ibn-Naír, When Omar had cleansed the dung from the Sakhrá, he said, Ye shall not pray therein until three showers of rain have fallen upon it. Moreover Al Walíd said, Shadád told me, from his father, That Omar went to the Holy City when it was nearly sunset; and his garments were soiled with the dung, and we were soiled with him in our garments. And he went, and we went with him, as far as the two fountains which are in the valley called the Valley of Hinnom. Then he returned, and we returned likewise, that we might pray in the place of the Mosque wherein the congregation pray. Then Omar prayed, and we prayed with him. And a tradition from Abú-Marian-Muwallí-Islám, who was also (an inhabitant) of the Holy City, informs us as follows:—I was present with Omar when he entered the Holy City. He went on until he entered the Mosque. Then he went in front of the Tower of David, and prayed therein. Then he read a Surát (of the Korán), and worshipped; and we worshipped with him. Yet, again, we learn from the author of 'The Book of Mankind,' in the history of the Traditions of the Tower, on the authority of Walíd-Ibn-Muslemin, as follows:—One of our Shaikhs informed me that the Apostle of God (upon whom be the peace and blessing of God!), when the Baitu-l-Mukaddas was manifested to him on the night he was carried thither, lo! on the right-hand side of the Mosque, and on the left, there were two burning lights. Therefore he said, O Gabriel! what are these two lights? And he said, That on the right hand is the Tower of thy brother David; and that on the left is above the Tomb of thy sister Maria (peace be upon her!).

Moreover, the author of the 'Book of Mankind' reports, whilst relating the capture of the Holy House, in his traditionary history in another chapter, to Obíd-Ibn-Adam and Abú-Soab, that Omar was in the village Jábít. Then Khalíd-Ibn-Al-Walíd came to the Holy City: and it was said unto him, What is thy name? And he said, Khalíd-Ibn-Al-Walíd. And they said, What is thy master's name? And he replied, Omar-Ibn-Al-Khattáb. And they said, Send him to us. So he sent him to them. It was also reported that they had said to him (*i. e.* to Khalíd), Thou art not he who shall enter into the possession of the Holy City; but Omar is he who shall enter, provided that Mount Cesarea be entered before the Holy City. Therefore go and enter it; then tell your master. Then Khalíd (it is said) wrote word of this to Omar; and Omar summoned men to advise upon it; and he said, They are the possessors of the Scripture; and with them is knowledge of the matter beyond you. Therefore they went to Cesarea and took possession of it, and came to the Holy House; and Omar capitulated with them, and entered among them. And he had upon him two perfumed outer robes. Thus, therefore, he prayed in the Church of Maria. Then he spat in one robe. And it was said unto him, Dost thou spit here, seeing this is the place wherein she communed with God? But this assertion Omar absolutely denied, as an invention of the Christians.

Again, it is said by the Háfez, Abú-Muhammad-Al-Kasim, in his narrative to Othmán, and also by Abú-Hareth, Palestine and its territory fell into the hands of Omar in Rabia the First, the year sixteen. Moreover we learn from Isḥák-Ibn-Bashr, Omar marched against Syria this year, which was the sixteenth, and left Al-Jabít, and Elia capitulated to him, which was the city of the Baitu-l-Mukaddas. Again, Abdul-Ali-Ibn-Muhmar relates, that he read in a book of Abú-Ubaidah, who says, The Holy City capitulated in the year seventeen; in which perished Moaz-Ibn-Jabíl, (with whom be God satisfied!) Moreover, it is said by Al Thirkashí, in his 'Directions of the Mosques' and in the 'Perfect Source,' that the fortunate moment caused the surrender of the city; and this fortunate moment fell out, whereby Omar entered it five days before the end of Dhí-l-Kaad, in the year sixteen of the Hijra, and from the decease of the Prophet (upon whom may the blessing and peace of God remain!) five years and (five) months.

We find, moreover, in 'The Marvels of the Baitu-l-Mukaddas,' by Ibn-Al-Juzí, Omar capitulated with the Holy City in the year fifteen. And we learn from Rija-Ibn-Haywah, who heard it from one who was a witness of the surrender, as follows:—When Omar rose up from Al Jabít to Elia, he went to the Tower of David (on whom be peace!) by night, and prayed therein, and did not delay until the morn arose, but commanded the Muezzin to summon the people. And he came and prayed with the men, and read among them a part of the Korán, and worshipped. Then he read in the second place, 'A Chief' and 'A people of the sons of Israël' (parts of the Korán). Then he bowed the head (performed the Rak'at); then he went his way. Then he asked for Kaab, and he came; and he said,

Where, thinkest thou, should we place the point of prayer? who replied, On the Sakhrá. And he said, By God! Kaab, thou wouldst make it like a Jew's. Nay, we will place the Kiblah in front, as the Apostle of God (on whom be the mercy and peace of God!) placed the Kiblahs of our Mosques, in front of them. Go away! And he said moreover to him, Thou art weak (thy advice), for we do not chiefly glory in the Sakhrá, but in the Kaaba.

Lastly, it is said in the Muthír Alfárám, "These are the historical features respecting Capitulations and Treaties, among varying paths and discordant bursts of eloquence. Whatsoever there is said therein, be it taken in good part." The capitulation of Syria, and of the sacred and glorious land, was in the time of the Companions, (of Muhammad) (may God be content with them!); nor did the holy and glorious places cease to be in the hands of the Moslems, from the period of the Capitulation of Omar, until the days of the Orthodox Kalífs, and after them until the year ninety from the prophetical Hijra. And Abdul-Málik-Ibn-Marwán (upon whom be God's mercy!) built therein Al Sakhrá and the Temple of the Baitu-l-Mukaddas. It is said that he spent upon this building the produce of a seven years' tax upon Egypt. Again, it is said by Sabat-Ibn-

Juzí, in his book on the 'Changes of Dynasties,' that Abdul-Málik-Ibn-Marwán began the building in the year 69 from the Hijra, and finished it in the year 72 from the Hijra. Also, it is said, Saíd-Ibn-Abdul-Málik-Marwán built the Chapel of the Baitu-l-Mukaddas and its outward covering. Again, we learn from Táher-Ibn-Rija-Ibn-Haywah, and Yazid-Ibn-Salám, a nobleman of Abdul-Málik-Ibn-Marwán, that Abdul-Málik-Ibn-Marwán, whilst they were building the Chapel of Al Sakhrá of the Holy City and the Mosque Al Aksá, came from Damascus to the Holy City, and dispersed a letter among all his (chief deputies), and to all chief cities, importing that Abdul-Málik wished to build a Chapel upon the Sakhrá of the Holy City, to be a free and lasting Chapel to Musalmáns; and did not wish to do this without the advice and will of his subjects. Therefore the subjects wrote to him their good-will (consent), and wrote what they would give for the purpose. Also a letter arrived from the chiefs, in reply to the proposal of the Commander of the Faithful, deeming it a faithful and orthodox design, "And we pray God Almighty to accomplish his intention of building this Chapel, and the Sakhrá, and the Mosque; and may God choose him as his vicegerent in the performance of this under his auspices; and may he cause his munificence to abide on him, and on all his relations who exist."

Then the Khalíf assembled the best artificers of all his workmen, and commanded them to labour diligently at the work of the Chapel, and made a vaulted crypt in it before he built the Chapel. Then he laid the foundation in the middle of the Mosque, and commanded that the Treasury should be built upon the East of the Sakhrá: and this is that which is on the farther side of the Sakhrá. Thus he built and loaded it with riches; and he nominated as commissioners for this purpose Rija-Ibn-Haywah and Yazíd-Ibn-Salám, and committed to the care of these the expenses of the building, and the things necessary for the undertaking; and that they should expend the treasure upon it to the last dínár, so as just to lay it out in the payment of expenses. They therefore undertook the building and the fitting-up until the work was finished, and the building brought to a conclusion; and there was not a word left to be spoken of it. Then they wrote (thus) to him—he being at Damascus—"God hath brought to an end that which the Commander of Believers hath commanded us respecting the erection of the Chapel of the Sakhrá—the Sakhrá of the Holy City, and the Mosque Al Aksá—and there remains not a word to be spoken about it.

Moreover, there remains some surplus above the money granted to us by the Commander of Believers to that end, after 100,000 dínárs have been expended thereon. Let the Commander of Believers convert it to the object he likes best." And the Khalíf wrote to them, "The Commander of Believers committed to your charge whatsoever should be fit and proper when he appointed you superintendents of the restoration of this glorious and blessed Temple." Then they wrote to him, "We have thought that it well deserved of us that we should augment the amount by the ornaments of our women, taking the superfluity of our wealth. Convert it, then, to the purpose you best like." Then he wrote to them, "A great sum hath been expended and paid by the public for the Chapel; therefore I will spend and lay out upon it (money for the purchase of) that which every one may look at—gold work, and ornament, a sort of common part, (which all may be permitted to behold) of mosaic, outside; and there also a second, to be a covering against rain and wind and snow." But Rija-Ibn-Haywah and Yazíd-Ibn-Salám had already surrounded it with a screen of lattice-work, with small interstices, and a curtain of silk hanging loosely between pillars.

Also there were, every day, two-and-fifty, to

whom were committed the saffron, which they were pulverizing and grinding. Some worked in the night, and perfumed it with the vapour of musk, and amber, and rose-water, for the purpose of making incense. Then the servants were ordered to come, before dawn, to the Baths of Solomon, which they entered and washed and purified. They afterwards went to the Treasury, which was behind, and threw aside their clothes. Then they took from the Treasury other clothes of meru, and of fine texture, and a stuff called Al Asb (a sort of variegated cloth from Arabia Felix), and girdles of leather, wherewith they tightly bound their waists. Then they began the descent of the structure behind the Sakhrá, and every part, as far as their hands could reach, was considered polluted until they had poured a stream of water upon the whole of it; and that which their hands could not reach, they washed upon the surface, (throwing water up to the roof). Then they ascended upon the Sakhrá, washing whilst there remained any thing polluted therein, and concluded the purification of the vessels of the structure. Then they came with censers of gold and silver, and aloës-wood of Kimar, and incense perfumed with musk and amber. And the curtain was all hanging loosely around the pillars. Then they took the incense, and made a circuit around (the Chapel) until the space between them and the Chapel was filled with abundance of the smoke of incense. Then they lifted up a corner of the veil, and the incense escaped, and the grateful odour was diffused until it arrived at the head of the market. Therefore the passers-by smelt the odour and the incense, and put a stop to the business in which they were engaged. Then a crier cried out among the people, "The Sakhrá is now opened to all men. Whosoever desires to pray, let him come." The people therefore, thus summoned, came up to the Sakhrá; and there were a great number of men who were enabled to compass (or continue to pray) two Rakás, and some of them four. Then the men went out; and whosoever smelt the smell of their incense said, This is from some one who has entered the Sakhrá; and they washed the soles of their feet, and slightly passed a moistened hand over their faces, at the thresh-hold of St. George, and napkins were wetted, and gates were split open, (*i. e. although they only slightly wetted their faces, and then wiped them with a napkin; yet, from the number who did this, the napkins were entirely wet, and from the rush of their entrance the gates were split open.*) Also, at every gate there were ten beadles. Also, the people never entered, except on the second and fifth day (Monday and Friday). On other days no one entered, except the servants.

Again, we learn from Abú-Bekr-Ibn-Al-Háreth as follows:—We fitted up the Sakhrá in the Khiláfat of Abdul-Málik-Ibn-Marwán, with tamarisk-wood of Midiam. And the beadles said unto him, O belóved Abú-Bekr! order for us candelabra, wherewith, if we be smeared, we shall smell sweetly. And he agreed to this. This is what was done herein, in the Khiláfat of Abdul-Málik-Ibn-Marwán. And Al-Walíd said, Abdarrahmán-Ibn-Muhammad-Ibn-Marwán-Ibn-Khálit narrated to us: My father (he said) told us from his father, on the authority of his grandfather, There was in the chain which was in the midst of the Chapel, over the Sakhrá, an incomparable pearl, and the horn of Abraham's Ram, (on him be peace!) and the diadem of Cyrus, suspended therein, in the days of Abdul-Málik-Ibn-Marwán. When, however, the Khiláfat passed to the sons of Hisham, they removed them to the Kaaba (which may God Almighty preserve!).

We have moreover traditionary information from the historian Ibn-Asákir (may God compassionate him!). He hath given a narration of the buildings of Abdul-Málik-Ibn-Marwán—the buildings of the Sakhrá and the Masjidu-l-Aksá. At this time there were, between the pillars, pieces of wainscot (wood), six thousand compartments of wainscoting, and therein fifty doors; and six hundred marble pillars, and therein seven galleries for announcing prayer; and for the candelabra four hundred chains, save fifteen; of these one hundred and thirty in the Mosque, and the rest in the Chapel of the Sakhrá; and the length of the chains was four thousand cubits, and their weight three-and-forty thousand Syrian pounds. Also five thousand candelabra; and there glittered in the candelabra a thousand wax tapers on the day of assembly, and on the middle of Rejib, and Shábán, and on the feast-nights. Moreover there were within the Mosque fifteen chapels (to match) to the Chapel of the Sakhrá. And upon the flat roof of the Mosque there were seven thousand seven hundred planks of lead, the weight of every piece seventy pounds, besides that upon the Chapel of the Sakhrá. All this was done in the time of Abdul-Málik-Ibn-Marwán. And he arranged in order for this work a fixed series of servants—three hundred servants—who were hired at the expense of five treasuries. Every one who died among them, his son occupied his place and rank, and his son, his (or some one of his household.) Thus it went on for ever in successive generations. Of cisterns (or tanks) in the Mosque, there were four-and-twenty great ones; of minarets, four; three in a row on the west of the Mosque, and one over the Gate of the Long-haired (a tribe of Arabia, Al Ásbat); and of Jewish servants, from whom no tribute was taken, ten men (and these had sons, and so became twenty), for the purpose of sweeping away the filth accumulated on the feasts (days of the assemblage of pilgrims for Mecca) of the winter and summer, and for the sweeping up of the sacred ablution-water which was around the place of meeting. And in addition to these, there were ten Christian servants, who obtained this service by inheritance, to superintend the (beasts of burden, asses, &c.) and to sweep out the conduits (channels of supply, pipes, &c.) which flowed into the cisterns of the water, and to cleanse the cisterns also, and for other purposes besides that. And there were also five Jewish servants, to superintend the glass for the candelabra, and the cups, and the spitting-basins, and for other purposes, as necessity summoned them. No tribute was taken from them, nor from the persons who purveyed the combustibles for the burners of the candelabra, according to a composition with them and their sons for ever, in successive generations, by the grant of Abdul-Málik-Ibn-Marwán, and his donation by way of wages.

We are traditionally informed also by Abdur-rahman-Ibn-Muhammad-Ibn-Mansúr, on the authority of his father, who refers to his grandfather, That all the gates were furnished with broad plates of gold and silver in the days of the Khiláfat of Abdul-Málik-Ibn-Marwán, and when Abú-Jafár-Almansúr-Al-Abbássí acceded to the throne, then the eastern side of the Mosque had fallen. Wherefore it was said to him, O Commander of the Faithful! the eastern side of the Mosque hath now fallen; and the western fell at the time of the earthquake, the year one hundred and thirty. Wilt thou not commission us to rebuild and restore it? But he said, I have no treasure whatever. And he then commanded to take off the plates of gold and silver which were upon the doors. And they took them down, and made them into dínárs and dirhems, and spent them upon the building until he had come to an end of them. Then there was a second earthquake, and the building which Abú-Jafár had commissioned to be rebuilt fell down. Then afterwards Al Mahadi acceded to the throne, and the Mosque was in ruins: which being reported to him, he commanded it to be rebuilt, and said, This Mosque was narrow and long, and was deserted of men: diminish from its length, and augment its width. And it was finished in his Khiláfat; and in the year 452 the vaulted (groined) roof of the Chapel of the Temple fell down, and with it 500 candelabra. When the Musalmáns then present beheld it, they said, There will be some great and extraordinary calamity in Islám. Again we learn from Atu, on his father's authority, The Jews purveyed the furniture (necessaries) for the Temple, but when Omar-Radh-Ullah-anhu-Ibn-Abdul-Azíz ascended the throne, he dismissed them, and placed therein some of the tribe of Khims (of Arabia Felix). And then came to him a man of the family of Khims, and said unto him, Give me some present. But he said, How can I give thee? for it thou shouldst strain thine eyes in staring. I have not a single one of thy dog's hairs (to give).

Abú says, The Holy City did not cease to be in the hands of the Musalmáns, from its surrender to Omar-Ibn-Al-Khattáb (with whom may God rest satisfied!) until the year 491: and in the year 492 the Franks besieged it more than fifty days. Then they became masters of it, on the dawn of the morning of the day of assembly (Friday) in the year 482, and killed therein a great number of Musalmáns for the space of seven days.* And it was said, that in the Mosque Al Aksá (they killed) more than seventy thousand; and they took from the Sakhrá vessels of gold and silver, wealth preserved in the strong boxes; and on this account the Musalmáns were agitated to the utmost degree of commotion, in every region; and Afdhál, commander of the armies, had received it from Sakmán-Ibn-Ortuk, on Friday, five days before the end of Ramadán, in the year 491 (it is said also, that this took place in Shabán, the year 489), and took the nominal government of it: but this governor had no power against the Franks, who therefore received it from him—yielded up to them.

Then the Franks obtained possession of many regions and shores in his days, and became masters of Jaffa in Shammál, the year 493, and Cæsarea in the year 494, and assumed the government over these regions and coasts, and over the castles and forts therein. And in these they ruled as princes; also over all the tracts of country, and productions of the soil, and fields therein, and received taxes from the fruits in the meadows of cities. And the devil impelled upon them their exactions, and the exhaustion these fiends made, and the injustice these vagabond tyrants com-

* See Note.

mitted; nor did the Holy City, and the neighbouring regions and coasts cease to remain in the hands of the Franks, destitute of help, for more than ninety years. Until that time came, the appointed season manifested of God, and (when God) revealed those events to which no parallel can be found, which may be called the greatest of events of that description; and when the night, darkened into gloom, broke forth into its dawn, and that period arrived which bears in its womb, among heavenly beings, the secrets of fate; until the time of manifestation be fulfilled, and that time came from that Only One, with whom assemble all the times and seasons of action, and from that King whose tabernacle is the Heaven; of which tabernacle the systems of constellations are the ropes, and the earth the expanded canvas, and mountains the fastening-pegs; whose gold coin is the sun, and whose silver coin is the moon; whose servants are the rolling orbs, and whose sons are the stars; and when the great Sultán reigned—a king of the age, the superexcellent, the accomplisher, the efficient executer. In that his rule made him chief among princes; for that the reward of the efficient actor was not lost unto him. He who granted the just desire. He who confided in God; for that he was to be trusted for preserving his servant in safety. He who firmly rested in God for the repulsion of every proud devil. He whose help was implored by a numerosity of number. He who was skilled in (explaining) God's truth among relatives and servants, faithful in the just obligations of lying secretly in ambush, and making sacred war with the tyrants and the proud : a destroyer, with contempt and scorn, of the drinking-spots of the infidels, and associators (Trinitarians). The intelligent Eye of his age, and illuminated by the glitter of lightning, the Sultán Al-Málik-Al-Násir, Saláh Addunya (as well as) Addín-Abú-Mustapha-Yusúf-Ibn-Ayyúb. May God rain upon him in abundance the rain of his compassion and satisfaction, and grant him to dwell in the higher mansions of the angels! And may God Almighty, according to his power, give such victories as he hath here tofore given, and such a descent of angels and spirits as he gave in the days of our lord the Imám-Al-Nasír-Uddín-Allah, Commander of the Faithful, descended in a right line from the Prophet's uncle, Al Abbás. May the peace of God be upon him, and upon his sainted fathers, and upon the just Khalífs and the orthodox Rulers! And these were the days in which those who then flourished saw him, and saw the accomplishment of their struggle, in the termination of the Holy City's humiliation. (Thus abundantly in those days was fulfilled the design) and thus arrived that which made those days supereminent in splendour, and acceptable in glory, and glorious in merit. Thus arrived that which exalted the brilliancy of their grandeur, and adorned them with ensigns of power, and blessed them with showers of blessing, and when the last watch of the night dawned with the light of prosperity in streams. And with respect to the Sultán-Al-Málik-Al-Násir-Saláh-Uddin, him did prayer assist, and victory claim. Him did the willing choose as chief, and the alien entrust with his affairs. He to whose rescript men appealed in their affairs. Skilled in command, submissive to wisdom, he was thrown forward (by Providence) for this distinguished capture; and he caused the second restoration of Islám to the Holy City. He obtained an exaltation to the satisfaction of martyrs, by means of his fixed design for the overthrow, for the second time, of the Trinitarians and Infidels. Him may God bless with the strength of Islám! May he bless him with the best of content! May he give him of his excellence and liberality in the other world! May covenants be executed, and content be complete! May a Refuge still remain in store for him, and may this turn of events bring him to the reward remaining for the good from God, who is the most potent causer of vicissitudes.

And this is the most potent of hopes, for whatever wealth one may barter it, and is true in the fulfilment of God's good promises, and in the prosperity he gives to the propositions of the hopes of men. He multiplies numbers, and routs enemies, and as a giver is liberal, and as liberal gives, and wishes to grant, and grants the wish, and causes the mean to expend, and makes the riches of the great vanish for others. And he (Salah-Uddín) was raised up for the complete deliverance of the Holy City from the Infidels; for he was the most exalted of lions, and the brightness of fire.

Now he set out from Damascus in the beginning of the year 583; and he knew victory to be sure, and was victor in his sure knowledge. And God saluted him chief, for the purpose of giving victory to Islám, and for the payment of the debt of the faith. And he wrote to regions and provinces, to demand a collection of money, an assemblage for the sacred war, and also the people already summoned, and the people prepared. So he went, and (good) intention stirred him up, and might made him earnestly desire; and the faith went forth with him, and victory was given him, and his assemblage came to the summoner, and his army to the furious one; and his troops formed a junction with him. Thus he went forth to the sacred war with the Associators, enemies of the faith,—(that war) which is the most just of sacrifices made to God's service, and the most direct of all roads. And there went out in the direction of the Holy City the people of those places, spoken of in 'The Book of Sacred Victories' with long explications. (In effect) a number of people went to the assistance of the throes of truth and right—the struggle with the people of the Associators—of existence with annihilation. Thus he thundered on, in taking possession of castles, and strongholds, and coasts, with the risk of his head; the accomplishment of his decree terrifying the market-places (of the Christians); and the earth was stripped bare, and its inhabitants; and the canterer (*i. e. the horse*) perished, and his food. Then signs appeared, and wonders shone, and ghosts (wandered). Then his torrent (of troops) flowed, and he was prospered in every respect. And He who gives vigour gave him strength; and He who gives firmness gave him victory. He who is the Happy, gave him brightness. He who is mighty made him illustrious; and the Conquering One was his guardian; and Islám gave him thanks, and God the glorious and mighty gave him victory, until victory brought him on to Ascalon, and gave him possession of all that was in the hands of the Infidels—castles, and land, and possessions, and produce, and strongholds, and provinces, and regions, and all that lived therein, by means of the happy accomplishment of his firm resolve. Then the power of the sacred summons to prayer was established, and the partners in mystery—the bells—belied their name, being silent, and the sight-deceiving tricks of the priests were made subservient.

Further, the author of 'The Sacred Victories,' in his account of the capture of the Holy City, says, Then marched the Sultan from Ascalon to the Holy and Glorious, beseeching, and proceeded on to victory from the Almighty, whom he rendered his friend, and towards a joyful change in circumstances, with a face averse from merriment; and the light of his army dawned forth in the accomplishment of the entrance into the plain; and the (noble) people abounded with the copious ness of power; and the companions of admirable deeds extended their dignity wonderfully; and the dust made, as it were, the dawn of day become the twilight of night. And he marched on his road, according to the narrations of history, and the expositions of lofty deeds, in noble works, and (by the road) which compilers of books have pointed out; a march by which hopes revived in abundance, and Conquest took her station, and rose up from her short sleep, rising up like the sun from among the false accusers who had exiled it. And Islám preaches among the saints, like a bride brought to the house of her spouse, and for a munificent bridal gift received souls; and the number of the slain is reported to her, to avert from her the kiss (*i. e. the number of the slain damped her exultation*); but (the bride nevertheless) enters the house with a countenance glad with joyful tidings, whereby gloom of face is made to vanish; for the loudly exclaiming voice of Al Sakhrá was heard, summoning to her succour against her enemies. Then also was the granting of her entreaty, and of her longing weeping. Then arose brightness in her sky, and then returned the exile, Faith, to her abode, and was restored to her habitation and place of repose. And the faith became superior by God's removing the Franks, and driving them with a curse from Al Aksá. And the chiefs fought for this capture with energy; and bells became stilled by the *vivá-voce* call to prayer; and the true faith drove away the Infidels; and it was purified from the pollution of filth and uncleanness of the approach of men; and good came upon the holy and glorious place by the arrival of the Sultán; and hearts therein flew away with terror; and minds became mad, and their breasts palpitated with dread of the army of Islám; and the Franks trembled and became weak when the news of it was divulged. Also, there were therein two chiefs of the Franks, Bálián-Ibn-Bázián, and the Great Patriarch. There were also two societies—those of the Hospitallers and the Templars, with their chiefs. Thus the Christians were occupied with Ibn-Bázián, and overflowed by these two illustrious parties; and their abodes became too narrow for the people; and every house in the city was shared with whoever was a Sharer (*i. e.* an Associator, a Christian). Also, those in the inferior people came forward to govern in places of dignity; and the (opinions) of the Infidels were at variance; and (even) Franks despaired of relief, and assembled together (to endure) the ruin of all that was most precious, and said, *Here* shall chiefs rush onward, and souls dissolve away, and blood be shed; also wounds and bruises shall be endured with patience by warriors untouched before, and we will freely give our lives as a gift to the mansion of the spirit (Jesus Christ); and our people shall closely surround him (the Messiah), and in the city shall arise the chieftains, and our clouds (of sorrow) shall wet us (with the rain of consolation). Herein is our bounden duty; upon her our indispensable vow: in her splendour is our splendour; in her safety, our safety; in her existence, our existence; and in her perpetuity, our perpetuity: and if we desert her, may blame and reproof be ours, and repentance come upon us! for within (this city) is the sought, the crucified, the sacrificed Victim, the offered oblation; herein the place of assembly of the Apostles; the place of the (Adoration) of Christ; the place of Descent (into the grave); the place of Ascent (into Heaven): (herein) is the place of magical incantations, the beds, the drinking place, the place for play, the fountains, the places whereto one may step aside (*i. e.* baths), the retired places, the places of usury, the squares, the places wherein mothers nurse their infants; also the inns, the inner apartments, the images, the figures, the paintings, the portraits, the mosaics, the bas-reliefs, and representations, and pillars, and tablets, and things corporeal, and things spiritual. Moreover, within that is the picture of the Apostles in their white robes, and of the Jewish scribes, and of the monks in their robes, and presbyters in their place of conclave: herein also the fascinating trick, and her net, and the priesthood with its spectres (illusions, dreams): herein the portraits of the Lord and the Lady (St. John Baptist and the Virgin Mary), and he that was born, and she that was strengthened (our Lord and the Virgin Mary), and the fish-ponds, the circus for horse-running, the place for polishing, the disciple, the learned man, the places of comfort, and the youth in the course of instruction, and the statue of the Ram (of Abraham), and the Ass (of Balaam), and the bells, and the secret lurking-places. Herein also (they said) is the Cross of the Messiah, and the Oblation of the sacrificed Victim : herein the Divine nature was produced, and the human nature presented to him. Here was the establishment of the insertion of the jewel into the ring (*i. e. the union of the Divine and human nature in our Lord's hypostasis*). Here was erected the cross ; here descended the light ; here was removed the darkness ; here abounded the congruity (of human nature) with the self-existing (God), and the commixture of existence with non-existence : here baptism confirmed the Adorable, and the Virgin Mary reared the son.

Thus they took up their abode in the slavery of this error, and strayed away thereby from the right path of just argument, and said, Beneath the Sepulchre of our Lord we will die, and on account of the dread of its separation from us will we be strong. From her will we procrastinate the evil day, and towards the relics in the City and the Sepulchre will we hasten. Wherefore shall we not fight? wherefore not battle in this quarrel? Nor will we give up. For what reason should we permit them to seize her? We will force from them the price of blood, until they have paid, to the last farthing, that which they compel us to pay, and escape (just as often as we escape), and contrive (what we contrive), and make no resistance (which we do not make), nor offer any defence in which we will not, in turn, strive to surpass them. And they erected machines for shooting stones, for their troops, on a level with the walls; and their Devils were burning, (*i. e. their machines for casting the Greek fire were prepared,*) and their harness-makers were preparing harness, and their insolent tyrants displayed their tyranny, and the dust (of busy preparation) flew up, and the waves (of bustle) rolled, and their heralds are summoning, and their spiteful vipers are running, and their priests are stirring the fire (of bravery), and their chieftains drawing out to the dregs all the milk (of courage); and their valour impels them; and their spies came to them, and reported to them what they had spied out respecting the approach of Christian armies—victorious soldiers, gracefully thin by vow for the purpose of attacking the enemy; engaged and bound down in the conceptions of their minds by the light of the way (*i. e.*, their religion), (an army) wasting away in thinness, sprinkled with the dew of hypocrisy (of opinion), full of confidence and assumption, hoping from God the superiority in the execution of their will. Then dust rolled like a torrent over the hollow places, and (the warriors agile as) fawns called loudly their words of reproof; and the light edges of the pennons of their spears (glittered) with fire; and the collars of their dresses flowed murmuring like a stream when moved by their breath, and their wide-stepping soldiers closed up the broad mountain-roads, and the waves of rolling dust were extended far along, and their spears were in motion like mountains, and their onset was as the onset of lions; and their advance came on magnificently; every one, bound by suit and service to his master, faithfully performed his obligation; and their arms were hidden by Indian white (sleeves), and the sounds of voices were confused by the thunder and lightning (of their swords and their arms).

Moreover, my author says, "The Sultan set out (accompanied) by the escort of Royalty, and a long train of brave warriors, and the escort of his sons and brothers, and the most promising of his Mamlúks and youths, and the most noble of his chiefs, and the most illustrious of his generals and aides-de-camp; and they came in the narrow passes in smaller parties, and the best cavalry in places where one could ride in larger bodies, and (there were) the yellow standard-poles for the standards which were made of yellow, white, and brown, and the horsemen, and whosoever, from zeal in the faith, was ready to barter his life and soul. And there came, in the dawn of morning, to question him, the greatest from afar, and the noble ones who were near, and companies from on high; and he relates what splendid victories God had given him; and says, If God will prosper us and be our guardian in casting forth his enemies from the Holy City, by opening the way for us (then), God will render us happy, if he will guide us in the work of our hands; for, truly, that Holy City hath been in the hands of the Infidels the long space of one-and-ninety years. God Almighty hath not been approached therein by the operators of his beauteous (will). With regard to this city, the minds of kings have slumbered, and for an age has she remained deserted, and for years suffered sorrow, and thus hath she been left desolate, and God hath made cheap her superexcellence. And how is it that we have not anxiously reflected upon the recovery of the Holy House, and the Mosque Al Aksá? for this city has its foundation upon the two most mighty and well-pleasing objects, the Sakhrá and the Kaaba. This is the abode of prophets, the shrine of chiefs, the place wherein the God-fearing adored, the place which *they* visited who barter things temporal for eternal—the holy Temple of the earth and of the angels in Heaven. Herein will the buried arise, and the dead revive, and herein, in that Sakhrá, the illustrious fame of which makes it be regarded as the loveliest among the lovely: herein the lightnings lightly played, and the thunderbolts rent (the earth); and on the night of the Prophet's gradual ascent to Heaven, that magnificent light, illuminated herein from the regions above, shone brightly: and herein is that Gate of Mercy (among its gates) by which alone every one must enter into Paradise, to all eternity. Herein is the throne of Solomon, and the Tower of David. Beneath it is the Fountain of Siloam, which, to any one approaching thereto to drink, hath the appearance of the size of a large fish-pond, full of water. This Temple, also, is the first of the two Kiblahs, and the second of the two houses, and the third of the two sacred places, and the only one of the three Mosques to which came the Prophetic Messenger. Truly, the burdens laid upon her have been excessive; and men have rendered useless her courts. Perhaps God will cause return to her, for our sakes, that beautiful state and form, according to the glory He ascribed to it among the most glorious of created beings, in his first *Surát*, saying, "Great is he who said, Praise to Him who brought his servant by night from the place of retirement to the Mosque Al Aksá."

In addition to this (it is to be venerated) by reason of the wonders and surpassing events which took place therein; which cannot be numbered or written. To this city, and in this city, was the night-journey; and to its soil was thrown open the Heavens. Herein prophets have succeeded to the footsteps of prophets, and chiefs to those of chieftains. Here is the place wherein were the Confessors of the (True) Way, and the grandeur of the great, and the most learned of the learned. Herein are the most blessed of all blessed places; and herein the place wherein God opened the minds of the dull. Herein is the long Sakhrá, and the first Kiblah, whereon the prophetic foot alighted. Within this place alighted our Prophet Muhammad (upon whom be the peace and blessing of God!) among the prophets, and in the company of the chief spirit (Gabriel), and ascended up the ladder therefrom to the height of heights. Thus he arrived at the appointed boundary of his felicity and grandeur, to the place wherein he was glorified, and reduced to silence, and exalted, and shot like an arrow to the summit of bliss, and brought into the Heaven, and lifted up, (wherein) his blessings were beatified, and his happiness blessed, and his adornments beautified, and his beauty decked out; and herein God revealed himself to him, and revealed the seven longer chapters of the Korán, by the word, magnificent and high, which we now pronounce when blessing him. Also, how many signs did God offer to his Prophet's view therein, and performed surpassing events which we have heard of, and which have been seen!

Then the Sultán described among his private counsellors and chiefs the measures on which he relied for the recovery of the places already bound by treaty; and he swore by God that he would never flinch until his vow was utterly performed. And he lifted up his standard on high, and set his foot on the road of the pilgrimage to the prophetic foot. Thus he marched, confident in Him who is the perfector of victory; and the army coveted the booty, whilst verging onwards to the succour of the imploring Sakhrá, and swore by God that they would make the Franks fly from the stony ground, like dust from the floor.

The Sultán then began to besiege the western side of the Mosque, on the eleventh day of the month Rajib; and the hearts of the Infidels palpitated, and the gestures of the Franks were alternately remarkable for anxiety of countenance and change of colour; and God's providence displayed God's grace. There were then Franks assembled in the Holy City, to the number of sixty thousand fighting men, composed of lancers and archers, who remained in the place, constantly coming down to fight, and keeping others from fighting (refusing to engage), entering the field of battle, and flinching aside, and going away untouched, making sallies, and exhausting all their courage, and lolling their tongues like dogs, and bragging, and retreating, and coming on, and running off like a ball kicked by the foot, and rolling about from side to side, and mingling in confusion like ants, and spying about, and twisting themselves like weeping boys. Then misfortune changed sides, and fate advanced headlong: then they fought bravely in battle, and came down to offer battle, and laid by their broad-swords in their caskets, lest the deer, thirsting for their lives, should quench that thirst. Thus continued they in dread, and partook all around of the cup of fate; but the combined Musalmáns raged like eager horses in cutting to pieces, and were all on fire, all merry, and attached themselves firmly to battle, and came forward openly to fight; and their ardour was unshaken, and their zeal full of confidence; and they said, Each one of us will cope with twenty, and each ten of us with two hundred. Thus, below the Temple of *Dust* (of the Resurrection) was found the *Dust* of armies, and beneath (the shrine of) Peace, the edge of peace is broken. Thus went on the war; and the thrusting and striking with spears remained as ever. And the Sultán arrived on Friday, the twentieth of Rajib, on the northern side, and encamped there; and the king hemmed in the Franks closely, and brought against them abundance of destructive engines, and erected his machines for casting stones; and from these heavy, full clouds rained copious showers, and the stone (Sakhrá) was overwhelmed by *stones,* and the sharp spear of their calamity pierced them even behind the walls. Therefore they who had returned (into the city) came forth from the walls, themselves and their chiefs, lest they should meet with misfortune and an unpalatable day; and they threw themselves upon the rocks—themselves and their chieftains—for the encounter of naked spears; and hearts rushed forward to dolorous slaughter, and hands upon the hilts of their drawn swords, and souls were deeply anxious lest the design be retarded. And the wall was also threatened; and the small towers, being found to be overthrown by stones cast from without among the Infidels, were a source of anxiety. Then played the slinging-machines, and the places of defence (discharged) shot, and masses dragged down masses, (*i. e. the masses of stone from the machines brought down masses from the walls,*) and men drew down men, and Calamity and Death became mothers, and brought forth sorrow; nor did we shoot one arrow from the bow, but entered right into a man's middle. Never shall he who passed by her ever once break his fast again; and as many horses as there are stars in the sky rush to disperse their cavalry; nor does this number suffice to express all—all the inflicted wounds, and the extreme sufferings of their broken battalions, and those random blows—the earnest of subsequent death. Nor can this number sufficiently denote the batteries they constructed, and the forts they ran up; nor was there any cessation to the lightning of their Devils (their machines for casting the Greek fire), nor the agile twisting of horses' bridles (the horses being incessantly wheeled about). Then was the advance, and the overthrow, and the beating with clubs, and the striking of the riders, and the loud shout (accompanying) their attempts.

Also, the batteries continued to bear upon one single point the force of their stroke, and thus the collected works on the right weakened the enemy by dividing and wearing them out. And the buttresses began to lean on one side by the stroke, and the fastenings began to be injured in the clamping-places. Also, the drinking-places (outside the walls) had been much frequented by drinkers, until defeat caused the wall to be deserted, and frequent attacks made it impossible; so that, from thirst, ulcers like the water-lily infested the enemy. Also, trenches were dug, and mines were sunk, and light appeared from the aperture of the opening. Then the rough became smooth, and the narrow became broad, and difficulties were exchanged for ease, and the design was accomplished, and the place obliged to sue for peace—for trenches cut off resources.

And then came forth Ibn Bázián to make peace with the Sultán, and to bind him down by treaty. And he demanded the right of capitulation for his people, which the Sultán refused, and was high in his disgust, and said, I will not grant you security; there shall be no capitulation for you; none, except that we shall perpetuate contempt upon you, and class you with tributary slaves—the vile and contemptible—according to the decree of the Korán. "To-morrow we shall become masters of your Sepulchre, and we will make broad your slaughter and captivity. From the men will we pour out the blood, and upon the women and the imps (your children) will we seize and lead into miserable slavery." And he returned a peremptory refusal to their request. Whereupon they assumed a demeanour, the reverse of submissive, and put on indifference, and endeavoured to alarm (the Sultán) by (representing) the extreme effects of their terror if they were disappointed of the capitulation, and said, If the women be excluded from terms of peace, and if your Sultán really means what he says, and we be deprived of all hopes of your kindness—if this calamity be laid upon us, that we shall receive neither salvation, nor success, nor peace, nor safety, nor capitulation, nor the security thereof, nor kindness, nor generosity—then our way is, that we fight the battle of blood, and oppose Existence to Annihilation; and we will throw ourselves upon the hazard; nor will we be exposed to loss and shame also; nor shall one of us be put *hors-de-combat* until he have put ten into the same condition. Never shall the hands of our slaying warriors be closed whilst we see the nerves of our hand strung for slaughter. In fine, we will burn the Holy Sepulchre, and lay waste the Chapel, and leave for you, in our disgrace, the disgrace (desecration) of that building; and we will pull down the *Sakhrá*, and on that account ye shall endure the *Sigh*. Moreover, we will kill every one of the Musalmán prisoners who are here with us, who are thousands (in number), and it shall be known whether our speech be like that of the contemptible and vile, who smell, as it were, the water of bravery, and turn away without drinking, or that of the bold, who execute his plighted word. With regard to our wealth, we will conceal it, and not give it to you; and as to our jewels, them we will hasten to destroy, nor leave a part of them. What advantage, then, can there be expected to accrue to you in thus withholding quarter from us. To you (on the contrary) there will be every cause of grief in this refusal and this consequent utter destruction; for he who is cast down from Hope, Obstinacy comes on to meet; nor can the evil be repaired, or replaced on the equable basis of Peace (*the evils of refusal cannot be repaired, nor matters arranged* in statu quo ante bellum.) He who sets forward on his journey in the evening twilight, will stray in the darkness of night before the dawning of the day.

Then the Sultán assembled a meeting for consultation, and invited the presence of the chiefs of his victorious army, and advised with them on the capitulation, and caused arise the hidden counsels of their hearts, and uncovered the mysteries of their secret designs, and became acquainted with what was in them, and broke them in to adopt the just arrangement amidst vacillating councils, and gently prevailed upon them to choose the lucrative side of the question, and said, Truly that opportunity is at hand which we earnestly desired to seize. Truly, a (good) portion hath descended (from on high). Let us, then, praise God for the nuts he has given us to crack. If opportunity escape, she will not be laid hold of: if she goes off, she will not be mastered. Then they said unto him, God hath given thee a peculiar place in his blessing, and his servants sincerely honour thee for this. Thy counsel is just; thy design relating to the surrender is acute; and the affair thou mentionest, relating to granting terms to the people, goes to the root of the matter. We, however, must inform thee of the booty which should result from our capture of this glorious place, and of the wealth therein deposited, consisting of things desirable and things useful, and things all prepared, and things fit to swell out a contribution whereby our joy may be fully perfected, and whereby they may redeem themselves and their property, and whereby they may save their women, and their men, and their little ones; so that whosoever shall be found deficient in the payment, after forty days, of that which is necessary to be paid; and whosoever shall refuse, and not thus purchase terms of peace; upon him shall slavery be imposed. And in this appropriation of the booty to ourselves we are confirmed by justice, and by our patient endurance of so arduous an undertaking. This tribute therefore is, for every man ten dínárs, and for every woman five dínárs, and for every boy and girl two dínárs. Also the Patriarch, and the chiefs of the Templars and the Hospitallers, were detained as hostages. And Bálián-Ibn-Báziân ransomed the poor for thirty thousand dínárs; yet the Sultán stood to his engagement, nor waived the full amount of his claim. Whosoever, then, was allowed peace and security, departed from his house in safety; but returned not as an inhabitant.

Now the (city) surrendered on Friday, the twenty-seventh of Rajib, upon these terms of tribute; and they surrendered it with the loathing of compelled reluctance—a surrender of rage, not of confidence. There were in the city more than 100,000 men, women, and youths; therefore the gates were shut upon them, and their personal property and necessary clothing being guarantied to each individual, a trusty person and a principal chief were appointed at every gate to keep guard over all who wished to pass forth. Whoever, therefore, wished to pass out, passed; but whosoever could not stand to what was imposed upon him, remained shut in, and endured deprivation of joy. Moreover, if all the money thus obtained had been justly kept, the treasury would have abounded with wealth; but in the affair there was a complete dereliction of duty, and universal corruption; and every one made some plausible colouring, in some way or other. Also, the collectors were turned aside from the straight path of (entrusted persons) by means of bribes. Thus some of them were let down from the walls by ropes; and some of them also were carried out, as if in the pains of labour, in litters; and some who pretended to remove their women; and many of the army went forth in this disguise. And there were some of them upon whom an obedient madness fell—a madness which had never preceded the surrender. There was also, among the holy ones, a Grecian princess, who had remained hidden in retirement among the adorers of the crosses of the Crucified. She was inflamed by the fire of grief, and, being firmly bound by the ribbon of the deepest mysteries of her religion, her sighs ascended the highest ladder of sorrow, and her tears descended like drops from the clouds. She had property, and wealth, and valuables, and possessions. The Sultán, however, granted to her, and to all who were with her, free egress, and agreed to the transportation of all the ready money, and all the property and rents she possessed. Thus she became joyfully at ease; and whatever tender vine-shoots were with her, sad and anxious, were also permitted to depart. In like manner, the wife of the captive king, daughter of the king Amaury, was residing among the holy damsels with her servants, and horses, and attendant ladies: she also was liberated, herself and all who were with her, and whosoever asserted that he was of the number of her companions or suite. In like manner, the princess, daughter of Falít, lord of Hanafa, besought that all her property in her treasuries should be weighed and fully paid; and that all her private attendants should be freely suffered to go with her. These amounted to five hundred people of the land, who were asserted to be of that prince's country, and that their arrival in the Holy Land was only an arrival in pilgrimage. Moreover, Muzaffar-Uddín-Alí-Ibn-Lájak, asked craftily for the liberation of a thousand Armenians who were, as he pretended, from Edessa. Nevertheless the Sultán agreed to their departure, according to his desire. With all this, the net proceeds which came to the treasury amounted to nearly 100,000 dínárs. Those who remained, remained in a state of slavery and captivity, on account of their delay in the discharge of the stipulated sum, and their inability to pay the quota demanded.

We hear also from Omad, (on whom be the mercy of Almighty God!) the surrender of the Holy City took place on a day that resembled the night of Muhammad's journey to Heaven. Then was accomplished that which threw light upon the broad road to victory and exultation. Then did our tongues abound with humble and devoted prayer. Then the Sultán took his seat, in the garb of humility, and the worn garment of modesty, to receive the congratulations of, and give audience to, the great men, and the Emirs, and the holy men, and the Ulema, and the Safís, and other pious men besides them. His face was bright with the light of the joyful tidings, and his hope prancing high with the great victory. His gate (of reception) was opened, his cup (of prosperity) presented, and his veil was raised (*i. e. he gave open audience*), and his own voice was heard, and his joyful merriment surpassed the usual bounds. Then shone forth the happy period of his life: then his design was sweetly scented. His chief men came openly before him to receive audience, but kept within their breasts the swellings of hope. There sat the readers, to read; there stood the poets, to recite; there are seen learned men, spreading the news; there pens are writing, to publish the glad tidings; and eyes, from excess of joy, are full of tears. Hearts yield themselves to lowly praise for joy at the victory, and tongues repress (their pride) in offering humble thanksgivings to God. Writers catch the odour of the news, and sweetly treat upon the subject. The flame (of the intelligence) widens and becomes broad, and proceeds with activity, and makes the unwilling to hear, and spreads far and wide. I also, said Omad, (upon whom abide the compassion of God !), wrote among those who announced the joyful tidings of this surrender, and diffused the grateful odour of this happy intelligence; and the Baitu-l-Harám (of Mecca) received the glad news of the liberation of the Masjidu-l-Aksá, (even as it had previously received the sad news of) its diversion from the service of the Muhammadan faith; and of the transformation of the White Rock into the Black Stone, and of the Spirit (*i. e. Jesus Christ*) having taken up his abode in the halting-place of the Night-journey, the resting-place of the Lord of Apostles, and Signet of Prophets, the resting-place of Apostles and Prophets, the Mansion of Abraham, which preserved the place of the foot of Muhammad the Elect, upon whom be the blessing and peace of God!

We are further informed by Omad as follows: —Men heard of this glorious victory and great conquest, and came to visit (the city) from all the distant highways, and walked into it from every path, and made a sacred procession from the Baitu-l Mukaddas, (Jerusalem, or the consecrated House.) to the Ancient House, Mecca, and joyfully sported among the flowers of generosity in the land of beauty. Still further, Omad informs us, The Franks were enjoined to sell all their goods, and to bring out whatever smaller matters they might have; such as would sell for a small price in the market of contempt, and be disposed of for a few dínárs, not amounting to ten. They therefore diligently bestirred themselves in collecting together all their property which they could find, managing matters well for themselves. Moreover, they swept up every particle of property from their churches, and took therefrom even the smallest things of value, and transported from them the vessels and candlesticks of gold and silver, and the silk of the curtains and napkins, and completely stripped their churches of all that was there laid up, and brought out from the recesses the hidden wealth. Also the Great Patriarch collected all the broad plates of virgin gold or silver, and the unwrought masses of bullion, which were in the sepulchre, and collected all the treasure, and valuable (offerings and relics) which were in the Church of Holy Resurrection. Then I said to the Sultán, This is absolute wealth, and evident property, amounting in value to nearly 100,000 dínárs; and the capitulation spared only their lives and personal property, not the property of their churches. Surely, if I may advise, we will not leave it in the hands of these cheating liars. Then the Sultán said, It is a pity. Nevertheless they will allege against us a breach of faith, among those who are ignorant of the real state of things. Let us therefore permit them to report how purely we observe the capitulation; nor let them object, against the people of Faith, a violation of an engagement; but let them tell how many valuable things we waived from it. Thus they left those valuables that were of heavy weight, and carried away that which was light of carriage. The greater men emigrated to Tyre; yet there remained 15,000, who refused the proposed impost, and were reduced to slavery according to the agreement. When, therefore, the holy places were purified from the footsteps of the Franks, that wicked race, and the squinting-eyed (sly, insincere) people had put off their garments, and the Christians had put on the honourable rate of a large amount of tax, if they departed; then they humbly besought permission to remain, and not remove. Thus they offered, in exchange for this privilege, loads of their wealth, and sought our favour in every way that is most degrading, by prostration, and salutation, and standing upright with joined hands. And they gave from their hand the tribute of slaves; for they were small, and we were victors superior to them. Thus, then, they entered into the compact of security, and came forth under protection, and occupied themselves in servitude, and employed themselves in servile offices, and accounted this degree of mercy as a privilege.

Again, we are informed by an author of 'The Surrender of the Holy City,' as follows:—The Sultán brought forward to view many beautiful places, and destroyed many bad places; for when he had concluded the capitulation, he commanded that the Tower of David should be brought out to view; and the Emir of the nobles received a royal command to execute this design; for the Templars had built, right before it, a wall, and left this (*i. e.* the Tower) for spite, in front. It was said that they made use of it as a privy and a brothel. Also they had built (upon the western side of the Kiblah) a large house and a lofty church: therefore Salah-Uddín commanded the covering to be lifted up, this veil to be raised from the wall of the Tower. He also destroyed all the buildings which stood before it, and commanded all the garments to be cleansed and purified; (also those places) wherein men assembled when they met in open places (not in the Mosque). Also he erected the Pulpit, and exhibited the purified

Tower, and destroyed those places of which they had informed him, between the walls; and they extended a wall of great height. Also, the candlesticks were suspended, and the Sacred Revealed Book was near, and Truth was righted, and Folly came to nought. Then also the Korán bore sway, and the Gospel was removed. Then were established the adorations; then did Worship utter praise; then was the restoration of prayers and the supplications; then took place glorious blessings of God, and magnifyings of Him; then were mysteries revealed, and the verses of the Korán became rulers, and the Sign-posts (of the Faithful) were erected on high; then the *vivâ-voce* call to prayer was heard, and the bells were silent; then were the Muezzins present, but the priests were hidden; then the lucky stars were on the ascendant, and the luckless stars on the wane, and the banished Faith returned to her native abode; then the Glorious One was sought in his "dread abode," and the religious-thirst-slackening draughts were desired; then assembled the Self-Denyers, and the Adorers, and the Devoted, and the Pillars; then the Holy One was adored; then were found the adorer, the offerer of the head-bowing and body-prostrating worshipper, the humble, the chaste, the wise, the confessor, the holy warrior, the diligent, the stander, and the sitter, the abstinent, the sparing, the watcher, and the worker, the visiter, and the frequenter, the pilgrim, and the ordinary attendant. Then the joyful news (of religion) was proclaimed in purity, and the hypocrite became manifest; then the stammerer was (challenged to dispute); then the Resurrection was asserted, as well as the assemblage of all on the day of judgment; then the Ulema (civil lawyers) recited sacred words, and were responsively answered by the Fukara (priests); then the sacred traditions were reported, and the narrators of religious tales recited oral traditions; the offerers of prayer were restored to safety, and, when restored to safety, prayed. The performers of the sacred ablution then took up the execution of that divine precept. Then those who were interpreters (of the Korán) enjoyed good fortune; then also those who were preachers were kindly treated.

And there were many who panted that the (person to whom) the office of preaching (was assigned) (should be made) known with clearness and perspicuity, nor was there any thing spoken among them but, Who is the appointed Preacher? Who is nominated to preach? Would that the fire of eloquence were mine! Would that I could try the clear explication, and polish words fit for the place, and harangue in a surpassing style of eloquence from the place above! Therefore their necks were eagerly stretched forward to obtain a positive assurance of the person appointed; nor was there one who did not contend for the office, and ardently desire it, and seek for that good work, and hope for that accession of honour; nor one who did not offer himself as a candidate for it, and humbly supplicate for it, and most fervently request it, and make intercession for it. And every one put on the garment of gravity (modesty), and sat still in modest forbearance; and every fifth struck the sixth, and lifted up his head, to obtain this headship.* Nevertheless, the Sultán did not yet designate any particular person; neither did he appropriate the office to any individual, nor set apart one from the other, nor point out any one.

When, therefore, the Day of Assembly (Friday), the fourth of Shabán, arrived, men came in the morning, inquiring respecting the choice of the Preacher by the Sultán. The place of assemblage was full, and the congregation hurried about in confused discordancy: eyes and ears caught anxiously the least sight or sound; the receptacle of tears poured out a full shower from the over-

* *i. e.* Men touched their next neighbour, to excite their attention. It is also a proverb.

flowing channels of hearts; eyes were staring in expectation; opinions are divided; and they say, Who will preach? To whom will the exalted post be given? They began, therefore, to weigh the respective merits of individuals, and remained for a long time considering, and talking of the most noble and most singularly-gifted personages. Then the standards were lifted on high, and the pulpit is furnished with drapery and ornamented with precious stones. Then voices are raised, and the crowd rush on together, and the people are more confused than a heavy shower of rain, and are driven against each other like the waves of the sea; and the clamour, to those who were well-informed, seemed like the crowd on Mount Arafát, in the ceremonies of the pilgrimage to Mecca, till the haughty Striding-one (the Sultán) came, and suspense ceased, and the offerer of prayer ascended the steps, and the guard advanced swiftly. Then the Sultán proceeded to elevate a person to the office of Preacher, and publicly declared the choice of his will, after examination, and summoned to his command the Kadí Muhammad Addín-Abú-Al-Umállí-Muhammad (a descendant of Othmán). Him did the Sultán ordain to ascend these stairs of honour, on account of the loftiness of his knowledge. Therefore this experienced man mounted up, and assumed the honour which his good stars provided him. The waving (tapestry) of the pulpit bent towards him in eager delight, and the passage of the place of stumbling (*i. e.* the stairs up to the pulpit) recognised him.

He therefore preached, speaking with a clear and intelligible voice, whilst they continued silent. He began a most eloquent discourse, speaking good Arabic, with much originality, and skill in foreign learning; and he gave a lucid account of the excellence of the Baitu-l-Mukaddas, and its purification since its pollution, and of the silencing of the bells, and the expulsion of the priests: and he first commenced his sermon (after having caused all the people to rise up from their seats and remain standing) by opening it with the perusal of the Surát Al-Fatha (the first chapter of the Korán) to the end. Then he said, So may all the followers of the people who work iniquity be cut off! and praise be to God, Lord of the universe! Then he read the first Surát of the chapter called 'The grace and favour of his power.' Then he read that beginning with "They who deny their Lord, shall receive a just reward." Then he read the Surát 'Praise,' and said, "Praise be to God, who never will accept a son (as heir) to his power; who has no equal or associate fit to express his will, or to magnify him in might." Then he read the first Surát of the chapter called 'The Cave,' and said, "Praise be to God who hath sent down from Heaven, to his servant, the book of the Three Signs!" Then he read from the chapter called 'The Ant,' "Say, Praise be to God, and peace upon his servant, who hath clearly revealed the Sign." Then he read the first Surát of 'The Captives,' "Praise to God, whose are all the wondrous things in heaven and on earth." It had also been his intention to recite all those passages of the entire Korán, which contain the words "Praise to God;" but he felt unwilling so to do, on account of the length of time it would have occupied; and therefore said, "Praise be to God, who hath magnified Islám by his aid, and humbled the Associators (Trinitarians) by this glorious victory! Praise be to him who hath by his command shifted the course of affairs, and augmented his grace by this abundant gift; who, by his skilful design, hath brought down the Infidels (a few steps)—that design which Time, in his revolving course, effectuated through the just and necessary decree (and foreknowledge) of God; and which the Appointed End accomplished in harmonious order, according to the Excellent Power of God. (It is God) who hath, of his bounty, given of the spoil of the Infidels to his servants, and manifested the accomplishment of his firmly-bound resolve, to all the faith. It is He who, high above his servants, gives them victory without denial, grants conquest to his Khalíf without dispute, and performs that which he willeth without gainsaying. He it is who finally executeth that which he desireth without delay. I praise him, in that he hath crowned his well-beloved (Sultán) with triumph and glory and might; and in that he hath aided him who aided His cause, and hath purified His consecrated House from the filth and footsteps of the Associators. Praise be to Him who hath granted unto Muhammad the conception of his inward secrets and his external acts! Truly, I bear witness, that there is no God but one God. He has no partner. He is the One, the universal Parent, who never begot, and who never was begotten."

"This is the preliminary confession of him whose heart openly proclaims the Unity. May the satisfaction of his Lord rest upon him! I testify also that Muhammad is His servant and His Apostle—the Resolver of doubts—who trippeth up the heels of the Associators, and knocketh the liars on the head. He who was brought by night from the Venerable Mosque to this far-distant Mosque, and was made to ascend up to the highest Heaven, to the lotus-tree of the utmost exaltation—fast by which is Paradise—and who took up his resting-place in that (seat) most glorious to the eye, and most lofty. Upon him dwell the benediction and peace of God, and upon his lieutenant (Khalíf) Abú-Bekr, the sincere, the first-fruits of the faith! and upon the Commander of the Faithful, Omar-Ibn-Al-Khattáb, the first who removed from this consecrated House the representations of the cross! and upon the Commander of the Faithful, Othmán-Ibn-Afán-Dhí-Núrain, the compiler of the Korán! and upon the Commander of the Faithful, Alí-Ibn-Abú-Tálib—he who changed the fortune of the Infidels and made the Associators tremble, and broke the idols to pieces! Also upon his family, and companions, and all who follow after his good deeds! O be joyful at the good tidings of the satisfaction of God, whose satisfaction is the highest point of eminence, and the loftiest degree of glory! Praise Him for the prosperity he has granted to your hands, in driving away error from this place, and for causing Islám here to repose, after it had endured a sad reverse of fortune by remaining in the hands of the Associators nearly one hundred years; and for this purification of that House, wherein His name shall be pronounced and extolled by the living voice; and for the expulsion of the Associators from its streets (ways), after that the cheating magicians had remained for a long time therein, and for causing his name again to be established therein! Truly, the corner-stones of this House are raised upon the doctrine of the Unity. Upon this is the building placed, and the structure ascends upon Praise, and its buttresses, behind and before, are the Confessions of his Might. This is the place wherein your father Abraham abode. This the spot from which your Prophet ascended to Heaven. This is the direction (Kiblah) towards which ye prayed at the commencement of Islám. This is the reposing-spot of the Prophets. This the tending-point (pole, or place, towards which the wish is borne). This the burial-place of the Apostles. Here descended the Revelation (of God). Here came down the Command and the Prohibition. Upon this land will take place the Resurrection. In this spot the Assemblage of the judgment-day. This is among those holy lands which God makes mention of in the Mysterious Book. This is the Mosque wherein the Prophets prayed to the Lord of the Universe, with Prophets, and Apostles, and the Angels nearest to God's throne. This is the region to which God sent his servant, and his Apostle, and his Word, which he cast upon Maria; from which came that Spirit, Jesus, whom God honoured by his Apostleship, and by his glory, and by his gift of prophecy; but never removed him from the station of a servant of himself."

Then said the Preacher moreover, "Of a truth, Christ never disdained to be the servant of God: neither would those angels nearest to His throne disdain so to be called. They are liars who assert a co-equal with God; and they err most widely. God never assumed a son: he never had posterity, nor desire (of offspring). All his children are those whom he hath created; whom he exalts one above another. Praise be to God! in that his mysteries are clearly revealed to the world; and may He be exalted far above that to which they would associate him as a partner. They are Infidels who have said that Christ the Son of Mary is God, on account of the miracles which God strengthened him to perform. Moreover, this is the first Kiblah, and the second Mosque, and the third place of veneration. The full complement in the number of Mosques shall never extend beyond this: never shall a finger's breadth be bound up in addition to the places of God's repose beyond this (*i. e. no other Temple shall ever be founded beyond Al Aksá*); for unless we had been of the number of those whom God elected as his servants, and chosen to be the inhabitants of His sacred territory, then God would not have appropriated to you, above others, those surpassing gifts with which the course of time can offer nothing that coincides, and with the glory of which no rival events can vie. Happy are ye for those blessings which are so pre-eminently yours—the miracles of the Prophet, the stout warriors of the field of Bedr, the mighty acts of the Sincere One (Abú-Bekr), the conquests of Omar, the armaments of Othmán, and the skilful valour of Alí. Ye have renewed the time of the introduction of Islámism—those holy times!—the closed ranks of Yarmúk, the infantry-struggles of Khaibir, and the brave lieutenantship of Khálíd. Truly, God hath given to you a good lot. To you hath God given a gift in exchange for all that you have poured out in his service; a superabundant lot. He hath graciously accepted all the blood poured out by you as an offering to him, and in return hath given to you Paradise, that house of joy, that resting-place of bliss! O, then, become capable of possessing it! May God in his mercy grant you a claim to the possession of this gracious gift! for you have established the necessity of receiving this grant; for his munificence towards you is exceeding great, in setting apart for you this favour, and bringing you up for this service (in Heaven). The victory he will give you is, that the Heavens shall throw open her lofty gates, and opening clouds shall pour their splendour upon enraptured faces, and the chief angels shall exult over you, and the most intelligent prophets and apostles shall bring you near (to God). Behold, therefore, the favour he will effect for you—for the army which hath conquered on his behalf—the Consecrated House in the other world! Behold the good things which your swords have confirmed to you by means of the number of wounds (received) beneath the prophetic standards of the Faith! God shall hasten to unfold to your power these his similitudes (shall give you the reality of his types and proverbs). This, moreover, is the Temple which God Almighty hath mentioned in his Book, and hath raised to eminence among the most illustrious places of preaching, and hath rendered it one of the most established places (in the world) for dignity and antiquity."

Then he said, "Praise be to him! May his praises be exalted, who brought his servant by night to the Mosque Al Aksá, from the Baitu-l-Haram! May the precinct thereof be blessed by us! This is the Temple which the true religions have raised to magnificence, and whereunto apostles were sent, and wherein were given the four Books which came down from God the mighty and glorious. This is the Temple for whose sake God, the great and glorious, heldback the Sun, at the word of Joshua the son of Nun, the son of Job, and caused the time of its setting to recede, in order that victory might prosper, and good fortune be brought near. This again is that House which God the glorious and mighty enjoined Moses to command the children of Israël to choose for him to dwell therein; and this they refused to ratify—all but two men. God, therefore, was angry with them on this account, and cast them into the desert as a punishment for disobedience. Praise, then, God! who hath brought home to you those necessary precepts, from which the children of Israël have swerved, and hath prospered you in those undertakings wherein the people who have preceded you have failed. And for this purpose he hath collected your Divine commands, which had been dispersed, and hath given you prosperity in those matters which, as I said before, were obtained by your fiery swords. And thus it hath become your exalted privilege to be mentioned by God as those who are his; and he hath made you to be his army, when, before, ye had been the army of a low estate.

"I exhort you also to praise those angels who have brought down to that House, which they have now given you, the sweet gift of the Unity, the Sanctified Knowledge, the words of Praise. Remove not, then, from this path into the path of the Associators, the Trinitarians, the Binders of Deity with Humanity, the impure perpetrators of iniquity. May God of his compassion continue this gift to you, and confirm from age to age this favour among you! By that potency of God, of which if a man take a firm hold, he is at peace; and by the handle of which, if a man grasp, he shall be preserved, and be defended against sin. Beware of the downward path! Beware of falling upon that rock! Beware of returning to (the practice of) retreating and turning your backs upon the enemy! Be zealous in seeking every opportunity of fulfilling the necessary precepts; nor decline the performance of that which is the very jewel (of Divine commands)! Fight, therefore, for God, the due and just holy war. Sell your lives, O servants of God! Obtain God's satisfaction, in order that he may make you of the number of his most excellent servants. For, alas for you! if the Devil should cast a stumbling-block in your way; and if the Serpent should enter you, and so fill you with fantasies, that you may trip, and say that this victory was won by your own sharp swords and your own swift steeds. Your vigour, on the contrary, consists in boldly using your sword in the place of martyrdom and honour. God is the Great One; nor can any victory be obtained but from God the Mighty Orderer.

"Dread then, O servants of God! since God hath granted to you this glorious and noble victory, this pre-eminent gift, and since he hath set apart for you this distinguished capture;—dread lest you be suspected of the greatest of things forbidden, and become the greatest of rebels, and be like those nations who, having once been powerful, have greatly diminished in power, on account of their breach of God's covenant, and become as those who, having received our signs, have put them off, like a cast-off garment, and have followed Satan, and have become of the number of demons. The sacred warfare, the sacred warfare, is the most excellent of your services—the most glorious of your round of duties. Assist God, and he will assist you. Think upon God, and he will think upon you. Praise God, and he shall encrease you and give you good gifts. Be zealous in cutting off the diseased part, in overthrowing the desire of your enemies. Purify the rest of the earth from these impure (wretches), with whom God and his Prophet are enraged. Cut off the heads of the Infidels; destroy from the earth their root; then, at length, the world will be illuminated with the light of

Islám and the Muhammádan religion! God is great! May God give us conquest! May God give us victory! May God grant us success in battle! May God render us conquerors! May God frustrate the Infidels!

"Be wise! If God in his mercy grant you this opportunity, then eagerly seize it. If he offer this booty to you, gird up yourselves to fight for it. If he present these good gifts of fortune, then gather them up. If he bring forward these beautiful and easily-acquired things, go out to receive them. These are your objects of pursuit. March forward to meet them. Go on towards them nobly. These are your magnificent offers. Rush forward to seize them, as if you were rushing upon a wounded foe, to despatch him. In these occupations is to be found happiness; in these treasuries ample competence; and a great booty is now openly displayed before you, to be won from these enemies, now separated from their friends. They are equal in number to you, or even exceed you. But how much? For even if ten should stand forward against one of you, God Almighty hath said, 'If there be among you ten abstinent persons, they shall conquer two hundred. If there be one thousand among you, they shall be victors over two thousand.' By that spoken word of God, which is with the abstinent, God shall aid us; but it rests upon you to perform his commands, and refrain from that which he hath prohibited you. The allied Moslem shall be strengthened by victory from him, if God will aid you; but none of you will be victorious if he frustrate you. Who, then, is he that can conquer you after that his most glorious word hath been spoken with certain determination? His darts shall penetrate: the word from his bow shall cleave the mark. That word, whereby knowledge is revealed, shall pierce through. That word is One, Single, Mighty, Omniscient!

Then he said, "My refuge is in God!" Also, "Bismillah." Then he read the first Surát of the chapter on the Assemblage of the Day of Judgment. Then he prayed for the Khalíf, the Commander of Believers, Násir-Addín-Allah, and for the Sultán, and said, "O God, grant a long life to the Sultán thy servant! He who reverently humbles himself before thy terrors, and thankfully accepst thy benefit, and acknowledges thy gifts—thy cutting, glittering sword; thy bright arrow; the Defender of the might of thy Faith; the remover of reproach from thy sacred abode; the intangible Lion; the King; the most glorious; the Conqueror. He who reunited the words of faith, and struck back the Cross; Peace of the World, as well as of the Faith; Sultán of Islám and of

Moslem; Purifier of the Holy City from the Associators, who saved it from the Infidels—Victorious Father, Joseph son of Job. May the Commander of the Faithful cause his dynasty long to live! May God grant to him the turban of an extended rule! May thy angels encircle him, and bless and strengthen the orthodox might of the Faith, and give to the Great One of the Muhammadan faith good gifts, both in body and in mind! O God! let Islám be diffused, and the alliances of men be broken, and the true prayer be announced from East to West. O God! since thou hast given us entrance into this consecrated Temple, after opinion-expresses had suspected (the practicability of so doing), give us also entrance into the remaining portions of the land, whether far or near, and make us masters of the fortresses of the Infidels, and of their chieftains; nor let them ever be enabled to join their broken ranks, nor re-assemble their scattered troops; nor let them receive any accession of numbers; but let them fail in obtaining the stake for which they are running. O God! I will praise thee for our Lord Muhammád (upon whom remain the blessing and peace of God!). May he have the pre-eminence; and may his command and his prohibition penetrate from East to West. O God! shower thy benefits upon the midst of this land and its paths, and grant hope to the king and to his army. O God! this is the incense-receptacle of the Infidels; this the place which the noses of the iniquitous eagerly desired. May the sweet odour of this victory be spread far and wide into the palaces of the king in the chief cities. O God! I would invoke a blessing upon him, as well as upon his posterity; and I would also make mention of his son, the Puissant, the Fortunate. O may his arm receive strength from the rest of his sons! Amen!"

Then he wound up the whole by saying, "Truly God doth command whatsoever is equitable and good!" Then he came down and prayed in the pulpit, opening his prayer with the "Bismillah" in the name of God, the merciful, the compassionate! Then he commanded the Book to be brought. Then he commanded these verses to be read; viz. "Thus hath come to a close this divine gift of mercy. Thus hath been perfected this grant of grace." And when he had finished his prayer, the people began to talk out, and felt less embarrassed in speaking or looking about; and then they formed into a compact body, and elbows were pushed about, and (many) were drawn away from their standing-places; and joy reigned supreme. Then the Sultán, standing in front of the Chapel of the Sakhrá, uttered a prayer; and all the others, in ranks, prayed in the space beneath the dome. And the people prayed that Victory might for ever abide with the Sultán Málik-Al-Násir. (Whilst praying) they remained humbly upon their knees, with their hands raised over him, and their supplications audibly expressed. After this (our author proceeds to say) I saw the Sultán preaching in the Mosque Al Aksá. However, I waived his discourse, and reposed myself upon the steps (of the Mosque).

Omad (on whom may God show mercy!) proceeds to say, To return to the Sakhrá—the Franks had built a church upon it, and had never ceased to lift up their hands in blessing it, and raising their eyes to salute and extol it. Therefore, they had adorned it with images and candlesticks, and had dedicated therein a place for monks, and a repository for the Gospel: also they framed an excuse for all this exultation and veneration, and erected, separately from the other buildings, just by the place of Muhammád's foot, a little chapel, raised upon marble pillars, and said, This was the place whereon Christ set his foot. This place, therefore, was regarded as consecrated and fit for prayer; and therein were images delicately carved in marble. Omad said also, I saw, among all this imagery, carvings of swine; and the Sakhrá was hidden from the passenger, being covered over by the buildings upon it. Therefore the Sultán commanded this veil to be raised; this intervening curtain to be drawn up; this coat of marble to be stripped off; this building to be taken to pieces; this disguise to be torn away. Thus he brought it out openly in sight for pilgrims, and purified it from Christians. He removed the clothing which covered it, he brought home this bride with pomp: he caused this pearl to come forth from the shell; this full-moon arise from the obscuring mist: he destroyed the place wherein she was incarcerated; he hastened the redemption of this detained pledge; he displayed her beautiful face, and clearly revealed her unsullied splendour; he restored her to her jewel-arrayed condition, to her exceeding preciousness, to her highly-raised permanency. Thus the Sakhrá was restored, as it was in old time. But the Christians had thought to adorn its beauty by a slight tattooing. Before the capture (of the Sakhrá by the Christians), no cutting nor severed portion had been externally visible; but the Infidel people have left somewhat of this sort behind it. Now, at this time it is most beautiful externally; all passengers sweep it; candles are glittering above it; there is light upon light. There hath been made upon it a splendid covering of new net-work, and it is an object of care to this moment and at this time, praise be to God! who shall augment (this attention) every day.

Also, the Sultán founded in the Chapel of the Sakhrá, in front, a most beautiful place of residence for religious men, and enriched them with fame, and gave them a famous name among religious sects, surnaming them the Seven Readers, although there were ten, and agreed with them to collect and promulgate traditions and histories. This convent he enriched and endowed, and presented it with his patronage, and settled upon them houses, and lands, and gardens, and gave them, in free endowment, a most beautiful house, and provided herein, and in the Tower of the Mosque Al Aksá, libraries of books, and tents, and large squares, in order that pilgrims might alight upon the couches raised up before them, and placed upon the pavement. And he decreed that this Chapel should be set apart as private, but the Mosque be open to the public, in order that the old women should manage their affairs properly veiled, and the old men perform their devotional service in regular order. Many therefore presented themselves. The listeners to preaching were again arranged (as flowers in a parterre). Humble devotees again honoured the place; the soft whisper of humility was again heard; tears flowed in a full stream from the eyes of the self-devisers; the ranks of the learned (theologians) were again established there: nor, throughout this consecrated assembly, could one be seen who was not adoring his Lord, nor one who did not hope for piety. Every one, with dusty and dishevelled hair, used his best endeavours to obtain from God the gift of piety to him: every one was quite alive, and stood firm, and penetrated deeply into truth, and greatly valued it. All were reading the Korán, and singing chants, and driving off the devils, and obtaining a clear insight into their knavish contrivances, and frustrating them: all became as well acquainted with them as were the most knowing of the conjuring priests; and all put them to flight, by making their necks touch the ground, through the quotation of texts and traditions. Truly, the blessedness of this place was as when angels came forward to visit it. Truly, hearts full of joy now supplied their place. The Sakhrá was accompanied with a tent, which was fastened by a clasp (or button). On the morning of every day, those who were occupied about it, and who cleansed the nearest part of the externally visible surface, led the way to it. Moreover, the Franks had cut off a piece from the Sakhrá, and had carried it to Constantinople. A piece of it was transported to the country of the Slevi

(Russians), who, it is said, bought it for its weight in gold : thus did they make a gain of it. When, therefore, the place of the fracture was seen, hearts were cut when the place of cutting appeared. Nevertheless, it is now guarded and concealed from their eyes, and shall be so for the rest of time, as a sacred treasury for Islám. Moslems shall watch and guard it with due reverence.

The Sultán, moreover, took order to issue an injunction respecting the repair of the Tower of the Mosque Al Aksá, and the encasing it with marble ; and commanded that the work should be dispatched. Therefore the princes, sons of Job—those of them upon whom the marks of excellent virtues were deeply imprinted, and who united to virtue the love of diligent endeavour—earnestly laboured and panted in the work. Truly the tongues of men praised them for the illustrious and beautiful piety they displayed, for the action they performed—an action which takes the place of honour beyond all other deeds, and for that gift which they gave (the gift of personal exertion) the most noble of offerings.

The Sultán also enjoined the most pious of the learned men, and the most virtuous of the holy men, of those who sat (in his audience-hall) to build a college for religious of the sect of Sháfí. These, therefore, consulted upon this subject. Also, he ordered a residence to be constructed for the upright sect of the Sufís, because he possessed for this purpose some beautiful buildings. Therefore, for the college he set apart the church called Sindahnah; and for the residence of the Sufís he set apart the house of the Patriarch, near the church called the Church of the Resurrection; and endowed them with great possessions, and granted them, as a free gift, to these two sects: for the highest of his dignitaries had won him over to this. Also, he enlarged the colleges of these sects, in order that he might assemble them together (to dwell) in those habitations thus granted to the most skilful, the most excellent, the most faithful, the most upright of learned men. In addition to this, the Sultán gave orders that bolts should be fastened upon the gates of the Church of the Resurrection, and that all pilgrimage thereto should be forbidden the Christians until the Imám of that church assented thereto, and that the people had agreed to give him a compensation for that privilege.

There were some who advised that the building should be utterly destroyed, and its very traces obliterated; that the road of pilgrimage to it should be concealed; that its images should exist no more; that its vanities should be banished far away; that its expounders should be sent off, and its chatterers have the lie given to them: for they said, If thou wilt destroy the building, bring down the lofty spire to the dust, unroof the sepulchre, utterly sweep away and quench the lights, extinguish and wipe off all the marks of their observances, reduce to oblivion, and plough up, and sow the earth, and destroy the length and the breadth;—then all means of continuing the pilgrimage will be cut off; then will these seekers of flesh, these longers for Hell, be wearied of setting off to visit this place. As long, however, as it stands entire, so long will the pilgrimage continue. However, the greater number of men said, There will be no advantage in destroying it, nor in demolishing it; nor will there be any reason to induce the Infidels to cease the pilgrimage, even if we stop up the ways to it: for that which they adore is, the *site* of the Cross and of the Tomb, not the *buildings visible* to outward sight; nor will Christendom ever be cut off from this journey, even if you disperse the soil into the sky. Also, when Omar-Ibn-Al-Khattáb, the Commander of the Faithful, obtained an entrance into this consecrated house, at the commencement of Islám, he gave them the right of remaining unmolested in this place, and gave no commandment respecting the destruction of the building. This reasoning prevailed upon the rest; and they who were inclined to demolish the church, gave up. Then the (proposal) of the Sultán was ratified, and the publishers of glad tidings wrote word respecting this distinguished victory; and the aiders of the faith of God, and the Khalíf of the faith of God, the Commander of Believers, came in public to the gates.

Omad (upon whom may God's compassion dwell!) says besides, (and the report of a certain learned man corroborates his statement,) I saw, in several military arrays, that the Sultán Saláh-Uddín-Yúsuf-Ibn-Aiyoub, (may God be merciful unto him!) inasmuch as the possessions of the Infidel people upon the coasts were very many, and their archery and force in charging were capable of causing great loss and suffering, made no strenuous effort to obtain an entrance into Jerusalem;—on account also of the great multitude of warriors who were therein, and the great number of men and slingers, and because it was the principal seat of the Christian faith, and of the good things which the Franks had seized, where their force was concentrated. Now, at that time, there was in the Baitu-l-Mukaddas an old man, sprung from the people of Damascus. He wrote a stanza in the sacred language, and sent it to the Sultán Saláh-Uddín; viz. "O Prince! who, with regard to the place wherein crosses are engraved, art slothful and supine, surely the obscurity (of forgetfulness or shame) hath come over thee. All Mosques derive their purity from the Baitu-l-Mukaddas; but here, upon its glorious spots, rests pollution." Then (zeal) seized upon Islám, and this stanza was the urging inducement to Saladin to undertake the capture of the Baitu-l-Mukaddas. It is said also, that Saláh-Uddín found among the old men the author of this noble stanza, and appointed him Chief Preacher; in which office he still continues. Now the Sultán Saláh-Uddín died in the month Saffar, the year 589. May his reward for this distinguished victory be delineated in the Beautiful Volume! and I hope that God will give him an abode in the most splendid of the highest tabernacles of Paradise.

This Temple, from the time of the great victory, hath remained in the hands of the Musalmáns, to be sought by pilgrims, and to be magnified in all successive ages; and still to remain in the power of Islám, with glory, perpetuated (if it please God Almighty) until the day of judgment (account) shall arrive. May, then, the lover of symmetry enjoy much good in this clear collection of accounts respecting this victory! May God Almighty grant much profit therein! May he, in his just clemency, afford to him true blessings, with the most perfect of favours! May he support by his aid this cessation (this resting-place, as after a journey) from the composition of this Book! May those who are addicted to pluck the pleasant fruits of literature from those who arrange reasons, remember that which is said in the first chapter! May he confirm by the signet (of his approbation) this chapter; for this is one of those favourable expressions, by which a design undertaken may probably be brought to a close—by which we may repose from useful performances. These are the words by which a period may be most fitly put to a work, and useful deeds be consummated.

To proceed—When God Almighty had transferred the consecrated Temple (to the Moslems) from the hands of the Christians, and had purified it from their dirt and their filth; when the victory was consummated, and affairs reduced to order, and matters brought to the state just described;—the Sultán Saláh-Uddín (upon whom may the mercy of God remain!) began to consider the means of perfecting that which God Almighty had established; namely, to exalt the rallying word of the Faith; to exhilarate the quivering hearts of the Unitarians; and to join together the wounds of the subterraneous places (*i. e.* to heal the wounds of Islámism).—[*The author alludes to the pieces cut from the Sakhrá.*]—Therefore, for the rest of the year

583, he occupied himself in arranging large collections of money, making that a regular payment which had before been an extraordinary grant. He wrote therefore to the people of the open country and to the dwellers in the chief cities, begging them to collect armies for the sacred war, and to send troops for the purpose of accomplishing those designs which his breast entertained respecting cutting off all places of strength or of value from the people of error, and deviators from the right road, and adversaries of the truth. To this they agreed, and came to join him from all quarters. And in the year 580 the Sultán Saláh-Uddín set off from the Holy Land, and left the city, and all those coasts near to it of which he had obtained possession when he marched from Syria, to its inhabitants, to cultivate in security. He proceeded on to the citadel of the Kurds, and laid siege to it. And his army laid waste the lands of the Franks far and wide, and cut down their trees, and all the constructions of these wanderers from truth, that were to be found. Then he went to Tarsus, which he took by storm. Then he went to its mountain-citadel and the fortresses around it, which he took by storm. Then he went to Laodicea, which he besieged some days (a short time); then he took it, and obtained a great booty from it. Then he went to

Antioch; but the lord of that city, who is the Prince of Antioch, begged for a truce: therefore he made a truce with him. Then he marched to Sahyún, which was a citadel upon the very top (of a hill). He besieged it, and took it by capitulation after three days. Then his army, and his sons, and his guards, dispersed (in different divisions), and took the different fortresses of this part of the country; such as Palátinus, and Kalat-ul-Jáhír, and Bikkás, and Shaar, and Tasmania, and the pass of Shák and Bifrás. Then he went on to Shúbak, and took it by capitulation. Then he marched to Sapphirus (Safad), and began to storm it. Here his brother, Prince Adil-Abú-Bekr, arrived with his army. The siege of Safad lasted until the ninth of Shawwál, when it was taken by capitulation. Then he marched to the fort of Kúkía, and stormed it and besieged it, and took it, in the middle of the month Dhúl Khaadát, in the year 584,—a year remarkable for the blessings it conferred on the Moslems.

And in the year 585 the Franks began to bestir themselves, and to burn with rage, and to be full of boiling fury, and made a sally from the city of Tyre, making towards Akká; and all the priests and monks, and all their most eminent men, assembled, and they put on black garments, publicly to denote their indignation and sorrow about the

Holy City. And the Patriarch (he whose splendid house near the Church of the Resurrection the Sultán had taken, and made it into a convent of Súfís, wherein the mighty Korán might be read, and the vocal summons to prayer clearly pronounced, and wherein wise men might compose histories,) took all the sacred vessels, and set off with them to the country of the Franks. So they began to make processions all around, and to call for aid, and to beseech help from all the princes and great men of the Christian Religion. And they made an image (or picture) of Christ, and a picture of the Prophet; and represented the latter as beating Christ, and driving him off,—and the blood flowing over his face. Now this made a mighty impression upon the Franks, and indignation seized upon them—the filthy indignation of folly. So they assembled until the number of men, and the wealth that was collected, surpassed computation. One who was with them relates that they arrived at the appointed station, in small transports, at Greater Greece. Then (says he) we marched forth out of these, and loaded our camels from the holds (of the vessels). Again, Ibn-Al-Attír reports, The Franks marched by rough ways and easy ways, by land and sea, going over every deep lake and ravine, in the belief that they would become masters of Jerusalem, and wrest it from the hands of the Moslems, and restore it to the condition wherein it was whilst in their hands, (God, however, forbid but that its light should still remain, even though the Infidels detest it!) Then the Franks, therefore, besieged Akká in the middle of the month Rajib in the year aforesaid, and invested it until no passage remained to the Moslems to approach it by. And the Sultán Saláh-Uddín came, and an army of Unitarians with him; and many great battles fell out between them. In one of them, Takí-Uddín, son of Saláh-Uddín's brother, made, by a feint, a charge upon the right of the Franks, which drove them back, and intercepted them from their entrenchments. Then the Sultán Saláh-Uddín became master of their magazines and their ground and the higher suburb of Akká; and the Sultán entered the country, and gave entrance to any number of men who were willing. And, upon the twentieth of Shabán, the Franks assembled a council of war; and the opinion they expressed was this:—If we attack the Musalmáns to-morrow, whilst in a state of confusion and carelessness, probably we shall gain the victory over them before they shall receive any extension of force, (which will not be the case) if the army of the Moslems be augmented by those who have been left at a distance; some before Antioch, from a dread of the treachery of its prince; some in Emessa, befóre Terapolis; some before Tyre and the army of Egypt in Alexandria and Damietta. So the Franks rose in the morning, looking with an evil eye for slaughter; and the Sultán rose in the morning, having changed the strict order of battle-array; and the Franks sallied forth, resembling a wide stream of locusts, and filled the land with their length and breadth. Then they began to attack single men. Then the Moslems hastened, and some of them stood their ground, and firmly closed their ranks. Then some of the Moslems returned, and the Sultán made with them a charge in right earnest, and made a tremendous slaughter of the Franks, and took the whole of them prisoners: and the number of those slain on that day was ten thousand. So the Sultán commanded them, and they cast them into the river, of which the Franks drank. Also it is reported by Omad, (may God compassionate him!) that those of the Moslems who stood their ground drove back one hundred thousand Infidels; and that one would say, I killed thirty; and another, I killed forty. And the whole land was infected with the odour of the putrefying bodies of the slain; and the temperature of the air was changed; and the Sultán fell sick; and they advised him to quit that part of the country, and to leave contending with the Franks in confined quarters, and to set off for the open country. So the Franks continued to besiege Akká; and those Moslems who were therein made sallies upon them every day, and fought with them until the middle of Shawwál. Also, there arrived Adil-Abú-Bekr with the Egyptians and a great number of others, who accompanied him to the siege. And when they entered upon the month Safar in the year 586, the Prince went into winter-quarters. Then several great lords came to the Sultán; and men also came from all quarters, out of those warriors who were near Akká. Therefore battles continued between the Moslems and the Franks for eight days, being incessantly renewed by each party.

And there set out the King of Almán (Germany), who marched forward among the greatest of the Franks, as regards the number of his troops, and was the most eminent for insolence and haughtiness, and had expressed the most confident opinion that he would recapture the Consecrated Temple, and was most ostentatious in his indignation and sorrow. Therefore he collected an army, and went forth in the direction of the country of the Moslems, desiring that victory might ensue for the people of his religion, and that he, with those whom he had under him, might seize Jerusalem from the Moslems. Their number was about 160,000; but, one day, their king went down to bathe himself in a river near Antioch, and was drowned in a place where the water did not reach the middle of a man; and his son took the command after him. Nevertheless, the force of the divine and providential destiny of the Lord caused them to perish on the road; so that there remained of them only about one thousand men who arrived at Antioch, and set off to return to their country; but their barks were sunk, and not one of them was saved. Glory and power be ascribed to God! Praise be to him! Let him be exalted who brings forward his command and procrastinates not his decree; for he determines in equity.

Now there still continued much fighting with the Franks who were in Akká. Also the Associators received a re-inforcement, which arrived by sea from the islands afar, in such numbers, that they filled the land and the sea. There came also re-inforcements to the Sultán. Also, the great Patriarch forbade them, under pain of God's curse, to enjoy any pleasure, and shut the gates of the churches. And they clothed themselves in mourning garments, and were straightly prohibited from approaching their wives. Nor were they to cease these observances until they should obtain an entrance into the Holy City. They set off, therefore, on their intended expedition; and whilst they were marching one day in a state of negligence, then the Sultán returned upon them, and completely enclosed them (in a circle, like a serpent's coil). Then they marched forth another time; and in this expedition made use of great towers of wood, with loop-holes all round: every tower was seven stories high. They constructed also a terrific ram; they constructed it of wood, and employed upon its head several hundred weights of iron in forming the horns, (which they sharpened) for the purpose of butting against walls, and overthrowing them. Thus they brought them out against the Moslems; and the towers shot at them stones, and caldrons of naphtha (Greek fire), and set every thing on fire. As to the ram, however, it stuck in the mud through its extreme weight, and was inefficient; and it was very easy to avoid its attack. Between these two parties, then, several affairs occurred throughout a long period, which are related in the 'Book of Histories.' The siege of Akká lasted two years, and more than 100,000 Franks were killed in it. And in the year 588 peace took place between the Sultán Saláh-Uddín and the Franks, notwithstanding great unwillingness with respect thereto.

And, in the latter part of the aforesaid year, the Sultán fell sick, and his malady became severe, and he was removed to Damascus, where he died in the month Safar, the year 589. And God hath transported his pious spirit to its place of repose among good angels, with those prophets and sincere ones, and martyrs and pious men, to whom God's blessing hath been granted. These hath he mercifully given as his companions. He was buried (may God be merciful unto him!) on the northern side of the Mosque of Umaiyah, in the western porch—that which is made of marble. His tomb is still visible on the road of the pilgrimage. When good people heard of his decease, there was great grief and wailing and tumult in the neighbouring regions, and a great agitation; and by God he was worthy of it. He left behind him seventeen sons; one, surnamed Azíz, became lord of Egypt, and Fadhl, lord of Damascus, and Táhir, lord of Aleppo; besides others:—also one daughter.

With respect to his son Azíz, he came before Damascus, and his uncle, Prince Adil-Abú-Bekr with him; and his brother Fadhl defended Damascus in battle; but the army closely (begirt) Damascus, and he and his uncle Adil obtained an entrance into that city. Then Al Azíz returned to Egypt, and Adil remained in Damascus, and assumed the government thereof, and expelled thence the children of his brother Saláh-Uddín, and gave Afdhal the city of Sarkhad. Then Adil demolished Jaffa, after taking it by the sword in the month Shawwál, the year 593. But the Franks attacked Bayroot, and became masters of it without much difficulty. In the year 594, news arrived of the decease of Tufankín, who was brother of Saláh-Uddín. He was lord of Yeman. His son Ismaël ruled after him, who was unjust and reckless, and who designed an evil expedition, aspiring to the Khiláfat. He surnamed himself 'Leader of the Way;' yet he never accomplished the matter. In the year 595, Al Azíz died. His brother Afdhal had been hastily sent for before his death, and had arrived in Egypt, and made the son of his brother Al Azíz king; which son was a boy: therefore Al Afdhal became Atábeg (Regent). Then Al Afdhal took the army of Egypt, and came before Damascus, and besieged it, and carried on the siege with spirit, burning all the suburban villages, and doing every frightful deed. Then he entered the country, and arrived at Báh-Al-Baríd, where the comrades of Prince Adil attacked him and those with him, and routed them disgracefully, and returned to the place whence they came; but Al Afdhal re-organized his troops, and the siege proceeded. At the entrance of the year 596, Al Afdhal and his brother Záhir, with their army outside Damascus, dug a wet trench, full of muddy water, from the place where they were, by the side of that which their uncle Adil had filled up. Thus there ensued a great scarcity at Damascus, and Adil expended his stores upon his soldiers. In this way the Musalmáns exchanged war with Franks for war with each other. Then they made use of the expedient of buying off; and Al Kámil assisted his father Adil with four hundred thousand dínárs, with which he prevailed, and Al Afdhal returned to Egypt. Upon this, Adil made haste, and followed him, and came up to him at Al Ghirabí, and entered Egypt, which Al Záhir then ruled. Upon this Al Afdhal returned to Sáckhad. Adil therefore appointed his son Kámil Sultán of Egypt; and they made a solemn agreement and consent to this. In the year 597, Al Afdhal and Al Záhir again returned to the siege of Damascus, wherein there then was Al-Muzim-Issá-Ibn-Al-Adil; but the siege went on slowly and tediously: therefore, at last, this celebrated siege was given up; for unexpected differences fell out between the two aforesaid brethren; and they marched from Damascus. After this Záhir died, in the year 613, in the winter, and Adil in the year 615, in another winter, outside Damascus. They brought him in a litter to Damascus, and buried him in the citadel. He was however, after four years, transported from the citadel to a tomb in the little mosque of the house of Adil, and there interred.

Adil left behind him twelve sons; the most remarkable of whom were Kámil Muhammad, lord of Egypt, and Muzim-Issá, lord of Damascus, and Al-Shirref-Músa, and Al-Násir-Daood, and others besides them. And when Al Muzim ruled in Damascus, he was earnestly pressed to fulfil his design of dismantling the castle of Mount Sinai, and the castle of Tabnín, and of Bányás; and subsequently (in the beginning of the year 616), from an apprehension that the Franks might make an attempt upon them, and for the purpose of preventing them from undertaking such expeditions under pretence of (the Holy City) being blocked up (guarded) against them. This design, then, he resolutely undertook; and the Holy City, when Muzim destroyed the walls, was one of the most strongly fortified cities. He also exhausted the city of the greater part of its inhabitants, and returned to Damascus.

Now, with regard to Kámil Muhammad:—Whilst he ruled Egypt, the Franks took Damietta, in the month Shabán, the year 616, whose inhabitants had been wasted and exhausted with famine and pestilence, and yielded upon terms to the Franks, who, being enraged with them, slaughtered and took captive and gave the whole country to the Church. Now when this took place, Al Kámil was engaged in war with the Turks or

Tartars; and he routed the Christians in the defeat of Búkas, and drove them, and those who were embodied with them, to Damietta. Terrible battles ensued between them and Kámil, wherein God granted the superiority to the Musalmáns; nor did Al Kámil cease a vigorous prosecution of war with the Franks who had taken Damietta. He at that time built a city, and named it Al Mansurah, upon the creek (or bay) of the sea Hálwa, and colonized it with his troops; for there were present with him many troops and armed men from all quarters. Truly the matter was an important one, and the experiment very great. Afterwards, in the year 618, Al Kámil expelled the Franks from Damietta in the following manner:—The Franks, one day, marched forth in complete array, with a zealous desire to possess themselves of more remote territory. It being then the season of the inundation of the Nile, Al Kámil opened the sluices upon them; so that the water completely begirt them on four sides, every where, so that they were unable to communicate with Damietta.

We learn from Ibn-Al-Athir,—Although the Prince Kámil prolonged for one day the execution of his merciful intention of taking them prisoners in this their extremity; yet, after he had sent to them his son, Prince Saláh-Najur-Uddín-Aiyoub, he granted them quarter. Then their kings came with Najur to his army, when he treated them kindly. Now there were there, in company with him, his two brethren, the Sultáns, whose names were Al-Muzim-Issá and Al-Ashraf-Músá, with their troops and attendants. And the Sultán Al Kámil displayed that day a great assemblage at his levee. There were present the princes of the Franks; and his brothers Issá and Moses, in splendid dresses, stood in the lines. That was a public day: the people and the privileged were present. There fell out also, among other strange things, a strange coincidence; which was, that Kámil's name was Muhammad; Al Muzim's, Issá (Jesus); and Al Ashraf's, Músá (Moses). Then stood up Rajib, the most accomplished and polished poet, and recited before Al Kámil this beautiful stanza:—" Truly, let tongues spread throughout the world, with a loud voice, this state of things. Let it be noised abroad, in both horizons, O servants of Issá! that Issá and his companions, and Músá together, are allies of Muhammad!"

I will omit the enumeration of all that happened between the year 719 and 725 to Al Kámil and his brethren, and their sons, and their uncle's successors, as also of their transactions with the Franks, and the Tartars and others—the expeditions, the numerous pitched battles, and the wars, the storms, and the sieges, and the migrations; because the minute explication would be long. However, Al Muzim died, and the investiture of his sovereignty in Syria passed from Kámil to the son of his brother Al-Násir-Dáood-Ibn-Muzim, in Safar, the year above mentioned. In another year, Al Kámil presented himself before Damascus, and Asad Aduddín, lord of Emessa, came to him. Then Al-Násir-Dáood shut the gates of Damascus, and summoned to his aid his uncle Al-Ashraf-Músá, who arrived from Khilat. Upon this, Al Kámil began to slacken and hold his hand, and prosecuted the matter no further; saying, I will never fight with my brother, with Ashraf; which expression arriving at Al Ashraf's ears, he said to Al-Násir-Dáood, My brother hath now withdrawn himself, and the matter will now be brought to a conclusion with him in an amicable way. Then he marched towards him, and joined with him, and became an ally *against* Al Násir—not *for* him. The two brothers then engaged in conjunction to expel Násir from Damascus; and Al Kámil called in the assistance of the Franks; upon which, Al Abrúz, king of the Franks (Frederic Barbarossa), came forward with a great army; and Al Kámil gave him the Holy City, whose walls had been destroyed. This affair caused great grief to the Moslems; for the inhabitants of the Holy City were left in the same town with the Franks; and the sound of the bells was plainly heard, whilst the *vivâ-voce* summons to prayer was mute. The people were deeply grieved at this, and the Faith was struck dumb with surprise; and the orphan religion was seen from every quarter to frown upon Al Kámil. Al-Násir-Dáood then marched to meet his uncle; and an agreement took place between him and Kámil as to that point; but both contended who should haste to besiege the city (Damascus); and the two brothers arrived, and begirt the city, and besieged it a month, and cut off all intercommunication and subsistence from it, and plundered all the means of supply, and devastated all its means of superiority. Much destruction was effected; and all the dispersed inhabitants were slain, and their villages burnt; so that, for a month, there was exceeding calamity and a great cry. In the end, however, peace was established, on the first of Shabán, upon the terms that Al Násir should turn aside to Karak, and there dwell, and that its sovereignty should remain in his hands. Al Málik then entered the citadel of Damascus. After this, he sent his army to invest Hamah, and gave to his brother Al Ashraf, in lieu of it, Haran and Ruhan (Edessa), and Rás Áyu, and Rika. Then Al Kámil marched to this city, to assume the government; and the lord of Hamah came forth and submitted himself. After this, Al Ashraf besieged Baalbak, in which was Al Majd, among others. Al Majd came to Damascus and dwelt in his house there. In the year 627, Al Ashraf gave to his brother Sálah Ismaël the lordship of Baalbak; who received its submission, and entered therein.

Now, with respect to Málik-Al-Kámil, he besieged Amida, and erected battering-engines against it, and captured it in the year 630, and took it from its lord, Prince Masúd-Maudád-Al-Anabkíl. Al Kámil appointed his own son, Sálah-Najur-Uddín-Aiyoub, viceroy of Amida. In the year 635, Prince Al-Ashraf-Músá, lord of Damascus, died, and his brother Al Kámil ruled the country after him. Al Kámil also died in the citadel, six months after the death of his brother, Al Ashraf. After Al Kámil, the Prince Al-Jauwad-Ibn-Dáood-Ibn-Al-Adíl became Sultán in Damascus. He expended his treasure, as well as the cities of Bedee, and Asraf, and Shára Al Násir, and received their value in exchange.

Now, with respect to Egypt, its sovereigns were these:—First, Adíl-Ibn-Al-Kámil. Now, Al

Jauwad took in Damascus a Sinjáb (سنجاب), a sort of squirrel.* Upon this the Sultán, Prince Saláh-Najur-Uddín-Aiyoub-Ibn-Al-Kámil, cast a longing eye; for Al Jauwad had written to him a description of it; which description caused his own ruin; for the Sultán, Prince Sálah-Najur-Uddín-Aiyoub-Ibn-Al-Kámil, prepared to advance upon Egypt, and sent a messenger to summon his uncle, Prince Sálah Ismaël, from Baalbac. Then he went to Báblis, and described the thing to his uncle. Thus he stirred the inclination of both towards it. Upon this, Sálah-Omad-Uddín-Ismaël made a sudden attack upon Damascus, and seized it, and so cut off the matter from Sálah-Uddín-Najur-Aiyoub. Then the comrades of the lord of Karak, Násir Dáood, marched against him from Karak, and seized him, and went with him to Karak. And Násir Dáood, lord of Karak, threw him into prison, demanding for the release of his brother Najur-Uddín-Aiyoub (a ransom), saying that he would barter him for 100,000 dínárs. His uncle, Sálah Ismaël, lord of Damascus, sent to Al Násir again, to demand Najur-Uddín-Aiyoub from him, and offered in exchange a ransom to a great amount. But Al Násir refused to send him to Sálah Ismaël, nor would he accept any part of

* See note.

the proposed ransom. After this he became reconciled to Najur Uddin, and proceeded with him to Egypt, to conquer it and become partners in its government. Then all the chiefs (Omras) of Egypt absconded from Al-Adíl-Ibn-Al-Kámil, and wrote to his brother Najur-Uddín, and incited him to hasten his arrival. He therefore arrived, and seized his brother Al Adíl, and assumed the government of all the Egyptian country without difficulty, or loss, or fatigue. This happened in the month Dhi-l-Kaada. With regard to Al Násir Dáood, he showed him no favour, nor gave him any countenance, so that he returned without success to Karak.

Now, when Al-Násir-Dáood had arrived at Karak, he anxiously desired to effect the liberation of the Holy City from the hands of the Franks, and to purify it from their filthiness and their pollutions; and he began openly to express what had remained hidden in his mind (his sentiments) respecting the avarice of Al Kámil, who, for the sake of obtaining aid and support in his affairs from the Franks, had given to them the Consecrated Temple. So much for the affairs of Al-Násir-Dáood, lord of Karak.

Now for the affairs of the Franks. When Al Kámil had given them the Temple, and had so bountifully granted it to them, they returned thereunto, and entered it and remained therein; the Moslems remaining also; for in every quarter where *those* were, *these* were also, even (associating) in their prayers, in their worship, and in their commemorations; for the same place was used for their Infidelity, their Trinitarianism, and Temple of public concourse (for worship). From these causes the Moslems were much confined and straitened, and greatly depressed in mind. Now it happened that the king of the Franks, when Al Kámil had given him the Consecrated Temple, and he was proceeding to enter it, was met in the road by a certain individual, who was said to be from Náplias, a Kádí there, and in Syria. He came near the king of the Franks, and politely offered to assist him in whatever was required during his advance; nor did he cease to accompany him (as a comrade) until he entered the Holy City with him; and this Kádí then began to conduct the king, and those who were with him, all round the city, and made him visit the most remarkable places, the great spots of the Divine Law, the venerable places of the Covenant. This preacher then became highly esteemed by the king, so that he was willing that he should remain in the Holy City and take up his abode there; and he exempted him from taxes. This said Kádí then entered the Mosque Al Aksá, and ascended the pulpit, and forbade the Muezzins to call their cry loudly, or to utter the "Praise to God!" at the hour of chanting, that night. When, then, the king rose in the morning, the Kádí was present with him; and he asked about the Muezzins, and remarked that he had not that night heard this service of the loud voice from the minarets, nor the cry of "Praise to God!" And the Kádí said to him, I have forbidden that, in honour of the king. For this, thy complaisance, may God repay thee, O Kádí!

Now, when the Prince Al-Násir-Uddín, lord of Karak, had changed his course of conduct with respect to meddling with these trifling matters on the part of the princes, and had ceased to squander away his time in transacting such things, he earnestly desired to accomplish that his blessed design, which hastened him on to rescue the Consecrated House from the hands of the Franks, —that wicked race (who sit on one side in the saddle), hoping to receive a recompense both in this world and in the next. He assembled, then, a great array, and arranged them for the purpose of making a sudden attack upon the Franks, on the feast of the Temple, at a time when they would be negligent. He arranged all his army, therefore, in divisions, and divided them into sections, and prescribed for every section (a distinguishing watchword), and appointed for every company a certain quarter of the city, in order that they might summon from thence men to join in the sudden attack; thereby to raise up the sound of Alláh Akbar, and to expect victory over the Infidels, the Trinitarians, the enemies of the Faith, on the day of their greatest feast, whilst they were assembled to enact infidelity, and to drink fermented liquor, and to lift up the Cross, after their custom on the seasons of their feasts. Therefore the man came, and those who were with him, on the night of the feast; and he stationed every band in the place which he had assigned unto it. Now the Christians were all occupied with their errors, their games, their infidelity, their Trinitarianism, and their drunkenness. Then the Musalmáns kindled their lights, and raised up their standards, and cried out, Alláh Akbar! and before the dawn of morning suddenly attacked the Christians in the very shrine of their infidelity and their Trinitarianism. Therefore they were astounded and stupified when they heard the cry, Alláh Akbar! from every quarter of the city. The Moslems then laid the sword on them, and continued to slay, to carry captive, and to plunder. The king then came to Al Násir and his army, and began to call out loudly upon Al Násir for an explanation of what had occurred. But he drew his sword, and cut off the head of the king of the Franks. Upon this the Moslems shouted the Alláh Akbar, and chanted the jubilate of praise. This massacre was terrific; nor did the dawn arise before the brilliant valour of the Moslems had prevailed, and they had succeeded in their design of tracking the footsteps of the Franks even to the deepest and narrowest passages whereunto they had in consternation betaken themselves. Thus God graciously prospered this sudden attack (and that eager craving of his people which had caused them to adjure him to grant his aid), and thus graciously apportioned his favour to his people. Thus did the Beneficent One illustrate his saying, "The work incumbent on you shall not be a grief."

Now Al Násir took care to establish all those sacred rites (especially the sacrifices of victims and the praise of Mecca) which his uncle Sálah Uddin (whom may God compassionate!) had established. He also commanded that they should write to all the princes, to announce the joyful tidings of this distinguished victory and great success. They wrote, therefore, and answers of acquiescence were received in return; amidst a number of which there was an Ode, or Didactic Poem, by Ibn Nábát, the Egyptian, wherein Al

Násir was panegyrized. This poem was of the kind called 'The Long.' The following couplets were contained in it:—"Truly a regular recurring train of vicissitudes seems to be the lot of the Mosque Al Aksá. It undergoes one change, and again reiterates a similar course. First, its turn was to be an abiding-place for the Infidels; then God sent unto it Násir (a protector). Thus Násir purified it first, and Násir purified it last." Now Násir, having accomplished this remarkable victory, returned to Al Karak. This greatly-meriting deed of his hath been inscribed in the volume of good actions. Then did the tongues of men utter prayer and praise; and now, at this moment, may we praise the Giver of good success! He who is worthy of praise; He who marketh out events; He who hath assembled Victory, Power, and Conquest, in one abiding-place, which is the Baitu-l-Mukaddas—that point of direction, and goal whereunto we must perform pilgrimage; which we must magnify, until the conclusion of the revolving course of years! Praise be to God, the Almighty, the Omniscient!

CHAPTER X.

Account of all the illustrious Prophets and Chiefs of the noble Company of Confessors and Followers of Truth, (the satisfying favour of God be with them all !) who have entered the Holy City. Account of others who did so: also, who of them departed this life here: and their tombs, &c. &c.

Now the number of these Prophets is said to be 124,000. Muhammad said, God sent consecutively 80,000 prophets; 40,000 of the sons of Israël, and the rest of all men. Muhammad also made to Dhurr, one of his disciples, the following declarations:—Before me there were sent 313 apostles—a great number taken all together. (The greater blessing, said Dhurr.) Of these, the first was Adam; also, of prophets, who were apostles in addition, there have been *four* Greeks (or Ionians), Adam, Sheth, Enoch (who is Idrís, and who was the first who employed characters written with the pen) and Noah, and *four* Arabians, Húd, and Shaíb, and Sáleh, and myself.

The first prophet of the children of Israël was Moses; the last, Jesus: the first apostle, Adam; the last, Muhammad. Of books of divine revelation sent down from God, there have been 140;—fifty tablets to Sheth, thirty tablets to Enoch, ten to Abraham, and unto Moses the Law, containing ten tablets. Also, the following were divine revelations;—the Law, the Gospel, the Psalms, the heaven-descended book of the Korán. Others say that God sent, as his prophets, first Idrís, then Noah, then Abraham, then Lot, then Húd, then Sáleh, then Shaih, then Moses and Aaron; Abraham being surnamed Al Khalíl (the Friend).

Between Adam and Noah intervened ten patriarchs and one thousand years: between Abraham and Moses, seven patriarchs; but the number of years not recorded: between Moses and Jesus 1500 years; and between Jesus and Muhammad 700 years. This last is the sum and end and chief of all. Again, from Adam to the building of Babel, elapsed 1718 years; and the whole duration of the reign of Nebuchadnezzar was 45 years; 19 of which passed before the destruction of the Holy Abode and the building of Babylon, and 21 after the death of Adam. Adam is said to have died at the age of one thousand years, or 1000—70 years, or 900 years. His tomb was in Abú Kabish;

but, at the time of the flood, Noah took him out, and brought his coffin into the ship, and afterwards replaced it. Some say he replaced it in the Holy City, and that his tomb is there. Some say also that it was Shem son of Noah who took the coffin into the vessel, and afterwards buried it in the Valley of Mecca, near the Mosque Al Khaif. Adam, when he was first sent down upon earth, is said to have been so tall, that his head just brushed against the sky. He would prostrate himself, in worship, upon the Rock of the Baitu-l-Mukaddas. When his head was thereupon, the distance to his feet was thirteen miles. He first came down to earth in India. Also, (but this tradition is weakly supported,) on the day of judgment, the mark of his footsteps shall be rendered visible. Also, now that he is buried, his head is in the Rock, and his feet in Abraham's Mosque, between which is a space of thirteen miles. On the day of judgment God shall stand over his feet and say, O Adam! I call back to life thy offspring; but I will not resuscitate thee among those of thy people who are mine.

Again, Noah's ark is said to have hovered about Mecca one week; about Jerusalem another week; and then rested upon Ararát. Abraham, also, when he came forward from Egypt, dwelt between Ramlah and Ælia. He remained in Palestine, and did not die until he had sent Isaac unto Syria, and Jacob unto Canaan, and Ishmaël unto Jarham (Gomorrha), and Lot unto Sodom. These, by the decree and grant of Abraham, were all prophets. A commentator asserts that he saw in Syria, upon the Rock of the Holy City, the engraved jewel of the signet, just as it is described in the Law. Also, to quote from others' assertions, we find that Jacob was surnamed Israël because he was *carried by night* (*Saray*) unto the seventh Heaven. The children of Israël had ten prophets —Noah, Núd, Saleh, Lot, Sheth, Abraham, Ismaël, Isaac, Jacob, and Muhammad, (God's peace and blessing rest upon the whole !). As to Jacob, it is said that he, when he was journeying to the land of his uncle (for his father Isaac had enjoined him never to marry a wife from the Canaanites, but to marry a daughter of his uncle), whose dwelling was in the Sacred Land. Whilst, then, he was making his way thither, the night overtook him in a certain road. So he passed the night there, using a stone for his pillow ; and, whilst sleeping, he saw a ladder, whose top was fixed upon one of the gates of Heaven, and the angels descending and ascending thereby. Then God revealed himself unto him thus : "I am thy God ; the God of thy fathers, of Abraham and Isaac. To thee will I give, as an inheritance, this land—

this sacred land—unto thee, and unto thy sons after thee. I will bless thee and bless them, and make you blessings. Unto you will I give the Book, the distinguishing touchstone of right, the gift of prophecy. I am with thee: I will be thy guardian until I bring thee at last unto this place; and I will make in this place a House, wherein thou and thy seed shall serve me." From this it would seem that there were some doubts who founded the Baitu-l-Mukaddas; Jacob, or Shem, son of Noah. There is some variation and difference of opinion; but God knows.

Now, when Jacob drew near his end, he summoned his sons and his sons' sons, and enjoined them, and commanded them in his will, and enjoined also Joseph (peace be with him!) to preserve his body until they should finally fix it in its place of rest with his father Abraham and Isaac, in the Holy Land. Joseph, therefore, placed it in a waggon, and carried it in haste from the land of Egypt, until they arrived at the Holy Land, and placed it in the spot which Joseph had commanded. A commentator says, By God he and his brother Esau died on one day. Their age was 147 years.

It is also known by certain eminent divines, that God made Moses a saviour, an apostle, and a prophet, for he says, "We have brought him nigh on the side of the mount—the right side. We have caused him to know our secret mysteries. Of our mercy we have summoned his brother Aaron to become a prophet. Then he said, Thee have I chosen to cause men to see my desire and my words. Receive, then, that which shall come unto thee, and be among the Pagans. Muhammad also said that Moses was a man of extreme bashfulness; so that no part of his skin could ever be seen, by reason of his exceeding bashfulness. Whence some of the sons of Israël said, He only conceals himself under this veil, on account of some defect in his skin; either leprosy, or hernia (rupture), or some mal-formation. God, however, was willing to rescue him from the scandal of their assertions. One day, he retired into a solitary spot, and, placing his clothes upon a stone, proceeded to bathe; which having finished, he went towards the stone to take them, when, lo! the stone marched off with them. Moses took his staff, and threw at the stone, and began to cry out, My clothes, you stone! my clothes, you stone! until it arrived, at last, right in the midst of the sons of Israël. So they saw him naked; the most beautiful creature God ever made. Thus God defended him from their slanderous accusations. So the stone stood still, and he took the clothes, and dressed himself, and began to aim at the stone a blow with his staff, when, by God! the stone received the mark of the scars of three or four blows of the staff. To this man is to be referred the verse, "O ye who believe, be not as those to whom Moses was a sign, when God sent him unto Pharoah, who regarded him not; neither be hard-hearted, nor put off the time, nor refuse, like the King, to make a just arrangement with the sons of Israël, but was a foe unto them, and made them slaves, and kept them close, and separated, and cut off, and thus lived amongst them forty years. Then God sent Moses, whose adventures are described in the Korán. His Kiblah is said to have been the Rock of the Holy House. And it is also related, that he asked God to bring him within a stone's-cast of the Holy Land. He was at that time upon the borders. Moses asked this blessing—to be in this corner, near the Holy Land, and to possess a tomb on the frontiers, near the red sand-hill. This tomb is near Jericho, and was seen by the Prophet on the night of his ascent. Upon this spot a Chapel is now standing, built by Prince Al-Záhir-Bíbris, the year 660. Záhir is said to have come hither in pilgrimage, and, having fallen asleep, to have seen in a dream a Chapel upon the spot, wherein was a certain personage, of a dark-olive complexion. He saluted him, and said, Art thou Moses, the Converser (with God)? He replied, Certainly. Then he said, Speak something unto me. Upon which he made a sign unto him with four fingers (whose length Záhir described). Then he awoke; but knew not what he said. He applied unto a certain Shaikh, who said, You shall have four sons; which proved to be the case.

Again, Muhammad said, Never hath the sun been kept back from rising and showing his face, except by Joshua the night he went to the Holy House; for God (as others say) appointed Joshua the son of Nun to succeed Moses, and commanded him to march against Jericho, and fight therewith, and war with the Giants. Therefore he went against them with the children of Israël, and fought for the whole of Friday. Now, the Sabbath drawing nigh, he prayed God, who kept back the sun, and added to the duration of that day's light half as much again. Then he utterly defeated the Giants, and laid their gate flat, and killed them.

Again, it is said that Jerusalem was the seat of David's kingdom long before he received the injunction about building the Temple; without accomplishing which he died. He is said to have had most skilful deputies, and most useful advisers, in the composition of the Psalms which he published. David is said to have had four hundred appointed commissioners, who welcomed him on the day of lamentation. These remained quiet until certain signals were heard. Not an individual was seen; but the voices were beautiful which were heard behind the curtain. He began with a loud voice to chant the Psalm by himself, which was taken up until the full chorus was completed by the addition of the last. David's tomb is said to be in the church of Sion, much accounted of by the Christians. David's prayer is said by Muhammad to have been as follows:—"O Lord! grant unto me the love of thee! Grant that I may love those who love thee! Grant me to perform such deeds as may at length procure thy love! O Lord! make the love of thee to be dearer to me than myself, my family, my wealth, and even than cool water!"

As for Solomon, he is said to have beseeched God, after he had concluded the building, for the gift of three friends, and to have prayed on the Rock, near the Gate Al Sabát. Again, one says, Solomon reigned fifty-three years: he was thirteen years old when he began the building, four years from the commencement of his reign; but God knows.

Now for Sháib, who is mentioned in the gospel of Jesus, and by Muhammad. When he was slain by the children of Israël, God caused them to be conquered, and became an enemy unto them, and put them to flight, and destroyed them. Then came the Assyrian, laying Syria waste for seven years; also the king of Babylon.

Now for Jeremiah. The children of Israël having again become polluted with new abominations, and becoming averse to their faith, some of them disliked the Baitu-l-Mukaddas, and wished to injure and pull down the Temple; so that the Temple began to totter. This violently enraging Nebuchadnezzar, he attacked them; but upon their expression of penitence towards God, he repulsed Nebuchadnezzar from them. After this, they returned to greater pollutions than ever: upon which God sent Jeremiah the prophet (peace be with him!) unto them, to inform them of God's anger. But they beat him, and put him into chains. Then God permitted Nebuchadnezzar to slay them, to burn their city, and carry away captive their children, and to devastate and ruinate the Holy Abode. Then Jeremiah went forth unto Egypt, and there remained; but being commanded by God to return unto Elia, he looked down upon the devastated city, and said, O that God would cause me to live again after my death! God, therefore, caused him to die for one hundred years, and restored him to life when the Holy City was rebuilt. It is said to have remained in ruins seventy years. This last story is also attributed to Azír (Ezra), who was not a prophet, but was one of the captivity, and one of the most learned doctors. He restored, from memory, the Law to the children of Israël, which had been destroyed. In the latter days of Ezra, the kingdom of the Holy Land passed to the Ionians, sons of Javan.

Now for Zachariah. It is said that Imrán married the sister of Zachariah's wife, and by her had Maria. Maria's father dying, Zachariah supported and brought her up. When he was old, God, of his gracious goodness, granted unto his wife a son, named John (with whom be peace!), and no other son besides. Three years after the birth of John (or, as some say, six months) Maria had a son. Then the sons of Israël raised a vehement clamour against Zachariah on Maria's account; therefore he fled from them, and went into a hollow tree, which they cut through the middle with a saw, and so killed him.* When, it is said, the saw began to cut his back, he groaned. Then God revealed unto him, Verily, all blame shall be removed from Maria; and for her sake will I turn away my face from this land. Then he remained silent until he was cut through the middle. John is called the Faithful Reporter of God's word—the Lord—the Chaste—the Pure Prophet: for

Muhammad once said, On the day of judgment all men shall be found to be polluted with some guilt, except John the son of Zachariah. Then, taking up a very small stone, he said, His whole quantity of crime, in comparison to that of other men, is no more than this pebble. Therefore he is named the Lord and Master (of his passions)—the Chaste. John is said to have baptized Jesus in the river Jordan; and Jesus is said to have sent John with the twelve Apostles to give knowledge to men. It is said that a certain king of the sons of Israël asked John's advice about the marriage of a wife; which John declared to be a wicked act. Upon this, the wife laid snares for him until the king killed him, and his blood remained putrifying. This was before the Ascension of Jesus; and after the Ascension of Jesus, a certain king of Babylon, being enraged at John's murder, marched against them, and, when he saw John's blood corrupting, killed a great number upon it, and demolished the Holy Abode. It is said that, in the matter of the wife, John defined and decreed that a son may not marry his father's wife. For this the king struck off his head. After his head was cut off, it said, It is not lawful unto him; it is not lawful unto thee. But many think that the story of Nebuchadnezzar being enraged with the Jews on account of John's murder, and of the devastation of their city in consequence, cannot be true; for the overthrow by Nebuchadnezzar took place about 400 years before the birth of John. A certain holy man observed, The heavens never wept on account of any one except John the son of Zachariah, and Hussain son of Alí (peace be with them both!); and the tears were red. Also, the following revelation came to Muhammad from God:—"For John son of Zachariah I killed seventy thousand; for thy prophet I will kill sixty thousand."

A holy man says, John son of Zachariah, when he was eight years old, came on pilgrimage unto the Holy City to behold the people of the Holy House; and, observing their manner of transacting their affairs, and their persons and appearance, he saw them dressed in vests of hair and cloaks of wool. So he returned unto his parents, and begged them to put on him a vest of hair; which they did. Then he returned unto the Holy City, where he remained shut up all day, but prayed and praised every night, until he was twenty-five years old. Then he began to think of fasting, and remaining engaged in devotion in the desert of Jordan. It happened that once, being very thirsty, he felt great delight in bathing his feet in the water, and found much refreshment. Then he said, O God! I will never taste fresh water until I know whether I am on the road to Paradise or to Hell. Then his father began to weep, and to beseech him to eat some handfuls of barley which he had, and to drink of this water. Then his father brought him back to the Holy City, where he remained weeping and praying, which made Zachariah also weep until he fainted; and all the servants of the mansion wept; nor did John cease weeping until his tears had burnt through and worn out his hanging (sleeves), or other part of his robe. Upon this his mother procured two pieces of cloth, and fixed them upon his hanging (sleeves), so that his tears might therein collect. Then she came and squeezed the cloth until all the tears flowed from it; which when John saw, he said, O God! these are my tears; this is my mother; I am thy servant; and thou art the supremely Merciful.

Now, with regard to Jesus (peace be with him!), a most authoritative tradition asserts, Muhammad prayed upon the spot where Jesus was born; and also that Abdallah-Ibn-Omar-Ibn-Al-'As sent olive-oil to supply the lamps burning over the spot where Jesus was born (peace be with him!). A tradition also says, Jesus son of Maria entered the Baitu-l-Mukaddas whilst the children of Israël were buying and selling therein. Hereupon he cut his garment into strips, and began to beat them, and reprove them, and say, O ye sons of parent serpents and vipers! make you the Mosque of God a market-place? Again, When Jesus was eight days old, he was circumcised according to the Law of Moses, and was named Joshua. Then they fled with him unto Egypt, where they remained twelve years, and then returned unto Syria, when he was thirty years old. Then Revelation came unto him. Again, God put out the life of Jesus for the space of three days; after which he raised him up to Heaven. At the time of his Ascension, the Holy City belonged to Rome; and when the king of Rome received tidings of all the glorious things he had done, then he took down the Crucified, and represented him carved into wooden crucifixes, which he honoured greatly, and slew a great number of the Jews, putting an end to their predominance in Palestine. Thus did the Christian faith commence in Rome. The name of this king was Constantine. It is he who built Constantinople.

Again, it is said that the Jews conspired to kill Jesus. Then God sent unto him Gabriel, with this writing beneath his wings:—"O God! I beseech thee, by the name of the One Great, the One Lord of all, the Mighty, the Essential Unity of Essence, the High and Lofty, the Ruler of all existence, relieve me from the danger at evening, from danger in the morning." Then God revealed this unto Gabriel:—"I will carry up my servant to Heaven, unto myself." Again, Muhammad, by revelation, asserted that Jesus said unto his companions, This shall be your prayer. Never think its accomplishment delayed or tardily executed; for with God is all good, which he fulfilleth as a reward in the end to all who confide in him. Also a holy man observes that Jesus said, Let not a learned man of my people repulse and drive away a youth; for truth shall be revealed unto no others; for they will become fools, and conceal the truth which has been laid down; (for it is said, they know that Jesus has been taken up to Heaven). Also he said, Whoso shall conceal and whisper secretly a secret of harmonious verity, let him not lay by for the morrow; for if he lay by any thing in hope, truly the season of accomplishment shall fail beneath him, and all the redundant profit upon which he counted shall come to nought: and he shall eat his corn without good digestion or effect. Again he said, Not many words shall be said besides this—"Harden not your hearts; let them be soft; for truly the hard heart is last accounted of by God. They who are like lords will not know, nor look into their sins. But look into your sins—you who are in the form of servants. If there be any who have been tried with grief and restored by God, then let them support and confirm the restored, and pity the tried." Also Jesus said unto his companions, "Take ye fixed places to dwell in, and houses to abide in, and eat the herb of the earth, and be saved from this world in peace, and drink the pure and limpid water." Also he said, "Consider your houses as inns, wherein to lodge your possessions, as inns by the way-side; for ye are travellers and wayfarers." Also, "I tell you the truth: the love of the world is the root of all sin. By the single glance of the eye, the seed of wickedness is sown in the heart, whence the tree of sin grows to full height." As to St. George, we have spoken of him already.

Now, for Al Mahadí (the True Guide), who shall live in later times, the Prophet said, "In the latter times great misfortunes and trials shall fall upon my people from their Sultáns, such as never was heard of before, until the wide earth shall be too narrow for them. The earth shall also be full of injustice and oppression. Then will God send down a man to fill the earth with justice and equity, as it was before filled with injustice and wrong. Then shall the dweller in the heavens and the dweller upon earth be well-content: neither shall the earth be deprived of one drop of the copious showers which I will pour down upon it, nor the heaven of those streams I cause to flow. This man shall live with them seven, or eight, or nine years. His life or death shall be fixed and determined by the good which God wills to be effected for the people of the earth." Again, "Mahadí shall be born in Medína, of the family of Muhammad, and of the same name."

Now, for the Expedition to the Baitu-l-Mukaddas, Muhammad-Ibn-Hanífa-Abbás said, Truly the black standards of the Prophet shall march forward; and from Khorasán another black and white array shall advance; in which array there shall be seen a man called Shaíh-Ibn-Sáleh, prince of the sons of Akama. He shall put to flight all the comrades of Sufián, until he attack the Holy City, in order to smooth the way for the assumption of the sovereignty thereof by Mahadí. Mahadí shall come thither from Syria. Also, between the commencement of the march and the final accomplishment of the proposed object, shall elapse 73 months. Others say that Shuaib shall suddenly and secretly march upon the Holy City, in order to prepare an abiding-place for Mahadí, when he shall hear of the march to Syria. The number of the army shall be twelve thousand. Again, By the hands of Mahadí shall the ark of Shechinah (Divine Presence) be brought forward, and exposed to view, from the desert of Tiberias, and shall be carried and placed before him in the Holy City; which when the Jews behold, they shall all become Moslems, except a few. Then Mahadí shall die. Again, justice and truth shall be perverted; men shall be avaricious; the world shall act perversely; not an instant shall pass unmarked by some evil deed or word on the part of created beings; and none shall show and follow the right way, but Jesus son of Maria. It is also a common and well-founded tradition, that never shall the Holy City want; never shall there cease to be found therein a man to do the good deeds of the house of David, and never shall there be wanting a chief of the company of David's comrades to enter the Holy City.

Now, of those who have entered the Holy City, Omar-Ibn-Al-Khattáb has already been mentioned. Abú-Ubaidah set out to pray in the Holy City; but his last hour came upon him when his journey was but half-accomplished. He died, and said, Bury me west of the river Jordan, within the Holy Land. Some say that he said, Bury me where death has seized me. He died of the plague at Emmaus, which is four miles from Ramlah, near the Holy City, in the year of the Hijra 18. His tomb and station are objects of pilgrimage to the inhabitants of the village of Hamash, beneath the Mount of Ajalon. He had already been on pilgrimage several times, and had entered the Holy City as commander of the forces raised by Omar. Abú-Ubaidah died at the age of fifty-eight.

Saad-Ibn-Wakás also entered the Holy City. By him it was said, "I never wept but three times in my life:—on the day when the Prophet was seized with the date fever,—the day Othmán was murdered,—and to-day I weep for the truth—I weep over the truth of Islám." He died in Mecca. Abú Dhurr also entered the Holy Abode at the time of its capture by Omar. He died at Mecca, and was carried to Medína. The people of Cúfa assert that he died there in the Khiláfat of Moáwiyah; that his body is still in the mausoleum of Moáwiyah. Abdallah-Ibn-Amín came to the Holy City, but refused to visit the Rock, or to join in the public prayer. He forbade the people of Hakim to enter the Baitu-l-Mukaddas. Amr and his friends also attacked Moáwiyah, to demand vengeance for the blood of Othmán. The following treaty was, however, concluded between them:—"In the name of the most merciful God! This is a treaty and agreement concluded in the Holy Abode between Al-Moáwiyah-Ibn-Abí-Sofyán and Amrú-Ibn-Al-'As:—that each of these two shall grant a truce and peace with the other; that we shall unite in the observance of God's law, by mutually aiding, by mutually defending and preserving, by mutually following, each other's good advice in the matters relating to God and Islám; that neither shall in any way weaken or injure the other, nor cease to maintain a friendly familiarity with him; that no dissensions shall fall out between either ourselves or our children, whilst we live, as far as we are able to effect this." *Moaz-Ibn-Jabbil* also visited, fasted, and prayed in the Holy City. His tomb at Damascus is an object of pilgrimage, and procures a favourable hearing for prayer. He was thirty-three years old when he died. As to Abú Dhurr;—A certain holy man entered the Baitu-l-Mukaddas. A thought struck him; and when the man came out, the holy man asked him, saying, Tell me whether I ought to perform the Rakás, and prostrations, in even or odd succession? He replied, I know not. The other said, Who, then, doth know? The man replied, "My friend, Abú Kasim, told me." At this name all the worshippers of God wept, and cried, prostrating themselves, May God raise him up a degree of glory, and remit him his sins, and decree a reward unto him! Then said the holy man, Tell me, who art thou? Who replied, I am Abú Dhurr, companion of the Prophet. Upon this (said the holy man) veneration struck my soul. Abú Dhurr died in Medína. (Sulman)-Al-Farsí-

Khálid-Ibn-Al-Walíd surnamed 'The Drawn Sword of God' entered the Baitu-l-Mukaddas to acknowledge the capture of Damascus. He died in Emessa, where his tomb is an object of pilgrimage. When the Prophet shaved, men eagerly strove to obtain his hair. He kindly gave to Khálid the precious gift of the forelocks, which Khálid made into a cap, or bonnet. He was the son of the daughter of Maimúna, one of the Prophet's wives.

A holy man remarks, I knew Omar-Ibn-Al-Khattáb, Talha-Ibn-Abdalláh, Moáwiyah Ibn-Sufián, and Amrú-Ibn-Al-As. The first was most remarkable for piety and divine knowledge; the second, for profuse liberality and generosity; the third, for mildness and courtesy; the fourth, for circumspection in his walk, affection to his friends and relatives, and ardent fondness for deep mysteries and secrets, on account of the loftiness of his conceptions. I was also intimately acquainted with Al-Mughíra-Ibn-Shabat, who had, in his house at Medína, eight gates; from every one of which gates no person ever departed without some liberal gift. All these entered the Holy City.

Abdalláh-Ibn-Salám-Abú-Al-Háreth, the Imám, is said positively to be in Paradise, amongst the highest ranks of the great company. He it was, who witnessed the capture of the Holy City. He departed in the year 43. Also, Yazíd-Ibn-Abú-Sufián. He was sent by Abú-Bekr into Syria. The account of his overthrow and destruction is to be found in history. When he died, Omar appointed his brother, Moáwiyah, in his room. Moáwiyah is said to have engaged and stipulated with three men for the murder of his brother. These were Amrú-Ibn-Al-As and Habíb-Ibn-Solmah. After his elevation and inauguration to the Khiláfat, these marched on and came to Elia. Here they prayed with the incantations and magic rhymes which had given them power. The story is well known:—Omar-Ibn-Al-Khattáb gave the government of the province of Damascus, which had belonged to Yazíd-Ibn-Abú-Sufián, after the death of the latter, unto Moáwiyah. When Omar was assassinated, Othmán gave the command of this province unto Moáwiyah also, and joined the whole of Syria thereunto. He (Moáwiyah) had governed Syria for twenty years, when he was saluted Khalíf; and all men joined him after the murder of Alí. He reigned twenty years, and died on the fifth night of the week, the middle of Rajib, the year 60, aged seventy-eight.

Abú-Huraira came to the Holy House, and died in Medína. He was not buried in the building which is between Ramlah and Gaza; but several of his children departed there. He died in the year 57. Abú-Mansúr dwelt (but it is not unshaken authority) in Bedr. He died in the year 39. He is said to have entered the Temple accompanied by many others, and to have said, "I heard the Prophet say, Unto whatever adorer God imparts inspiration, from him shall that inspiration never be cut off; neither shall he flit about the narrow entrance of the forbidden place, but shall enter by whatsoever gate of Paradise he will." He departed in Egypt, in the Khiláfat of Moáwiyah, the year 35.

Shadád came to the coasts of Palestine with the army. He was a man of learning and judgment. Of him it is said, that when the Prophet's decease was drawing near, he stood up; then he sat down; then stood; then sat down. The Prophet inquiring the reason of this, he replied, "O Apostle of God! it hath fallen into my mind, that Syria shall be conquered, please God! and that thou, and thy sons after thee, shall be rulers therein, please God!" He died in the year 58, aged seventy-five. Some say his tomb is yet visible, and visited by pilgrims, on the west of the Gate of Mercy, adjoining the Mosque Al Aksá.

Tamím-Ibn-Awís, with his brother, assented to

the pretensions of the Prophet, and became Moslems, in the year 9. They were great supporters of Muhammad. He remained in Medína until the assassination of Othmán, and then emigrated into Syria, and became governor of the Holy City. Rúh-Ibn-Rabbáh says, that he one day entered his house, and saw him picking out his hair with his nail, and then standing up, so that the hairs hung upon him, and adhered to him. Upon my exclaiming, What satisfaction can that afford thee? he said, The Prophet said, Whosoever shall pick out and select hairs in God's path, and let them fall upon him, and adhere to him, shall receive for every hair a blessing. Others say, that he and his brother were Jewish scribes, and that Muhammad cut off their feet and put out their eyes, which was the only occasion when he exercised such severity. Tamím had been overthrown by the errors of his doctors, but that the people used proper means with him; so he repented. Tamím was the first who gave lamps to the Mosques. He died in the year 40, and his tomb is said to be near a certain Syrian village named Al Kasút. Al-Dibber-Ibn-Sarír also came to the Holy City in consequence of a vow which he had made, that he would pray there if God would grant Muhammad to recapture Mecca; which came to pass. Also, Fírúz-Al-

Dílamí. He was a Persian; one of those whom Khosroes sent to Yaman. The army of the Persians conquered this province, and obtained by force a domicile in the Holy Abode. His tomb is said to be there. He died in the Khiláfat of Othmán. Also, Abú-Mahmúd-Al-Ján, or Al Najarí. He was of opinion that the singularity of the Essence of the Deity existed of necessity. Abadat-Ibn-Al-Sámat observes, that in this he declared falsely. He died in the Khiláfat of Omar.

Also, Muhammad-Ibn-Rabiah. Of him it is said, that he became a disciple of the Prophet at the age of five years, fully comprehending and penetrating all the arguments and reasons brought forward by the Prophet in his presence. He came, with his family, with the army which attacked the Holy City. He is said to have circumcised Abadat. He died in the year 99, aged ninety-three. Moáwiyah and all his family also prayed in the Mosque of the Companions. They were all muffled up, heads covered, and limbs contracted, and prostrate. No Imám was there.

All these just enumerated were Companions of the Prophet, who entered the Holy City. Now for the Followers of the Prophet, and others who did so,—Awwís-Al-Karaní is said to have been taught by Omar, whom he met when upon pilgrimage, to repeat the prayer whereby forgiveness is attained, at the Mosque Al Aksá, and by the heap of sand. He afterwards went as a soldier to Armenia, and subsequently, with two friends, went to the tent-inhabiting tribes. There he died. He had at that time a wallet and a cup. Then the two men said, We will go and dig a sepulchre for him; for we have beheld in his wallet certain garments which are not of this world. So the two men came and said, We have made a sepulchre deeply hewn in a rock, which our hands fell in with in a minute. So they coffined him, and buried him; and when they looked back, they saw nothing. He died in the year 37. Kaab-Al-Habbár (*i. e.* the Scribe) a Jew, who embraced Islámism in the Khiláfat of Abú-Bekr, or Omar. Al Abbás once said unto him, What induced you to embrace Islámism at the injunction of Omar? So he said, My father wrote several books of the Law for me, and gave them to me, and said, Be diligent in observing this. He also sealed several books, and bound me by my duty to my parents never to break the seal. When, however, I saw the religion of Islám, my heart became purified and enlightened. I said then within myself, Perhaps thy father wished to remove knowledge far from thee, and to conceal it, lest I should read it. Therefore I broke the seal, and found the full description and account of Muhammad and his people. Upon this, I immediately embraced Islámism. Kaab dwelt in Syria and was very learned. He was once telling stories (*i. e.* traditions), it is said, in Syria, when a man said unto him, O Kaab! I heard the Apostle of God say, "No one shall tell traditions but the governor, or he who is commanded so to do, or he to whom the option so to do is granted." Kaab hereupon went to Moáwiyah and obtained his permission. He died at Emessa, in the year 32. Amín-Ibn-Suaid was appointed by Omar to be governor above Othmán. Othmán had himself been governor of Syria, and Ibn-Suaid also obtained this province. Othmán greatly exalted him, and named him Al Moáwiyah (the roaring-lion cub). Also Ibn-Shadíd-Ibn-Awwis. He is said to have been present at the capture of the Holy City, and to have visited it, for the sake of prayer, subsequently. He was a native of Emessa, and converted in the Khiláfat of Abú-Bekr. On his authority we have the following saying:—"Five properties and dispositions are ugly and unbecoming:—Passion in a king, Cupidity among the learned, Moroseness among old men, Avarice in the rich, and Excess of Modesty in deserving people." Abú-Naím was the first Muezzin of the Holy Abode. When Abadat-Ibn-Al-Samut was governor of Elia, he delayed, one day, for some time, before he came forth to morning prayer; Abú-Naím therefore led the devotions of the people. Abadat, coming out afterwards, prayed with the others, after Abú-Naím. Also Abú-Jafar: he says, I once entered the Mosque of the Holy City with Abadat, and saw a man praying there, who had placed his slippers on his right hand and on his left. Then said Abadat, If thou wert not now engaged in secret converse with thy Lord, I would have cleft thy head with this stick. Do thou as the people of the Book do. Also Khálid-Ibn-Moad, who prayed every morning forty thousand morning prayers. These are, he said, many in the Holy City; but if a man go six miles off, truly there they will not amount to five effectual prayers.

Also the Khalíf Abdul-Málik-Ibn-Marwán, who built the Chapel of the Baitu-l-Mukaddas. It has been reported that the Prophet said, Whoso doth not make a hostile siege, or attack, and doth not prepare and arrange a siege or attack, or who doth not follow up those good actions by good conduct, God shall make him a comrade with supreme misery. Ibn-Omar also remarked, Men have sons, but Marwán had a father born to him; viz. Abdul-Málik. Ibn-Marwán-Amrú-Ibn-Abás remarks, Marwán displayed a beautiful and cheerful mien to those whom he met. He spoke pleasingly when he conversed. He listened gracefully when others spoke. He was modest in his personal arrangements when he was opposed. He never sported with any who distrusted his good faith; nor did he ever frighten them; and he never spoke any thing which required apology. Abdul-Málik-Ibn-Marwán died at Damascus, in the year 86. The Khalíf Abdul Azíz is also said to have visited the Holy City when Khálid was there; to whom he said, O Khálid, what have you for us? This, from God, replied Khálid:—"God's ear hears, though thou see him not." Then the Khalíf trembled and shook, and drew back his hand (for he had taken Khálid by the hand). Then said Khálid, Hereafter thou shalt be a just Imám. Khálid kept his house at the latter part of his life, and said, Nothing is now to be found among men but envy, and ill-will, and unlucky faces. He died in the year 90. Abdul Azíz died in the year 101. It is said that there were five just Khalífs:—Abú-Bekr, Omar, Othmán, Alí, and Abdul Azíz (God's mercy be with them!). Also a Kádí, Ibrahím-Ibn-Abel-Ablah, a saint of great acumen. He asserted that he once prayed with the Prophet before the two Kiblahs. He asserted, moreover, that the Prophet said, upon occasion of some cavilling about the necessary existence of Hell,

"If ye give unto a slave his liberty, God shall, for each of his limbs, give to each of your limbs freedom from the bondage of Hell. This saint died in the year 52. (God be merciful unto him!) Also Muhammad-Ibn-Wása, of Basra. He became governor of the Holy City. Of him is told the celebrated story relating to the prayer which he offered up (in deprecation) every day:—"O God! since the Evil One hath obtained the mastery over us, beholding acutely our faults, and hovering over the recesses of our hearts, that he may see them; therefore, O God! make him to despair of us, as he despairs of thy mercy! Make him to be hopeless of us, as he is hopeless of thy benefits! Set him as far from us as he is far from thy Paradise!" It is said that Iblís appeared unto him, and said, O Ibn Wása! what is the prayer which thou prayest every day? Repeat it unto me. So he recited it. Then said Iblís, I charge thee never to make known this supplication which thou hast just offered. Upon which Ibn Wása replied, I tell thee, God enjoins me never to conceal it from the people of God whilst I am in life. He departed (God's mercy be with him!) in the year 117. Also Al-Walíd-Ibn-Abdul-Málik-Ibn-Marwán, who built the Mosque of Damascus, and the Mosque of Egypt, and repaired the Baitu-l-Mukaddas. May God (says an historian) be merciful unto Al Walíd, and to all who are like Al Walíd, who demolished the church of Damascus, and built a large Mosque on its site. God be merciful unto Al Walíd, and to those who are like Al Walíd, who gave a large silver dish, and apportioned it for the reader of the Baitu-l-Mukaddas! He died in Damascus, in the year 76. (God be merciful unto him!) Also Sulaimán-Ibn-Abdul-Málik, the Khalíf, came to the Holy City; whither also came the envoys, to inaugurate him. He sat in the middle of the great area (under the dome) of the Baitu-l-Mukaddas, near the Sakhrá. His carpet of state was spread near the Chapel (and the Rock). Upon this were placed the cushions and the throne. Having taken his seat, proclamation was made unto the public, who came and took their seats upon portions of the throne, and on small pillows. The magistrate, collectors, and the registrars were by his side. He had some idea of taking up his abode in the Holy City, and fixing his household there. He communed with Al Zabari and Házim; from which latter he asked questions and received advice. Some say, that in his way to Mecca he passed through Medína, and inquired if any comrade of the Prophet had survived so long as that period. Házim being sent for, and presented, Sulaimán said, Wherefore do we hate death?

Házim replied, Because you are always demolishing the other world, and building up this world; therefore you detest to pass from restoration to demolition. Then he said, And how can I arrive at a healthful state with regard to God? Házim replied, Truly good deeds shall be like secrets presented before the public; but evil deeds shall be like a runaway slave who comes suddenly in front of his master. Sulaimán, upon this, wept, and said, O that I knew how I am with God! Házim said, Turn aside your attention to the Book of God. Sulaimán replied, In what part shall I find it? Házim said, Here—"Truly the pious are careless about good, and the wicked are careless about Hell." Upon this, Sulaimán said, Where, then, is the mercy of God? He replied, Very near to good doers. Then said Sulaimán, Which of God's servants is most noble? He who is first in manly fortitude and manly abstinence. What prayer is most acceptable? The supplication of a good man who does good. What alms are most meritorious? Those given to a poor suppliant with liberality by one who has but little, when no benefit and no repayment is to be expected. What word is most equitable? The word of justice and right, said by one who hopes or fears. What believer is most wise? He who performs obedience unto God, and leads men thereto. Who is most foolish? He who, when his brother injures him, falls into wrath, and turns love into anger; and he who sells the next world for this. Then said the Khalíf, What wilt thou say of us? Házim replied, O Commander of the Faithful, pardon me! The Khalíf replied, Speak truth and probity, which thou shalt also meet with from us. Then said Házim, thy father conquered the people with the sword, and seized these kingdoms without the advice of the Moslems; nor did he obtain their acquiescence until he had made a great slaughter of them. Upon which, one of the attendants said, O Házim! you are insolent in what you say. Then said Házim, Thou art a liar. Would that God would begin to thrust forth doctors who would openly manifest the Book to men, and not conceal it! Then said Sulaimán unto him, How, then, shall we act rightly? He replied, Let your pasture be straightforwardness, your dwelling manliness, your rule and measure equity. Then said Sulaimán, How shall I most properly manage my wealth, received hence (from my subjects)? Házim said, Let us take it legally, and allot it among the people. Then said Sulaimán, Thinkest thou, Házim, that what is fit for us is fit for thee? He said, My refuge is in God! Also he said, I fear lest I should incline and yield to thee the least thing, and so be made to taste half life and half death. So said Sulaimán, Remove thy dubious expressions. He replied, I mean, mayst thou save me from Hell, and cause me to enter Heaven! Then said Sulaimán, This is nothing to the purpose. He replied, I have no other difficulty to solve. Then said Sulaimán, Pray, then, for me! Then he said, O God! if Sulaimán be thy friend, give him all happiness and prosperity both in this world and the next; but if he be thy foe, seize by the forelock all that he loves, and all that contents him, whether in word or deed. Upon this, Sulaimán said, O Abú Házim! speak weightier words to me, and more of them. Upon this, replied Abú Házim, I abbreviated the matter. If thou art of the household (of God), I have spoken abundantly; but if thou art not of the household of God, wherein should I profit if I shoot an arrow from a stringless bow? Then said Sulaimán, Give me some precept. I will give thee a precept, he replied—a very compendious one;—it is, "To magnify thy Lord, and consider that he sees thee wheresoever thou arrivest, and can frustrate thee wherever thou art engaged." When, then, Sulaimán departed, he sent him one hundred dínárs, and wrote to him—"Spend these, and you shall receive many such from me." But he returned them, and wrote thus unto him, O Commander of the Faithful! God be thy refuge! If thou didst design this in joke, then my rejoinder to thee is sufficiently broad, being thy own munificent gift. These things do not satisfy and content thee; how then can they satisfy and content me? This is the chief event which Sulaimán has to boast of. He began to reign in the year 96, and died in the year 99, aged forty-five.

Also Sulaimán-Ibn-Tarkhán. He dwelt at Basra, and asserted that when he entered the Holy Abode, his breath never entered him, nor did he respire until he came out. He died in the year 143. Also Abú-Ambah-Al-Khawás. He is the author of the following tradition:—"There was a Shaikh eminent for silence, for rigid abstinence, and for poetry, who, in the Holy City, wished to barter with me for a black vest and a black turban. I said to him, God have mercy on thee! dost thou not know that *this* is thy robe? dost thou not perceive that white becomes thee not? Then he wept and said, This is like the garment of sorrow. Whilst we are in the world, let us not wear mourning; for unto that we are reserved. Then he covered the robe over. Also, Thúr-Ibn-Yazíd. He is said to have lived in a village of the Holy Land. Every morning he came with the dawn, and prayed all the prayers in the Temple, returning, after the last evening prayer, to his village." Thúr is the authority for the following tradition from the Prophet :—" If any one sees or meets with any thing to terrify or alarm him, God is the unequalled, the unparalleled, the one, the mighty Conqueror." Whosoever thus says, from him God will not be separated, although a wall of iron should be between them. This man was, one night, going along the road, when some lions met him, stopping up the path. He repeated the above words; when God put them to flight, and he went his way. Then he met an ass, all in a flame, opening his mouth wide, whence issued fire. He wished to eat up his hand; but he repeated the words. Then the ass drew near, saying, No thanks to you, Thúr, for your deed.

The Imám Muhammad-Ibn-Idrís came to Jerusalem. He declared that the Prophet said, " Imitate my successors, Abú-Bekr and Omar." Now it is said that Omar imposed the precept of the Truce. This Imám died in Egypt, the year 204. His tomb is an object of pilgrimage. Over his sepulchre a great chapel is built; and on the summit, where the Crescent is placed, is a small ship, into which the Crescent is formed. It is made of iron. Certain men assemble every night in the beginning of every month, in parties of four, to read the Korán over his resting-place, until the whole is read through. It has been said that certain poets of that age came on pilgrimage to the tomb of the Imám, and were surprised at the size and loftiness of the structure, and at the ship placed above. So they wrote upon the wall the following verses:—"Truly, the chapel of the Maulá is lofty: the lodging well tallies with the greatness of his reputation. Truly, unless the sea were beneath, the ship would not be above." Also, Basar-Ibn-Al-Harith, who said, No good people are ever too merry in the Holy Abode; for there sober thoughts will enter; nor can the soul be lifted up on high. Also, I have nothing more in this world to wish for, than to prostrate myself on my side, beneath the sky, in the place where is held the public congregation in the Baitu-l-Mukaddas. He was born A. H. 226. Also, Abdallah-Al-Omarí. He said that a certain monk of the Holy City observed, when he asked him what was the first requisite for those who enter upon God's service, That hunger is so. Upon which I said, Why? He said, Because the body of creatures is made of earth, and the soul of the angels of Heaven. If the body be satiated, it is weighed down to earth; but if it be not satiated, it is born upwards to the angels. I replied, And wherefore does hunger effect this? He said, Because it necessitates thought and humility.

Also, Rakthum-Al-Záhad. He said, I saw at the gate of the Baitu-l-Mukaddas a monk who was said never to have shed a tear. This terrified me; and I said unto him, O monk! give me some counsel which I may remember. He replied, Be ever like a man who is terrified at wild beasts or sandy places, and is terribly alarmed lest he should be overlooked or forgotten, and he should be bitten, and thus passes a night of dread. Truly, here the fearful are in safe confidence: here the morning of mercy arises: here the barterers of present for future good are rewarded with mercy. Then he turned from me and quitted me; but I said, Add something more to your exhortations, for me; something which God may firmly establish to my profit. He said, O thou that thirsteth! he shall satisfy thee with the water of his joyfulness. Also, the Imám Abú-l-Fadhl, a most illustrious historian of the marvels of the Baitu-l-Mukaddas. He published his work in the year 448. He removed to Bagdad in the year 467, and subsequently returned to the Holy City, and performed the pilgrimage to Mecca. He died at Bagdad, A. H. 507. Also, Abú-Muhammad-Al-Nasarí. Of him it is said, that he related the following tradition from the Prophet:—"Whoso believeth in God and in the day of judgment, either let him speak what is good, or remain speechless;" and "Let the believer love his brother as he loves himself." This theologian died in the Holy City. Abúl-Hasan-Al-Málikí wrote the book called 'The Diligent Exercises,' and dated it from the Mosque Al Aksá, A. H. 596, on the tenth of the middle of Ramadhán.

Thus having related all the different paths and ways whereby to honour the Holy Abode, and all the superexcellent merit of performing pilgrimage thereunto, I will use the words of the author of the 'Minute Text-Sifter,' with which he concludes his last chapter—"Know that this glorious and consecrated country is the place wherein all the constant adorers of God continually assemble."

CHAPTER XI.

Upon the supremacy of our Lord Abraham, and the merit of performing pilgrimage unto him. Account of his Parent, and the story of his Strength in the Fire. Account of Abraham's hospitality and generosity. Account of the meaning of the word *Khalíl*, or Friend, and unto whom it is especially appropriated, &c.

KNOW that the great God, of his goodness and bounty, placed man above all creatures, and said, "This pair is glorious and great; for we have honoured the sons of Adam, and made them our vicegerents by land and by sea. We will give them abundant support from all good things, and exalt them above all that we have created." Then he proceeded to make distinctions and divisions among them, and to exalt some, by certain degrees, above others. First, prophets were promoted above all other men. Then he added to certain prophets the augmented glory of the apostleship; and thus they formed a separate class among prophets. To certain of the apostles he appropriated the superior rank of Declarers of the Divine Precept, and made them people of ordinances—scriptures—appointing unto these the firmly-ratified gift of the most privileged of privileges; lifting them high in the ranks and orders of his favour. Thus, in the first order were the people; next, prophets, whose rank and order of glory is firmly established; thirdly, the apostles; fourthly, those of the apostles unto whom the word of their Lord was granted. These are thus honoured for the high order of their knowledge, the acceptable nature of their pious service, and their fair excellence. The first of the Declarers are five;—Noah, Abraham, Moses, Jesus, Muhammad,—all prophets too. Unto each of these was assigned, as an especial mark of distinctive rank, the right of repeating the especial God-praising word (Subhán). Some of these, as an additional mark of grandeur, received the friendship of God; and some, in addition thereto, the very speech and word of God, as a mark of grand pre-eminence and especial distinction. But the whole of these concentre in Muhammad, the absolute verity of the whole company—the universality of all the utmost-limit-of-perfection-attainers, and the divine-precept-deliverers. He is the unique confluence of all new oracles.

Next in grandeur to him is the Lord, the Father of the prophets, Abraham-Al-Khalíl. He was made a Perfect Lord and a Supreme Father. In him dwelt the sacred words of Praise and Exaltation. In his book was the mode of specifying and distinctly describing God's supremacy and glory by numerous signs mentioned in articulate words by the Prophet. Immediately after our Lord, as to the right of prophecy, and the garment of especial gifts, follows our Prophet. Upon them and upon all our prophets and apostles be invoked the abundant harvest of prayer, the kindly growth of peace! God, then, I say, hath manifested the right of using the words of prayer and praise in the Great Book (unto the Prophet-Apostle). This on account of their Venerable Station and their Election as God's Chosen; for their great power, their glorious gentleness, which exceeds description. Nevertheless, all their wondrous excellence, all the account of their peculiar gifts is surpassed by the glory of Abraham; for the Almighty says, "God hath taken Abraham as his Friend," and so on, in about thirty verses; all showing the propriety of men magnifying their Parent and their Imám, and the blessings promised to those who firmly resolve upon obeying the faith of God, and especially three things therein contained; viz., The Indispensable Command, the Cheerful Offering, the Choice of Love. The *Indispensable Command* is a perfect obligation, of confirmed excellence, glory, greatness, and importance, of great rank and authority. The *Cheerful Obedience* is the performance of that in which there is some doubt or mystery, and is also to show honour and humility in hearing His name, and at hearing accounts of different traditions relating to the Pilgrimage and the Tomb, and a lowering of the voice, and an abstinence from all things prohibited in the Law, as if the Prophet had expressed it in so many letters; also to maintain the fact, that he and all the prophets are still living in their sepulchres; for, truly, none but a fool would deny that the prophets live in their sepulchres—a fool, who ought to dread some consequent punishment as a requital from God. The *Choice of Love*—This he performeth who bears witness to his *(the Prophet Abraham's)* grandeur and glory, and every day sets forth (mentally) on pilgrimage unto him, and represents the figure and similitude of his grandeur and intercession, firmly confiding in the marvellous merit of this noble prophet and merciful father, in those blessings which God hath granted as especial privileges unto himself alone, —the prophecy, the apostleship, the right of originating a sect, the right of conducting into a road, the word, the prayer, the ministering in front of the congregation, the vicegerency of God, the patriarchate, the intimate friendship, the eternal dwelling, the effectual merit, peace, prosperity, mildness, knowledge, the right belief in clearness and perfection, long life, generosity, accomplishment of wishes, election, safety, calm repose within, greatness without, firmness in the faith, contentment in Islám, &c. &c.

Now, we are informed by a certain writer that the Prophet asserted that Abraham was the best of men, and that whosoever, deeply impressed with the greatness of glory of Abraham, should visit his tomb, should pray in the Mosque, and, turning to the tomb, use another prayer and perform other ceremonies (*which the translator omits*), repeating them several times, should obtain forgiveness of sins, and the accomplishment of all his wishes. The following prayers are the most effective:—"O my Lord! O Friend of God! I bear witness that God is the only God, and has no partner, and that thou art the Friend of God;" and "Peace be upon thee! peace from God, from angels, from prophets, from apostles, from sincere believers, from martyrs, and from confessors; from the people of heaven and earth, O father of the prophets! O friend of God! and upon thy son, the

Revealer, the Signet—Muhammad." Then turning round to our Lady Sarah, let him say, "Peace be upon ye, O family of the prophets! O mine of apostleship! the mercy also and the blessing of God! By ye may the people of the House be enabled to put off their impurity, and by your purity be rendered pure." Let the pilgrims do the like unto Isaac and Jacob and their wives, and, after washing his face, repeat the same ceremonies before Abraham's tomb; for all wise and learned men agree that Abraham is the most meritorious agent in prayer, and the very signet of consenting acquiescence from God. Also the Prophet said, upon another occasion, Whoso cannot fulfil all the pilgrimage, let him at least visit Abraham's tomb. A tradition also tells us that if the way of the pilgrimage be stopped, Abraham's tomb should, however, be visited by pilgrims. Whosoever shall perform the pilgrimage and the prayers at the tombs of Abraham, Isaac, and Jacob, and Sarah, and Rebecca, and Leah, shall receive forgiveness of sins, and all ample support and prosperity in this world, and a blessed mansion in the next. He shall not return to his own house before the forgiveness of his sins is confirmed; nor shall he depart from this world before he hath seen Abraham the Friend, and hath heard his positive declaration, that God hath forgiven his sins.

Kaab also says, that no one who visits duly the tomb of Abraham shall depart without beholding the accomplishment of his wishes, sooner or later; for none shall ask a gift in Abraham's name, but God shall grant it. A certain historian, moreover, has the following:—"A certain man of Baalbec said, We were performing pilgrimage at the tomb of Abraham, and with us was a certain man of Baalbec. We heard this man, whilst visiting the Chapel, weeping, and saying, O my friend! O Abraham! ask of thy Lord that such a one, and such a one, may be requited on my account; for they have injured me. At this we laughed, and were surprised at his speech; but on our return, after a space, to Jaffa, a relative arrived from Bairoot, wherein was a man of Baalbec. From this quarter news arrived that the three persons whom the man had named were dead. Blessed, says another learned person, is he who hath visited Abraham's tomb; blessed is he whose sins God doth remit, although they were every one like a mountain; for God hath established a conjunction of will between himself and Abraham."

Now for all that is told of his parent, and the

story of his endurance in the fire, &c. When God willed to send Abraham as a sure sign and evidence unto his people, and as an apostle for his service, Nimrod saw in a dream a star which, rising, outshone the sun and the moon, until no light remained. Being greatly alarmed at this, he assembled the priests and sorcerers, and questioned them about this. They replied, A child will be born this year, in this country, who will destroy thee, and seize thy kingdom into his hand. Upon this Nimrod commanded every male child from within that year, to be put to death, and commanded the men to be separated from their wives, and appointed a trusty person to guard every pregnant woman, who murdered the child when born. Thus, all the women were shut up, except Abraham's mother, whose pregnancy they knew not, and its visible appearance was concealed. Nimrod, it is said, also assembled all the males into one army, and secluded them from their wives, dreading the birth of the aforesaid child; and whilst engaged with this army, if Nimrod found any needful business to be transacted in the city, he trusted no one but Azar. This was before the pregnancy of Abraham's mother. He sent then to Azar, and entrusted him with the work of necessity he wished to be performed, and said, I should not have sent for thee, had I not perfect confidence in thee; but I positively enjoin thee not to go near thy household. Azar replied, I will hold to my promise in that matter. Azar accordingly entered the city, and, having completed his commission, began to bethink him of entering his household, to inquire how they were, and to arrange any affairs; but he here forgot the injunction and prohibition of Nimrod, and his wife in consequence conceived. When he was as yet unborn, the idols were overturned, and the stars of Abraham rose brightly. They were two small stars; one in the East, and one in the West. Nimrod, seeing these, felt his anxiety renewed, and his fear augmented. When, then, the time of his birth drew near, God sent unto Abraham's mother an angel, endowed with the most beautiful form ever assumed by the sons of Adam. He touched her with his hand, and stilled her fear, and gave her joyful intelligence as to the great estate and authority to which the infant was destined.

But when the time of her delivery drew near, he said, Come with me. She rose up then, and followed him. He conducted her until he brought her into a cave, wherein were all things necessary, and which was remote from men. Here she easily (by God's aid) gave birth unto Abraham, on the night of Friday—the tenth night—a night lengthened tenfold; and in the morning Gabriel came and clothed him in white raiment. Then the mother returned to her abode, leaving the child in the cave.

Also Nimrod, having been for a long time absent, returned to his country to settle and arrange affairs which were of importance. Whilst, one day, then sitting upon his throne, a tremendous crash was heard behind him, and a voice cried out, "He shall perish who believeth not in the God of Abraham." Then he said to Azar, Didst thou hear the voice which I heard? He replied, Certainly. Then he said, Who, then, is Abraham? But Azar said, I know not. Then he sent unto the priests and soothsayers; but they could inform him of nothing by their learning. This happened on the day Abraham was born. After that, voices continually pursued Nimrod, and beasts and birds began to speak articulately the same words; so that Nimrod could not pass by any place without hearing the cry, "He shall perish who believeth not in Abraham's God." Nimrod also saw another terrific vision. He saw the moon rising up from Azar's back, whose light appeared like a pillar of fire, extending between heaven and earth. He heard also one saying, "Truth hath come, and folly shall perish; and truth shall triumph over idols, which shall be overturned from their pedestals." This struck him senseless with alarm. He related his vision to Azar, who was in fear for himself, and said, This is to warn me to augment my adoration of thee. Now Nimrod, being sometimes very foolish, was satisfied with Azar's word, and held his peace. He afterwards went with Azar to visit the idols. They were standing upon their pedestals; but, when Azar's eye fell upon them, they all fell down from their pedestals. And when Azar fell down prostrate to worship, God gave them the power of articulate speech, and they said, "O Azar! truth hath come, and vanity shall be annihilated. That against which Nimrod took such precautions hath been accomplished unto him."

After this, Azar entered his house, having surmised that his wife was pregnant; and seeing her very merry, he asked the cause; when she said, He who took care to provide that no son should be born is as he who should provide that no wind should blow. Then he cast his eyes upon her and saw the truth. Thus God caused forgetfulness and incautiousness to possess Nimrod in the matter of Abraham. His mother then continued to visit the cave once every three days, to see how he was, and to provide for his comfort; and once, when she came there, she found cattle and birds at the gate of the cave. She was alarmed and struck down with fear, thinking her son had perished; but, upon entering the cave, she found him quite safe and well upon his fine linen cushions, and properly perfumed and anointed. When she saw this, she knew that he was reserved unto some great station, and that the Lord would exalt him. So she found him gently sucking his fingers, his forefinger, and his thumb; from one of which he was drinking milk, and from the other honey. He grew up as much in one day as another boy does in a month, and as much in a month as another boy in a year. He only stayed in the cave fifteen months.

One day, he said unto his mother, Who is my master? She replied, I am. And who is your master? Your Father. And who is my father's master? Nimrod. And who, then, is Nimrod's master? She replied, Be silent! and he was silent. She then returned, and said, I have seen a boy who declares that he will change the religion of the people of the land, but did not say he was her son. Then she informed his father of the matter, and of the place wherein he was. His father thereon came unto him, and beheld him, and was delighted with him. Upon saying to his father what he had before said unto his mother, Azar bade him be silent when he mentioned Nimrod's God; which he obeyed. One day he said unto his mother, Take me from this cave! which she did, one evening. Coming out, he beheld and considered the creatures of heaven and earth. He said, He that created me, and sustains me, and gives me to eat, and gives me to drink, he is my God: I will have no God but him. Looking up then on the heavens, and beholding a star, he said, This is my Lord. But when it began to wane, he watched it until it departed, and then said, I love not things that set; for his genius, and acumen, and knowledge, convinced him that things which set could not be divine. Looking then at the rising moon, he said, This is my Lord. Then he followed her with his eye until she was intercepted and departed, and then he returned, no longer believing her to be his Lord; but turning to other objects. He then said, Will no one show me the right way to my Lord? he who is a safeguard among people in error; that is, who will lead me the right way to my Lord; for truth and harmonious evidence is in his hand? Then the sun arose, and he said, This is my Lord; this is the greatest. But when the sun set, he returned to seek his Lord with a true and humble heart; and he found him, found his face in verity, in sincerity, in certainty, and began publicly to preach among the Pagans the Distinctive Doctrine, and said, O people! I am wearied with your Paganism; I turn my face unto him who created out of nothing the heavens and the earth, embracing his true Moslem religion; for I will not be of the number of the Pagans. God, after this, translated him from the Sure Evidence of Knowledge unto the Sure Evidence of Sight. After this, his father imposed silence upon him.

He continued, however, to grow up, and to augment in perfect excellence, until God gave him the glorious gift of signs, and glories, and splendour; and thus he clothed him with the honourable robe of his Friendship, and appointed him Chief of Divine-Ordinance-Imparters and Apostles, Father of Prophets, Crown of the Elect, Light of the World, and Glory of his People. Most people assert that he was born in Kútha, in the region of Babylon in Irák. Nor was the faith imparted to any man before Abraham. He first brought forward the whole: for, says Ibn-Abbás, It is evident that God opened Abraham's heart from these words of the Great Book:—viz. "So Abraham was tempted by his Lord, but yet saved him." The words, also, which God sware unto him are among the most noble divine injunctions in Islám, and the most powerful in opening the hearts of the people of the earth to the faith which Abraham possessed.

Thus, then, did God tempt Abraham by his word; yet Abraham was perfect, and his will was perfect. He was consummate and perfect, whether we inquire into his faith, or his soul, or his property, or his son; and he displayed consummate excellence when Nimrod made a slinging-engine for him, and cast him into the fire. Then shone forth the truth and verity of resistance to temptation, and the reality of his Chieftainship; for, being placed by his enemies in the slinging-machine, the angels then prayed that help might be granted unto him, saying, "O our Lord! thou knowest what thine enemies have done unto thy friend." Upon this, God said unto Gabriel, Go unto him; and if he entreat for aid, then aid him, and join with my corner-stone and my friend. Gabriel then went to meet him whilst he was shooting, like a sling, through the expanse of the atmosphere unto the fire. Then said Gabriel unto him, Hast thou need of any thing? And he replied, If from thee, no; if from God, yes; for he is my guardian-protector from danger and ill. None but God can aid me. He shall be the asylum of my sorrow, when he sees fit. Nevertheless, I quietly submit to the decision of God, relying in full acquiescence upon his ordinance to dispose of my life. With this, he called upon God by his Two Names; and God saved him from the flame, and said unto it, O fire! become cold and harmless unto Abraham! (Some intelligent persons remark, that the word 'harmless' was added, lest the *cold* should destroy Abraham.) Upon this, the fire submitted; and it has been said, that from that time there is no fire, either in the East or West, but will submit to a duly and deliberately-uttered divine word.

It is said again, that when he was placed in the slinging-machine, his garments were torn off from him. He fell down then into the glowing mass of embers, all in a blaze. But they separated and parted, and nothing of the heated mass came in contact with him, or marked him at all. Those also who were near, and beheld him, saw that the ground in which he alighted was of bright green, and uninjured. Here he sat, safe and sound in person and appearance—the most beautiful sight ever beheld. After this, he received a vest from Paradise; and Gabriel broke his chain and fetter, and said, Peace dwell with thee! The Lord of Peace saith unto thee, Know that the fire shall not injure my beloved. Then said Abraham, God is my guardian and my provider. Abraham was the first who had his garments torn from him in God's cause; for which reason God granted unto him a Vest on the spot; and he shall be clothed in a robe, the first of all men, on the day of judgment. All this happened as a testimony among men, who, when they saw it, glorified God; and a great number believed, unknown to Nimrod. Abraham then walked from the spot, and Gabriel departed from him. He then advanced from the place of his descent, and Nimrod sent unto him to inquire about his dress and his companion; when he said, This truly is an angel whom God sent unto me. Then he told him the story, and Nimrod said, Surely the God whom thou servest is a great God. I will offer sacrifice unto him on account of the glory and the might displayed by him in regard to thee, because thou hast persisted in serving him. Hereon he sacrificed 4000 oxen. After this, he again differed from Abraham, and broke off from him, saying, One day, I beseech thee to depart from my country whereunto thou wilt. He consented; and, departing with his household, came to Edessa. After this, he removed in succession to Aleppo, Syria, the Holy Land, and Mecca. He was the first who fled from his abode of the God-endowed, in order to preserve his faith; and, for that he did this, God in requital granted unto him that all believers should penetrate unto and centre in him, from all extremities of the earth.

Now for his generous hospitality; also his Friendship and its approximation unto him of especial right. It is said that whenever Abraham made a feast, or wished to eat, he went out a mile or two, to lay hands on some one to eat with him. Therefore he was surnamed the Father of Hospitality; and truly he was sincerely devoted unto hospitality; whence hospitality is in great repute even unto our days. And he never allowed day or night to end without having some guest to eat with him; whence, unto this day, no place can be closed at night against a guest. It is said that a certain powerful nobleman, having a large clan of followers at Damascus, and of great worship, came unto our Lord the Friend, to visit him, at certain appointed seasons. Upon these occasions Abraham always presented a feast, according to his usual custom, unto all visitants. During the feast, Abraham would look on, but eat nothing. This man, then, once coming, found Abraham sorrowful. Being urgently pressed to tell the reason, he said that he eagerly desired to pick up whatever was left in the dish, and whatever remained of the pieces of bread and crumbs, and to eat them. This I beheld him do, said the abovenamed nobleman; and he, moreover, said unto me, I should not have eaten any part of our feast, had not thy visit previously taken place. Since this has occurred, I now eat.

It is, moreover, traditionally asserted, that God

granted unto Abraham abundance of possessions and servants, and that he then constructed a house of hospitality. This house had two gates; by one of which the stranger entered, and by the other departed. Here he made a pavilion, and laid up summer and winter clothing, and had always a table ready prepared with food upon it. Then the guest ate, and was clothed if he were naked. And thus liberally Abraham behaved at all times. Also, when Abraham presented a heifer unto his guests, and saw their hands not raised in prayer, he said unto them, Wherefore do ye not eat? They replied, We will not eat food except we pay the price. So he said, Then have you not the price? Then I will tell you the price. Call upon the name of God when ye eat, and praise him when ye finish. Hereupon they said, Praise be unto God! If it were fit and proper that God should choose a friend out of his own creatures, surely, Abraham, he would take thee. And God *did* choose him as his Friend; and the angels beheld Abraham's augmented good, and the gifts he received of worldly wealth; yet, in his admiration of all this, he was never drawn aside from God during the twinkling of an eye.

It is said that, though externally good, he knew no sure revealed means of adoring God; but praised him within his heart. God, therefore, taught him how to speak articulately the Praising and Exalting Words; for he commanded two of the most glorious of the angels, Michael and Gabriel, to descend unto him. These angels were commanded to ask hospitality of him, and to converse with him about his Lord, and, raising their voices, to sing the words ascribing thanks and holiness unto God. They came therefore, and besought Abraham to listen to their entreaty. He immediately gave them audience in his house (they were in the form of the sons of Adam). Then he agreed to their desire, and gave them a splendid abode, and appointed them a place wherein to lodge. It happened, then, on a certain night, when Abraham was talking with them by the light of the moon, that one of them lifted up his voice and said, Praise to the Holy King! he who is possessed of power and dominion. Then the other lifted up his head and said, in a voice which Abraham had never heard before, Praise be to the Holy King! This threw Abraham into a fainting fit, and he was no longer master of himself, from his eager desire and restless feelings. After a time he rose up again, and said, Repeat unto me the words ye have just pronounced. They said, Why should we do so, unless thou give us something of value. So he said, Take whatever you choose. But they said, Give us what thou wilt. So he said, I will give you all my sheep, which are very numerous. This satisfied them: therefore, raising their voices, they chanted as before. Abraham again therefore fainted away; and when he arose, knowing that they would not chant without some valuable gift, he gave them all his cows. And he thus continued to be deeply delighted and drowned in pleasure at the chanting of these words, and to add to his gifts, until he had given them all his property and all his household; and nothing remained but himself. Then he sold himself to them, and begged them to regard him as their slave, and fixed his manumission at a high price. They accordingly consented to receive him himself. After this, he said unto them, Now give me one more chant as a free gift. Then they said, Truly it is just that God should choose thee for his Friend. Then they intimated to him that they were angels; and Abraham smiled, and said, Truly my guardian and provider is God. Then they said, Take hold of God's blessing upon thee and upon thy race. And God graciously gave good gifts unto the rest of his race, and all their posterity, and augmented their blessing and their joy, and caused his line to extend from that day to this, and to the day of judgment, please God!

Moreover, a certain Kádí observes, that some difference of opinion exists with regard to the explication of the word Khullat (خلة), or Friendship, and the correct derivation thereof. A Friend is said to be one who is absolutely set apart and devoted unto God; from which devotion and separation he never falls away; so that Love is of necessity appropriated and defined to be his. The synonym of the word translated 'Friendship,' is Election. Abraham is called the Friend, because *he* inclined to or broke off from others, as *God* inclined to or broke off from them. This Friendship, thus entertained with God, gave him victory, and constituted him Imám and Superior over all posterity. The word Khalíl (or Friend) has another synonym, or root, signifying *Poverty*, a state of *Want*, or of great *Need*, from the *sourness* and *constraint* attendant upon that condition. Abraham is so called because he referred all his wants to his Lord alone, and cast all his anxiety and thought in fulness upon Him, choosing no guide or friend but him, as when he said unto Gabriel, when they were about to shoot him from the slinging-machine into the fire, and Gabriel asked him if he could aid him; when he replied, Not thee. Again, the whole meaning of the word, as applied unto Abraham, rests upon that choice Love which of special necessity belongs to him alone, and by which he became Participator of Secrets. The synonym of the word is Love, Affection; and the meaning refers unto 'Right of Near Access,' 'Subtle Penetration,' 'Loftiness of Rank,' 'Power of Intercession.' This Right of Friendship is most powerful in prophets, if they be among enemies; for God says, If your wives and children be your foes, such enmity, if accompanied by *The Friendship*, shall be of service unto you. Now, this Friendship has been granted unto Abraham and Muhammad: that is, an especial devotion unto God, beyond all other men; a recurrence in need to God alone; a right of an interchange of secrets, standing face to face; and also a right of urging reasons and arguments; a visit granted of peculiar right by God to these two; a manifestation of subtleties; a sort of intermingling of divine secrets in their inmost souls, and a deep perception of mysteries; a surpassing knowledge, granted by Elective right unto them; a purification and sifting of their hearts, whereby they, being emptied of all things but Him alone, retained no loving principle to any but Him. Therefore the word Khalíl means, He who expands his heart to no intimacy but God's; which explains the Prophet's words, "If I could choose any friend but my Lord, I would choose Abú Bekr the Sincere; but all Islám are brethren."

Learned men, masters of mysteries, differ also upon this question; viz. Whether Khullat (friendship) and Hubbat (love) are both upon an equality, or one expressing a higher rank than the other. First, it is said that Khullat is Hubbat, and Hubbat, Khullat; but that Khullat is the distinctive property of Abraham, and Hubbat of Muhammad. Referring to the words of Muhammad, quoted above,—"If I could choose any Khalíl," &c. we might say that Khullat is the higher. Nevertheless, it will readily be determined by all noble hearts, that Hubbat is the higher; for the degree of Muhammad is higher than the degree of Abraham. Moreover, the synonym and explanation of Hubbat is, a certain preponderating inclination towards some object that engages our love, even although that object is in its nature averse to reciprocal inclination or swerving. Now the former is precisely the case with created beings; for the Creator is too glorious and exalted, and is far removed from all this. His love unto his servant was that which aided him by his blessing and support and guardianship, turning all events unto his good, and, by reason of his sacrifice, his feast and hospitality, fulfilling his compassion upon him; for they tell, how that the veil was removed from his heart, so that he (Abraham) could see him (God) with the eye of his heart, and behold him with his heart's glance, just as the tradition has it,—"When I loved him, I became unto him ears whereby to hear, sight to behold, and tongue to utter." Now, by no possibility could it be compassed, that any one should be so intelligent, but he who was utterly devoted unto God, cut off from all beside him, turning away from all but him, having cleansed his heart for God, and freely yielding to its motions unto Him.

Abraham, it is said, was circumcised when he was one hundred and twenty years old, and lived ninety years after this. Also it is said again, He also circumcised Ismaël at the age of thirteen years, and Isaac at the age of seven days. He also is said to be the first Musalmán, the first who broke idols, or wore slippers, or lifted his hands in prayer at every falling of the voice. Every morning he offered four *Rakás*, which God accepted from him as the full complement of prayer.

Abraham was, also, the first who displayed hospitality, or broke bread into crumbs, or parted the hair, or cleansed with water, or cut his nails, or kneaded and shampooed his bones. He was the first also who shook hands, or laid his hands on the neck in embracing, or kissed between the eyes, on the spot which strikes the ground during adoration. He was the first whose hair ever became grey; upon which he said, What is this? And God said, This is to make thee look grave and reverend. Then he said, O God! make me still more grave and reverend; and he ceased not his entreaty until his beard also became white. Another story has it, that, upon a certain day, Abraham saw a hand coming forth from the sky, and holding a white hair between two of its fingers. It continued to approach until it seized hold of the hair of his head, saying, "Be whitened!" and it was whitened, and became grey. God then spake in revelation unto him, desiring him to be clean; whereon he performed the sacred ablution. Then he said to him again, Be clean; whereon he bathed. Then, again, he said, Be clean; whereon he circumcised himself. Another story has it, That men then arrived at a great age without symptoms of decay; but, that once a father and son were amongst the people, and the father said, Ye cannot distinguish between father and son. Then said Abraham, I will do something whereby a distinction can be made. Then he made his head and beard white. He was perfect in the right way before he arrived at the full knowledge thereof, and he invited the world to truth by the tongue of correct argument from youth to age, according to the Word, "This is our argument and proof; that which Abraham brought unto his people." He was the first whom God named the Orthodox. He first began to entreat and invite the Jews and Christians, which is testified by the Word, "Abraham was neither Jew nor Christian, but an orthodox Musalmán." He was not a Trinitarian. He is the Guardian of all Moslem youth, and Prince of the people of Paradise in its whole extent. He built the Kaaba; he first broke idols, and set up the worship of God, and raised the dead by his prayer. He, on the day of judgment, shall first put on a white robe, and be placed on a pulpit to the left of the General Assembly. He is said to have been the first who preached in a pulpit or held a staff. He is the best of prophets, and his people the most excellent of people, if they follow his injunctions.

Abraham is said to have lived 195, 175, or 200 years. Between him and Noah elapsed 1142 years. Between his birth and the Hijra of the Prophet intervened 2932 years. Abraham is said to have visited Mecca three times, and to have invited men to perform the pilgrimage on the last occasion of his doing so. They obeyed him; and the first who did so was Jurham, Prince of the Amalekites. They became Moslems; and Abraham, returning to Syria, died, aged 200 years. When the angel of death came in to cut off his breath, he saluted Abraham; which salutation Abraham returning, said, Who art thou? He replied, I am the angel of death, and am about to kill thee. Then Abraham wept until his son Isaac heard his weeping, and, coming in, said, O friend of God! wherefore weepest thou? Because, he said, here is the angel of death who wishes to take away my life. Then Isaac wept until his weeping exceeded his father's. The angel of death then departed to God, and said, O God! thy servant Abraham grieves deeply at death. Then said God, O Gabriel! take some sweet herb (odoriferous basil) of Paradise, and set off with it unto him, and revive him therewith, and say, "Truly it is now a long time that friend has been separated from friend. Long hast thou been divided from thy friend!" Gabriel then came and delivered the message of his Lord, and presented the sweet herb. Then said Abraham, It is true, I have long been separated from thy friend. Then, smelling the herb, he took it in his hand, and said, I will gladly go when God willeth. When God willeth, let him take Abraham.

The angel of death was sent unto him in the form of a very old man; and it is said that Abraham once gave a very great entertainment, of which numbers partook. Whilst they were feasting, an old man was seen walking in the outward enclosure. Abraham therefore sent out an ass to fetch him, which carried him to the table; and when the old man took up a mouthful and put it into his mouth, it came out at his eyes and ears. Then he put it into his mouth again, and made it enter his belly; but it came out behind. Now Abraham had entreated of God, that his life never should be taken until he himself asked it. He said therefore unto the old Shaikh, when he saw his condition, Wherefore doest thou this? He replied, Because I am very old. Then said Abraham, How old? So he told him his age, which was twenty years above Abraham's. Then said Abraham, There are twenty years between me and thee. When, therefore, I arrive at thy age, shall I be like thee? He said, Certainly. Then said Abraham, O God, take me to thyself before this. Then the old man rose up and cut off his spirit; for he was the angel of death. God's peace and blessing be upon them both!

There are other versions of this story. Abraham, it is said, was always given to hospitality, compassionate unto the poor and wayfaring men. Once it was very late, and no guests had arrived, so that he began to be scandalized, feeling uncertain whether any would come. At this, he went out to seek some hungry person. And there passed him the angel of death in man's form. After mutual salutations, Abraham said, Who art thou? He replied, A wayfaring man. So Abraham said, Why should one like you remain here? Come along. So he went with him unto his abode; and Isaac saw him, and, knowing him, began to weep; which when Sarah saw, she wept also. Then the angel went up to heaven. When, therefore, Abraham arrived at the upper chamber, he was enraged, and said, Wherefore did you weep in the guest's face, so that he hath departed hence? Then said Isaac, Blame me not, O my father! I saw the angel of death with thee. Then Abraham gave him a certain command and injunction (to be silent). Now Abraham had a certain pavilion, wherein he adored God, and which none entered but himself; and whenever he went forth, he locked the door. When, then, Abraham came to open the door, he saw a man sitting. He said, Who art thou? and wherefore hast thou entered my house? He replied, By permission of the Lord of the Pavilion have I entered. Then said Abraham, The Lord of the Pavilion has the full right thereto. Then Abraham, going to one corner of the pavilion, prayed therein as he was accustomed to do. Then the angel of death ascended again, and when he was asked, What didst thou behold? he said, O Lord! I have just come from the devotions of thy servant. Surely, in the whole earth, there can be no one so good as he. There is not a single one of thy creatures for whom he omitted to pray, supplicating for them peaceful quietness, and the enjoyment of all the happiness of life.

After this, Abraham still lived an additional space; as long as it pleased God. But, upon a time, again opening the door of his oratory, he saw a man sitting, who said that he was the angel of death. Then said Abraham, If thou be really so, show me a sign whereby I may know that thou art the angel of death. Then he said, Turn aside thy face, O Abraham! Which having done, the angel said again, Turn round now thy face, and look; which doing, he beheld him in the form which he assumes when he takes away the lives of believers—a form of such surpassing light and brilliancy as God alone can comprehend. Then he said, Now turn aside thy face, O Abraham! which having done, the angel said, Turn it in front. And then Abraham beheld him in the form in which he cuts off the infidels. Then was Abraham seized with dreadful horror; his limbs trembled under him, and he almost gave up the ghost. Then he said, I know and see who it is that hath commissioned thee. Return then unto him.

Then the angel ascended to heaven again, and received commission to deal gently with Abraham in taking away his life. So he came unto him at vintage-time, in the guise of a very old man. Abraham, beholding him, had compassion on him. Taking, therefore, a basket, he gathered some grapes therein, and, coming up, placed them before him, saying, Eat! So the old man began to seem as though he ate and masticated; but it all flowed over his beard and breast. Abraham was surprised, and said, Is nothing left unto thee? How many years are upon thee? So the old man, in a weak voice, said, So many years. Then said Abraham, I have almost arrived at that age. I never wish to be in this condition. Therefore, O Lord! take me to thyself! Then Abraham gently breathed forth his soul, and the angel of death seized his spirit on that instant.

It is said also, that the angel of death said unto Abraham, O Abraham! I have commandment to seize thy life. He then said, Grant me a delay, until Isaac be born, and be strong. And when at length the angel came to him, he found them both so closely embraced that they could not be separated. Therefore the angel returned unto the Lord, and said, O Lord! I saw thy friend in grief, on account of his approaching death. Then said the Lord, O angel of death! go unto my friend in his sleep; which he did, and took away his life. Thus Abraham died without contempt and without disease. Abraham, David, and Solomon died, it is said, suddenly. This death is pleasant for believers, but dreadful for infidels. It is a mark of clemency and compassion to God-fearing believers, graciously arranged by God. When Abraham, it is said, came unto his Lord, the latter said, O Abraham! how didst thou find death? He said, O Lord! I found my breath gently drawn out, smoothly and softly as butter. So he said, We tamed and softened death for thee, O Abraham!

On the day of judgment, Abraham shall be first clothed, on account of his friendship with God; then Muhammad for his apostleship; then Alí. Between Abraham and myself, said Muhammad, there shall be a flash of lightning, whirling us, like a furious wind, to Paradise. Abraham, on the day of judgment, shall first be clothed in fine Egyptian linen: Muhammad shall come with naked feet, uncovered, alone. Both he and

Abraham shall then, by God's command, be clothed in white raiment. Muhammad shall then be placed on a glorious seat, in front, where all the first and all the last shall look on him with wistful admiration. All men, on the day of judgment, shall rise naked-footed and uncovered. Abraham shall be the first arrayed; then Muhammad; then all men, according to their stations and rank (in piety).—So much for this matter.

CHAPTER XII.

Account of Abraham's temptation regarding the sacrifice of his son. Account of the age of Isaac, and the age of his father and mother when he was born. History of Jacob, and his age. Also some part of the history of Joseph; his beauty; length of his separation from his father Jacob; duration of his residence in a foreign land; his sepulchre; and the space of time which intervened between him and Moses.

Know that God Almighty, in order to exalt the Friend, sent him various temptations, particularly that respecting the stars, which he was tempted to adore. But, having escaped from all these, he arrived, as has been already mentioned, at a most glorious degree of prosperity in this world, and rank in heaven. All this has been already described. After all these things, God gave him, of his favour, a son. This son, having arrived at a set age, and beginning to intermingle with his heart, he was then tempted to sacrifice him. He immediately obeyed the command, and hastened, without hesitation, to perform his duty, not swerving therefrom. He said therefore unto his son, O my son! I have seen a dream which directs me to sacrifice thee. Consider, then, what is thy opinion. Isaac said, O my father! do as thou art commanded. Thou shalt find me patient and submissive, please God! Now Abraham had proposed this question to prove Isaac's docility and submission to God, not as wishing to set his opinion against God's command. But when both were ready, two goats fell down on the earth, and a voice was heard, exclaiming, O Abraham! I declare, of a truth, that for this deed blessings shall flow upon thee. Then he (God) redeemed him with a great offering, and blessed him (Abraham) and his son in both worlds, and added unto Isaac the joyful rank of a prophet, choosing from their race the prophet-apostles. Some difference of opinion, however, exists, as to the question, *which* young man was commanded to be sacrificed—Isaac or Ishmaël. Some say that the words of the Korán, "We give him the joyful tidings of a son," certainly referring to Isaac, and certainly uttered after the sacrifice, prove that Isaac was the youth intended to be offered. The Khalíf Omar-Abdul-Azíz, however, asked a certain Jewish learned man, who had become a Moslem, Whom was our father Abraham commanded to sacrifice? He replied, *Ishmaël;* remarking that the Jews knew this very well, but were envious on that account; it being a notorious assertion of the Arabs, that their father Ismaël built the Temple, together with his father Abraham. Al Moáwiyah also asserted as follows:—I was once with Muhammad when a man came in, saying, O son of the Two Sacrificed! Then the Prophet laughed, and said, Who are the Two Sacrificed? He replied, When Abraham was digging Zemzem, he vowed, that if God would make his work easy unto him, he would sacrifice one of his sons. The lot fell upon Isaac; but his uncle's family protected him, and said, Redeem thy son for one hundred camels. These, then, he offered at dinner-time; and offered, secondly, Ismaël.

Isaac is said to have lived 190 years. Abraham was thrown into the fire at the age of sixteen years. When his wife, Sarah, gave birth to Isaac, he was aged ninety years. When he was commanded to sacrifice him, Isaac was seven years old. Others say that, when Isaac was born, Abraham was 112 years old; and when commanded to sacrifice him, 117 years old. Sarah, daughter of Abraham's uncle, was ninety years old. Isaac also was blind, and married Laiká, daughter of Bítawíl, and had Esau and Jacob when he had passed his sixtieth year. Sarah died, aged 117 years.

Again it is said, that three women have been prophetesses; viz. Sarah, and the mother of Moses, and Maria, daughter of Imram; for Sarah received by revelation the joyful news of the birth of Isaac; Moses's birth was divinely communicated to his mother; and Maria received from an angel the happy tidings of the birth of Jesus. It is notorious also, that all these were faithful and true.*

* See note.

CHAPTER XIII.

Account of the Cave wherein Abraham and his glorious sons were buried. Account of his purchase of this place from a king who was a crafty, powerful giant. Also, who was first interred there. Also, account of the Tombs discovered there, &c. &c.

Now whilst Abraham was dwelling in Midian, Gabriel and Michael came down unto him. They were seeking the family of Lot. Abraham then came forth to sacrifice a calf, when it fled from him, and did not stop until it arrived at the cave of Hebron. Then it cried out aloud, O Abraham! peace be upon the bones of thy father Adam! These words sank in his mind. He killed the calf, and offered it to them. And then took place that which is related in the Korán. Abraham went with the two angels until they came near unto the houses of the family of Lot, when they said, Sit down here! which he did, and then heard the voice of the cock in the sky, crying, "This is the truth, the convincing evidence, which surely knoweth the overthrow of the people." So said Abraham, This is the site of the Mosque of the Convincing Evidence. It is about one parasang from Abraham's land. Then Abraham returned, and asked Hafrún to grant him the cave, and purchased it of him for four hundred dirhems; the weight of each dirhem was five dirhems. So the bargain was struck, and the property transferred, and the cave became a burying-place for himself and those of his family who should die after him. Sarah was the first who died, and was buried within these walls. It is said also that Hafrún, insisting upon the above price and coin, Abraham received the amount from Gabriel.

Abraham was buried over against Sarah. Isaac was buried there over against Rebecca. Jacob was buried at the gate of the Tomb-Cavern; Leah over against Jacob. Then the sons of Jacob and Esau, with his brethren, met together, saying, Let us keep the door of the cave open, and bury therein whosoever dieth amongst us. Some dissension ensuing, one of the brethren of Esau was enraged, and killed one of the sons of Jacob.

Then the others struck Esau, and knocked off his head, in the cave. They carried away his trunk, and buried it without the head, leaving the head in the cave. This they then closely blocked up, and put tombstones, inscribed, "This is the tomb of Abraham," &c. Then they closed up the entrance. All, then, who came thereunto, went round the spot, and missed it; so that no one could find it until the Greeks came. They opened the gate, and, entering, built a church. Afterwards, God giving victory to Islám, the Moslems seized all the sacred buildings, and destroyed the church.

There is a tradition that Wahab-Ibn-Mauhab said, I met with the tomb of Abraham, and found an inscription thereon, as follows:—"Foolishly do we change our dwelling. He dies who meets with his appointed season. No craftiness shall avail him herein. Many learned and brave men have been on pilgrimage; but nought will accompany them to the tomb, except their deeds." He said also, I met with Muhammad-Ibn-Al-Khattáb, preacher of the Mosque of Abraham, who relates, that certain holy men went unto the tomb of Abraham, and remained there three days. On the fourth day they fell in with an inscription, cut into the stone, opposite the tomb of Rebecca. This they ordered to be washed, so that the engraving became visible, and the letters were transferred unto some tablets which they had; an exact fac-simile being made. When they returned to Ramlah, they made every inquiry among those who were skilled in languages; but none could be found who could translate the inscription. They at last were referred to a Shaikh of Aleppo. To him they carefully sent the engraved fac-simile; and he sent the translation from Aleppo:—"In the name of my God and his God, the overshadowing Tabernacle, the Conqueror, the Leader into the right way, the Mighty, the irresistible Compeller; the tombs here found are these:—This first is the tomb of Rebecca, wife of Isaac; that, similar to it, is the tomb of Isaac; that large one opposite is the tomb of Abraham; that opposite to this last, on the eastern side, is the tomb of Sarah; the farthest tomb, answering to Abraham's tomb, is that of Jacob; the tomb near it on the east, is the tomb of Leah. Esau wrote these characters."

A most learned man asserts, upon positive evidence, the following:—That Abú Bekr, the cobbler, surnamed the Pious, asserted as follows:—The tomb of Abraham is in the place which now exists; and I have seen and beheld it with my own eyes; for I had devoted unto the doorkeeper, and the place generally, a great endowment and gift—nearly four thousand dínárs. All the pious men and monks would frequently come unto me also, to converse upon subtle, and pleasant, and glorious matters, and examine the root of things. One day, they being all assembled together, I said unto them, I beseech you to allow me to pass the entrance to the cavern, that I may descend to see the prophets. They replied, We will consent to this; for this is our established right: but this is not the season; for there are many night-travellers. Therefore be patient until winter comes. When, then, winter began, and January commenced, I went unto them. Then they said, Remain with us until the snow falls. So I remained until the snow fell and cut off all night-travellers. Then they came unto a spot lying between the tomb of Abraham and the tomb of Isaac. They raised the pavement, and there went down with us a man named Salúk, who was a man of probity, excellence, and good faith. I went with him. So he walked on, and I after him; and we descended seventy-two steps; and then I beheld, on my right hand, a great sarcophagus of black stone, upon which was an old man with scanty hair, long beard, and in a green dress, and lying on his back. So said Salúk unto me, This is Isaac. Passing on then a little, we came unto a larger sarcophagus than the first.

Thereon was a Shaikh, lying on his back, between whose arms all was grey-haired, his head and beard being white, his two veils (or eye-lashes) and the borders of his eyes (eye-brows) being white also. Beneath his grey hair was his green robe. His person was most beautiful, and the wind gently waved his grey hair on the right and left. Then said Salúk, This is Abraham. And I fell on my face, and prayed to God the prayer which occurred unto me. We passed on, and came to a lightly-skilfully-carved sarcophagus. Thereon was a brown dark old man—very brown indeed; his beard was short, crisp, and curly, and thick. Beneath his shoulders was his green robe, most resplendently green. Then said Salúk, This is Jacob. Then we turned aside, and went on to examine the deep venerable Recess.

Here Abú Bekr, the cobbler, swore that his story was finished: but Salúk being subsequently entreated by the narrator to tell him some excellent idea as a means of preservation from sin and wickedness, and being moreover asked concerning this adventure, and more especially what they saw, and what occurred in the Venerable Recess, at first made some difficulty, saying, Hath not Abú Bekr informed you? But the narrator replying, I wish to hear it again from you, he said, When we turned aside towards the Recess, we heard a loud voice exclaiming, "Turn ye away from the Forbidden Place! God be merciful unto you!" Upon this, we fell into a swoon. After a time we arose and stood up; but we despaired of our lives, and all others despaired of us. Nevertheless, both Abú Bekr and Salúk lived after this adventure many prosperous days. God's mercy be with them!

A certain Kádí of Palestine is said to have pointed out the true site of Abraham's tomb to an old man, a youth, and a boy, successively; observing, that the best way of preventing dissensions in preserving traditions was to communicate them simultaneously unto successive generations; whereby novelties and heresies were avoided. In the book entitled 'The Wonderful Novelties of the Superexcellence of the Rule of Islám,' in the chapter on the village of Abraham, it is said, Herein is a stronghold of great extent, thought to have been built by genii. It is built of great stones, sculptured and carved. In the midst is a chapel of beautiful stone, over the tomb of Abraham. The tomb of Isaac is in front, in a niche, and the tomb of Jacob at the farther end, over against the tomb of all his wife's sons. The Genii constructed this Mosque, and built around it a convent for devotees. Here is contrived a cloister on every side; and there monks have a canal of water flowing unseen. In the middle of this village is a place of public hospitality; and on each side of the village are rooms for travellers, vineyards, grapes, and apples, the yearly produce of which is carried into Egypt. In this village is kept up continual hospitality; herein are cooks, and bakers, and servants, who are appointed to present olive-berries and lentils unto the pious divines present. When they have partaken, it is presented to the rich.

As for the discovery of the tomb of Joseph; that tomb is said to be in the platform behind the wall, over against Jacob's tomb. The Khalíf Al-Muktadir-Billah came to the Holy Land, and was informed by an old woman, who was standing in the Baitu-l-Mukaddas, that this place was really Joseph's burial-place. The Khalíf employed workmen, and, having purchased the spot from the owners, cleared it of all building, and examined it, and found a great stone. He broke off a piece from it, and lifted it up, and saw Joseph, in all his beauty and gracefulness of form. The air of the spot was deeply impregnated with sweet scent. Then came a vehement wind, and the workmen closed up the stone of the pavement as it was before; and the Khalíf built the chapel thereon, which now remains.

A most veritable story is told, of an excellent

man (an Imám) who went to sleep with his head reclining on the lowest step of the pulpit; when, in a dream, a voice came and informed him of the site of Joseph's tomb three times before daylight. This man told the old woman, who told Al Muktadir. Again, it is said that Joseph's tomb was believed to be merely the burial-place of some one of the tribe of Israel; but a man came from Khorasán, and asserted that he had been directed in a dream to go to the Holy Land, and point out the tomb of Joseph. The Sultán commanded his son to go out with the man; which he did. Coming unto the spot, the workmen ceased not to dig until they came to a wooden waggon, which was crumbled into dust. Our old women never ceased to look for this dust, desiring to use it as a remedy for sore eyes.

Now, respecting a Grant made by the Prophet to Tamím Addarí and others. Abú-Hind-Addarí said, We went and presented ourselves unto the Apostle of God, being six in number,—Tamím-Ibn-Awís, his brother Nain, Yazid-Ibn-Kais, Abú Abdalláh (author of the tradition), his brother Al-Taib-Ibn-Abdalláh, and myself. So we saluted the apostle, and requested him to cut off an allotment for us out of the land of Syria. He replied, Ask whatever part you will. Hereupon, we rose up, and went aside to consult what place we should request.

Then said Tamím, I think we should ask the Baitu-l-Mukaddas, and the adjoining territory. But Abú Hind said, The Baitu-l-Mukaddas is now exempt from foreign rule; is it not? Then said Tamím, Yes. Then said Abú Hind, I fear we shall never effect the foundation of an Arab kingdom there. Then said Tamím, Let us ask Gabriel's house. To this replied Abú Hind, That is a greater and more populous country than the other. What then, said Tamím, thinkest thou we should ask? Abú Hind replied, Let us ask the village and territory, wherein we may construct wells on the spots marked out before by Abraham. So said Tamím, Thou hast hit upon the right nail, and hast well settled the point. They returned then to the Prophet, who said, O Tamím, will you inform me what you have just agreed upon; or shall I inform you? So he said, Thou shalt inform us, and shalt precisely hit upon our opinion. Then he said, You thought one thing, O Tamím! and this man (Abú Hind) thought differently; and the opinion of Abú Hind is assented unto. Then the Prophet asked for a piece of parchment, and wrote a grant thereon; of which the following is a copy:—"In the name of the most merciful and compassionate God, this writing commemorates a gift made by Muhammad unto the Dárians, when God shall grant unto him the land. He giveth unto them the House of Fountains, and the moist muddy place, and the House of Abraham, and all that is therein, to belong unto the Dárians for ever.—Witnesses, Abbás-Ibn-Abdul-Mutallib, and Hamár-Ibn-Kaís, and Shazil-Ibn-Hasan, and the writer." Then he went into the house with the writing, and, in transferring the writing to cloth, ratified it, adding besides something which is unknown, and fastened it outside the cloth with two fastening straps, and brought out the instrument folded up.

It is said that men appointed Abraham to be chief of all, and his posterity to succeed him; and this is the prophet who governs and directs all who believe in God (as the chieftain of believers). Then said he, Depart until ye shall hear that I have fled. Therefore, says Abú Hind, we departed until we heard that the Prophet had fled unto Medína; then we presented ourselves, and requested him to give us another and a more extensive grant. Hereupon he wrote the grant of which the following is a copy:—"In the name of the most merciful God! This is the grant made by me, Muhammad, apostle of God, unto Tamím-Al-Dárí, and his company. I grant unto you Bait-Ainúm and Hibrún, and Al Martoom, also the House of Abraham, with all the suit and service-owers therein, and every thing else therein, an absolute gift perpetually alienated and freely given unto them and their heirs after them for ever and ever; and may God trouble whosoever shall trouble them herein!—Witnesses, Abú-Bekr-Ibn, Omar-Ibn-Al-Khattáb, Othmán-Ibn-Afán, Alí-Ibn-Abú-Tálib, Moáwiyah-Ibn-Abú-Sufián, and the writer." And after the decease of the Prophet, and the accession of Abú Bekr, when the army was warring in Syria, Abú Bekr gave us also a grant (copy):—"In the name of the most merciful God! from Abú Bekr to Abú-Ubaidah-Al-Jiráh. Peace be upon thee! I praise God (he who is the only God) for thee. After the usual solicitations, I hereby prohibit every one who believes in God and in the last day from plundering the village of the Dárians; and if its inhabitants have evacuated the territory, and the Dárians wish to sow therein, let them sow; and when the produce comes, it is theirs and their due right. Peace be with thee!"

CHAPTER XIV.

Account of Ismaël; his removal to Mecca, and the visit made to him by Abraham, upon Al Burák. Also his mother Hagar; her death and burial. The time that Ismaël lived; his tomb; and the interval between him and Muhammad.

Ismaël, son of Abraham, was the eldest of his children, father of the Arabians and of the Apostle, the lord of both worlds, our Prophet Muhammad. His mother Hagar was handmaid to Abraham. On her account Sarah was full of haughtiness and pride. She sent her to Abraham, saying, Take her. Perhaps God may grant thee a son from her. For Sarah had greatly desired a son, but despaired of one; and Abraham had beseeched God to grant him this blessing: yet the prayer was delayed till Abraham became old, and Sarah barren. Hagar then had a son; and Sarah grieved deeply that her time was past.

Others say, that Sarah and Hagar were both pregnant together. The two boys grew up, and once, on a certain day, they were throwing stones at each other; and Abraham caused Ismaël to sit upon his lap, placing Isaac by his side. This Sarah seeing, was enraged, and said, "Thou shalt not put my son in the rank of the concubines." Afterwards, Ismaël and Isaac fighting one day together as boys do, Sarah was enraged, and said unto Hagar, Thou shalt not dwell with me in the same land for ever. She commanded Abraham to remove her and Ismaël; to which, having received God's consent in revelation, he agreed. Abraham went with them unto a spot whose frontiers are guarded by the proud Amalekítes. He leaned upon a stony place, and caused them to alight, and commanded Hagar to place a seat thereon; which she did. Then Abraham prayed: —O Lord! I take up, as a resting-place for my offspring, a valley never sown, hard by thy Venerable House of Marvels (or signs). Some say that Ismaël was a suckling at this time; some deny it. Then did Abraham place them (some say) beneath a great tree. They had with them nothing but an old skin of water. At that time there was no one in Mecca, and no water there. He also placed with Hagar a vessel containing dates. Then he returned, and Hagar called loudly after Abraham, O Abraham! whither fleest thou? Wilt thou leave us in this place, wherein there is no man? This she said unto him many times; but he turned not round his head towards her. Then she said, God hath commanded thee to do this. He said, Yes. Then she said, God therefore will not permit us to perish: I am content. Then she returned, and Abraham proceeded until he came to a declivity where no one could see him. Then he prayed the prayer just quoted, turning himself towards the spot where Mecca afterwards stood, as his Kiblah. Hagar, however, went back, and continued to suckle her little boy, and to drink the water, until the skin was exhausted. Then she began to thirst, and he began to thirst. Seeing him struggling for thirst, she could not bear it. She went up, therefore, unto a neighbouring hillock, to see whether any one was near whom she might call to her succour. Here she leaned upon the stony and flinty place, called Marwat. She did this several times, going round and round. At last she thought she would look at him, how he did. Then she heard a voice; and she then cried out, Help, if you can! Then, lo! she beheld Gabriel strike with his heel, and the water flowed from the earth, and voices sang around Ismaël. Hagar was astonished, and, going up, found Ismaël sucking up with his hand the water which gushed from a fountain flowing beneath his hand. She began to stop up the stream, in order to fill her vessel, to preserve some for Ismaël, and also to widen the mouth, and dig into it. Had she not done so, assuredly the fountain Zemzem would have flowed bright and clear. The angel then said unto her, Fear not destruction. Here is the place wherein thy son shall build a temple unto God. Never shall God destroy his family. Here shall the temple rise above the earth, like a lofty hill, strong as mighty torrents, extending on the right and the left.

Here, then, Hagar remained, drinking and suckling her son; but some genii passing, or, as some say, a company with camels passing by, saw some birds hovering and flying about in the low hollow of the valley of Mecca. Then they said, Surely these birds must be flying over water; yet we never met with water here before. So they sent to examine, and found Hagar and Ismaël by the water. They returned, and told the story: upon which the company went and met with Hagar by the water-side. They said, Suffer us to dwell with thee. She replied, Yes; but you shall have no right in the water. They replied, Very well.

Ismaël, however, neglected this, and, loving the men, dwelt with them; and, sending for their families, they dwelt also there; so that houses were built. The youth also grew up, and learned Arabic, and filled them with admiration. At a proper age, he married one of their females.

After this Hagar died, and Abraham came to offer his blessing. Not finding Ismaël, he asked where he was; and his wife said, He is gone to seek us some game. Abraham then asked of their welfare and their comforts. Then she said, We endure great straits, and suffer under poverty. Abraham doubted her, and said, When Ismaël comes home, salute him from me, and tell him "to change the threshold of his door." When Ismaël returned, and asked if any one had been there, his wife said, An old man, of such and such an appearance, came; who asked me about our way of living; when I told him we lived in great struggles and straits. Then said Ismaël, Did he give you any command? Yes, said the wife, he told me to salute thee on his part, and to say that thou must change the threshold of thy gate. Then said Ismaël, That is my father. I shall dissolve all connexion with thee and thy family. So he divorced her, and married another. Abraham in like manner came unto her in Ismaël's absence, and asked about their welfare. She replied, We live in great comfort and abundance; which blessing I impute to God. So said Abraham, What is your food? She said, Meat. And what your drink? Water. Then he said, O God! bless their meat and water! Then he said, When thy husband returns, salute him from me, and tell him to stand firmly by the threshold of his gate. When, therefore, Ismaël came back, he said, Hath any one come unto thee? Yes, the wife said; a Shaikh of beautiful appearance came; and so told him what had happened. He replied, That was my father; and thou art the threshold I am commanded to keep and hold fast.

After some delay, Abraham came whilst Ismaël was sharpening his arrows under a large tree near Zemzem. When he saw Abraham, he rose up, and they both did what sons and fathers do. Then he said, O Ismaël! God hath commanded me, and I will do it. Make me, then, thine eye, and I will make thee my eye (follow my directions, and I will make thee my deputy); for God Almighty hath commanded me to build a temple here. Then he pointed to Mecca, which was a rising ground. Hereupon the corner-stones were placed, and the foundations were laid. Ismaël collected all the stones, and handed them up to Abraham; and Abraham built. Also, they said,

O Lord! prevent us; for thou art the All-Hearing and Omniscient One.

Hagar the Egyptian died before Sarah in Mecca, and was buried in the Sacred Pavement. For her sake Muhammad ordered, that when Egypt was conquered, the Egyptians should be treated kindly, and spared to become subjects (owing suit and service, not slaves). Ismaël died at the age of 137 or 130, and was buried in his mother's sepulchre. Whenever Abraham came to see Ismaël and Hagar, he was carried upon Al Burák. They passed over Syria, and came to Mecca, and spent the evening in Mecca, and passed the night with his household in Syria. Between Ismaël's death and Muhammad's birth elapsed about 2600 years; or, as the Jews say, about 2400 years; but God knows. Lot was interred in the village called the Blessed Vault, about one parasang from Abraham's Mosque; others say, in the western cave.

CHAPTER XV.

History of Lot, and site of his sepulchre. History of the Mosque of the Sure Evidence, and of the Cave on its eastern side, and other matters contained in this chapter.*

The site of the cities of Lot is near the Mosque built by Abú-Bekr-Al-Sabakí. Here is Abraham's Reclining Place, sunk into the soil about a cubit. It is said that Abraham, seeing the cities of Lot in a blaze, fell down here and slept, saying, I testify that this flame is the True, the Sure Evidence. Whence the name of the Mosque. However, an author observes, that he has never, in any work, met with any information respecting the death of Lot, his age, or his burial-place.

* See Note.

CHAPTER XVI.

Legend of Moses, son of Amrám. The description of him given by the Prophet. His kindness towards the Moslems, and mercy and compassion unto them. Some account also of his miracles. Relation of the cause for which he was named Moses. Account of his age, and how he prayed in his tomb; and the blessed result of his entreaty that he should be brought within a stone's-throw of the Holy Land.

MUHAMMAD asserted that, in his night-journey, he saw Moses on one side of the Prophets. He was a spare, thin man, like all abstemious persons. He saw also Jesus and Gabriel, and asserted that he himself more nearly resembled them than any one else. Moses, he says, was graceful and very tall. Jesus was a middle-sized man, with a red and white complexion, and hair not curly, but flowing loosely. He saw also the

Angel Warder of Hell, and Antichrist. Adam was also there, of a very dark brick-dust complexion; for he was made out of reddish earth; whence his name Adam. [*In describing these, Muhammad used certain corrupt words of the dialect of Yemen, which the author explains by quotations from lexicons and grammarians.*]

There is another story, told by Al Abbás. He asserts that he was once walking with Muhammad and others in a certain valley, when the latter said, What is this valley? They replied, The Valley of the Provident Sustainer. Then he said, Lo! I behold Moses son of Amrám. He afterwards described his complexion and his hair (but this is not recorded). Then, putting his fingers into his ears, he continued to repeat devoutly the proper formulæ of prayer all the time they remained in the valley. Then we came unto Fool's Hillock. Asking the name, we told him; and he then said, Lo! I see Jonas (Jonah) son of Mattay. He is riding upon a young (dun) she-camel. He is clothed with an inner vest of wool, and the bridle of his camel is of twisted hemp.

About this story learned men differ. Some say all this was in a dream, because it is not found in the received collection of traditions, and because he said once, "I was asleep, and the

Kaaba-encirclers beheld me." However, in the story of Jesus son of Maria, it is said, "Many truth-telling persons say that this was seen by eye-sight, not in a vision, or in a dream, just as all the orthodox assert that he saw on the night of his ascent, when he saw by the eye, and not by vision or in dreams. In like manner, there is some difference of opinion upon the question, how it was possible for Moses to perform the pilgrimage to Mecca. One illustrious divine asserts, that this takes place openly, actually, and visibly; for all the Prophets (he declares) live after their death, just as martyrs do, but more gloriously: and if they live, surely they will not cease performing the Pilgrimage, the Prayers, the Oblations unto God, as far as they can; for, after their decease, they remain in this world, the world of Deeds, until their appointed season be elapsed; hereafter to enter the other world—the world of Spirits, whence deeds are excluded and intercepted, which they for a time procrastinate; for they love these good doings (he adds), and serve in those matters which their souls earnestly desire, as willing agents, and not bound by necessity. Thus do the heavenly spirits offer praise and adoration; as it is said, They shall utter, by spontaneous intuitive inspiration, thanksgivings, as do spiritual beings; which expounds the verse,

"They shall supplicate thee in praise, O God! and live in thanksgiving." And again, "They shall pray, glory to God, Lord of the Universe!" for Paradise is not a place of constrained obedience, since this verse bears upon the face of it Spontaneous Intuition. Thus will it be with the Pilgrimage and Prayers of Prophets. Others say that the Apostle only meant to refer to the conduct which they pursued whilst they were in life, and brought them forward as giving the portraiture of their deeds; meaning, *whilst* they *did* live, they did so and so. Others assert, that Muhammad was only describing a revelation at that time made unto him, revealing that Moses, &c. *did* so act.

Respecting the existence of the prophets in their tombs, we have the following:—Muhammad said, I saw Moses praying upon a dark-coloured sandy heap, in his tomb. He was standing. Whence it is evident that Moses is alive within his tomb. It is plain also that Muhammad, when he saw this, was in the body; for his night-ascent was corporeal.

Two men, again—a Musalmán and a Jew—came to high words about the election and rank portioned out by God to Muhammad and Moses. The Muhammadan asserted that Muhammad was the most elect and pure: the Jew said, that it was Moses. Hereon the Moslem lifted up his hand, and, giving the Jew a box on the ear, carried him to Muhammad, and told him the affair. Then said Muhammad, Do not make comparisons, or prefer me to Moses; for when men shall be terrified, be overthrown by an earthquake, cry out with terror, and faint away; then I shall be the first who shall be raised up. But Moses will then be quite strong, and by the side of the Great Assembly. I know not, therefore, whether he will then have fainted away at all, and have been raised up before me, or whether God will raise him up second to me. For I do not know whether he will be before or after me in the Fainting of Sinai. Now this is a powerful proof that Moses, and Muhammad, and the prophets, will all be alive; and this is corroborated by the fact, that the departure of Moses was intercepted and unknown; and that the fainting, which shall seize upon all men at the blast of the trumpet on Sinai, applies only to those then living in the world. But they who died before, do not swoon away; for that would be an absurd conclusion. Whence it may be taken for a truth, that Moses will be alive, living like the martyrs, but more gloriously. This argument is confirmed by the assertion of Muhammad, that he saw Moses standing and praying, and also by the verse, "God forbids the earth to eat up the bodies of prophets." For they had said unto him, How shall we present our prayers before thee?

Now, however, I perceive an expedient which may reconcile these learned men. The death of prophets is not like the death of other men; but they are merely translated from one state to another, and depart from us, whither we know not. Thus they continue to exist in a state of being, just as the angels live and exist; yet no one of our race beholds them but he unto whom God grants that especial blessing. Thus it is true that God allows them to melt away from this world, and to taste of death, as Abú Bekr said to the Prophet, Truly, death is written down for thee by God, and thou shalt taste it. If, then, they live, they are made alive by God after their deaths. But in this case it will be necessary that they die twice over; a second death being inflicted when the trump sounds in Sinai; and thus they will taste a greater death than others. To this it may be answered, that when the trumpet sounds, all beings, both in heaven and earth, will faint away; and there can be no doubt but that all besides the prophets will then have fainted away with the fit of death. But the fainting-fit of prophets is merely a temporary failure of sensation. It is that fainting-fit which has the appearance of death in others; so it needs not that they die twice. It is merely an externally visible fit. Thus the two Imáms, Al Babakí and Al Kurtubí, and others, have decidedly adopted the opinion that the fit on that day shall only be a swoon, not a cessation of the soul. This is proved by the Prophet's expression, "I know not whether Moses be *raised* up before me." He does not say, be *re-vivified* before me.

From all this we may finally determine, that the trump will sound twice, and will raise up all who are lost in the trance, and revivify all who are absolutely dead. The result is, that our Prophet spake truth in asserting that he should be brought out of the tomb first, before all other men and prophets, except Moses. With regard to him, some discrepant difficulty results, whether he be raised from the dead before Muhammad, or, whether he remain in the same state in which he was before the sound of the trump, and the trance. This, then, is all that is fit to be said upon this part of the tradition. No controversy exists as to any but Moses; nevertheless, God knows.

With regard to that expression of Muhammad's, "Do not exalt me above Moses," learned men (God be satisfied with them!) view the matter under different lights. One is, that he said this before God informed him of his overflowing supremacy above others; for when God informed him of this fact, he cried out with a loud voice, saying, Truly I, the son of Adam, am Lord. Another is, that Muhammad forbade any contention about pre-eminent supremacy in the prophetical office, for this reason,—because that is a degree of rank absolutely *single*, *one*, and *indivisible*. No superiority can herein exist.

Another is, that this is all to be referred to the Prophet's good manners and humble-mindedness. This view of the case gains the palm. It may itself be regarded in several points of view:—One, that the Prophet forbade this discussion, because that a comparison of the varying supremacies of prophets by no means determines the just claim of any one; for we cannot point out distinctions between the Excellent and the Most Excellent, the Perfect and the Most Perfect; whereas most men, in determining relative superiorities, chiefly rely upon some diminution, or loss, or lowering, sustained by one, when assimilated or compared with another. But the supreme excellence of some prophets over others, exists in such sort, as that each is to be regarded as having attained unto the utmost limit of supremacy, which is not a whit diminished when one is placed by the side of another. The Prophet then abstained from this controversy, lest he should aid and abet in diminishing the rank of prophets, or excite any idea of inferiority or diminution in their rank, among those who were chary of receiving what was not perfectly clear. Another opinion is, that the Prophet did not abstain from a positive definition herein, but for this reason :—he dreaded lest the matter thus put in men's minds should stir up any strife or dissension among Jews and Moslems ;—but God knows.

Ibn Abbás says, Admire how that the Right of Friendship belongs to Abraham, the Speech to Moses, the Seen Vision to Muhammad. The Spoken Word of God unto Moses is peculiar to him. God spake to Moses, and Moses heard the words of God uninjured ; and his words were far from such as can be expressed by letters and vowels, just as when the Moslems shall behold God on the day of judgment: he shall be very different from any objects towards which our eye can be directed, or our eye-sight embrace. This is a most excellent opinion, well worthy of true acceptance.

Now for his compassion towards the Moslem people, and his pity with regard to them :—This consisted in the remission of the original number of prayers imposed, which was lowered from fifty to five. Now for some of the miracles of Moses : —When Pharaoh's guards, commissioned to sacrifice all the male children of Israel, came unto his mother, his sister said, O mother! the guards are at the doors. Then his mother rolled him in a cloth, and put him in the oven, which was then blazing, not understanding what she was doing. The guards then came, and found the oven blazing. The mother did not change colour, or make any sign which might discover her son. So they went away, and, her senses returning unto her, she said unto Moses's sister, Where is the little boy? So she said, I know not. But hearing a weeping voice in the oven, she opened it, and lo! God had made the fire blazing around him cool and safe. Many other remarkable and eminent wonders and miracles were performed by him, which are enumerated among the miracles of the prophets. He was named Moses for this reason:—After his mother had cast him into the sea, he was found in the water and among the trees of Pharaoh's demesne. Then they asked Asíat, Pharaoh's wife, to name him; when she said, I name him Moses; for in the Egyptian language (موسي), مو is the name of water, and سي is the name of a tree.

When Moses died, no one of the children of Israël knew where his tomb was, or whither he had departed: therefore the people were all in a swelling tumult, and wandered about hither and thither, sleeping neither day nor night: and on the third day there came unto them, in the evening, rapidly passing over them, a swiftly-moving cloud, wherein was a crier, who cried with a very loud voice, "Moses is dead; but his soul is not dead." This he repeated three times, so that all might understand, and know that he was dead; but that no mortals knew where he was. Again the Prophet said, No one can attain to the tomb of Moses but the vulture (or pelican), and God hath bereft her of understanding, lest she should show any one the way thereunto. This is found in a comment upon the verse, "O ye, who believe, be not like unto those who troubled Moses, saying, He had killed Aaron his brother; and unto this Moses did angels reveal the time of his death; nor does any one know where his tomb is but the pelican. This was done by God, your ineffable Lord." Moses died at the age of 120 years. Aaron died one year before Moses; being older than Moses by one year. Moses died on the seventh of Adar, and was buried in the valley where he died. Aaron was born a year before Moses; and it is said that death abstained from cutting off the old men of the sons of Israël: therefore the Egyptian chiefs said unto Pharaoh, Death abstains from those people; therefore very soon will they become great and opulent; therefore slay the infants. Then he commanded that they should slay one year, and spare the next. And Aaron was born in the year of indulgence, and Moses in the year of slaughter.

Now with respect to Moses' entreaty to be brought within a stone's throw near unto the Holy Land, &c. &c.—First, Moses, it is said, prayed unto God, saying, O Lord! let me die within a stone's throw of the Holy Land! Muhammad also said, " If I had not conversed with him, certainly I would have shown you his tomb, by the side of the road, adjoining a red sand-mound." Now Moses, some say, did not ask permission to breathe in the Holy Land; nor did he request any fixed and known spot to be appropriated unto him, which men should have cognizance of; but he besought to be buried a stone's throw from the Holy Land. To this it is replied, that he wished to be buried a stone's throw *from* it, that he might look down upon it; and wished not the place to be known, lest men should adore it. Also, the great multitude of traditions assert nothing about this stone's-throw cast, (as applying to his *tomb*). One of these is, that his tomb is now to be seen in the Holy Abode; for (the tradition states) Moses besought of God one thing; and God gave him a gift far beyond and above his request. And this is surely the usual custom of the generous, to grant more than the petitioner requests. To this day, all the people of the Baitu-l-Mukaddas, and others, act upon this last ancient tradition; for they consider that he was buried *in* the Holy Land, and that his tomb is a fit point of direction for Pilgrimage unto the chapel mentioned before. Hither, then, they bring pieces of cloth of gold; and here they pass the night, doubly sounding the praise of God. Here they also barter their property for meat and drink, and permission to observe this custom. This is done both by the men and women, natives of the Holy Land, and the visiters thereunto. They cease not unto this day. Thus asserts the historian Dhí-Addín-Al-Mukaddisí:—It is said that this tomb, thus remarkably signalised, is to be found in the Holy Land, near Jericho. Hard by is a red sand-mound, by the side of the public road.—But God knows:—I have done.

CHAPTER XVII.

On the Wondrous Supremacy of Syria. Upon the miracles, tales, and traditions hereunto to be referred. Account of its boundaries. Traditions which the Prophet uttered regarding those who dwell therein. The pledge entered into by God on behalf of this land and her people. How this land is confirmed to be the Temple of believers, and how the corner-stones of the Faith exist herein. How that Syria is the precious choice land of God, beyond all lands, therein to fix for ever the chief blessings which he distributes among his adorers. Supplication of the Prophet that it might be blessed. Account of the building of the Mosque of Damascus. Account of its restoration and ornaments. Origin of the building. Of the relics of Martyrs and Confessors whereunto Pilgrimage is most commonly performed. Account of the favourable audience granted unto supplication herein offered, and the happy effects of meditation upon her.

As to its Wondrous Supremacy, we may refer not only to what has been already said of the Holy Abode, but also to the examination which the people of Islám have made of those ancient words, in the verse, "Truly I will cause you two to sing praise in the lofty mound wherein is the sure dwelling-place." This lofty mound is declared by one to be Damascus; by another, Jerusalem: another pointedly says that the Prophet himself interpreted it to mean Syria, the land called the Ghút, *(watered, moist, and wooded,)* and also one of its chief cities, Damascus. There is another verse—"I will cause you both—people who were regarded as weak—to sing praise in the Eastern Land, in the western part thereof, which we have blessed." This is referred to the western part of Syria.

Again, there is another verse:—"The children of Israël took up their abode in the unshaken mansion of truth." The word *truth* is here spoken metaphorically, as beauty is; meaning good, advantageous, happy; so called because this abode is full of religious blessings and all good gifts; which is the actual case of Syria and the Holy Land; they having most choice blessings, with the utmost possible abundance of all the necessaries for the support of life—fruits and trees. Some say that the "western part" mentioned in the above tradition is Egypt. Some differ as to what may be called precisely the Holy Land. Some say only Mount Sinai and its neighbourhood; some, Elía and the Baitu-l-

Mukaddas; some, Ascalon and the river of Jericho; some, Damascus and Palestine; some, Jordan; some, all Syria. None positively assert that the term "Holy Land" may not be applied unto Syria.

With regard to the reason of the name of Shám, or Syria, hereunto applied, writers upon idiomatic expressions remark, that the word is both masculine and feminine. It is either Mushám or Shám. It is so named, either because it lies to the *left* (or *north*) of the Kaaba, just as they call all the low-lying country, to the right of the Kaaba, by the name of Yemen; or because the companions of Noah, when they came out of the ark, took possession, some of the country right of the Kaaba, and some of the country left; whence the names Yemen and Syria (Shám.) Some say that the mountains here being white, the land is by contrariety called *black* (Shám). Some name it after Sám, son of Noah, who first dwelt here; and that the Arabians, who looked down upon it from their dwellings above, disliked to call it Sám, because that is a name of death (*unlucky*); so they called it Shám, on account of the number of villages therein, and their proximity to one another. Some say that a people, sons of Canaan son of Ham, came in bands, and blackened all over the country (by their numbers) or took possession of the left or north side. Hence the name Sám. As to its boundaries:—On the west, the Salt Ocean, on whose coasts are many great cities, and on whose sides are *Ramul* Misr (sandy heap of Egypt) and Al Arísh; then the desert of the sons of Israël and Mount Sinai; then Tabúk; then Dúmat-al-jandil, (Dumah the Stony). On the east, the Desert Samáwít (lofty, heavenly,) stretching unto Irák, inhabited by Syrian Arabs. On the north, the parts adjacent to the east; also the Euphrates, along the land of the Peninsula (Mesopotamia), extending in length from Al Arísh to Irák, twenty days, or more: in "the Book of Roads and Possessions," however, it is said to be twenty-five days, taking the whole extent of space between the two into account. As to the width of the country, its widest part is of eight days' journey in extent; and the narrowest, three. These boundaries are noted by the historian Shamsuddín-Al-Zaharí, in his publication "The Two Provinces."

Again, from other authors:—The first town in Syria is Báyas (بایاس), and the last, Al Arísh. Syria is divided into five provinces, or sections:— First, Palestine, so called because first inhabited by Philistin son of Kusín, son of Mutí, son of Yúmán, son of Yafíth, son of Noah. Its first frontier town is on the Egyptian road Rafah, or

Al Arísh: next to this is Gaza, then Ramula, or Ramlat Phalistín. Of great cities in Palestine are, Elía, which is the Baitu-l-Mukaddas, eighteen miles from Ramlah (this holy city was the residence of David and Solomon), and Ascalon, and the city of Abraham, and Sebaste, and Neapolis. The whole extent of Palestine is, in length, two days' journey to one who rides at the rate of a slow-moving beast; and in width, from Japha to Jericho, about as much. Secondly, Húran, (Auranitis,) whose remarkable places are, the Great Tiberias and its lakes, which is mentioned in the tradition of Gog and Magog. A certain historian says, that in the time of Waládat, the lake of Tiberias had nearly dried up; and this lake is only its middle. The rivers of Palestine are, Al Ghúr, (the low-lying Netherland,) the Yarmúk, (Hieromax,) and Bísán (Pisan), from whose palm-trees pitch is sought; whence its name, Al Dijjálat (the Tigris). Also the Ordono, or Jordan, so remarkable in the Divine Law, and mentioned in the Word, "Your trial is the River." Thirdly, Al Ghút (the irrigated land), wherein are many traces of sacred events. Its chief city is Damascus, said to be the Temple of Noah. On the coast is Terapolis. Damascus is said to be within the Holy Land. Fourthly, Emessa, wherein, it is said, no serpent or scorpion can find entrance. Here dwelt five hundred companions of the Prophet, by whose labours the city became safe from venomous creatures. One of its dependencies is the city Salamít. Fifth, Kinnarin, whose chief city is Aleppo. Its dependencies are Samwíl and Antioch. Here is the tomb of Habíb-Al-Najjár. Each of these provinces is again divided and subdivided into five Prefectures and Sub-Prefectures.

As to Syria, all learned men fully agree that it is the most eminent of regions, after Mecca and Medína. One, in his work 'The Privileges and Desirable Gifts of Islám,' says, that God says, By us the faith is beloved; the infidels, and the rebellious and wicked, are hated. We have appointed the people of Syria to be blessed unto the end of time. We have made it the abode of prophets, and apostles, and saviours; and its shores are full of elect angels. The Lord of the universe is her surety and pledge, and hath granted unto her people the right of superiority, so that her confines shall receive no injury unto the day of judgment. It is the tending point of believers, the refuge of fugitives; especially Damascus. This possesses a sure stability, a peculiar consecration, as all agree. Hither descended Jesus son of Maria, to magnify the faith, to aid the Unitarians. Within its watered land is the tent (Fostát) of Moslems, annexed (to its other good gifts). God hath, of his bounty, blessed the coasts and the surface of Syria, by flowing rivers and fountains of water, in the midst of houses and temples; and on its surface hath he given to grow grains and fruits and flowers, and hath made it the beloved Magazine of Adorers, the Market of the Cream of Piety. With regard to the traditions of the Prophet respecting Syria,—Offerers of prayer are best in Syria. Then the frontier-land next in sanctity is Irák, and then Yemen. Let any one seek after the fatness of Syria, and quench his thirst by her rain; for God is surety and pledge for Syria. Then said one of the Prophet's followers, turning round, If God is her surety, she shall never perish. A man also said, I would go forth; for I desire to visit the most surpassing place in the sight of God. So said the Prophet, That is Syria; for all the blessings taken from other lands are added unto Syria. All the earth shall be destroyed forty years before Syria is destroyed. Muhammad also said, Mecca is the Glorious Sign; Medína is the Mine of the Faith; Al Kúfa is the Tent of Islám; Al Basra, the Glory of Worshippers; Syria, the Shrine of Piety; and Egypt, the Nest of the Devil, his asylum, and his abode. The Two Seas (Al Bahrain) are the Dwelling-place of the Blessed; and the

2 D

Continent, the Robbers' Mine. Also, the hearts of Yemen are noble; nor shall ample abundance, or supreme rule, ever be stripped off from the Kuraish. Also, the people of the sons of Hishám shall bear sway. Also the Prophet said, Let there be frontier garrisons, to guard Syria, and Yemen, and Irák; for God recognizes the inhabitants thereof as his primary people. Syria is for you; but if you dislike Syria, then Yemen. From her streams let each quench his thirst; for God pledges himself for Syria and her people. Again, when two persons asked the Prophet's advice as to the place in which it was most desirable to dwell, he replied, Syria for you; for that is God's choice place, wherein he fixes all good things to dwell. He who will not choose Syria, let him attach himself to Yemen instead. Ata of Khorasán says, When I meditated changing my abode, I advised with learned men of Mecca, Medína, Kúfa, Basra, and Khorasán, about the best dwelling-place for my family. All agreed to recommend Syria. Next to Syria is Ascalon; for when the Prophet said, "The mill shall be grinding among my people; Ascalon shall be quiet and plentiful," &c.; he said again, "Shall the good things of the people of Irák be transported unto Syria, and the bad things of Syria be carried to Irák?" Again, the Prophet having conducted the

Prayer of Dawn, came forth, and, standing before the people, said, O God! bless us in our city! bless us in our weights and measures! bless us in our Harams! bless us in our Syria and our Yemen! Then a man said, And Irák too, O Apostle! But he said, Who is he that is so perfect in putting forth the horn of Satan, and stirring up strife? In a comment upon the verse, "Enter ye the Holy Land," it is said, There were six men carrying bunches of grapes, four carrying pomegranates, and two carrying figs. Syria is said to be blessed from Al Arísh unto the Euphrates.

John son of Job, and Zaid son of Thabat, were once collecting and transcribing the Korán into tablets, when the Prophet said, "Happy Syria! for the angels of the merciful hover around thee. They overshadow your city, Damascus, all the night, and at the dawn they place divisions and battalions, with standards and ensigns, by its gates, and then ascend, praying, O God! diminish their sick, and cleanse their mud!" Again, "All good things are divided into ten parts; a tithe is given to the other parts of the world; the other nine portions to Syria. All evil things are in like manner divided. One is apportioned unto Syria; the rest to the other parts of the world." Again, "Iblis (said the Prophet) shall enter Irák, and accomplish his desire therein. Then he shall enter Syria; but they shall repulse him until he be overthrown. Then he shall enter Egypt, and therein shall dwell, and rejoice, and widen his dæmon power."

This was reported as from the Prophet, when all were cavilling at Moáwiyah, except Syria, which had made peace with him.—Syria, the people thereof, their wives and children, constitute the great outworks and guards of the Continent. They are the firm constant warriors in the path of God. They are to be preferred as the corner turrets and outworks of a city, or the picket-guards and frontier positions on the enemy's borders. When Syria is destroyed, no good shall remain unto my people. Syria is God's whip, wherewith he punishes those of his creatures he willeth to punish. The people of Syria are God's sword of swords, to punish the rebellious of the earth. Syria is my quiver (says God); and when I am wrathful with the people, from that quiver I shoot my arrows. When Moáwiyah had conquered Egypt, the people of Egypt began to abuse the people of Syria. Then said Awf, lifting his face from his cloak, Dispute not, O Egyptians! with the people of Syria; for I heard the Prophet say, Therein are the martyr confessors; therein the ever-sustained, the ever-victorious. Moáwiyah also said, I will never curse or reproach any one of the Syrian people; for therein are the martyr confessors. Again, pious men from Syria, generous men from Egypt, worthy men from Irák,—martyrs are supplied to Syria in perpetual succession; just as when one man dies, being taken away by death, God places another in his room. They shall drink of abundant rain; they shall conquer their enemies; and all their pain and punishment shall be transferred to their foes. Of confessors and martyrs, twenty-two are in Syria for nineteen in Irák.

Again, it is said, Abdarrahwán-Ibn-Jahír-Ibn-Naghirat-Yazíd-Ibn-Alí-Sufián, and those with him, wrote unto Abú Bekr, unto Khalíd-Ibn-Al-Walíd, who was in Irák, or, as it is called, "The Shore of the Fountains of Yemen," after God had given the Moslem possession of Ferganah and Jalúla; the commander of the army then being Said-Ibn-Abú-Wakkás. The letter requested that he should detach 13,000 cavalry to assist his brethren in Syria, with the very utmost dispatch; for, said the writer, "By God, some of the *villages* of Syria have been given by God to the Moslems, more beloved by me than the borough-towns of Irák." Khalíd did, therefore, as he was commanded; and, after a difficult and toilsome march, accomplished his design, and, arriving with his men, found the Moslem army in Jabít (*i. e.* the

Great Tank, a village near Damascus). There he united with the other generals to prosecute the war. Again, the Prophet declared, That mosques and mufties should never, by God's decree, be removed from Syria. Among the other gifts wherein Syria surpasseth all other lands, there are therein 10,000 fountains, studded all over the land by the Prophet.

Thus said Kaab the scribe, "This is he whom I most prefer—he who is not coarse and rude; not unkind and sour; not he who brawls in the market-places, or who recompenses evil with evil; but he who forgives and forgets. Such was Muhammad. His birth-place was at Mecca; his place of refuge in Medína; his kingdom in Syria." To this assertion of Kaab the scribe, regarding the might of the kingdom of Syria, the greatness of its frontier garrisons, by means of its bold warriors, and all the valour of the country, all eye-and-ear witnesses assent. Syria and her people were chosen by God to dwell and lodge within. God hath blessed all its contents and surface; nor shall one place be particularly set apart, or enclosed, more than another. Syria is to be common to all in its whole extent unto its frontiers. Such is the tutelary guardianship and care bestowed upon Syria. Also, all good men, and witnesses, both ancient and modern, prove by their arguments that Damascus is the best province of Syria, and the king of Damascus the most choice of the kings of Islám.

One proof that Damascus is the most glorious city in the land of Syria, next unto the Holy Abode, is to be found in the fact, that herein are very many offerings presented, and a constant circulation of good deeds: also, because the mosque is so great, that, for the longest night or day, it never wants the sound of the reading of God's book and the recitation of traditions. Herein are ever to be found the instructors and the instructed.

It is related, that a certain woman sold a dish in the copper-market of Damascus: the purchaser discovered that the dish was of gold. Hereupon he said unto the woman, I bought it of thee, supposing it to be of yellow brass, and, lo! it is gold; therefore it is thine: but she said, I received it by inheritance as yellow brass; if, then, it be gold, it is thine. The dispute was referred to Walíd-Ibn-Abdul-Málik, who deputed Abdar-Rijá-Ibn-Haiwút to examine the matter. This last decided against the man, (decreeing him to *keep* the dish,) who came near to present himself, and said, O Commander of Believers, I give her the price, and now cast it down into the treasury of the Moslems. I saw (says Zaid-Ibn-Jábir) a vessel, used for domestic purposes, hanging among the candlesticks of the mosque of Damascus: it was of gold, and weighed thirty pounds. No one came for it; therefore (the mosque) took it. Damascus is gloriously alluded to in the verse, "In the mountain Kásiyún will I build in thy stronghold, in thy midst, a temple wherein I may be adored." Again, the verse wherein the word "Figs" is named, alludes to the fact that the gainful Damascene commerce is the supply of figs to Egypt.

As to the erection of the mosque of Damascus:—first, A.H. 96, the whole company of workmen under the direction of Abdul-Málik-Ibn-Marwán finished the building of the mosque of Damascus. (May God recompense him this good deed towards the Moslems!) It had been commenced A.H. 86, and was ten years in building. The Great Mosque was founded upon the site of the spot wherein the Greeks had worshipped of old. They had there adored the seven stars;—the Moon in the sky, Mercury next, Venus next, the Sun next, Mars next, Jupiter next, and Saturn next: they also made seven gates in Damascus according to the number of the stars they adored. Saturn's statue was placed over the gate of Kisán; the Sun's over the eastern gate; Venus over the gate at Tum; Jupiter over the little gate; Mars over the gate Al Jábít; Mercury over the gate of Paradise (Firádis); and the Moon over the second gate, now called the Gate of Islám. As to the Gate of Victory and the Gate of Gladness, they were places of worship, and a yearly feast was held at each. These Grecians also appointed Astronomical Observers, who should note the motions of the stars, and observe when they were at the ascendant. Thus they built Damascus just as the lucky star was rising. But what they most preferred was a reservoir by the side of the water, which flowed from between two great mountain-channels. They changed the course of the streams, causing them to flow into high and low places. They built, then, this place of worship, and prayed towards the North Pole; their most holy spot facing the north. The gate of this temple was in front of the Kiblah, where the tower now is, as eye-witnesses plainly declared they saw when some of the walls were cast down, at the two extremities. This gate is very beautiful, built of stones, all slanting from right to left. There are two (other gates) small in proportion to this. The western side of the building is a lofty tower, whose walls are supported by pillars arranged in the gate: the eastern is the citadel of *Jírún*, who is said to have built Damascus, which is said to be "the Iram of the Pillars" mentioned in the Korán. Others say it was built by Al Ariz (i. e. Eliezer), the young slave of Abraham, who was an Abyssinian, given unto Abraham by Nimrod. His name was Dimashk, after which he named the city Dimashk.

It appears also that in the time of Al Moáwiyah, there was in Damascus a pious man, who was visited by St. George,* at the season of the Pilgrimage, *(not the Hajja.)* This coming to Al Moáwiyah's ears, he came unto the pious man on foot, and said that he was very desirous of meeting with St. George, and communicating with him. The pious man, accordingly, informed St. George of Moáwiyah's wish; which the latter refused to gratify, saying, There is no reason for this. The pious man informed Moáwiyah of St. George's refusal; who replied, Say to him, We have sat down with and communed with one who is better than thee and than ourselves, who is Muhammad. But ask him about the origin of Damascus—how it was. The pious man then asked St. George, who said, Once I passed by, and saw the site of this city all covered by the sea, wherein was an abundance of water collected. After this, I was absent five hundred years, and then, returning, beheld a city commenced therein, where many were walking about. The Gate of Jírún was built, by order of Solo-

* See Note.

mon, as it is said, by a certain devil of that name. Some say, that Damascus was built by a slave belonging to Alexander the Great, whose name was Dimashk. This Dimashk built three gates;—the gate Jírún, the gate Al Barid, and the Iron Gate, (this is outside, near the Gate of Paradise, hard by the "Bucket of Ancyra").

This city, then, Dimashk built; and here all the servants joined, and built a church to worship God in. Some say, however, that this church was built by the Greeks; for Abdalláh-Ibn-Abbás, having marched against Damascus, and besieged it, demolished the walls, after he had entered the city by storm. Then there fell down a stone, having certain letters inscribed thereon in the Greek language. They therefore sent to bring a certain monk who could read Greek: but he said, Bring me, in pitch, the impression of the letters on the stone; which he found to be as follows: "Wo unto thee, mother of shame! Pious is he who inflicts upon thee with usury the ill which God designs for thee in retribution. Wo unto thee from five eyes, who shall destroy thy wall after four thousand years." Now, Abdalláh's entire name was Abdalláh-Ibn-Alí-Ibn-Abdalláh Ibn-Abbás-Ibn-Abdul Mukallib.

Again, the historian Ibn Isakír says, When God had granted unto the Moslems the possession, as conquerors, of the whole of Syria, he granted them, among the other cities, that of Damascus, with its dependencies. Thus God sent down his mercy upon them; and the commander-in-chief of the army, (besieging Damascus,) who was either Abú Ubaídah, or, as some say, Khalíd-Ibn-Al-Walíd, wrote a treaty of capitulation, and articles of surrender. By these he settled and appointed fourteen churches to remain in the hands of the Moslems. The church of which we have spoken above was left open, and free for future consideration. This was on the plea that Khalíd had entered the city at the sword's point by the eastern gate; but that the Christians at the same time were allowed to surrender by Abú Ubaídah, who entered at the western gate, opened under articles. This caused dissension; but at length it was agreed that half the place should be regarded as having capitulated, and half as stormed. The Moslems therefore took this church, and Abú Ubaídah made it into a mosque. He was afterwards appointed Emir of Syria, and was the first who prayed here; all the company of Companions praying after him in the open area, now called the Companions' Tower; but the wall must then have been cut through, hard by the leaning tower, if the Companions really prayed in the "Blessed Precinct." At first, the Christians and

Moslems entered by the same gate, which was "the Gate of Adoration and Prayer," over against the Kiblah, where the great tower now stands. Afterwards the Christians changed, and went into their church by the gate facing the west; the Moslems taking the right-hand mosque; but the Christians were not suffered to chant aloud, or recite their books, or (strike) their bells (or clappers), in order to honour the Companions with reverence and fear. Also, Moáwiyah built, in his days, a house for the Emir, right opposite the mosque. Here he built a green chapel. This palace was noted for its perfection. Here Moáwiyah dwelt forty years: nor did this state of things change from A.H. 14 to A.H. 86; but Al-Walíd-Ibn-Abdul-Málik, began to think of destroying the churches, and of adding some to those already in the hands of the Moslems, so as to construct one great mosque; and this, because some of the Moslems were sore troubled by hearing the recitations of the Christians from the gospel, and their uplifted voices in prayer. He designed, therefore, to remove them from the Moslems, and to annex this spot to the other, so as to make one great mosque. Therefore he called for the Christians, and asked them, whether they would depart from those places which were in their hands, receiving in exchange greater portions in lieu thereof; and also retaining four churches not mentioned in the treaty;—the church of Maria; the church of the Crucified, just within the eastern gate; the church Talla-Al-Habn (hill of the dropsical); and the church of the Glorious Mother (B. V. M.), occupied previously by the burnishers. This, however, they vehemently refused to do. Thereupon the Khalíf said, Bring me, then, the treaty which you possess since the time of the Companions. They brought it therefore, and it was read in Walíd's presence; when, lo! the church of Thomas, outside the gate of Thomas, hard by the river, did not enter into the treaty, and was one of those called, "the greater of churches left open" (for future disposal). Therefore he said, This will I destroy, and convert it into a mosque. They said, Nay, let it alone, O Commander of the Faithful! even although not mentioned among the churches; for we are content that you take the chapel of the church. To this agreement then he held them, and received from them the Kubbat (or chapel vault, dome) of the church. Then he summoned workmen able to pull down; and assembled all the Emirs, chiefs, and great men. But the Christian bishops and priests, coming, said, O Commander of the Faithful, we find in our books, that whosoever shall demolish this church will go mad.

Then said the Khalíf, And I am very willing to be mad with God's inspiration: therefore no one shall demolish it before me. Then he ascended the western tower, which had two spires, and called "the Almonries," which was a monastic cell. Here he found a monk, whom he ordered to descend. The monk making difficulties, and lingering, Al Walíd took him by the back of his neck, and ceased not pushing him until he had thrown him down stairs. Then he ascended to the most lofty spot in the church, above the great altar, called "the Altar of the Martyrs." Here he seized the ends of his sash, which was of a bright yellow colour, and fixed them into his belt. Taking then an axe into his hand, he struck against the very topmost stone, and brought it down. Then he called the Emirs, and desired them to pull down the building as quickly as possible. Hereupon all the Moslems shouted, "God is great!" three times; also the Christians loudly cried out with their wailing and wo upon the steps of Jírún, where they had assembled. Al Walíd therefore desired the commander of his guard, whose name was Abú-Nábal-Ríah-Al-Fasálí, to inflict blows upon them until they should depart; which he did. The Moslems then demolished all that the Christians had built in the great square here—altars and buildings and cloisters—until the whole square was one flat surface. He then resolved to build a splendid pile, unrivalled for beauty of architecture, which none could hereafter surpass. Al Walíd therefore commissioned the most eminent architects and mathematicians to build the mosque according to the model they most preferred. His brother chiefly moved and stirred him up to this undertaking; and next to him presided Sulaimán Abdul-Málik. It is said, that Al Walíd sent to the king of Greece, to demand stone-masons and other workmen for the purpose of building this mosque in the way he desired; sending word, that if the king refused, he would overrun his territory with his army, and reduce to utter ruin every church in his dominions, even the church of the Holy City, and the church of Edessa, and utterly destroy every vestige of the Greeks still remaining. The king of Greece sent, therefore, numerous workmen, with a letter, expressing himself thus, "If thy father* knoweth what thou doest, and permits it, then truly I accuse him of disgraceful conduct, and blame him more than thee. If he understandeth it not, but thou only art conscious, then I blame thee above him." When the letter came to Walíd, he wished to

* See Note.

reply unto it, and assembled several persons for consultation. One of these was a well-known poet; who said, I will answer him, O Commander of the Faithful! out of the book of God. So said Al Walíd, Where, then, is that answer? He replied, this verse,—"David and Solomon, lo! they assume a right to the corn-field, (they are decreed) a right to the place where the people are shearing their sheep. Also, we are witnesses of their decree; for Solomon hath given us to understand it, and both (David and Solomon) have come down to us as judges and learned men." Al Walíd, by this reply, caused great surprise to the king of Greece. Al Fírsúk alludes to this in these verses:—"I have made a separation between the Christians and their churches, and between the people who shine and those who are in darkness." —"I neglected for a season thus to apportion their happiness, I being a procrastinating vindicator of their grievances."—"Thy Lord hath made thee to resolve upon removing their churches from those mosques wherein good words are recited."—"Whilst they were together in one place, some were praying and prostrating themselves on their faces, slightly separated from others who, behold! were adoring God and idols."—"How shall the people of the Cross unite to ring their bells, when the reading of the Korán is perpetually intermingled?"

—"I resolved then to remove them, just as did those wise men when they decreed themselves a right to the seed-field and the flocks."

When Al Walíd resolved to build the chapel which is in the midst of the cloister, called "the Vulture's Chapel," (a name given to it by the country people, because the porticos on each side look like two wings,) he dug deep at the four corners of the intended chapel, until they came to sweet and limpid water. Here they first placed the foundation of the wall of the vineyard. Upon this they built with stone; and when the four corners were of sufficient height, they then built thereon the chapel; but it fell down again. Then said Al Walíd to some one of the mathematicians, who well knew the plan of the Vulture's Chapel, I wish you to build this chapel; for the injunction of God hath been given me, and I am confident that no one but thyself may build it. He therefore built the four corners, and covered them with wicker, and disappeared for a whole year; Walíd not knowing where he was. After a year Walíd dug down to the four corner foundations. Then he (*i. e.* the architect) said, Do not be in a hurry, O Commander of the Faithful! Then he found the mathematician, who had a man's head with him. He came to the four corners, and uncovered the wicker-work; and, lo!

all that had been built above the earth had fallen down, until they were on a level with the earth. So he said, From this (work have I come). Then he proceeded to build, and firmly fixed and supported a beautiful fabric.

Some person also said, Al Walíd wished to construct a brilliant chapel of pure gold, whereby the rank of the mosque might be magnified. Hereupon the superintendent said unto him, You cannot effect this. Upon which Al Walíd struck him fifty blows with a whip, saying, Am I then incapable of effecting this? The man replied, Certainly. Then he said, I will, then, find out a way to know the truth. Bring forth all the gold thou hast; which he did; and Al Walíd melted it, and formed it into one large brick, which contained one thousand pieces of gold. But the man said, O Commander of the Faithful! we shall require so many thousand bricks of this sort, if thou dost possess them; nor will this suffice for our work. Al Walíd, seeing that he was true and just, presented him with fifty dínárs; and when Al Walíd roofed the great precinct, he adorned the roof, as well as the whole extent of the pavement, with a surface of gold. Some of Al Walíd's family also said unto him, They who come after thee will emulate thee in rendering the outer roof of this mosque more commodious every year.

Upon this, Al Walíd ordered all the lead of the country to be collected together, in order to construct therewith an exterior outward covering, answering to the interior, which should be light upon the roof, and on the side-posts that supported the roof. So they collected lead throughout all Syria and many other countries; and whilst they were returning, they met with a certain woman who possessed a weight of lead—a weight of many talents. They began to chaffer with the woman for it; but she refused to sell it, except for its weight in silver. So they wrote to the Commander of the Faithful, informing him of this; who replied, Buy it from her, even for its weight in silver. When, then, they offered this sum unto her, she said, Now that you have agreed to my proposal, and are satisfied to give the weight in silver, I give the weight as an offering unto God, to serve for the roof of the mosque. Hereupon they marked one corner of the weight with the impression of a seal—"This is God's." Some say the woman was an Israëlite; some say that they sought for lead in open ditches or holes, and came to a stone sepulchre, within which was a leaden sepulchre; whence they brought forth a dead body, and laid it on the ground. Whilst dragging it out, the head fell to the ground, and the neck being broken, much blood flowed forth from the mouth; which terrified them so much, that they rapidly fled away. This is said to have been the burial-place of King Saul. Also, the guardian of the mosque came unto Al Walíd, and said, O Commander of Believers! men say that Al Walíd hath expended the money of the treasury unjustly. Hereupon, Al Walíd desired that all the people should be summoned to prayer. When all were assembled, Al Walíd mounted the pulpit, and said, Such and such reports have reached me. Then he said, O Omar-Ibn-Al-Muhájir! stand up, and produce the money of the treasury. Now it was carried upon mules. Therefore, pieces of hide being placed in the midst, beneath the chapel, he poured out all the gold and silver, to such a height, that those who stood on either side could not see one another. Scales being then brought out, the whole was weighed; when it was found that the amount would suffice for the public use for three years to come, even if nothing were added to the amount. Then all the people rejoiced, praising and glorifying God for this. Then said the Khalíf, O people of Damascus! you boast among men of four things;—of your air, of your water, of your cheerfulness, and your gracefulness. Would that you would add to these a fifth, and become of the number of those who praise God and are liberal in his service! Would that, thus changing, you would become thankful suppliants! In the Kiblah of this mosque were three golden scimitars, enamelled in lapis lazuli. Upon each scimitar was engraved the following sentence:— "In the name of God, the Merciful and Compassionate! There is no God but God. He is the ever-living, the self-subsisting Being, who never slumbers nor sleeps. There is no God but one God. He has no partner. We will never adore any but our Lord, the One God. Our faith is Islám, and our Prophet is Muhammad. This mosque was built, and the churches which stood on the site of the chapel were demolished, by order of the servant of God, the Commander of the Faithful, Al-Walíd-Ibn-Abdul-Málik-Ibn-Marwán, in the month Dhúl-Kaáda, A.H. 86." Upon another tablet was inscribed the whole of the first chapter of the Korán. Here also were depicted the stars; then the morning twilight; then the spiral course of the sun; then the way of living which obtained after the arrival of the Faithful at Damascus. Also it is said, that all the floor of this mosque was divided into small slabs, and that the stone (carving) of the walls extended to the utmost pinnacle. Above was a great golden vine; and above this were splendid enamelled knobs of green, red, blue, and white, whereby were figured and expressed all countries and regions, especially the Kaaba, above the tower; also all the countries to the right and left (of Mecca), and all the most beautiful shrubs and trees of every region, famous either for their fruits or flowers. The roof had cornices of gold. Here was suspended a chain of gold and silver, which branched off into seven separate lights. In the tower of the Companions were two stones—beryls —(some say they were the jewels called pearls); they were called "The Little Ones." When the candles were put out, they inflamed the eyes by their brilliant light. In the time of Al-Amín-Ibn-Al-Rashid, Sulaíman, captain of the guard, was sent by that Khalíf to Damascus, to steal these stones, and bring them to him; which he did. When Al Mámún discovered this, he sent them to Damascus, as a proof of his brother's misconduct. They afterwards again vanished, and in their place is a glass vessel. In this mosque all the gates, from the dome (gallery) unto the entrance, are open, and have no bars or locks. Over each is a loose curtain. In like manner there is a curtain upon all the walls, as far as the bases of the golden vine, above which are the enamelled knobs. The capitals of the pillars were thickly covered with dead gilding. Here were also small galleries, to look down from, enclosed on the four sides of the skirting wall. Al Walíd also built the northern minaret, now called "the Bridegroom's Tower." As to the western gallery, that existed many ages before;—in each corner of this was a cell, raised upon very lofty walls, and used by the Greeks as an observatory. The two northern of these fell, and the two opposite remained. In the year 740, part of the eastern had been burnt. It then fell down; but was built up anew out of the Christians' money, because they had meditated the destruction (of it) by fire. It then was restored after a most beautiful plan. This is the tower (but God knows) upon which Jesus son of Maria will alight; for Muhammad is reported to have said, I saw Jesus son of Maria come forth from near the white minaret, east of the mosque, placing his hands upon the wings of two angels, firmly bound to him. Upon him was the Divine glory (the Shechínah). He was marked by the red tinge of baptism. This is the mark of original sin.*

Jesus (it is also said) shall come forth from the White Tower by the eastern gate, and shall enter the mosque. Then shall the word come forth for Jesus to fight with Antichrist at the corner of the city, as long as it shall please God. Now when this mosque (the slaves' mosque) was completed, there was not to be found upon the face of the earth a building more beautiful, more splendid, more graceful than this. On whatever side, or area, or place, the spectator looked, he still thought that side or spot the most preferable for beauty. In this mosque were certain talismans, placed therein since the time of the Greeks; so that no venomous or stinging creature could by any means obtain entrance into this enclosure; neither serpent, scorpion, beetle, nor spider. They say also that neither sparrows nor pigeons built their nests there; nor was any thing to be found there which could annoy people. Most, or all, of those talismans were burnt by the fire that consumed the mosque; which fire took place in the night of Shabán, A. H. 461. Al Walíd frequently prayed in this mosque. One night (it is related) he said to his people, I wish to pray to-night in the mosque: let not any one remain there whilst I pray therein. So when he came unto the Gate of the Two Moments,* he desired the gate to be opened, and, entering in, he saw a man standing between the Gate of the Two Moments and the Gate of St. George, praying. He was rather nearer to the Gate of St. George than to the other. So the Khalíf said unto his people, Did I not charge you that no one should

* See note.

remain whilst I was praying in the mosque? Then one of them said, O Commander of the Faithful! this is St. George, who prays every night in the mosque. Again,—One prayer in this mosque equals thirty thousand prayers.

Again, a certain man, going out of the gate of the mosque which is near the Jírún, met Kaab the scribe, who said, Whither bound? He replied, To the Baitu-l-Mukaddas, therein to pray. Then said Kaab, I will show you a spot wherein whosoever prayeth shall receive the same blessings as if he prayed in the Baitu-l-Mukaddas. The man, therefore, went with him. Then Kaab showed him the space between the little gate from whence you go to Abyssinia; that is, the space covered by the (arch of the gate), containing about one hundred (yards), to the west, and said, Whoso prayeth within those two points shall be regarded as praying within the Baitu-l-Mukaddas. Now this spot is said to be a spot fit to be sought by pilgrims. Here, it is asserted, is the head of John son of Zachariah (peace be with him!). For Al-Walíd-Ibn-Muslim, being desired to show where John's head was to be found, pointed with his hand to the plastered pillar—the fourth from the east corner. Zaid-Ibn-Wákad says, At the time it was proposed to build the mosque of Damascus, I saw the head of John son of Zacharias brought forth from underneath one of the corners of the chapel. The hair of the head was unchanged. He says, in another place, Being nominated by Al Walíd, superintendent of the building, we found a cave; of which discovery we informed Al Walíd. He came, therefore, unto us, at night, with a wax taper in his hand. Upon descending, we found an elaborately-carved little shrine, three within three (i. e. *within the first a second; within the second a third*). Within this last was a sarcophagus, and within this a casket; within which was the head of John son of Zacharias. Over the casket was written, "Here is the head of John son of Zacharias. Peace be with him!" By Al Walíd's command we restored the head to the spot whence it had been taken. The pillars which are above this spot are inclined obliquely to the others, to distinguish the place. There is also over it a pillar with a head in plaster. He asserts again, that when the happy event occurred of the conquest of Damascus, a certain person went up the stairs which led to the church, then standing where the mosque now stands. Here the blood of John son of Zacharias was seen to flow in torrents, and to boil up; nor did the blood sink down, and become still, until that seventy thousand had been slain over him. The spot where the head was found is now called

Al-Saka-Sak (perhaps, the Nail of the Narrow Cave).

In the days of Omar, the Christians requested that he would confirm their claim to the right of meeting in those places which Al Walíd had taken from them and converted into mosques. They therefore claimed the whole inner area as their own from Omar. The latter thought it right to restore them what Al Walíd had taken from them; but, upon examination, he found that the churches without the suburbs were not comprehended in the articles of surrender by the Companions; such, for example, as the great church of the monastery of Observants or Carmelites, the church of the convent behind, the church of St. Thomas, and all the churches of the neighbouring villages. Omar therefore gave them the choice, either to restore them the churches they demanded, demolishing in that case all the other churches, or to leave those churches unmolested, and to receive from them a full consent to the free use of the open space by the Moslems. To this latter proposal they, after three days' deliberation, agreed; and proper writings were drawn up on both sides. They gave the Moslems a deed of grant, and Omar gave them full security and assurances of protection. Nothing was to be compared to this mosque. It was said to be one of the strongholds of Paradise; and it is said, that no inhabitant of Damascus would long for Paradise when he looks upon his beautiful mosque. Al Mamún came to Damascus in company with his brother Al Motasim and the Kádí Yahyay-Ibn-Aktam. Whilst viewing the mosque, he said, What is the most wondrous sight here? His brother said, These offerings and pledges. The Kádí said, The marble and the columns. Then said Al Mamún, The most wondrous thing to me is, whether any other could be built at all like this.

A writer (on Sháfá's authority) observes, There are five wonders in the world; namely, first, the Steeple of the Two Pinnacles at Alexandria; secondly, the Companions of the Cave at Rome; thirdly, a Watch-Tower by a gate of Spain,—the gate of her chief city (here a man sitting, and looking down, can behold his comrade at a distance of five hundred parasangs); fourthly, the Mosque of Damascus, perfect in beauty, brightness, and grandeur; fifthly, the Marble and delicate Sculpture therein, the manner of placing which is not precisely known; but it is thought that the marble was hammered, kneaded, and modelled, because it softens in the fire.

Now, with regard to all the traditions and excellent privileges pertaining to the mountain Kásídún. First, Muhammad, being requested to enumerate the blessed relics of Damascus, said, On the western declivity of the mountain Kásídún, was Adam's son killed, and Abraham born. Here God entertained Jesus; here Jesus bathed, and prayed and supplicated God not to cast him off frustrated of his desire. Being requested to describe the place, he said, It is in a moist watery plain, where is the city called Damascus. God hath spoken of this mountain, that the supplication of him who prayeth here shall never be invalidated. Being asked if this place was the asylum of John son of Zacharias, he replied that it was, and that it was set apart for any one who should justifiably slay a man, who should remain in the cave which is beneath the blood of Adam's son. Here Elias the Prophet found a hiding-place from the king of his people. Here prayed Abraham, Lot, Moses, Jesus, and Job; and all their prayers were granted. Here is the place, or open plain, Biraz, of which the following tradition is told:—The king of this country attacked Lot and his household, and took them prisoners. Abraham came forward to reclaim him with 320 of the people of Bedr, and came up with the enemy by the Rock of the Covenant. Here he arranged his right, and left, and centre, being the first who ever fought in this battle order.

They fought; and Abraham routed the enemy, and brought Lot and his household back again. Also, coming unto the spot where the open place now is, he prayed there, and built a mosque. Some say, however, that Abraham was born in Kútha of Babylon. Whosoever shall pray four Rakás in the cave of this plain, shall be cleansed from all sin as completely as he was the day he was born; nor shall he ever be frustrated in any desire. Of this several proofs are given. Upon several occasions of drought, the people prayed in this cave, when God caused great quantities of rain to fall. The earth being saturated, they prayed again that the rain might cease, which ceased accordingly. Kaab the scribe visited the cave, and prayed very earnestly upon the spot where the blood of Adam's son fell. Being asked what supplication he had so earnestly offered, he said, I prayed that God would cause peace between Moáwiyah and Alí; that he would grant me sufficient sustenance, and give me a son. Soon after this Moáwiyah sent Kaab 1000 dirhems and a gown, and wrote to Alí, offering peace; the terms of which they agreed upon. Upon the high ground of the monastery of Marwán is seen a great quantity of parched dry herbage. This marks the spot stained by the blood of Adam's son, and is most propitious for prayer. Again,—

Without the "Gate of the Awful Moments" is a Rock, whereon offerings are to be placed. If the oblations be acceptable, fire comes and burns them up; if they be rejected, they remain as they were before. Now, Abél was the owner of sheep; and his abode was in a village; and Kabíl (Cain) was, among his people, a tiller and sower. Now, Adam being in his chamber, where he passed the night, and Eve being in her own chamber, Abél came with a fat ram of his flock; which, being placed upon the stone, was consumed by the fire. Then came Cain with some barley mingled with wheat, and laid it on the stone; but it remained as it was. This inflamed Cain against his brother; so he followed him to the mountain, and resolved to kill him. Here, then, he did kill him; whereupon Eve cried out with a loud voice, and Adam said, "Be it upon thee and upon thy daughters! not upon me, or upon my sons!" The same divine, who mentions the above traditions, says, I mounted up the mountain Kásíún, to the spot marked by the blood of Adam's son. Here I beseeched God that I might perform the Pilgrimage: I *have* performed the Pilgrimage. I besought him to grant me, that I might have the honour of providing a horse for the sacred Border warfare (against the Infidels): I *have* done so. I besought him to grant me the blessed privilege of praying in the holy Baitu-l-Mukaddas: I *have* prayed there. I besought him to grant me good profit in buying and selling: he hath now made me rich, and granted me competence. Also, I saw (says that divine), in a vision, whilst I was standing in prayer upon this spot, the Prophet, Abú Bekr, Omar, and Abél. Whereupon I said, I beseech thee, in the name of the one unchangeable God, in the name of thy father Adam, in the name of thy mother, and in the name of this Prophet, to tell me if this is thy blood. He said, By the one unchangeable God, this is my blood. This blood hath been appointed by God for a sign to the universe; for I beseeched of the Lord of my father Adam, and my mother Eve, and this Prophet, that my blood might be the asylum for every prophet and sincere believer; and that whosoever should pray there, his requests should be granted unto him. So God granted this, and sent as many angels as there are stars, to be guardians here; and allowed that no prayer, here offered, should fail of acceptance. To this the Prophet added, that it was true that God, of his generous grace, had so ordained; and that he and his comrade, Abú Bekr and Abél, come, from time to time, to pray there. If men (says the same author) knew the supreme merits of this cave of the blood, they would neither eat nor drink but within it. Again, it is said that in this cave, beneath Abél's blood, the prophet Elias sought refuge from the king of his people for ten years, until God cut off the king, and another ruled. Here Elias arrived at full perfection, and was converted to Islámism, and made a great number of his people Moslems. Again, it is said, Here in this cave dwelt John son of Zacharias, and his mother, for forty years. Here prayed Jesus son of Maria, and the apostles. The prayer and supplication of him who cometh here never shall be fruitless. It is the spot of Acceptable Audience. Whoso would arrive at the Hill of Firmness and Distinction, let him come unto the lofty Nairáh (place of offence,—great misfortune), and mount up to the cave of the mountain Kásíún. There let him pray; for it is the house of Jesus and his mother,—their asylum and stronghold from the attacks of the Jews. If he wish to behold Iram of the Columns, then let him come to the river in the trench of Damascus—the river named Baradún—to the spot in Kasiyán known by the name of the Caverns: for a Shaikh of Baalbec asserts, that a distinguished Shaikh of Damascus told him, that he, in company with other Shaikhs, went to see the Cavern: that, having heard that it contained something worth inquiry, they resolved to dig therein. After permission obtained, they entered the cave, and, digging hard by the door, exposed to view a large portion of pavement. Removing this, they went down, and found a cave, about five ells square, or more. On the northern side was a cloister; lying in which were seven individuals, very tall, and placed transversely in their coffins, after the manner of the Arabs. They felt two much awe to approach them; therefore they returned and replaced the pavement.

In Damascus very many holy and devoted persons took refuge; adoring and worshipping here, many also died and were buried here, whose tombs are still here. Among these was Umm Habíb, wife of the Prophet, according to some accounts. But the historian Al Akshabree asserts that she died and was buried at Medína, on the faith of the following tradition:—Ayesha asserted as follows: Umm Habíb, daughter of Abú Sufián, said to her, whilst at the point of death, Since we have lived as became the co-wives of one man, pray to God to pardon me! To this Ayesha replied, God hath already pardoned thee; and thou shalt be sent to Umm Solmat (Jerusalem). She died in the Khiláfat of Moáwiyah, A.H. 44. That she did not die in Syria, is confirmed by the author of 'The Mothers of Believers' and many others. But these appear to refer only to Khadíjah Maimúna. But God knows.

To conclude the whole, I will mention certain places in Syria, of most especial pre-eminence and peculiar privileges. Thus, Palestine. Whatever is taken (they say) from the rest of the earth, is added to Syria. Whatsoever is lessened from Syria, is added to Palestine, (or, what is little in the rest of the earth is much in Syria; what is little in Syria is much in Palestine.) Abú Kaab the scribe met with a certain man, whom he asked, Whence art thou? I am, replied the man, one of a certain people of Syria. Art thou, then, said Kaab, one of that host, of whom seventy thousand shall enter Paradise without being brought to a reckoning? Who are they? said the man. The people of Emessa, replied Kaab. No, said he then, I am not of Emessa. Art thou, then, said Kaab, one of that host who shall be distinguished in Paradise by green garments? Who are they? said the man. The people of Damascus, replied Kaab. No, then, I am not of Damascus. Perhaps, then, of that host who shall be within the shadow of the All-Merciful's throne? Who are they? said the man. The people of Jordan, said Kaab. No, then, said the man, I pertain not to them. Perhaps, then, of that host upon whom God looketh down twice a-day? Who are they? said the man. The people of Palestine, said Kaab. Then the man replied, True, I am one of them. The name of this man is asserted to have been Al Hanífa.

Again, in another Collection of Traditions, from Kaab:—In Tarsus, of prophets' tombs are ten: Al Masísa (*Mamista in Cilicia*) five: in Al Thugúr, *the frontier fortresses* of the coasts of Syria, are one thousand tombs of prophets. In Antioch is the tomb of Habíb Al-Najjar. In Emessa are thirty tombs; in Damascus, five hundred; in the cities of Jordan, the same; in Palestine, the same; in the Baitu-l-Mukaddas, one thousand tombs; in Al Arish, ten tombs. Also in Damascus is the tomb of Moses (but this others deny, as mentioned in a former chapter).

When (said Kaab) all the world shall be full of distress and scarcity, Palestine shall enjoy opulence and abundance. Syria is the Blessed: the Holy Land is the Sanctified: the Holy City is the Holy of Holies. The holiest part of the world is Syria; the holiest part of Syria is Palestine; the holiest part of Palestine is the Holy City; the holiest part of the Holy City is the Mount; the holiest part of the Mount is the Mosque; the holiest part of the Mosque is the Chapel. Damascus is the most privileged and glorious of all the plains of Syria; nor shall the Holy City ever fail of full sufficiency of support.

Also Lydda. At the gate of Lydda, said the Prophet, shall Jesus son of Maria (the peace and blessing of God be upon him!) engage in battle with Antichrist, who shall tarry in that country a short time. Jesus (it is said by others) shall take three stones from the Holy City. Over one he shall say, In the name of the God of Abraham; over the second, In the name of the God of Isaac; over the third, In the name of the God of Jacob. Jesus, and the Moslems with him, shall then march forth against Antichrist. When Antichrist sees him, he will be put to the rout, and fly from him. Jesus will overtake him at the gate of Lydda, and throw one stone at him, which will hit him between the eyes; then a second; then the third, which will fell him to the ground. Then Jesus will kill him, and will slay the Jews, until the stones and trees cry out, O Believing Ones! this will be sufficient to convince the Jews that Antichrist hath perished and is slain. Then will Jesus quickly descend as a just judge among you, and will break the crosses and kill the pigs.

Also Ramlah (the palm). This is said to be the place called, in the Korán, The Hill of Confirmation and Division: but this is upon weak proof. Muhammad (it is said) asserted that Dajjal would be posted on the east of *Jordan*, and the Moslems on the left; and that they will not cease fighting until Dajjal be slain by the sword. But (says Abú Idris) By God! I do not know, at this day, where a Jordan can be found among God's cities. And in this Muhammad-Abán-Kúfi is blind and weak. God revealed unto Moses that he had thus revealed unto Abraham, "I will cause thy son to dwell in a land overflowing with milk and honey." So that the believers shall be weak as regards riches, but assuredly never weak as regards an ample sufficiency of bread. This is said to apply to the *Jordan*.

Also Gaza. Of this it is said, Happy is he who takes up his dwelling-place with one of the Two Brides, Ascalon and Gaza. This tradition is of the *second-hand* (quoted) and abrupt (unconnected) kind. Several commentators look upon it as weak.

Also Ascalon. Here a tradition is quoted as emanating from the Prophet himself; viz. that he said, Ascalon is one of the Two Brides, whom God will raise up, sanctify, and glorify, on the day of judgment. Here will be seventy thousand martyrs, who will come forward together as ambassadors unto God. Of these a certain number will hold in their hands their heads, which had been cut off, whilst the blood flows in streams from their jugular veins. So they will cry out, O Lord! perform unto us that which thou didst covenant with thy Apostle! Then will he say, O my faithful servants! I will wash you in the White River. So they will come forth from this river white and pure, and, with joyful merriment, enter Paradise whenever they will. Now, this tradition is not among the sound and genuine ones. Ibn Omar tells us, that the Prophet prayed in a certain cemetery, and, being asked the reason, said, This cemetery is in the land of Ascalon, and, on the day of judgment, shall be opened; when there shall arise therefrom seventy thousand martyrs, who shall intercede for men, by the formula Rebid, Modar, and the Spouse of Paradise—Ascalon. This is a tradition certainly to be received. In the collection of a Portion of the Wondrous Virtues of Ascalon, by the historian Ibn Asákir, the compiler notes them as *genuine, unsound, hypothetical,* or *unconnected.* Ascalon is said to be given to excess in eating, drinking, and adultery. The intelligent say that the cause of this is to be found in the fact, that Ascalon is a dépôt for sacred cavalry, a frontier town, ever guarding against the frequent attacks of the enemy. Even now, in these days, although many sacred-cavalry-quota-contributions are to be found in other places, yet it is far from being no longer a point of attack by the enemy. As to the asseverations of two other authors, that the above tradition* is genuine, they are in the habit of producing authorities from other books.

Again, Bethlehem. This is the place where Jesus was born, and Muhammad prayed, the night of his journey.—A most genuine tradition.

Again, Emessa. In Emessa, Sufián Ibn-Omar and Sharíb-Ibn-Ubaid declare, God confirmed the law, and sent the plague, which he with difficulty removed. The historian Al Thahabí says, that this plague was, perhaps, that which took place in the time of the Companions, since our era, and in the early part thereof; yet this plague was by no means a severe one, only inasmuch as female children died therein.

Also, Kinnasrín, or Kinnissín. Of this the Prophet said, God revealed unto me as follows:— Thou shalt descend, and the stages of thy flight shall be Medína, Al Bahrein, and Kinnasrín. This is a foreign tradition;—only on single authority. Two others declare it to be genuine.

Also Antioch. Yúsúf-Ibn-Isbát said to his wife, When I am near death, then bring me to

* See note.

Antioch, and there place my sepulchre. Upon the verse, "I will strike upon them as I struck the lords of the cities;" Abú Sálik asserts that allusion is here made to Antioch; but herein doubtful points arise;—and God knows.

And now, thus says the compiler:—"May God confer upon him the benignant gifts which are His alone! May he have compassion upon him, and grant him Paradise, in requital for all that hath been carefully arranged and polished in this fortunate work! May God bring him safe at last into his glorious presence, and grant him the full consummation of near approach unto him, and everlasting grace! We beseech him, of his supreme excellence and compassion, that he would grant unto us a share in those glories, which he hath apportioned to the first believers, and the faithful doers of good works; and that he would forgive, both us and them, all our sins, all our stumblings, all our faults, all our falls. Multiply upon us, O God! thy gentleness and mercy! for long hast thou protected us; greatly hast thou forgiven us; often hast thou been moved to wrath. Thou art the Veriest Perfect One; chief of all glorious ones. Thou art the Bounteous One; all bounteous in pre-eminence and grace! We beseech thee, O God! to grant unto us the performance of the Pilgrimage,

Islámism in our religion, Peace in old age, Blessing with competence, the gift of Firm Evidence, Penitence before death, and Pardon after death, Joy and Abundance in this world and the next. And this we ask of thee, O thou most Compassionate One! O Light of Heaven and Earth! O thou Glorious and Majestic One! O thou that hearest the cry of the crying ones! Thou Refuge of the seekers for succour! Thou that fulfillest the wish of the suppliant! O thou that givest gladness to the sorrowful! O thou who lovest the prayer of the poor despised! I offer unto thee the prayer of one who is weak, defenceless, and poor. With suppliant groans I offer the submissive prayer, and present the fearful and timid entreaty. I am of those who, before thee, humble the neck; in fear of thee, shed streams of tears; who maketh vile his body, and submitteth utterly unto thee. Let not, O God! my supplication offered unto thee, my Lord, ever be miserably rejected! but be gentle and merciful! O thou best of prayer-receivers! thou dost direct all events that concern me by thy hand; thou dost not leave my soul to itself even for the twinkling of an eye, nor the soul of any one of thy creatures. Grant unto me, then, this one gift out of thy treasures, this merciful share of the favours thou givest unto thy servants —that thou wouldst conduct me by the way thou willest unto thy broad path, the path of God, King of Earth and Heaven, towards whom all events converge! Thus prays the compiler, whom may God Almighty pity and pardon! This book was finished on the second holiday, the thirteenth of Saffar, the happy morrow of the New Moon, the year 875, in the Holy City. Praise be to God, Lord of the Universe! His peace be upon our lord Muhammad; also upon all the prophets and apostles; also upon their noble families, and the whole company of their comrades!

> Well-pleased, I close. O Merciful and True!
> Forgive the Reader, and the Writer too!"

The other, and later, MS. concludes thus:—"Praise be unto God, Lord of the Universe! the First and the Last (or from first to last), internally and externally! Peace be upon our lord Muhammad, Prophet of the Merciful One, Intercessor for his people, Reliever of their cares! Upon his family and comrades also, upon his wives and offspring, may he ever distinguish them, and grant them favours in perpetuity, unto the day of judgment! God is our Resource, our

Provider, our Master, and our Guardian. There is nothing above us, or around us, but the Omniscient God."

To this in the same MS. is appended the following:—"The copy of this blessed work was concluded in the Taleek character, in four nights, by the hand of the poor little servant of God, who, most of them all, needs remission and abiding forgiveness from the Lofty King who doth pardon sins; viz. Ibn-Músa-Ibn-Alí-Al-Kamil-Al-Abdhal. May God preserve him! establish a covenant with him! think upon him! Peace and salutation also be upon our lord Muhammad, and on his family and comrades!

To the older MS. are also prefixed two couplets upon the work.

SOME REMARKS

ON

MUHAMMADANISM.

SOME REMARKS

ON

MUHAMMADANISM.

The subject of Muhammadanism and its founder has been treated by various authors, continental and British. Mill (author of 'Muhammadismum ante Muhammaden'), Prideaux, Gagnier, Gibbon, White, Mill (author of the 'Hist. Crusades'), and Forster (author of 'Muhammadanism Unveiled'), may be mentioned as the most esteemed English writers upon this curious object of research. The works of Reland, Ockley, Pococke, Sale, Lee, Renaudot, Savary, and many others, may be regarded as having illustrated different points in the inquiry.* The labours, however, of those who have investigated the history of Mu-

* Maracci's learned edition of the Korán is also highly valuable.

hammad and his religion have scarcely sufficed to clear the subject from some considerable degree of obscurity and incorrectness. There is a spirit of laboured and eager partizanship,—a want of philosophical calmness and clear induction of facts, sometimes also of sincerity—to be observed in some of the above writers, which leaves the mind of the reader in a state of uneasy dissatisfaction and painful confusion, far removed from resolute conviction. Much of this result may be attributed to the age and circumstances of the respective authors. Dean Prideaux lived at a period when infidel sentiments began to be more openly and systematically expressed; and he naturally felt much indignation at the invidious attempts to exalt the character of Muhammad. That character must surely be estimated by the moral standard set before him, and the moral opportunities afforded; and is only so far important, as it affects his veracity in claiming to be a divine teacher. When, however, it was covertly and insincerely portrayed in bright colours, in order to mislead the uninformed, Dr. Prideaux rightly endeavoured to counteract such an impression; and, if we judge by the rule of enlightened Christian morality, has not misrepresented the pseudo-prophet: but his coarseness revolts us, and seems unsuitable when applied to a poor illiterate Arab factor, bred amidst the debasing examples of a fierce and corrupted race. Sale and Ockley wrote at a time when (as Bishop Butler observes) the question of Christianity was generally, among the upper and better-informed classes, regarded as decided in favour of scepticism. They therefore enter but little into a *causa finita*, although Sale's notes and dissertation are very useful as a popular introduction to the subject; and he is not fairly described by Gibbon as a half-Musalmán. Gagnier, rather an elegant writer (although accused of inaccuracy), was contemporary with Sale, and (perhaps for the reason just hinted) appears to decline much discussion. The learned author of the 'Decline and Fall' regarded the introduction of a new religion as a matter so easy as scarcely to merit much investigation; and by this unfortunate opinion was drawn aside from an inquiry to which he would have brought, certainly, considerable ingenuity and erudition, however misdirected and misleading. Mill, again, although he treated the subject of Muhammadanism in a distinct work, and although evidently capable of writing powerfully, is in general very vague, and content to offer, in the room of original discussion, ill-digested extracts and second-hand Gibbonism. The eloquent White seems to have given more attention to his periods than to his facts: he is painfully inconclusive and unsatisfactory; and no writer ever presented more valuable points of attack to an adversary. Scarcely any writer appears to enter upon the discussion in a calm, unprejudiced spirit. There is a lurking insincerity to be traced, and a mere desire of victory which is most especially unpleasing: nor is there wanting much of that virulence and ill-will which Orientalists have been accused (not wholly unjustly) of entertaining towards one another.

The Rev. *Charles Forster*, chaplain to Bishop Jebb, published, about 1828, a work intitled 'Muhammadanism Unveiled.' The design of this learned writer is to examine, in fuller and more accurate detail, the causes of the origin and progress of that religion; and he has so far succeeded in the undertaking, as to have directed attention to the proper objects of inquiry, to have unfolded many new and original views, and to have placed the discussion upon a right and profitable basis. Whatever light may yet be thrown upon this subject, Mr. Forster may claim to have led the way in illuminating one of the obscurest regions of literary curiosity. Still, it is to be regretted that this author should have determined to pursue his researches in a manner so exclusively theological. As far as the *history* of Muhammadanism is connected with that of the Jewish and Christian religions, it is plain that it must be considered as a theological subject: but why did Mr. Forster embarrass and restrict himself by entering into theories and disquisitions connected with prophecy—a province of dogmatical divinity? Very probably, perhaps doubtless, the origin and success of Muhammadanism were objects pointed out by prophetical inspiration: but before we adapt prophecies, we should ascertain facts; and it would seem that our facts, as relates to early Muhammadanism, are as yet not so fully classed and verified, as to warrant us in forming a decision from them upon any minute accomplishment of prophecy. That is a task which may well be delayed for a season, until the literary and theological world, whose attention has been drawn to the subject, have sufficiently weighed the mass of matter presented to them, and augmented it. The result of a too premature recurrence to prophecy by Mr. Forster is, that a cloudy, unsatisfactory indecision oppresses the reader throughout a considerable portion of his otherwise excellent work. Resolved to confirm a doubtful theory (for to his interpretation of the prophecy of Daniel there are endless objections), he exaggerates or misplaces facts, or adds to certain facts an undue importance, or suppresses at one time facts which he brings forward prominently at another. To mention but one instance:—Considering the 'king of fierce countenance,' (Daniel viii, 23.) as Muhammad himself, and hence as a personification of his religion, he desires to explain how "he by *peace* shall destroy many;"—certainly a strange distinguishing mark of the author of the Surát of "The Sword" and the "Warrior Faith." He refers for this purpose to certain treacheries and cruelties perpetrated by the Moors in Spain upon their Christian subjects. Now, not to mention the comparative small importance of Spain, compared with the immense Saracenic empire, we may justly imagine that the brief words of a prophetical definition would point to a grand and marked outline of the distinguishing, uniform features of character, or policy, by which we might at once recognise the object of the prediction. But Islám was neither established nor promulgated by *peace;* nor did the Moslems, generally, practise treachery; but, on the whole, observed the faith of treaties with much sincerity: and Mr. Forster, subsequently finding it necessary, for the interpretation of another part of his prophetical theory, to *exclude* Spain from the list of Musalmán possessions, does not hesitate to remove a point necessary to establish the truth of his position, in order thereby to introduce another point, equally necessary to the proof, although irreconcilable with the excluded step. The desire also of establishing an exact parallelism between the founders of Christianity and Muhammadanism, often misleads us by overstraining facts. These two religions can be assimilated only in the grand leading points—in having a definite founder, and in having, from small beginnings, overspread most parts of the world. They certainly possess no similarity; but are, rather, contrasted in their details. Thus Muhammad can hardly be said to have been *rejected* by his brethren in the sense that Christ was rejected. Muhammad, on the contrary, was in the end *accepted* by his brethren, and in his own lifetime was raised to the chieftainship and sovereignty of his countrymen. Upon the whole, it is to be lamented that so learned and ingenious a writer should have selected a line of argument which, however well treated, still leaves us room to desire some clear, popular, and conclusive work on the subject. It is not the *promulgation* (asserts Gibbon), but the *permanence* of Muhammadanism, that may excite our wonder. Although this be a position to which Forster adheres, it is one which we may justly question: it is beset with contradictions. If the causes which produced existing circumstances *continue* in operation, it is plain that antiquity, custom, and education, will add to them a tenfold intensity. Even if the original causes cease, the effects will long remain; for it is not so easy a matter, as some writers have supposed, to change suddenly the habits and sentiments of masses. But is not the opinion of *permanence* applied inconsistently to Muhammadanism by an author who himself asserts that it is hastening to decay? Is it wonderful that men should follow the habits and opinions of their ancestors and countrymen? What process of thought is more natural than that which instructs us to look for the original causes of things with the confident expectation that we shall thence trace the causes of their continuance? Who wonders at the permanency of Hindooism, entrenched by a barrier of ancient prejudice? But who does *not* wonder how so debasing and tyrannical a system *first* obtained an ascendency? The promulgation of Muhammadanism, *after* it had acquired power, is by no means so surprising, although not destitute of difficulties. Could a system of Paganism have been so promulgated among the Christians of Asia and Africa? Did Arianism long maintain its triumphs and supremacy? But the questions to be resolved are: How did Muhammadanism *acquire* that power at first, which it subsequently so successfully wielded? How did the illiterate prophet find means to defy, to engage, to overwhelm the power of interest, envy, and pride, which he was compelled to encounter?

There must assuredly have been some predisposing cause, some preparatory feeling or opinion or prejudice, that facilitated, in the first instance, the prophet's success. To suppose the contrary, is to suppose a state of things repugnant to the usual course of men's motions and actions. An Arab (certainly of noble birth, although by no means the chief of his family) calls upon his countrymen to obey his commands, and accept his doctrines, as emanating directly from the Deity. He assumes the title, and demands the due veneration, of the Elect of all created beings—the Last of the Prophets: and this he does, not only without producing miraculous attestations of his mission, but absolutely disclaiming any miraculous powers whatever. He produces no fact which appeals to the senses, no sensible evidence whatever, although constantly importuned to do so. Those, therefore, who believed in him with any sincerity, must have believed upon grounds abstracted from, and antecedent to, his own personal asseveration. It is impossible to imagine that the mere assertion of the son of Abdulláh, taken singly, could have influenced and swayed them in so remarkable a manner. Some of these predisposing grounds of belief may be thus briefly stated :—

There is a peculiar principle, which, from the remotest antiquity, has prevailed among the various nations of Asia. It is a principle which, although one of the most influential and deep-rooted that ever governed the mind, is very difficult to conceive clearly, or define. It may be called the principle of division, distinction, or separation. It led the mind, in a very forcible manner, to affix ideas of approbation and horror, delight and detestation, in an arbitrary manner, to matters in their nature and essence indifferent. Among the many ways in which this principle displayed itself, is the distinction of classes, and the distinction of meats. It appears to have prevailed among the ancient Chaldeans, the Egyptians, the Assyrians, &c. We have no proof that it was universal: the tribes of the Grecian peninsula and continent seem to have lost it, if they ever possessed it. It appears to have been observable among the Mexicans, &c., and among the inhabitants of the islands of the Pacific. It can be modified, or weakened, or destroyed, as among the Cingalese, the Siamese, and the Chinese. Its origin and extent it would be almost impossible to explain. Whether originally inculcated by the Patriarchs, and connected in some inexplicable manner with the moral principles of right and wrong, is equally uncertain. It seems to have always been allied with notions of sacredness and reverence. No sentiment or rule of action was ever more real in effect, or more shadowy in description. Whatever this feeling be, it probably existed long before the birth of Abraham (Genesis vii. 2, 8; also Genesis iv. 4, 5, et seq.:) but under the Patriarchs the principle to which we allude received a new and especial sanction; was consecrated by being connected with the promise of the Messiah; and was embodied in a new (or then renewed) observance—that of Circumcision. This rite was enjoined not only on the child of promise, but upon Ishmaël also—upon all, indeed, who were born in the Patriarch's family. It was evidently designed as a work of distinction, even more than of honour, except only as applied to the chosen seed: for Abraham's collateral family appear to have been held in higher honour than his own offspring by Hagar and Keturah; and from the former an alliance was sought both for Isaac and Jacob, although there seems no reason to believe that circumcision was adopted by any of Terah's descendants, in addition to Abraham. These last observing, in all probability, the principle of distinction of which we speak, did not think any rule designed to enforce and confirm that principle, to be of retrospective or necessary obligation upon themselves. However this be, those descendants of Terah, who are not included in the promise, must have peopled a great portion of Asia. They include the offspring of Abraham's brother, and sons by Keturah, of Ishmaël, and of Esau. All these tribes may have retained some notion of a common origin, as well as many customs and opinions of their great ancestors. All would be disposed to cherish those observances, which reminded them of their superiority over others, and which, superadded to the peculiar principle which prevailed around them, and which they shared, rendered them distinct among the distinct. The most eminent of these tribes was that of Ishmaël's descendants; into which the others most probably, in a great measure, merged; and from whom, as Mr. Forster proves, the nobler tribes of the Arabians sprang. These would inherit many traditions and precepts, all tending to exalt the principle of separation and division, as sanctioned and confirmed by the divine approbation. It appears, indeed, to have been connected with sentiments of delicacy, dignity, honour, morality, and religion; and its degeneracy consisted in becoming disjoined from these sentiments, and existing only as a superstitious prejudice, not opposed to the most depraved state of worship and manners. How do we know but that this feeling may have originally been the real *lex non scripta*, the law of natural conscience,—the unerring, "never-dying echo of the eternal voice?" It had prevailed for many centuries among the merely natural descendants of Abraham, when, among his spiritual descendants, it was renewed, augmented, and sanctioned by the Divine Revelation and Will. The Mosaic Law applied the principle of separation to a whole people; extended, ratified, and guarded it by stronger and more definite barriers. The Israëlites had probably observed very many of the rites of their Law, long before it had been promulgated; and they had lived amongst a people who, although in no way derived from the Abrahamic stock, carried the indefinable principle to which we allude to a most superstitious height. The Mosaic ritual added to the ancient observances some borrowed from the Egyptian, and others original; and was enjoined upon the chosen people, as an unalienable and solemn pledge of the distinction, separation, and division to be kept up between them and the Gentiles. The juxtaposition of some of those observances, which are merely ceremonial, by those duties strictly moral, and their intermixture and association in various injunctions and prohibitions, must convince us of the importance attached to the principle in question. The conquest of Canaan,—the establishment of the Jews,—their wars with the Philistines,—their kingdom,—the glories and commerce of Solomon,—the subsequent misfortunes, emigrations, and dispersions of the people,—the invasions of Judea,—the captivities,—the convulsions of the time of Alexander the Great,—the persecutions of the Syro-Grecian rulers,—the grandeur of the Maccabees and of Herod, contributed to maintain a knowledge of the Jewish religion among the neighbouring nations. The Arabians, at the period of the Exodus, were probably, in general, worshippers of the True God; for Job and the father-in-law of Moses were both Arabs. They seem to have subsequently declined to hero-worship and Sabeanism. Their error would appear to have mainly consisted in an adoration of certain symbolical representations of the creative power of the Deity; to which power the cherubim of the mercy-seat may have possessed some references: but in their idolatrous practices, the Israëlites willingly rivalled them; nor did much practical distinction exist between the subjects of Jeroboam and his successors and the surrounding and bordering Arab tribes. To both, the notions of repugnance to the "τὸ κοῖνον," (see Rev. xxi, 27.) the principle of distinction, would be a sentiment sacredly cherished. With both, the practice of circumcision prevailed; to both were prophecies addressed, and Jewish prophets sent; and, as might be conjectured, many of the Arabs, the Idumæans, and others, professed at last the Jewish religion. This faith, no doubt, would have been still further promulgated among the Arabs, had not a natural prejudice rendered them unwilling to degrade their great ancestor Ishmaël, or diminish his dignity by acknowledging the supremacy of the offspring of Isaac.

The manner in which Christianity dealt with this innate ancient Law, and its upholders and recipients, was remarkable. With the Mosaic obligations Christianity came into direct collision; and nothing can be more admirable than the readiness with which the first evangelic teachers prohibited the imposition of customs and ceremonies intertwined with every occurrence of life, and dear to the feelings of pride and veneration, to a degree which we can hardly conceive. Even circumcision, common to the Jewish and Ishmaëlite race, and regarded as the seal and pledge of the Abrahamic covenant, was no more enjoined; yet, whilst any prospective promulgation of these rites was discountenanced and prohibited, those who had already received and practised them were suffered to retain them; and, moreover, by an express decree, the grand eastern law of separation was recognised and recommended. The mandate of the Apostles, from Jerusalem, contains *four* prohibitions only—forbidding the eating of meats offered to idols, of blood, of things strangled, and fornication. But the principle of separation and division is plainly to be traced in it; and it involves the same intermixture of ritual with moral "vetita" and "inhonesta," as is observable in the Mosaic code. It was addressed to the Christians of Antioch, Syria, and Cilicia; but was probably communicated also to those Christians whose origin or country would lead them to entertain the same scruples as those which agitated the above churches, and would be accepted as a pledge that those feelings, regarded as sacred for ages, would not be rudely violated, but purified by the introduction of Christianity. No doubt this decision removed a powerful obstacle to the progress of the Gospel, which spread rapidly in Asia Minor and Egypt, and obtained a deep footing in Abyssinia. Still, it must not be denied, that the general spirit of Christianity opposed the excluding principle we speak of. The apostolic mandate was, in all probability, addressed to those only who needed it, and was designed to be only of local and temporary authority. Among the European Christians it was perhaps unknown, as well as the principle from which it proceeded: the intercourse of the Christians of the different portions of the Roman empire would soften and level prejudice; and an increasing jealousy and dislike of the Jews, no longer the depositaries of truth, would lead the Eastern Christians to desire to obliterate any traces of community of sentiment or practice which had prevailed. A feeling of jealous contempt for the Jews is probably alluded to by St. Paul (Rom. xi. 15 and seq.); and indeed one may almost imagine that we can observe, in the heretical notions of the East and West, a kind of struggle between the two principles of confusion and communion, and separation and distinction. The Gnostic heretics, in all their ramifications, seem to confound good and evil, by deducing the origin of the latter from some Æon, or emanation from the supreme Fulness of the Deity. They considered Jehovah (see Tertullian, adv. Hæres.), the God of the Jews, as a distinct being from the Great God, and as by no means entitled to our regard. This confusion in right and wrong they practically followed up, and there is a remarkable analogy between their notions and the mythology of the Hindoos; whereas the *Manicheans* asserted the eternal existence of the two distinct principles of right and wrong, and the connexion of this distinction with certain earthly symbols of perpetual repugnance and incongruity. Whether this be correctly stated or not, there is yet reason to believe that Christianity, as regards Arabia especially, was placed in an unfortunate and unnecessary state of opposition to the Eastern prejudice. The Abyssinians, indeed, who boasted of their descent from Solomon, and who had long practised many of the Jewish ceremonies, readily received the Gospel; but their remote situation left them at liberty in the profession of their semi-Judaized Christianity, undisturbed by the opposition of Western zeal. The Arabians were under different circumstances. The proximity of Palestine—the resort of Western pilgrims—no doubt often produced occasions for the excitement of mutual scorn and pride: the tribes of Jews who dwelt among the Arabs contributed to renew and maintain the feelings and traditions already so powerful; yet, to embrace Judaism, involved the acknowledgment of national inferiority, and the deprivation of the eldest-born of Abraham of his legitimate supremacy—to change their ancient Kaaba for Jerusalem. Some of the Jewish tribes, also, are said to have been cruel persecutors of the Christians, and perhaps others, in their proselytizing zeal. There were then feelings and prepossessions in the mind of the Arabs, which precluded a cordial reception either of Christianity or Judaism. It is not therefore surprising that their country should have been fertile in heresies. The divinity of Christ, the doctrine of the Trinity, and of the Atonement, were occasions of offence, and subjects of error. All was distasteful that implied universality, and appeared to disappoint the lingering hopes, that were still cherished, of spiritual importance and superiority.

May we not, then, regard Muhammadanism as a grand and opportune reaction of the Eastern principle, in its Ishmaëlitical form, as a systematic incorporation of opinions which only needed some rallying-point to combine and coalesce as an ingenious and popular heresy? The heretics of the ancient Church stood, in the strictest sense, upon separate unconnected ground. They often rejected or mutilated all that the Church had taught or received from the beginning—the Scriptures inclusive. Muhammad was not a greater heresiarch than Valentinian (of whose whimsical notions an account is given in the latter part of Tertullian adv. Hæres.); * but the assumption of the title of *Prophet* by the Arabian, in addition to that of Apostle, was a proof of great foresight and acumen; so much so, that the non-assumption of

* See Note.

this title, long before, by some pretender, is surprising, unless, indeed, Muhammad's stories about the people of Ad and Thamud, and the prophets Hud and Saleh, may refer to some tradition of an unsuccessful attempt of the kind. The Koraish knew enough of the miracles of our Lord and his Apostles, to perceive the value of miraculous attestation, and to demand it of their kinsman. As a *prophet*, however, he might, without too palpable an acknowledgment of want of power, elude and refuse this. It is difficult precisely to define the nature and privileges of the prophetical office of the Jewish Scriptures. It would seem, however, that the prophet's message was not confined to the Jewish nation, and that miracles were not of necessity demanded or expected of him. He made use of known principles, but did not profess to introduce original ones. His warnings and threatenings presupposed a knowledge, in those he addressed, of Him in whose name they were presented; and his mission therefore needed not that confirmation by miracles, which are necessary to insure the credibility of the author of a new dispensation. It was to this persuasion that Muhammad wished to bring, and in the end did bring, his countrymen. His mission and doctrines were, in their estimation, antecedently, probable and flattering. In such a case miracles (he said) were superfluous, and the pretensions to them presumptuous: the Prophet's message afforded its own internal proof—the proof which prejudiced haughtiness regarded with complacency. When Muhammad, therefore, once obtained a footing, he soon succeeded in his designs: he soon transformed visions into miracles, and found followers to guaranty them. His object was to gain over some of the wise, more of the weak, and, by their united influence, to prevail over all; and this object he at length attained. But how did he attain it? How did he at first win leaders, and afterwards conciliate and appropriate his conquered enemies? Probably, as the mass of Arabs would deem his pretensions unfounded, the wiser portion would demand some proof of the divine commission of *Muhammad,* in preference to *Omaîyah.* To secure the silence and favour of these was the prophet's aim; and, but for their aid, his enterprise would either not have succeeded, or been brought to nothing upon the event of his death. This is a subject of great interest; but can here be but superficially sketched and hinted at.

The best method of arriving at some confident conclusion in this inquiry is, to endeavour to enter into some individual detail. To examine the state of thought and feeling in different individuals, is the best criterion of the state of general sentiment. It is to be regretted that our means of conducting such an examination into the springs of early Muhammadanism are in comparison so limited. The Korán contains little besides hints and riddles; and the stream of tradition cannot be regarded as perfectly unsullied. Perhaps, however, the main points of interest may be depended upon.

Premising that our facts can be only stated with brevity, with little detailed explanation, the following may probably merit our attention. When Muhammad retired to the cave in the mountain Hará (حرا), previous to the first alleged revelation of Gabriel, he was *accompanied by his family or some of his household* (اهله); and upon his assumption of the prophetical office, his wife Khadijah consulted her uncle, Warakah-Ibn-Nawfal (ورقه بن نوفل) a Christian, who could read the Law and the Gospel, upon the subject of her husband's pretensions. Warakah, it is said, having consulted the sacred books, replied, That Muhammad was that person whose advent the Law of Moses predicted, and was the prophet of his nation :—

لقد جاءه الناموس الاكبر الذي كان ياتي موسي بن
عمران و انه نبي هذه الامة

But it does not appear that Warakah embraced his kinsman's religion.

The prophet having thus opened his commission, proceeded to solicit converts; but of the circumstances attending the conversion of his first partizans, it is evident that we can possess no record or tradition deserving our confidence;—the "thing was done in a corner," and was never brought to light. When, however, the prophet began to excite more attention, and his doctrine and assumptions became more notorious, the various conversions which augmented the number of his friends and supporters would evidently become the objects of remark and history. By examining into the circumstances which attended those later conversions, we shall be enabled, probably, to obtain some retrospective insight into the motives which influenced the first followers of Islám. Hamza, uncle of Muhammad, was violently enraged by the report of certain insulting expressions used against his nephew. He sought Abú Jahl, the alleged author of the injury, and, after a violent altercation, wounded him, and thus excited the vengeance of his clan. This was the cause (says Abul Feda) which completed the conversion to Islám of Hamza. Al Abbás, another uncle of the prophet, had always zealously protected him from the attacks of the

Koraish, without, however, accepting him as a prophet. It was Al Abbás who conducted the negociations with the inhabitants of Medína on behalf of his nephew, in course of which he, as if it were a matter of no moment, addresses the latter as "the Apostle of God." After the flight to Medína, Al Abbás returned to Mecca, and at the battle of Bedr was taken prisoner by the Moslems, and presented to Muhammad. When we hear again of him, after a short interval, he had become a convert. Few more converts appeared for some time. Meanwhile, the prophet obtained repeated victories over the neighbouring tribes, especially the Jewish Arabs, by which he enriched his followers, and consolidated his authority. By presenting himself before Mecca, he had exhibited the force, number, and enthusiasm of his gallant followers; and in the eighth year of the Hijra, Khalid and Amr deserted, and joined him. The capture of Mecca soon followed, and the conversion of Abú Sufián presents some remarkable particulars. Muhammad's army, when he drew near to the city, amounted to ten thousand men. The capture of the place being now inevitable, Al Abbás began to be desirous to secure the safety of his kinsmen and friends there. He greatly desired (says Abul Feda) to meet with some straggler, by whom he might certify the Koraish of the utter helplessness of resistance, and advise them to submit by a voluntary surrender to the army of the victorious prophet. Advancing from the camp for this purpose, he met with Abú Sufián himself, accompanied by some of the principal Koraish, who had come out to reconnoitre. Al Abbás, in few words, explained the danger, and besought Abú Sufián to ride on, and claim from Muhammad personal immunity. Abú Sufián instantly saw his situation, and obeyed. Whilst riding forward to the prophet's tent, he was perceived by Omar-Ibn-Al-Khattáb, who, with an exclamation of joy at the opportunity offered, declared that he would at once despatch him; but Abú Sufián outrode the fierce zealot, and, coming up to Muhammad, begged his life; Omar arriving immediately after, with an entreaty for permission to despatch him. To the intercession of Al Abbás, however, Muhammad replied, "I promise him safety. Bring him hither to me, Al Abbás, to-morrow." Al Abbás, departing, entertained the chief, and the following day presented him to the prophet. "How!" said Muhammad, "is it not now time for thee, O Abú Sufián! to know that there is no god but God?" That truth, he replied, I acknowledge. But woe unto thee! said Muhammad; is it not time that thou shouldst also know that I am the Prophet of God? To this he replied, Be thou unto me as my father and my mother; but as to that other thing, I feel something within me that rejects it. Al Abbás here exclaimed, For heaven's sake, say the Confession! your head will assuredly be struck off. Upon this, Abú Sufián cried out the required creed or formula of acquiescence in the Musalmán faith. Having done this, the prophet said, "Al Abbás, go with Abú Sufián to the narrow pass of the valley, and let him behold the army of God." O Apostle! replied Al Abbás, he loves glory. Will you, then, grant my wish, and give him some especial privilege, whereby he may receive honour among his people? To this the prophet answered, "Whoso entereth the abode of Abú Sufián, he is secure. Whoso entereth the Temple of the Kaaba, he is secure. Whoso closeth his own gate, he is secure. Whoso entereth the house of Hakím-Ibn-Hazám, he is secure." After this, Al Abbás proceeded with his kinsman to the lower part of the valley, where the prophet's army passed in review before him. When the veteran troops of the immediate followers of Muhammad passed by, Abú Sufián was struck by their martial appearance. Who is this? said he. That is the Apostle of God, with the Helpers and the Fugitives, was the reply. Truly, said Abú

Sufián, the kingdom of thy brother's son hath now become a *great kingdom*. Ill betide thee! rejoined Al Abbás; you mean to say, the *prophetical rank* of my brother's son? O, ay! replied Abú Sufián, certainly.

Omar-Ibn-Al-Khattáb, the future Khalíf, to whom allusion has just been made, was a much earlier convert. He had resolved to kill Muhammad, but was dissuaded by a friend from a design which would have brought upon his head the irreconcilable vengeance of the prophet's powerful clansmen. At the same time he was advised rather to reserve his displeasure for his own sister, who, with her husband, had embraced Islám. To them Omar repaired in a rage; but the interview ended in his own conformity to the new religion. It is remarkable that Muhammad is said to have prayed for the conversion either of Abú Jahl, or of Omar, in order to strengthen his own authority against the attacks of the Koraish, and replace the loss of his uncle and protector, Abú Tálib.

The above instances present specimens of different converts; and into one of them may possibly be resolved most of the individual cases of early assent. After the storm or surrender of Mecca, the principle of compulsion was openly acted upon, and *outward conformity* was a matter of necessity. Some further hints may tend to explain the subject of preceding acquiescence and following zeal. Our facts are but slight; yet they may indicate the course of influential feeling. Umaiyah, father of Abú Sufián, died shortly after the battle of Bedr. He is said to have been skilful in reading books, and to have examined into the prophet's mission, which, from motives of envy, he denied. *He foolishly imagined that he himself would be the Sent One.* Had Umaiyah been content to hold the second place, his mind was, in other respects, prepared for Muhammadanism. His grandson, *Moáwiyah*, a forced convert, succeeded in wresting from the family of Muhammad himself all the splendid fruits of their founder's laborious fraud and success. A Meccan, named Makías, was resolved to revenge the death of a brother, a Moslem, killed by one of the Helpers, by mischance, the latter having supposed him to be one of the Infidels. Makías came to Medína, professed Islám, and after a time demanded of the prophet the price of blood for his brother. It was paid accordingly; but Makías, shortly after, killed the homicide, fled to Mecca, and there denounced Muhammadanism. At the surrender of Mecca he was one of the proscribed, and was put to death.

In the sixth year of the Hijra, Muhammad,

under the pretence of performing the pilgrimage to the Kaaba, determined to attack Mecca. He encouraged his followers by an alleged vision of happy omen; but he was refused admittance into the city, and for some reason declined to attack it; and entering into a truce, in the preliminary forms of which he consented to waive his prophetic title, he returned to Medína, to the deep vexation and disgust of his followers.

The circumstances attending these two occurrences would convince Muhammad of the necessity of diverting or destroying the feeling of clanship, and of the attachment of his countrymen and followers to the sacred customs and rites connected with the Kaaba. It is to be noted, that Muhammad, shortly after this, married by proxy the daughter of Abú Sufián, chief of Mecca. He had emigrated into Ethiopia with her husband, one of the early professors of Islám, who there embraced Christianity, and died. One of the Medinían Helpers professed to have received, by revelation, the precept of the *vivá voce* summons to prayer, as distinguished from the clappers of the Christians and the trumpets of the Jews. This revelation the prophet admitted and adopted. After the violation of the truce by the Meccans, the prophet resolved to march upon the city with all his forces before they had time to make preparation for effectual resistance; but one *Hátib*, a fugitive, sent a letter to the Koraish by a slave named Sara, informing them of the approaching expedition. This letter Muhammad intercepted, and called upon Hátib to explain his treacherous proceeding. The latter asserted his constancy in the faith; but declared that he wished to concilitate the Koraish of Mecca, in which city his family and children remained; adding his conviction of the approaching destruction of the Koraish. Omar upon this, crying out that Hátib was a hypocrite, desired leave to cut off his head; but Muhammad refused, and observed, It may be that God does reveal himself to those who fought at Bedr.

Abdulláh-Ibn-Saad was a writer of the Korán, under the illiterate prophet. He was accused of corrupting (probably by interpolating) the sacred signs; and, subsequently flying to Mecca, he renounced Islám. Upon the capture of the city, it was with the utmost difficulty that his brother scribe, Othman (afterwards Khalíf), obtained his pardon from Muhammad. Upon the same occacasion Muhammad ordered a poet, who had satirized him, to be put to death.

Do not the above instances display a politic willingness to admit any pretensions to divine intercommunication which did not interfere with his own supremacy, and a determination to visit with the utmost vengeance any one who should expose his fraud, or throw contempt upon his character? When the prophet's crier ascended the roof of the Kaaba, on the day of the capture, to proclaim the hour of prayer, the vanquished could not refrain from expressions of grief and indignation. Soon after the surrender of Mecca, a tribe of Koraish, named Hawá Zan, (هوازن) dwelling in a valley three miles distant, resolved to oppose the prophet by force of arms. In the conflict that ensued, the Moslem, for a time, gave way: the newly-enforced Meccan converts began to hope an approaching deliverance. Abú Sufián took out his divining arrows, which he had concealed in his quiver, crying out, "The sea alone will stop their flight." Calda exclaimed, "But charms are now useless! (i. e. since the prophetic light has appeared.)" "Be still," exclaimed his father Sufián: "God stop thy mouth! If a man of the Koraish *must* be my master, I would rather that one of the Hawázenites should lord it over me." The conflict ended, however, in the defeat of the hostile tribe, who fled and took refuge in the city of Táíf (طايف), a small rich city, at some distance east of Mecca. This place had incurred Muhammad's especial displeasure. At an early period he had attempted to obtain that footing in Táíf which he subsequently effected in Medína; his sagacious mind clearly perceiving the advantages of a *point d'appui;* but he was dismissed with some contempt. "If," said the Táífian chieftain, "thou art indeed the Apostle of God, we are not worthy to converse with thee: if thou speakest falsely, we waste our time in addressing thee." This city was now, however, compelled, after some resistance, to yield to the prophet-victor; the Hawázenites were taken captive; their chief embraced Islám; and they were dismissed with the forfeiture of their goods. The apostle hereupon, with consummate art, resolved to convince by bribes those brave men whom he could not fully bend by force; and he divided a great portion of the rich booty amongst that very Abú Sufián,* and the other Meccan Koraish, who had so lately displayed such distaste and disaffection to his recent authority. He left Mecca soon after, on his return to Medína, appointing, as governor of the latter city, a youth, *nephew of Abú Sufián,* and at the same time selecting Moáwiyah, *son* of Abú Sufián, and a man of consummate abilities, to be his secretary, and writer of the Korán. We hear no more of the race of Umaiyah, but as confirmed *professors* of Islám, although

* See Note.

generally but lax observers of its required duties, and scanty partakers in its peculiar prejudices.

Jealousies soon arose respecting *Alí.* When the prophet set off on his unfortunate expedition into Syria, he left Alí at Medína. It is (said some) that he may not be a burden; probably alluding to Alí's love of ease. Alí complaining of this, the prophet said, No; I leave thee as my vicar; but be content to be the Aaron to Moses; for no prophet shall there be after me. He expressed a similar sentiment to Abú Bekr, who, upon setting out with a message from the prophet to Mecca, said, O Apostle of God! will any divine revelation be made from God to me? By no means, replied the latter. No divine command shall arrive unto me, which shall not be published either by me, or by some man from me. Be content, Abú Bekr, that you were with me in the cave, and were my comrade at the fish-pool. I am content, replied Abú Bekr. It was probably some feeling of jealousy on the part of Alí or Ayesha, which, during the prophet's last illness, interrupted his design of writing a final book.

The apprehensions of Muhammad respecting rival prophets were verified during the latter period of his life. Musailama and Al Aswad (the latter of whom gained over the greater portion of Arabia Felix) both asserted the prophetical character. Al Aswad was slain whilst the prophet was upon his death-bed; but it was only by the prompt and vigorous exertions of Abú Bekr and Alí that the faction of the former was entirely suppressed.

May we not trace, in these brief notices, somewhat of the effects of a fixed and settled *design*, acting upon the spirit of *clanship*, *interest*, and *fear?* Can we not even detect an artful system of *fraud* gradually initiating others into its mysteries, and admitting them to share its benefits? But then this fraud and this design were employed in guiding towards a desired direction a current of feeling and prejudice which previously prevailed. Many an Arab would acknowledge the probability of the mission of some Arab prophet. To take the next step, and to allow Muhammad to be that prophet, he was either allured or compelled. It would seem almost probable that Muhammad scarcely obtained a convert who can be called, in the strict sense of the word, *sincere*. In truth, Muhammad himself appears to have vacillated in the details of his plan. The Korán is full of hesitation,* retraction, and evasion. He modified his system when expediency or conciliation required; but we are

* See note.

ignorant of the precise nature of his original design. We know, however, that if that design ever included the aggrandisement of his own family, it did not entirely succeed: his immediate successors appear to have been little more than ecclesiastical republican chiefs; and when a more extensive authority was established, it was in the person of Moáwiyah, a man whose conduct displayed so entire an insincerity in religious belief, and so much contempt for such of the prophet's family who were neither ambitious nor able, as to incur the suspicion and dislike even of the ignorant fanatics he governed, and, by outrunning the reigning spirit, laid the foundation of the future re-action which dethroned his race. Perhaps Muhammad was a nice judge of character, and knew well whom to admit into his mysterious councils and deeply-laid plans: he may have perceived that no one, even of his own family, would long continue to wield his dominion, unless he possessed the capacity to understand, and the skill to maintain, those arts by which it was at first constructed.* However this be, there is little doubt that the more we investigate the subject, the more we shall be inclined to believe that Muhammad fired a train already laid, and at

* See note.

a favourable crisis aroused a grand re-action of the Asiatic or Semitic principle, more especially as it existed among the Terahite and Ishmaëlite races. The world has twice or thrice arrived at a crisis which has terminated by the direction of the Supreme Ruler in some extraordinary change. At the time when the great Author of Christianity appeared, such a crisis had arrived: * the world was ripe for change. Had no divine revelation then existed, it is not at all to be imagined that this spirit of change would have originated a better system of religion and morals than then prevailed. On the contrary, the fraudful mysteries of the later Heathen philosophy exhibit far darker spells—the elaborate wickedness of seared and reprobate minds—than can be traced in the lighter superstitions of early mythology. The preparedness of the world, however, for some alteration, was remarked by the early Christians and the heathen sophists; the latter of whom probably invented the tale which represents Apollonius Tyaneus as lamenting his hard fate in having lived *after* Christ, instead of *before* him; but for which the world would have obeyed another master, and followed *his* doctrines. If, then, we may be allowed to speculate upon the

* See note.

possible consequences of a change in the moral government of the world, as we are permitted to reason upon the effects of an alteration in the active laws of physics; suppose that the introduction of Christianity had been delayed for a season; is it not, under all circumstances, highly probable that the religion of the *Jews* would have been very widely known?* is it not very probable that it would have been also appreciated and admired? We argue very much in the dark, indeed; for we know not how far Providence *designed* the books of the Old Testament to be dispersed, or whether it was his will to dispose the minds of the heathens to receive the truths contained in them. But in the main, it may well be assumed that truth, beauty, and piety would not be exhibited in vain. Yet, to the entire reception of the whole of the Jewish law by the heathens, insurmountable obstacles would exist; obstacles of a civil nature, as well as others proceeding from the distaste naturally felt towards so pure and perfect a law of morals and obedience. Perhaps, therefore, men might have settled down into a half-dreaming assent to the general truths which the Law revealed;—an assent mingled and corrupted with the Jewish and Pagan traditions.

* See Hor. Sat. iv. lib. i.

Under such circumstances, might it not be possible that many "false prophets and false Christs" would have started up in the various sections and among the various nations of the world, who, modifying their doctrines by the varying shades of popular feeling and prejudice, yet not losing sight entirely of the Hebraic ideas of religion, would "deceive many?" The perversion of truth is often more convenient and acceptable than direct falsehood, supposing the antecedent influence of prejudice or interest to be equal. The population of British India may, before any great period shall elapse, be imbued with a general knowledge of the history and truths of Christianity, and a general conviction of the folly of their own superstitions. Called upon to decide, yet unwilling to yield, they will then be precisely in a state which will dispose them to listen favourably (unless the Great Disposer of events shall ordain another result) to the invitations of any plausible system which shall profess to reconcile the outline of nominal Christianity with the opposing prejudices of deep-rooted pride, and ancient, endeared principles of distinction and caste.

Muhammadanism, probably, would not have flourished so long but for certain renewed impulses. The dissensions between the Ommiades and Abbassides rendered it the interest of the latter (as well as that of the Fátemite Khalífs of Egypt) to keep up the spirit of fanatical Islámism; and in the tenth and eleventh century, the fierce and hardy Turks conquered the degenerate sons of the prophet, and reunited his decaying stronghold of imposture, by embracing the faith of their prostrate foes. But for these circumstances, the Korán and its author might now have been almost forgotten amidst the gloom of the dark ages. Muhammadanism is now again breaking up and dissolving—it is to be hoped effectually and finally.

The present is not the proper opportunity for discussing the best means of winning the Moslems to Christianity. Perhaps any lengthened observations on the subject are not needed. Experience now begins to assure us that preliminary arguments upon these occasions are of no great importance. Men are individually nearly similar in passion and feeling, under all institutions; and the readiest way of influencing them will be found to place the sacred truths of the Gospel plainly before them, and so leave that manifestation of the truth to commend itself to the conscience. In these matters, therefore, a practical knowledge of the Moslem character will be the best guide in forming a judicious plan of proceeding. We may, however, remark, that Muhammadanism is a Judaic heresy, slightly Christianized. It is analogous with the Law rather than with the Gospel; yet it differs from Judaism in the grand point—believing Christ and Muhammad to be both of them Messiahs;—the latter the final one, who is never to be followed by any other. Perhaps, after all, however, the belief of the Messiah's future advent is rather the ostensible than the real tenet of modern Judaism. In arguing with Jews and Moslems, therefore, Bishop Kidder's rules may be judiciously observed.* The missionary also, becoming for the time a Moslem Moolla, may introduce discussion upon their own theology in their own way; and, amidst the perplexity of the doctors, dexterously sow the seed. He should remember that the peculiarities of Islám are not contained in the Korán alone: tradition, and the authoritative decisions of the most esteemed Imáms and Moollas, complete the otherwise defective system. Acquainting himself with these, as well as with the opinions maintained by the various sects and schools, he may learn to argue not so much in the logical method of modern refinement, as in the authoritative style of ancient simplicity, when reason did not disdain

* See Sale's Preface.

to borrow light and direction from imagination, nor failed in that way to arrive at truth. If, by exposing the absurdities of Islám, he may induce the acute Moslem to feel some doubts as to the soundness of his belief, he will have gained a point which may be of great service to the cause. But before we can do any thing, we must overcome that barrier of pride and bigotry which stands in the way of all argument or discussion whatever. Education partly, and the decay of fanaticism partly, will, we trust, effect this object; will afford us the means of entrance into the closed understanding and heart, and enable us silently to impart that knowledge which will burst forth into conviction at length, when "the people shall be made willing in the day of His power."

NOTES.

Page i. "*His Names are too high to be computed,*" &c.—The Muhammadans reckon up ninety-nine names, expressive of the various attributes of God. By these words the author would seem to intimate that he held the orthodox or moderate opinion respecting the essence and attributes of the Deity, asserting that the subject is beyond human definition, in contradistinction to the heretic schools of the Mutazilites, who denied the eternity of God's attributes, and confounded them with his essence, saying that he knew by his knowledge, but that his knowledge was his *essence*, &c. These heretics ran into innumerable subtleties upon this subject, as well as upon Predestination, Free Agency, Origin of Evil, &c. &c.

Ibid. "*The glorious Pilgrimage, the accomplishment of the Divine Precept.*"—The Pilgrimage to Mecca is positively enjoined as an act of *Muhammadan* devotion in chapter ii. of the Korán. "Perform the pilgrimage of Mecca, and the visitation of God; and, if ye be besieged, send that offering which shall be the easiest, and shave not your heads until your offering reacheth the place of sacrifice." By shaving the head, the pilgrim signified the completion of his vow: thus the Nazarite, in the Mosaic Law, terminated his separation (Numbers, c. vi. v. 13. et seq.): "And this is the law of the Nazarite, When the days of his separation are fulfilled, he shall be brought unto the door of the tabernacle of the congregation, and shall offer his offering unto the Lord,...and shall *shave* the head of his separation at the door of the tabernacle of the congregation, and shall take the hair of the head of his separation and put it in the fire which is under the sacrifice of the peace-offerings." The conditions of the Nazaritic separation are curious: "He shall separate himself from wine and strong drink, and shall drink no vinegar of wine, nor vinegar of strong drink; neither shall he drink any liquor of grapes, nor eat moist grapes, or dried. All the days of his separation shall he eat nothing that is made of the vine-tree, from the kernels even to the husk." Not only were the Muhammadans inclined to pay great regard to the sayings of those "who had received the Scriptures before them" (Korán *passim*), in matters not opposed to their own religion, or upon customs already received and popular among themselves, but they have also enrolled among their most authorized traditions many quotations (probably by Jewish converts to Islám) from the Old Testament. Thus it is not unlikely that the above verses may have come to the knowledge of the fanatical madman, the Khalíf Hákim-Biamr'-íllah, and have induced him to carry on, among his other fantastic acts of tyranny, his insane opposition to the sale or culture of grapes, under every form. He destroyed an immense quantity, both fresh and dried. Hákim* was son of a Christian slave, and nephew of *Orestus*, bishop of Jerusalem.

* See note B, at the end.

Page ii. "*The Baitu-l-Harám.*"—"The Venerable and Peculiar House;" *i. e.* the Temple of the Kaaba at Mecca; so called because it is one of the spots consecrated by the especial manifestations of the Deity himself.

Page ii. "*Praise be to Him who by night brought his servant from the Venerable Mosque to the Mosque Al Aksá.*"—These words commence the seventeenth chapter of the Korán, entitled the Night-journey.

Page iii. "*One of his most perfect creatures.*"—The Muhammadans assert that Jesus was born without sin, and their prophet was purified from original sin in his childhood.

Page vi. "*Lord of the first and the last prophets.*"—Muhammad, on the night of his journey to heaven, was saluted as chief by all the prophets and apostles. He is named 'lord of the first and last,' on account of his pre-eminence over both the prophets of the Law, and the apostles of the Gospel.

Page vii. A change from the first to the third person.

Page xii. "*On the third of Shabán, in which lights begin to be divided.*"—Probably meaning, when night and day begin to approach more nearly to equality. The third of Shabán, in the year of the Hijra 874, answers to the middle of March, A.D. 1470.

Page xiii. "*Near to Sohá;*" *i. e.* nearly equal to Sohá in beauty. Sohá is a very small star in the constellation of the Great Bear.

The reader may here be reminded that the two grand questions of Muhammadan controversy relate to matters of Discipline and of Doctrine. The disputes on discipline turn chiefly upon the right of succession to the Khiláfat, and the office of supreme Imám. The orthodox party, in the main, regard that office as limited in power, (and, in fact, the Khalífs were originally by no means possessed of irresponsible authority,) and not *jure divino* the right of Muhammad's immediate descendants. Their opponents assert the indefeasible claim of Alí and his posterity to the universal Khiláfat, and consider the maintenance of his pretensions to be an indispensable part of religious belief. The differences, in matters of doctrine, refer, for the most part, to the Essence and Attributes of the Deity, and to the questions of Freewill and Predestination. Some maintain the absolute singularity of the Deity, declaring that to ascribe Necessary Attributes to him, is in effect to assimilate or liken him to creatures, since (we may suppose they argue) it is only by adding infinity to *our own* notions of perfect Justice, Wisdom, &c. that we can arrive at any idea of the Wisdom or Justice of God. Some, on the contrary, consider the Attributes of the Deity as in fact his Essence. The shades of opinion upon this subject are innumerable. With respect to Freewill and Predestination, the vulgar opiniòn, countenanced by the Korán, is strongly in favour of the dogmas of Necessity and Fate; yet the doctors modify the doctrine by their tenet of *Acquisition.* God, they say, decrees Power and Will. He decrees also all our actions; but the *concurrence* of power and will with actual Deed and Performance, is of man's freewill, by which he *acquires* and takes hold of an action which before existed only in God's decrees unconnected with him. A man, for example, pressed by necessity, has it in his power to commit a theft. Now, in general, the Will of that man to supply his necessity, and the Power occasionally of so supplying it, are both decreed by God. Moreover, that very action of theft was decreed to happen; but the concurrence of that man's decreed will and power with that decreed action is the man's own acquisition or act. This argument (which only transfers the difficulty) is stated in various ways and with endless modifications. In truth, the discussions upon both these subjects are interminable. Other points of discrepancy relate to the eternity, or non-eternity, of the Korán, the rank of Muhammad, the comparative excellence of the Kiblah (or point towards which the face is turned in the act of praying), of Mecca or Jerusalem, &c. &c.

The following Works are quoted in the MS. originals. There are also several others, whose titles are expressed too indefinitely to render an exact transcription useful for any purpose of reference.

مثير الغرام by Shaháb-Uddín-Abú-Mahmúd. The first word appears to be derived from the root ثار, which in Conj. iv. signifies, "to stir up dust as by the wind—to scatter dust into the air;" and the other from غرم only used in Conj. iv. "to divide into small particles." Hence the title of the work may be rendered, "The Stirrer-up of Minute Subtleties;" or, more freely, "The Minute Text-Sifter." It is evidently a favourite theological work. The Translator cannot find the *precise* name of the author or the work in Casiri Biblioth. Escurial.

الرَّوض المغرس by Taj-Uddín,—"The Gardens of the Circus, or of Exercise." فرس signifies "to be skilful in horsemanship—to be a good equestrian."

كتاب الانس في فضايل القدس by Bíhá-Uddín, — "Book, or Writing, of Cheerful Communion with the Excellences of the Holy Places, or Saints."

الجامع المستقصي by Abú-l-Kásim, "The Carefully-compiled Volume," on the Masjidu-l-Aksá.

كتاب باعث للنفوس الي زيادة القدس المحروس By Barhán-Uddín-Al-Kazárí,—"Writing or Book of the Stirring up Souls to the Visitation of the Guarded Holy Spots."

كتاب المستصفي by Bíhá-Uddín,—"The Select or Lucid Writing."

تسهيل المقاصد لزوار المساجد by Shaháb-Uddín, surnamed الافقهسي Al Afkahsí,—"A Smoothing of the Road for Pilgrims to the Mosques." It is in the Escurial Collection.

جزؤ لطيف "The Elegant Volume," by Abúl-Hassan-Al-Málikí.

اعلام الفضايل الشام by Barhán-Uddín,—"Notices of the Wondrous Privileges of Syria."

There is another مثير الغرام "Upon the Pilgrimage to Abraham's Tomb," by Ishak-Ibn-Ibrahim. Al-Tadmírí, Tadmor, or Palmyra, was the name given, not only to the celebrated city of Zenobia, but also to one in Moorish Spain.

مناظرة لبعض اليهود Perhaps, "Mirrors, or Looking-glasses, for certain Jews:" but the points are confused in the two MSS. It is by Abú Aliat.

There is an Abul Faraj also mentioned, (*possibly* the author of "The Dynastics,") as Jerusalem was an object of veneration to Christians as well as Jews. *Omad*, secretary of Salah-Uddín, wrote a work upon that Sultan's reign in very difficult Arabic. He is frequently quoted in the ninth chapter.

Page 2. "*The Holy Spirit Gabriel.*"—The Muhammadans assert that by the Holy Spirit, mentioned in the Christian Scriptures, is intimated the angel Gabriel. Thus, in the Korán, chap. ii. "We gave evident miracles to Jesus the son of Mary, and strengthened him with the Holy Spirit."

Page 4. It is not called "the Venerable," or Forbidden Place; that being appropriated to the territory and the temple of Mecca, from which infidels are excluded; whereas they may approach Jerusalem, although they may not enter the Mosque of Omar.

Page 5. "*The Hidden Book.*"—The Korán was supposed to have existed from all eternity upon the preserved table of God's decrees; there remaining hidden until brought down, in parcels, by Gabriel to Muhammad.

Page 7. The "*Revealed Words,*" here quoted, were probably corruptions of Exodus xii. 11, 12. and xxix. 43. Psalm xcv. 8. Ezekiel xliii. 12. &c.

Ibid. "*The figs and the olives.*"—An allusion to the opening verses of the ninety-fifth chapter of the Korán, "By the fig and the olive, and by Mount Sinai, and by this territory of security," &c. &c.

Page 10. "*In the Psalms.*"—Psalm xxxvii. 11, 29. Isaiah lx. 21. &c.

Page 11. "*The Holy of Holies, in the seventh heaven, is a counterpart*," &c.—A Talmudic fable. There is a story, referred to by Tertullian, in his third book against Marcion, of a city which had been seen in Judea, suspended in the air, for forty successive days, in the early part of the morning, and said to be the New Jerusalem.—*Bishop Kaye, on Tertullian*, p. 367.

Page 15. "*God called David and Solomon to repentance*."—Yet some authors assert, from the Talmudists, that Solomon was not himself guilty of apostacy, but that one of his dependent demons, fraudulently obtaining his magic signet, assumed his form, and perverted the people in his name.—*Sale's Korán*, vol. ii. page 321.

Ibid. "*In the Holy House, or Baitu-l-Mukaddas, unto Maria, &c. were winter-fruits made to come*," &c.—The Virgin Mary, (the Muhammadans assert,) from a mixture of Jewish traditions and Christian apocryphal fables, was the daughter of Imrám (or Amram), by Hannah, or Ann, daughter of Fakudh. Being barren and aged, Hannah, one day observing a bird feeding its young, became very desirous of children, and prayed to God to grant her issue; promising to dedicate the child to his service in the temple. She had a *daughter, Maria*, who nevertheless was accepted by the priests, entrusted to her uncle Zacharias, and educated in the Temple. Here she was miraculously supplied with summer-fruits in winter, and winter-fruits in summer. After the conception of Christ, Maria was compelled to flee from the persecutions of the Jews. Her travail came upon her whilst leaning against the trunk of a palm-tree. It was a withered tree, and the season was winter; yet it revived at her prayer, shot forth green leaves, and produced ripe fruit; a rivulet, at the same time, starting forth to supply her with drink. She presented her child to the people, who, still continuing to calumniate her, were miraculously reproved by the infant, who declared her innocence and his own divine commission.

Page 16. "*The Strengthener.*"—The Muhammadans would seem to confound the Descent of the Holy Spirit at Christ's baptism, with the Descent of the Angel during his passion. The Arabic language expresses "baptism" by two different words; one simply implying immersion; and the other, corroboration, or confirmation. The practice adopted by the Greek and many Oriental churches, of conjoining the confirming chrism with the baptismal water, may have led to this etymological confusion. It is to be observed, that the Muhammadans draw a distinction between the "Holy Spirit" and "the Paraclete" of the Gospels. The former, they assert to be Gabriel; the latter, Muhammad himself. In drawing this distinction, they may possibly have copied from some Christian heretics. *Montanus*, towards the latter end of the second century, drew a similar distinction between the Holy Spirit and the Paraclete; asserting that he himself was the latter, appointed to perfect the Gospel by the addition of doctrines omitted by our Saviour (*Bishop Kaye's Tertullian*, p. 23); and the *Gnostic heretics* represent a succession of various *angels*, æons, or existences, as partakers of the nature of the Supreme Deity. Simon Magus gave out that he himself was the Holy Spirit. (*Epiphanius, Hæres.* 21. and *Walsh's Essay on Christian Coins*, &c. p. 15.) Yajúj and Majúj, Gog and Magog, now confined in Armenia by a wall constructed by Alexander the Great, will break out shortly before the last day. (Korán, c. xviii. and c. xxi. Ezekiel, c. xxxviii.)

Page 17. "*In the Holy Abode shall be the general gathering,*" &c.—A detailed account of the Muhammadan notions respecting the day of judgment, and the signs preceding it, is to be found in Sale's Preliminary Discourse, page 104 and seqq. The scene of the final reckoning will be (according to our author) the Sacred Land, into which all generations will be miraculously brought in troops, all being compressed in some way, so as just to cover the surface of Palestine; or, the various portions of the earth will be so arranged, that all men will have a clear sight of Jerusalem and the Divine Glory. Forty years before the blast of the trumpet of judgment, all created beings will, at the sound of another blast, either die, or be annihilated, &c.

Ibid. "*O flesh torn from the bones!*" &c.—Ezekiel, c. xxxvii.

Ibid. "*God grant to Solomon.*"—See the next chapter.

Page 19. "*By offering four* rakas."—"On appelle Rika, ou Rikat, une certaine série de rites et de prières qui doivent se suivre selon un ordre invariable; et chaque prière est composée d'un plus ou moins grand nombre de ces Rikas. Voyez Tableau Général de l'Empire Othoman, tome i. p. 165. seqq." (De Sacy, Chrest Arabe, vol. ii. p. 36.)

Page 20. "*Dajjál,*" or "*Antichrist.*"—This passage probably alludes to some floating tradition, founded on Revelations, chap. xii. Dajjál signifies *false*, or *lying*. For an account of the Consecrated Rock, see further, chap. iii.

CHAP. II. The Rabbins, not satisfied with the Scriptural account of the wisdom and greatness of Solomon, have thought fit to represent him as a mighty magician, skilled in the language of birds, and endowed with the power of controlling and directing the genii, or fairies, the afrites, or gnomes, and the evil spirits. These notions are probably of remote antiquity. The celebrity of Solomon spread far and wide in the East. The splendour of the Temple, the riches expended upon it, and the noiseless mode of its construction, were calculated to impress the mind. Solomon's knowledge of natural history would also easily pass for magic among the ignorant; and the natives of Syria, Arabia, and Tyre, would readily exaggerate and misinterpret the Jewish traditions: and thus it is that the Arabians held many wild and absurd opinions respecting him; some of which are to be found in this chapter. The distortion of the Scriptural narrative will be immediately recognised. The unrivalled kingdom, such as no other possessed, which Solomon prayed to God that he would grant him, is referred by the Arabians to his fancied dominion over the unseen powers. The idea of embodying second causes, and making of God's attributes a kind of really existent and active Being, employed in the works of Creation and Preservation, appears to be a very ancient corruption of the true doctrine of angelic natures. The Hebrew word "cherub" would appear to convey some allusion to the effects of the creative Power of the Deity. (Kirby's 'Bridgewater Treatise.') It is a word evidently derived from the verb قَرُبَ Karuba, *propè accessit*, and alludes, perhaps, to the immediately-derived energies of the Supreme Intelligence.

Page 35. "*Put wine in its place.*"—The capture of the Devil by Solomon recalls that passage of Xenophon's Anabasis, lib. ii. c. 2. respecting the Fountain of Midas at Thymbrion in Phrygia, where that ancient king is said to have caught a *Satyr* by mingling the water of the fountain with wine. It is not easy to decide whether this story were borrowed by the Arabian writers from the Greeks, or *vice versa.* Midas, originally a Thracian king, is said to have migrated into Phrygia; but several authors assert that it was in his gardens, in *Macedonia*, that the Satyr was caught. Ælian, in his 'Various History,' introduces a conversation of Silenus with the Phrygian Midas; and Ælian, it would seem, has been translated into Arabia. On the other hand, Ælian copies from the Chian Theopompus; which circumstance brings the tradition nearer to Asia Minor. The account given by Servius, from Theopompus, coincides remarkably with the text:—"Is enim apprehensum Silenum a Midæ regis pastoribus dicit crapula madentem et ex ea soporatum, illos dolo aggressos dormientem vinxisse, postea vinculis sponte labentibus, liberatum de rebus naturalibus et antiquis Midæ interroganti respondisse." The skill of this Satyr in antiquity and natural history tallies with the account of Solomon's demon. Midas, again, is said to have been a disciple of Orpheus, and to have filled Phrygia with superstitions; and, since the traditions respecting Solomon's general intercourse with spirits, and the knowledge obtained thereby, are confessedly of Asiatic origin, we may upon the whole, perhaps, refer this particular instance of this intercourse to the same source. (See Xenophon's Anabasis, lib. iii. cap. 2. ed. Schneider, Saxo.) The Satyrs of ancient mythology coincide with the evil spirits of later popular tradition, in many respects;—in their alleged acuteness, their capriciousness, and their unwillingness to converse with men; and the form ascribed by the monkish legendaries of the middle age, to the evil fiends, is evidently taken from the Greek Satyr. The monkish fiends appear to be beings of a more terrific and malicious character than the companions of Pan; but this variation may be accounted for by the comparatively greater barbarity and coarseness which distinguish the middle ages, and also by the effect of climate. The *fairies* of England and Scotland are evidently the same race of beings; yet how much more harmless and friendly is the one class described to be, than the other!

Page 38. See Solomon's Dedication-Prayer, Kings and Chron.

Page 44. The peculiar reverence paid to the Sacred Rock at Jerusalem seems to be one of the many instances of afterthought and addition to Islám since the time of Muhammad. The politic Moáwiyah encouraged this superstition, and directed the fanaticism of his subjects into this new channel, probably from a wish to withdraw their exclusive attention from the cities of Mecca and Medína, where the rival family of Alí chiefly resided. Jerusalem also, so often mentioned in the Jewish and Christian Scriptures, afforded a better field for the pilfering talents of tradition-hatchers than the desert-encircled and distant Mecca. Perhaps, Jewish tradition may also have really preserved the site of the Temple of Solomon. However this may be, the Mosque built by Omar has been embellished and enlarged by many of his successors, and is now one of the most sumptuous specimens of Muhammadan architecture. The following concise description of the Mosque Al Sakhrá, and Al Aksá, are extracted from Russell's 'Palestine,' who follows Alí Bey and others. (Russell's 'Palestine,' p. 171, 172. seqq. and p. 238.):—"The Sakhara is a regular octagon, of about sixty feet a side, and is entered by four spacious doors, each of which is adorned with a porch projecting from the line of the building, and rising considerably on the wall. All the sides are panelled. The centre stone of one panel is square; of another, octagonal; and thus all round, alternately, the sides of each running down the angles like a plain pilaster, and giving an appearance as if the whole were set in a frame. The marble is white, with a considerable tinge of blue; square pieces of the latter being introduced in different places, so as to confer upon the exterior a very pleasing effect. The upper story is faced with small tiles, painted of different colours—white, yellow, green, and blue; some also covered with sentences from the Korán. At the height are seen elegant windows on each side, except where the porches intervene, and there only six. The general appearance is light and beautiful, especially from the mixture of soft colours above, and the delicate tints of the marble in the main body of the structure. The interior fully corresponds to the magnificence and beauty just described. There are twenty-four marble columns placed parallel to the eight sides of the building, and three opposite each side, so as still to preserve the octagonal form. Eight of them are large plain pillars, belonging to no particular order of architecture, and standing opposite to the eight entering angles of the edifice, and deeply indented on the inner side, so that they furnish an acute termination to the octagonal lines within. Between every two of the square columns there are two of a round figure, well-proportioned, and resting on a base: they are from eighteen to twenty feet high, with a sort of Corinthian capital. A large square plinth of marble extends from the top of one column to the other; and above it there is constructed a number of arches, all round, which support the inner end of the roof or ceiling; the outer end resting upon the walls of the building. This is composed of wood, or plaster, highly ornamented with a species of carving, and richly gilt. This Temple owes its name and existence to a large irregular massy stone, of an oblong shape, which is in the centre of the edifice. It is a portion of the calcareous rock on which the city is built, and which prevails in the other mountains in the neighbourhood of Jerusalem, having very much the appearance of being part of the bed that might have been left when the foundation of the building was levelled. It rises highest towards the S. W. corner, and falls abruptly at the end where are the prints of the prophet's foot. It is irregular on the upper surface, as when broken from the quarry. It is enclosed with a wooden rail, four feet high, every where in contact with the stone. Al Aksá is an inferior building, within the same enclosure. Between the two there is a beautiful fountain, which derives its name from a clump of orange-trees overshadowing the water. The mosque is composed of seven naves, supported by pillars and columns. At the head of the centre wall is a fine cupola: two other naves branch off at right angles to the principal body of the edifice. Before it is a portico of seven arches in front, and one in depth, supported by square pillars. Alí Bey observes that the great centre nave of Al Aksá is 162 feet long by 22 broad. It is supported on each side by seven arches, lightly pointed, resting upon cylindrical pillars in the form of columns, but without any architectural proportions, with foliaged capitals which do not belong to any order. The fourth pillar, to the right of the entrance, is octangular and enormously thick, called 'the Pillar of Sidi Omar.' The walls rise thirteen feet above the tops of the arches, and contain two rows of twenty-one windows each. The roof is timber, without being vaulted: the cupola is supported by four large arches resting upon four square pillars: it is spherical, with two rows of windows, and is ornamented with Arabesque paintings of great beauty: its diameter is equal to that of the centre nave. Alí Bey observed that the curtain suspended over the Sakhara, which is of green and red silk, was very dusty. Burckhardt remarks that the Holy House is a group of buildings, erected at different periods of Islám, and in the then prevailing taste. It is not one mosque, but a group of mosques."

Chap. IV. This chapter contains the traditional dogma of Reduplication; by which is meant, that, within the Holy Abode, the merit and reward of all good words, deeds, and blessings, are multiplied in a certain proportion; nay, that *good* things are actually multiplied, or doubled, in amount as well as effect. By the Reduplication of evil things (evil words or deeds), which also takes place, it is, however, meant to imply only, that the *effect* or *retribution* of such things is doubled, otherwise men might be supposed to be necessarily compelled to commit sin.

Chap. V. In this chapter there is a story, from which Cervantes, doubtless, borrowed. The case which came before the sage governor Sancho, of two men, one of whom hid the entrusted deposit of the other in a stick, and, giving the stick to the claimant to hold, swore that the money had been restored.

Chap. VI. The discussions of the Muhammadan divines, upon disputed points of theology, are often acute and diverting. An amusing instance is given by Sale. (Korán, Preliminary Discourse, p. 219 and seqq.) "The Ashárians are a sect of the Sefátians, and are the followers of Abú-Hasan-al-Ashárí, who was first a Mótazalite, and then scholar of Abú-Alí-Al-Jobbáí; but, disagreeing from his master in opinion as to God's being bound (as the Mótazalites affirm) to do always that which is best or most expedient, left him, and set up a new sect of himself. The occasion of this difference was the putting a case concerning three brothers; the first of whom lived in obedience to God; the second, in rebellion against him; and the third died an infant. Al Jobbáí, being asked what he thought would become of them, answered, that the first would be rewarded in Paradise, the second punished in Hell, and the third neither rewarded nor punished. But what, objected Al Ashárí, if the third say, O Lord! if thou hadst given me longer life, that I might have entered Paradise with my believing brother, it would have been better for me. To which Al Jobbáí replied, that God would answer, I knew that if thou hadst lived longer, thou wouldst have been a wicked person, and therefore cast into Hell. Then, retorted Al Ashárí, the second will say, O Lord! why didst thou not take me away while I was an infant, as thou didst my brother, that I might not have deserved to be punished for my sins, nor to be cast into Hell? To which Al Jobbáí could return no other answer than that God prolonged his life, to give him an opportunity of obtaining the highest degree of perfection which was best for him. But Al Ashárí demanding further, why he did not for the same reason grant the other a longer life, to whom it would have been equally advantageous, Al Jobbáí was so put to it, that he asked whether the Devil possessed him. No, says Al Ashárí; but the master's ass will not pass the bridge; *i. e.* he is posed." This story is taken by Sale from Pococke.

Chap. VII. Several Gates are enumerated in the original, which, as possessing no interest, are omitted.

Page 143. The Musalmáns imagine that our Lord did not himself suffer, but was caught up to Heaven; Judas being substituted and crucified in his room. They therefore disregard all places connected with his crucifixion, burial, or resurrection.

Page 145. The inhabitants of Jerusalem have long suffered an indifferent reputation. Gregory, Bishop of Nyssen, brother of St. Basil, born in Cappadocia A. D. 332. visited Jerusalem, and was much disappointed to find it "a sink of iniquity and debauchery, the seat of envy, malice, adultery, robbery, murder, idolatry, poisoning, and bloodshed, where men assassinated each other for a trifling reward; so that in no place were more murders committed."

Page 146. It is not easy to say to whom this tradition of Dhahák-Ibn-Kais is to be referred; perhaps to some floating notions respecting Archimedes and the defence of Syracuse, or the siege of Tyre by Alexander the Great, or to the defence of Gaza, against the same monarch, by the eunuch Batis. (Mitford, 'Hist. Greece,' vol. ix. p. 381.) It is remarkable that the Tyrians are said to have venerated a Hercules; not the Grecian hero, but one worshipped by the Tyrians many ages before him in a temple the oldest known on earth. (Mitford, quoting Arrian.) Was this the Kaaba of Mecca, or some temple in Tyre constructed upon the model of the Kaaba? Dhahák-Ibn-Kais himself lived in the reign of the Khalíf-Marwán-Ibn-Hákim, the latter part of the seventh century.

Page 148. The talisman of the serpent is evidently a corruption of the Scriptural account of the Brazen Serpent.

Page 149. The prevalent impressions of the Muhammadans, respecting the future destruction of their religion, and the restoration of the Jews, appear to be faint outlines of ancient prophecy impressed traditionally upon the minds of men.

Ibid. The various traditions which introduce Muhammad as prophesying the future deposition of the house of Abú-Sufián from the Khiláfat, the elevation of the family of Al Abbás to the pulpit, and the commencement of that revolution by a revolt in the province of Khorassán, were probably brought forward subsequently to the event. The eventual rule of the *yellow-haired*, or Russians, has for many centuries been currently asserted among the Turks.

Page 159. Abú-Ubaidah is represented as nominating the Governor of Damascus, which city he had himself taken; but this was probably only during his absence, as the appointment belonged to the Khalíf Omar. Yazíd-Ibn-Abú-Sufián was nominated Governor of Damascus by Omar.

Chap. IX. This chapter contains brief notices of the capture of Jerusalem by Omar, the Crusaders, and Saladin. A rapid review is also given of the dissensions between Saladin's surviving family. One of these, Al Kámil, demolished the walls of the Holy City,—a wise and politic measure, for Jerusalem could not offer any important resistance to an invader; nor was it of much value in a political point of view: to maintain any effective garrison there would, therefore, be a useless expense. Al Kámil, subsequently, by ceding the possession of the defenceless city to the Emperor Frederic Barbarossa, (الابروز) Al Abrúz deprived the Western Christians of all pretext, upon religious grounds, of invading his territory. Muhammadan fanaticism, however, rendered such a tenure very insecure, and accordingly the Christians were in a few years surprised by treachery, and expelled. It would seem that there is some doubt whether Omar was actually engaged in the siege of the city *before* its surrender, or came from Medína merely to receive its submission. The object of the author is (it would appear) to maintain that the Treaty of Capitulation signed by Omar is irreversibly binding upon the Moslems and Christians, and not to be repealed by any future and inferior authority. So that the Moslems, in wresting the Holy Abode from the Christians by any means, were not liable to the charge of want of faith.

Page 195. The following lively description of the entrance of the Victorious Crusaders into the Holy City is extracted from William of Tyre:—"Intueri erat amœnissimum, et spirituali plenum jucunditate, quanta devotione, quanto pii fervore desiderii, ad loca sancta fidelis accederet populus; quanta mentis exultatione et spirituali gaudio Dominicæ dispensationis deosculabantur memoriam. Ubique lachrymæ, ubique suspiria, non qualia mœror et anxietas solet extorquere, sed qualia fervens devotio, et interioris hominis consummata lætitia, solet Domino in holocaustum incendere. Erat porrò tam in ecclesia, quàm per urbem universam, tantus populi gratias Domino exhibentis clamor, ut jam quasi usque ad sidera tolli sonus videretur, et de eis merito dictum crederetur, 'Vox lætitiæ et exultationis in tabernaculis justorum.' Fervebant sanè, pio succensa desiderio, per urbem universam opera misericordiæ. Hi Domino confitebantur deflenda quæ commiserant, voto se obligantes ne de cætero deflenda committerent. Illi in senes, valetudinarios, et egentes, profusa liberalitate cunctam erogabant substantiam, pro summis et sufficientibus reputantes divitiis quod hunc vidisse diem sibi fuerat concessum divinitus. Illi flexis nudisque genibus, cum singultibus et præcordialibus suspiriis, loca circuibant venerabilia, lachrymarum cuncta replentes aspergine, quorum vero sermo dirigebatur ad Dominum, 'Exitus aquarum deduxerunt oculi mei.' Quid plura? Difficile est ut nostro comprehendatur sermone, quanta in plebe fideli sanctæ devotionis esset immensitas; certatim enim se mutuo vincere cupientes in operibus pietatis unanimiter desudabant, cœlestis memores beneficii et gratiam præ oculis habentes divinam, quæ tantos eorum labores remunerare dignata est. Quis enim tam ferrei pectoris, quis tam mentis adamantinæ, cujus interiora non liquefierent, cum liceret tantæ peregrinationis fructum carpere dignissimum, et exhibitiæ militiæ numerare stipendia? Quibus tamen mens fuit altior, in arram futuræ retributionis qua sanctos suos se remuneraturum promisit Dominus, id muneris videbatur exhibitum, ut per collationem præsentium munerum, firma sit expectatio futurorum, et per eam quæ hìc peregrinatur Hierusalem, ad eam perveniatur cujus participatio est in idipsum. Porrò episcopi et sacerdotes in ecclesiis consummantes sacrificia orabant pro populo, pro collato beneficio gratias exhibentes."—(*Gesta Dei, per Francos*, p. 760. lib. viii. c. 20.)

"Very pleasant it was, and a source of spiritual delight, to behold with what devotion, with what fervour of pious zeal, did the faithful people approach the holy places; with what exultation of mind, and spiritual joy, they kissed the memorials of the stewardship of the Lord. On all sides are tears, on all sides sobs, not such as sorrow or suffering extort, but such as fervent devotion, and the consummation of delight in the inner man, commonly cause to flame up as a whole burnt-offering to the Lord. Indeed, both in the churches and throughout the whole city, so loud were the thanksgivings which the people offered unto the Lord, that the sound thereof mounted to the sky, and one might well believe that it was of them it had been said, 'The voice of joy and gladness is in the dwellings of the just.' Assuredly works of mercy, lit up by pious zeal, were warmly undertaken throughout the whole city. Here were beheld some confessing unto the Lord those grievous sins which they had committed, binding themselves by vows not to commit such sins again. There were others, who with profuse liberality spent all their substance upon the old, the sick, and the poor, deeming it to be the most surpassing and sufficing wealth, that Heaven had granted them to see this day. There were others, who upon naked knees, with sobs and sighs from the inmost heart, were making the circuit of the venerable spots, who might with truth direct that exclamation to the Lord, 'Mine eyes gush out with water.' But why more? Words of mine can but with difficulty express how great was the immensity of sacred devotion among the faithful people; for with one accord, vying with each other, did they zealously labour mutually to surpass one another in works of piety, mindful of the heavenly gift, and still keeping in view that grace divine, which had vouchsafed to requite their great labours. Whose heart, indeed, could be so steeled,—who could possess so adamantine a spirit, as not to melt within himself, when it was permitted to reap that most worthy fruit of so great a pilgrimage, and to count over the wages of accomplished services and terms of warfare? Some there were, however, of a more exalted spirit, who looked upon the gift thus granted as an earnest of that future recompense wherewith the Lord hath promised to requite his saints; since, from present benefits conferred, we deduce a firm expectation of benefits to come; and since it is through the Jerusalem which is now a stranger upon earth, that we must arrive at the Jerusalem wherein to be a partaker is a reality indeed. The Bishops also, and Priests, were in the churches, accomplishing the sacrifices (i. e. of prayer and thanksgiving) by *praying* for the people, and offering thanksgivings for the blessing imparted."

Page 205. The word translated *bells* may more properly be rendered *clappers*, which, being beaten, gave the signal for assembling in the churches. It is doubtful whether the Christians of Jerusalem possessed metal bells in Omar's time.

Ibid. "*Secret lurking-places*," &c.—Probably confessionals. Since the conquest of Jerusalem by the Crusaders, in A.D. 1099, the Latin church possessed the ascendancy in the city. The variations between the Greek and Roman churches form a frequent subject of remark and animadversion with the contemporary writers: the mode of confession varies considerably. Probably, these controversies, as well as the Eutychian and Monothelite questions, may be scoffingly alluded to by the author in several passages of this chapter.

Page 215. "*Balian-Ibn-Bazán*."—Belianus, or Belian, is a name that occurs in the annals of chivalry. The name of this nobleman was Balian of Ibelin. He commanded the Christians in the absence of the captive king of Jerusalem.

Page 216. "*Church of the Holy Sepulchre.*"—Literally, "The Round Building." The Temple Church in London, the Church of Maplestead in Essex, and the Church of St. Sepulchre in Cambridge, are remaining examples of this form.

Page 234. The Khalíf Othmán is called Dhi Núráin, or Dhú Núráin (possessor of the Two Lights), because he enjoyed the experience of his two predecessors, the first Khalífs, Abú Bekr and Omar, or because, upon his elevation to the Khiláfat, he engaged himself to abide by the precedents they had established.

Page 273. سنجاب Sinjáb, or Sunjáb, is an animal of the sciurus or squirrel genus, whose fur was considered extremely precious, and used to line robes of state.

Page 288. Shaib, or Shuaib, is a prophet, said in the Korán to have been sent to warn the Midianites. He appears sometimes to be confounded with Zacharias son of Barachias, and with Isaiah.

Chap. X. All this is evidently copied from the Gospels, although much corrupted.

Page 305. Abú-Mahmúd-Al-Járí appears to have held the dogma of the necessary singularity of the essence of the Deity. The theologians of this sect asserted that God has no attributes, because, to attribute unto him the qualities of Justice or Mercy, which are themselves separate and distinct qualities, is to introduce a principle incompatible with pure Unity, incapable of division into parts, and thus to resemble the Christians, who ascribe, they pretend, partners unto God.

Page 306. Kaab-Al-Habár, or the Scribe, was a Jewish Rabbi, who was won over to Islám by Omar-Ibn-Al-Khattáb, and proved a most fertile originator of traditions, from his knowledge of the Hebrew Scriptures.

Page 321. By "the Declarers," appears to be intimated, Promulgators of New Revelations.

Page 325. "*The prophetic signet*" was an excrescence, or *wen*, said to be found only on inspired prophets.

Page 357. The remainder of this chapter, not possessing sufficient interest, is not printed.

Page 358. "*Hebron*."—Russell's 'Hist. Palestine' contains the Cave of Machpelah, wherein Abraham and the Patriarchs were interred. It was formerly a Greek church, and is now a mosque. The ascent (says Burckhardt) is by a large and fine staircase, leading to a long gallery, to which the entrance is by a small court. Towards the left is a portico, resting upon small pillars. The vestibule of the Temple contains two rooms; one supposed to be the tomb of Abraham, the other that of Sarah. In the body of the church, between two large pillars to the right, is seen a small recess, in which is the sepulchre of Isaac, and in a similar one, on the left, that of his wife. On the opposite side of the court is a vestibule containing two rooms, in which are the sepulchres of Jacob and his spouse. At the extremity of the portico, to the right, is a door which leads to a long gallery, which is still a mosque. Passing thence, we observe another room, containing the ashes of Joseph, brought from Egypt. All the sepulchres are covered by rich carpets of green silk, magnificently embroidered in gold: those of the wives' sepulchres are of red silk. They are given by the Sultán, and renewed from time to time. Mr. Burckhardt counted nine on the sepulchre of Abraham, one above the other. The rooms which contain the sepulchres are covered with rich carpets; the entrances are guarded by iron gates and wooden doors plated with silver, having bolts and padlocks of the same. More than one hundred persons are here employed in the care of the buildings, &c. &c.

Page 359. "*The Cock in the sky.*"—This is the Celestial Bird, which, as the Musalmáns assert, from the Talmudists, crows every morning, and is heard by angels, animals, and genii, but not by men. By the cessation of this crowing, on the morning of the last day, all rational creatures, except man, will be convinced of the actual arrival of that event. Absurd as this fable is, it is far surpassed in childishness by the tales of its Rabbinical source.

Page 361. Palestine abounds with caverns, which appear to have been useful as reservoirs of water. William of Tyre seems to intimate that Jerusalem itself was thus mostly supplied with water in the time of the first crusade.

Chap. XV. This chapter is omitted, being already recorded in the Korán, and is a mere corruption of the Scriptural account of the destruction of the cities of the plain.

Page 394. There are three Palestines; one whose capital metropolis is Jerusalem; another whose capital is Cæsarea Maritima; a third whose metropolis is Bethsan, or Scythopolis. All Palestine is sometimes confounded with Syria by later writers. Syria-Palestina is the designation used by Herodotus and Arrian. The Talmudists represented the sacredness of their territory, not as stopping short abruptly, but as gradually diminishing and melting away; so that all Syria possessed a portion of sanctity.

Pages 396 and 420. "*To aid the Unitarians.*"—It is by no means easy to define the opinions of the Muhammadan divines upon Christ. Some attribute to him a rank which would appear to be above that of their prophet, although, no doubt, they would evade such a conclusion. None of the orthodox sects entertain the opinion of his simple humanity, at least in the Socinian sense. Many of them allow the doctrine of the Incarnation; but their notions are confused and inconclusive. An obscure passage in our author, which occurs in page 420, seems to imply that he was not free from original sin, since the *impress* of his baptism remained. Muhammad, they say, was purified from all taint, in his early youth, by Gabriel.

Page 404, &c. The Khalíf Abdul-Málik-Ibn-Marwán, often mentioned in the ninth and seventeenth chapters, was of the family of Ommia. He ascended the throne A. H. 65, and died A. H. 86. His son and successor, Al Walíd, built the Masjidu-l-Aksá.

Page 410. "*Hill of the Dropsical.*"—Perhaps alluding to some miracle.

Page 412. In the letter of the Grecian emperor to Al Walíd, the expression "thy father" evidently alludes to Muhammad, both as the originator of the Khalíf's religion, and as his collateral ancestor. By the reference to David and Solomon, the poet intimated that the spiritual ruler was entitled to the property of his subjects, and was supreme referee in all causes; his judgment being final. The passage of the Korán in question contains a story of Solomon's judgment. Some sheep having trespassed in a field, and injured the corn, David thought that the sheep should be forfeited to the owner, in compensation; but Solomon, then only eleven years old, was of opinion that the produce of the sheep only—the milk, lambs, &c.—should be given to the owner, until the amount of the damage was discharged.

Page 414. The head which the architect found was probably that of John the Baptist, mentioned below. Probably he was supposed to be a magician.

Page 421. By the "*Two Moments*" is meant, the moment when all creatures shall perish, at the blast of the trumpet; and the moment, forty years after, when all shall be resuscitated to the final reckoning.

Note A.

(REFERRED TO IN THE TRANSLATOR'S PREFACE.)

Our materials for an account of Jerusalem, from the apostolic period to the capture by the Khalíf Omar-Ibn-Al-Khattáb, are not very abundant. The storm and demolition of the city by Titus are, indeed, accurately described by Josephus; but of the restored city not much is recorded. The earlier Christians, perhaps, did not wish needlessly to excite the jealousy of their persecuting rulers by performing pilgrimages unto those sacred spots; and even after the predominance of Christianity, Jerusalem, being upon the frontiers of the Byzantine empire, was open to attack on the side of Persia and Arabia. It probably always remained an inconsiderable place, chiefly supported by the resort of pilgrims.

Soon after Titus quitted the scene of his success, many Jewish and Christian families returned to dwell among the ruins. Gradually beginning to restore the city, they alarmed Vespasian, who, to prevent any attempts to rebuild the place, established a garrison of 800 men on Mount Zion. He is said also to have put to death all the known descendants of David. In the reign of Trajan, the Jews, still numerous, and not entirely uprooted, revolted, but were defeated. Adrian expelled the Jews from Cyprus. He published an edict, forbidding circumcision, the reading of the law, and the observation of the sabbath. A leader at this time started up to head the desperate Jews. Barchochab (son of a star) asserted himself to be the true Messiah; and, being recommended by a famous Rabbi, Akiba, the Jews rallied round him, and seized the Holy City. Adrian resolved upon their utter destruction. After a desperate struggle, Barchochab was defeated and slain. In the course of this war, it is said that 580,000 were slain. Judea was reduced to a desert. Adrian now built the city which he had long projected; but in such a manner as to confound the topography of the original Jerusalem. This city was called Ælia Capitolina. To mortify and repulse the Christians, Adrian moreover erected a statue of Venus upon the Mount Calvary; another of Jupiter, near the Holy Sepulchre, and consecrated the grotto of Bethlem to Adonis. The Jews were forbidden to enter Ælia; and the statue of a sow was placed over the principal gate. By the establishment of Christianity, Jerusalem was partially restored to importance. Helena, mother of Constantine the Great, visited Ælia, founded the Church of the Holy Sepulchre, discovered, it was said, the true cross, with a number of other relics, and directed the attention of Christian zeal to this interesting and sacred spot. The attempt of Julian the Apostate to rebuild the temple, and its miraculous failure, are well known. In the next century, the recluse and monastic states began to prevail; and Palestine seemed to be a fit place for the retired piety of holy and contemplative men, whether in monasteries or hermitages: many of both were to be found. In the sixth century, Justinian contributed to the beauty of the city; but shortly after this, Palestine and Syria were invaded by Chosroes the Persian. This barbarian sacked Jerusalem, and nearly destroyed it. The Jews on this occasion rose, and, joining the Persians, murdered 90,000 Christians. Not long after this, Abú Ubaidah, lieutenant of the second Khalíf, Omar-Ibn-Al-Khattáb, besieged and took the city, which was thus subjected to the Musalmán yoke. At that time it probably contained but few inhabitants. Under the sway of the two dynasties of Khalífs, the Ommiades and the Abbássides, the Christians of Jerusalem enjoyed comparative security; but the decay of the Khiláfat subjected them to cruel and bigoted tyrants. Achmet, a Turk, who, from being governor of Egypt, had usurped its sovereignty, conquered Jerusalem; but his son being defeated by the Khalíf of Bagdad, the Holy City fell again under that government, A.D. 905. About thirty years after this, Muhammad Ikschid, a Turk, seized Egypt, invaded Palestine, and took Jerusalem. This dynasty was expelled by the Fátemites, who assumed the title of Khalíf and Imám, A.D. 968. (One of these Khalífs, Hákim,* cruelly oppressed the Christians, and demolished the church of the

* See Note B. p. 520.

Holy Sepulchre.) The emir Ortok, towards the end of the tenth century, made himself master of the Holy City. His children were driven out by Mustáli, Khalíf of Egypt. In 1076, Meleschah, third of the Turkish race, took Jerusalem, and ravaged the country. The Ortokites, however, returned, and maintained themselves in the city against Redouan, Prince of Aleppo. They were, however, expelled by the Fátemite Khalífs, who were in possession when the Crusaders arrived.

Ælianus Adrianus, (observes William, archbishop of Tyre,) fourth from Titus, built the city Ælia Capitolina, and in the (Acts of) the Synod of Nice we read, "Let the Bishop of Ælia be honoured by all." "But the city thus built (continues the archbishop) by Adrian varied in site from the original. The whole of the first city was placed upon a steep declivity, in such a way that, of the entire city, one part faced the east, and the other part the south, being founded on one *side* of both Mount Sion and Mount Moriah; the temple only, and the citadel of Antonia, being upon the summit. But Adrian transferred the whole to the top of the mount; so that the scene of our Lord's Passion and Resurrection, which had before been without the walls, were now included within their circuit. The town itself is less than the greater ones, and greater than the middling-sized ones. It is of an oblong figure, longer on one side—a tetragon, but hemmed in on three sides by very deep valleys; on the east by the valley of Jehoshaphat, where there is a church to the Virgin, and also the winter-torrent of Kedron; on the south by the valley of Hinnom, in the lot of Juda and Benjamin; on the west by part of the same valley, where the site of an old fish-pond, famous in the times of the Kings of Judah, is shown. This valley extends unto the upper fish-pool; now (*i. e.* the time of William of Tyre) called 'The Patriarch's Lake,' near the ancient cemetery called 'The Lion's Cave, or Den.' On the north is a flat, even road, leading to the city. The city is built upon two mountains, whose summits are within the walls; they are divided by a moderately deep valley, which also divides the city into two parts. Of these, the western is called Sion (which name is also sometimes applied to the whole), and the eastern, Moriah. On the western mountain, upon the summit, is built the church of Sion, near to which is the tower of David, a citadel that commands the town. On this western mount, but upon the eastern declivity thereof, is the church of the Holy Resurrection. It is of a round form: the summit of the mountain overlooks and renders it less conspicuous: it has a roof of timber, built up to a great height, and with wonderful workmanship, contrived so as to present the form of a round lantern, whence the needful light pours into the church: right beneath is our Lord's Sepulchre. The Golgotha, and the place where the Cross was discovered, as well as the place where the Body was anointed, were formerly small oratories, *without* the church. But the Crusaders enlarged the church, so as to include them. Upon the other mountain, the eastern, and upon its southern declivity, is the Temple of the Lord. It is somewhat of the following form:—There is a broad space, scarcely a bow-shot in length, and about as much in width, quadrangular, and contained by equidistant sides: it is surrounded by a strong wall, of a moderate height, entered on the western side by two gates: one, named 'The Beautiful,' is that near which Peter strengthened the ankles of the lame man, and set him upright; the name of the other is not positively known: on the north side there is one; on the east is another, which is, even to this day, named 'The Golden Gate:' on the southern side is that royal abode commonly named 'The Temple of Solomon.' Over each gate which adjoined the city, and at each corner of the above-named superficies, were very high towers, which, at certain hours, the priests of the Saracenic superstition were wont to ascend, thence inviting the people to prayer: some of these remain; some, by various accidents, have been levelled. Within these precincts no one was permitted to dwell; no one even to enter but with naked and washen feet; to enforce which, keepers were placed at every gate. In the midst of this area, thus enclosed, there is again another flat space raised higher, in like manner quadrilateral, and equidistant from the outer wall. To this area there is an ascent, on the western and southern side, of two steps; on the last, of one. In each angle were small oratories; some only of which now remain. In the midst of this last area is built a Temple, of an octagonal form, and octolateral, adorned, both within and without, with marble slabs (or panels) and mosaic work. It has a spherical roof, ingeniously covered with lead. Both of these spaces, the large outer and inner, and the contained area, are paved with white stone, so that all the rain-water, which descends abundantly in the winter season from the Temple and other buildings, flows clear, and unmingled with dirt, into cisterns or tanks, of which there are several. Within the Temple, in the centre, within the inner row of pillars, there is a Rock, rather higher than the floor. Beneath, hollowed from the the same rock, is a cave, over which the Angel is said to have sat, and sheathed his sword; thus arresting the pestilence inflicted for David's sin in numbering the people. This spot was purchased for six hundred sigli (σιγλοι) of gold, of just weight, and an altar built. All this existed thus when we entered the city; and, for fifteen years subsequently, the rock remained open and uncovered. Afterwards, those who presided over that place covered it with white marble, erecting an altar upon it, and building a choir, wherein the clergy might celebrate the divine offices."—(*Willielmus Tyrensis*, c. 8.)

Note B. (Page 488.)

(From De Sacy, 'Chrestomathie Arabe,' compared with Abulpharagius (Pococke). De Sacy's author is Taki-Uddín-Makrízí.)

The reign of the Khalíf Hákim Bíamr'-Illáh presents a curious example of the miseries of despotic rule in the hands of a capricious and extravagant prince, as well as a specimen of the practical effects of Muhammedan fanaticism and controversy. Hákím Bíamr'-Illáh-Abú-Alí-Mansúr was the son of Azeez Bílláh Nizár, one of the Fátemite Khalífs of Egypt, whose territory included Syria and Palestine. His father, Azeez Bílláh, appears to have been a mild and generous monarch. His mother was of Christian extraction, sister to Orestus, bishop of Jerusalem. The consequences of this last circumstance, probably, had considerable effect in the formation of the character of the future Khalíf. The jealous Musalmáns, doubtless, took care to breed the Christian's son in the most rigid notions of Moslem bigotry, and to imbue him with that hatred of the Nazarenes which became the Commander of the Faithful: and as a Fátemite, (or rather a *soi-disant* Fátemite,) the eventual participators in the divided Khiláfat, he would naturally become acquainted with the prejudices and controversies which divided and convulsed the Muhammadan world. All this, acting upon a mind wild, reckless, fickle, inconstant, perhaps partially deranged, yet without generosity, produced a reign at once whimsical and cruel. Azeez Bílláh dying at Bilbais at the age of forty-three, Abú-Alí-Mansúr was saluted Khalíf, by the surname of Hákim Bíamr'-Illáh, at Bilbais, on the afternoon of Tuesday the 29th Rhamadan, A. H. 386. He was born at the palace of

Cairo on the night of Thursday 23rd Rebia the 1st, and was consequently eleven years five months and six days old when he ascended the pulpit of Cairo.

Early as maturity is attained in the East, this age was as yet too tender to be entirely independent; and it was not for three or four years from this time that he began his career of blood and caprice by the deposition and execution of his prime minister. From this time his character began to display itself, and he proceeded to the extravagances which distinguish and disgrace his administration. His first act bore the affectation of humility (not an uncommon feature in similar characters): he pretended to revive the simplicity of the early Khalífs, and forbade the titles Said-na (our Lord) or Moollah-na (our Master) to be applied to him, contenting himself with that of Commander of Believers. All who disobeyed this rule were to be put to death without trial. In the year 391, being now sixteen years of age, he began to ride on horseback about the city, and was splendidly entertained by the citizens. The spirit of jealousy and suspicion so characteristic of the Moslem now induced him to publish some vexatious orders: he forbade that women should quit their houses at night, and desired that no man should remain in his shop during the night, but all retire to their houses. In the following years, his cruelty and zeal led him to put to death several of his ministers and a great multitude of other individuals, and to build the great mosque or *jami*, Báb-Al-Fotúh (Gate of the Victories). In the year 395 he manifested his cruelty towards the Jews and Christians, and his whimsical scruples respecting fermented liquors. He seems also to have borrowed and believed some of the prohibitory clauses of the Pentateuch. He commanded all Jews and Christians to wear the badges which distinguished them from Musalmáns, and ordered that none should eat the herb melookhia, or the rocket, or certain others. He extended his prohibition to all shell-fish; and commanded that no ox or bullock (unless attacked by disease, infirmity, or accident) should be killed, except only at the feast of sacrifices. He forbade the sale or manufacture of the beer, or liquor, called *Fokka*. He ordered that no one should enter the baths without drawers; that no woman should on any account appear with the face uncovered; and that fish without scales should neither be caught nor sold. All these ordinances were not suffered to remain inactive; they were vigorously enforced; and many received the bastinado for neglecting them.

The Khalíf's caprice now took a theological turn. He commanded curses and imprecations against the three first Khalífs, Abú Bekr, Omar, and Othmán, to be inscribed upon the principal mosques, shops, taverns, and cemeteries: he enjoined his subjects to write and paint these curses in different colours upon various places. By this he unfolded his inclinations for the sect of Alí. One of these tenets was certainly flattering; that which regards the Khalíf or Imám, as the immediate personification or representative of the Deity upon earth, and offers the veneration due to so divine a Being. Hákim's subjects took the hint, and rushed in crowds to proffer themselves of the Khalíf's sect. Two days in the week were appointed for their initiation at the palace; and it is recorded that several of the eager neophytes perished in the crowd. His restless mind had taken an unfortunate direction, and he was haunted by the idea that illicit intrigues were going on. He desired that no buying or selling, no traffic of any kind, should be carried on in the streets after sunset; nay, that no one should presume even to be seen there: in consequence the streets were deserted. His zeal now flamed against the forbidden liquor: he caused all casks and vessels containing wine to be broken, and the contents spilt. The Copts, who generally fill the offices of clerks, or scribes, and who, as Christians, had no doubt often violated the wine-prohibiting statute, were struck with dismay; but the capricious Khalíf granted them an amnesty and indemnity. He now ordered all dogs to be slain; and an immense slaughter ensued. Still dwelling upon his notion of the prevalence of intrigues, his suspicions fell upon his Rikabee, or running-footmen, as probable means of intercommunication. Of these poor creatures many were executed; but, probably convinced of his mistake, he pardoned the rest. He commanded that no one should enter the gates of Cairo on a saddle; and that no persons who let out asses for hire should presume to enter with their beasts: no one, whether on foot or horseback, was permitted to pass by his palace. He now proceeded to a more dangerous exercise of caprice; he killed the Cádí, and burnt him, and beheaded a number of eminent persons. A revolt soon followed, under the standard of Abú Rakwa, who asserted that he was of the lineage of Ommia, the deposed branch of the Khalífs. This general defeated several of Hákim's armies, but was at length defeated and slain by Abú-Fadl-Ibn-Saleh. This revolt recalled Hákim to some moderation. He ordered that the imprecations and curses against the first Khalífs should be effaced.

Internal calamities now troubled the Khalíf. The Nile, upon which the fertility and subsistence of Egypt depends, did not rise high enough to inundate a sufficient portion of the country. To satisfy popular clamour, he confiscated the property of the Christian churches, and burnt a number of crosses before the door of the jámi, or great mosque. In spite of this, the lowness of the Nile continuing, he ordered public prayers, and forbade all public assemblies, all promenades for pleasure on the banks of the river, and all sale of inebriating liquors. To conciliate the Sonnites (or Anti-Alíites) still more, he published a Declaration of Toleration, by which he permitted perfect liberty of conscience as regarded the various modes of performing the Five Prayers, the Funeral Prayer, and the Summons of the Muezzins. He ordered that no one should pronounce curses against the first Khalífs. He declared that all this was done from a sense of gratitude, on account of a lowering in prices. Still further to show his gratitude, he destroyed a number of churches, and gave up one to plunder. His jealous suspicions were excited against the eunuchs, clerks, and Sclavons. (The Sclavons, or Slavi, were probably the descendants of those Sclavonians who were driven out of Spain by the Visigoths in the fifth century.) Of these he killed numbers, having first amputated their hands, from the middle of the arm, by a hatchet, upon a block. He executed his victorious general, Fadl-Ibn-Saleh. His fury now exceeded all bounds: he destroyed the Church of the Holy Sepulchre at Jerusalem, which, however, he subsequently rebuilt. He established a court to take possession of, and administer, the property of those whom he had put to death; of which he was sometimes capriciously liberal. Many were publicly exposed, and beaten, for having in their possession beer, the herb melookhia, or shell-fish. He renewed his severity towards the Jews and Christians, and destroyed the monastery Daír-Al-Kasr. The general consternation, and the flight of several chiefs, did not arrest his career. His bigotry and jealousy continued; the orders against inebriating liquors were rigorously executed; many clerks, eunuchs, and *valets-de-chambre* were executed. He prohibited all pleasure-boats on the canal, and stopped up all windows, gates, or openings, that overlooked the water. Many were exposed, paraded, and whipped for selling fish without scales. His folly was unaffected by a revolt, in which the Emir of Mecca was saluted Khalíf; which however came to nothing. He forbade the importation or sale of dried grapes (raisins), and threw a great quantity into the Nile, or burnt them. He commanded that no woman should visit even her nearest relatives. Pleasure-parties upon the banks of the Nile were forbidden. No fresh grapes were permitted to be sold, except in portions of four pounds' weight at one time at most. Their importation was prohibited. Quantities were thrown into the streets, to be trodden under foot, or cast into the Nile. All the vines near Cairo were cut down, and directions sent to the different provinces, enjoining a similar proceeding.

A. H. 403, the Khalíf commanded the unhappy Christians to dress in their distinguishing habits; to bear crosses of wood, five pounds in weight, a cubit (18 inches) wide, and the same thick; to ride upon mules and asses only; to use wooden saddles, covered with black leather, and without ornament; to wear girdles around their waists; to retain no Moslem in their service, and never to purchase either a man or woman slave. In consequence of these rigorous measures many became Musalmáns. Hákim ordered several persons to be beaten for infringing the precepts of the Korán in playing at chess. Christian churches were every where destroyed and plundered. He desired that no one should kiss the ground before him, or kiss his hand or stirrup. He lowered his titles to yet greater simplicity, and forbade timbrels or trumpets to be played before his palace. His extravagance, as he approached the end of his reign, seems reducible to no conceivable motives. He became profusely liberal. He affected frankness, plainness, and simplicity. Completely reversing his former conduct, he commanded that all who cursed the first Khalífs should be beaten. He began to walk frequently about the town, by night and by day, often unattended. The Jews, as though not sufficiently outraged and degraded, were now commanded to wear little bells around their necks. Hákim forbade astrology to be spoken of, (a natural measure in a hated tyrant, whose death was earnestly desired,) banished all astrologers, and prohibited fortune-telling, or occult charms for the discovery of stolen goods.

At this time some feeling of remorse appears to have affected his mind, and he restored the lands he had confiscated. An instance of his capriciousness, or insanity, is recorded as occurring about this time. Offended with a certain Káid, or noble, and his secretary, he cut off both the hands of the latter, and one of the hands of the Káid himself. Changing his mind, he attempted to make amends to the Káid by sending him presents of gold and rich dresses; but, again returning to his first feelings, he then cut out his tongue. An instinctive feeling of insecurity now prompted several measures, but was insufficient to restrain the effects of his insane prejudices. He suppressed several imposts. Then again, enraged with the canine race as unclean, he ordered another massacre of dogs. He began to promenade more frequently on horseback, in order to observe if his orders were obeyed. He renewed his decrees prohibiting the appearance of women in the streets. Finding, probably, that these decrees were evaded, he shut up the women's baths, and enjoined the shoemakers not, for the future, to make or sell women's shoes. In a fit of motiveless liberality (and indeed all his actions were destitute of intelligible motive) he manumitted many slaves. Perhaps, however, this was done in order to secure friends in the event of a popular insurrection; and, to crown his absurdities, he, to the utter astonishment of the grave Moslem, paraded the city, both by night and by day, six times on horseback, once on an ass, once in a litter, once in a boat on the Nile; each time without his turban. This last practice proved fatal to him. Having, one night, promenaded as usual, being upon an ass, and accompanied by two attendants, (two of the same Rikabee or running-footmen against whom his rage had been directed some years before,) he arrived, towards morning, at a sepulchre, (قبر القفاعي or القفاعي *Al Kopháee*, Pococke,) near which was a fountain. Here, the men asserted, the Khalíf sent them back to the city. Not returning the whole of the ensuing day, his attendants proceeded, in the evening, to search for their master. They proceeded as far as the mountain Asfán (عسفان) and there saw the ass on which Hákim had been riding, with the fore-legs cut through, but still saddled and bridled. Following the marks of footsteps, they arrived at a small lake, or piece of water, by the side of which were lying the Khalíf's clothes, consisting of seven woollen vests, which had evidently been stripped from his body at once, and not separately, and in which were found rents and holes, evidently caused by the thrusts of poignards. Satisfied of the death of their master, the attendants returned to Cairo. This event happened A.H. 411, when Hákim was thirty-seven years old, and had reigned twenty-five.

The character of this Khalíf scarcely admits of accurate description. He is said to have been liberal and generous: he was skilled in astronomy, and indeed appears to have possessed some abilities, although deformed and perverted by his lively and restless inconstancy and caprice. Our indignation at his cruelties may be tempered by compassion, if we admit, what was probably the fact, that he suffered under a partial derangement of mind. He resembles, in many respects, Peter of Castile, and Paul of Russia; and, like them, forms an example of the disastrous effects, both to the governors and the governed, of that jealous despotism which makes no provision for the possible mental incapacity of the monarch. The contrivers and perpetrators of this assassination are not known. Makrízí tells us, that the imputation of fratricide was thrown upon his sister: but he denies that the report was well-grounded; and, on the contrary, declares that in the reign of Hákim's son and successor, a man, taken prisoner for some crime, confessed himself the assassin of the Khalíf. Being asked the motive of this murder, he replied, that he was induced by the glory of God and the good of Islám; and when requested to declare how he slew Hákim, he replied, "Thus!" and at the same time stabbed himself with a dagger to the heart. Both these accounts are reconcileable. Hákim's sister assumed the regency after his death, in the minority of his infant son—a proof, in an Eastern country, of the possession of remarkable talents—and by her arrangements contributed to heal the wounds that Hákim's absurd policy had inflicted. Nothing can be more probable than that she may have concerted with the chiefs of Egypt the means of the removal of so ruinous a tyranny. We may hope also, that self-preservation decided or originated the resolution of the princess to take advantage of the imprudent habits of her brother, and to employ the hand of some secret unsuspected assassin. That fickle and unreasonable jealousy which had long tortured Hákim's unhappy subjects may have appeared, to an acute mind, to be gradually verging towards his own family and Harem. In such a contingency, a sad alternative alone remained, and the doom of death must be endured or inflicted. It is one of the many blessings of

Christianity and civilization, that most of those occasions are, by their prevalence, removed, when men are called upon to become either the perpetrators or the victims of crime.

Page **463**. There is much in the historical traditions of nations to lead us to the conclusion that the mythological religion professed by most of them is a superaddition to a simpler system. The Hindú religion is not so ancient as is sometimes supposed: the Cingalese, Chinese, Tibetians, Tartars, &c. practise rites more recent even than those of the Hindús. This simpler system, which formed the groundwork of superstitions successively engrafted, was probably founded upon the adoration of the elements, and was in effect an atheistical confusion of nature with God. The Cingalese and Chinese, as well as the Buddhists, &c. still assert this terrible principle. It was the principle of the old philosophers and of the Eleusinian Mysteries. Perhaps in this chiefly consisted the first grand defection of men from truth, both before and after the Flood. Perhaps also, the principle of distinction and separation may have been at first divinely implanted in the minds of men, as a means of enabling them to separate between right and wrong, sacred and profane; and when men forsook God and truth, they either rejected the principle altogether, or disjoined it from its intended object, perverting it to sanction castes and customs, instead of moral obedience. The system of *feudality* bears some resemblance to the system of castes and distinctions. It is remarkable that feudal institutions prevail in Hindostan among the Rajpoots. Perhaps the system may have been introduced in Europe by means of the Muhammadan Spaniards.

Page 476. Abú Sufián entreated, it is said, of Muhammad three favours :—That he would grant him the command of his army ; that he would appoint his son Moáwiyah secretary ; and that he would marry his second daughter, having already married one. Muhammad agreed to all these, except the *last*.

Page 477. It is curious, that a different phrase is used in expressing nominal conversion to Muhammadanism, and sincere conversion. Of one who merely embraces Islám, it is said سلم "he hath become Moslem ;" but of the same man it may subsequently be observed that احسن اسلامه "he hath made good his faith sincere." Muhammad was satisfied with the first ; but intercourse with him often led to the second step. Many of the Koraish, for good reasons, thus cordially embraced that which had at first been forced upon them. There is a passage in the fifth chapter of the following translation, which asserts the descent of some verses *after* the decease of Muhammad. Perhaps this instance is not singular ; and many alterations may have been made.

Page 478. The account of the conversion of the renowned Khálid, given by the author of 'The History of the Afghans,' (Dorn's Translation, Part i. p. 27.) but quoted by him from an Arabian work, exhibits this warrior as acknowledging his motives with sufficient frankness :—" I contrived all means to lay violent hands on the prophet, but was unable to effect this design ; a circumstance that led me to the conviction that God was his protector, and that he would soon overcome us, and the Kuraish lose their whole power and strength. When peace had been restored between them and the prophet, I was well aware that I could not take refuge with the Abyssinian monarch Najáshi, he being attached to Muhammad; and that if I repaired to Heraclius, the emperor of Rúm and Shám, this prince would tender to me either the Jewish or Christian religion; one of which I should be under the necessity of embracing, although quite averse to them both. I was thus in a state of suspense; and on the prophet performing the pilgrimage, I left Mecca. When he had finished the ceremony, he inquired of my brother, who had turned Musalmán, where Khálid was; which induced my brother to send me a letter, as follows:—'Dear Brother, I am greatly astonished that thou hast not yet embraced the faith of Islámism; and when the prophet asked, Where is Khálid? I replied, God perhaps may bring him hither. When the prophet said, Khálid is not of that race, that the truth of Islám should remain concealed from him: if he should become a Moslem, and exert his bravery against the infidels and idolaters, he would fare much better, and I myself would receive him before any other. Make haste, therefore, dear brother, to partake of this happiness and blessing, for thou hast already lost much good from not knowing the value of the Islám.' On this letter being handed over to me, I felt great compunction at my former life: my inclination to the Islám grew stronger, and the idea of meeting the prophet pervaded me with joy; in consequence of which I set out for Mecca, and thence proceeded to Medína,"—(where Muhammad received him with open arms).

Ibid. Paley admits the genuineness of the Korán; but nothing can be more doubtful. Muhammad's reveries were only partially written, being partly committed to memory: his scribes are plainly intimated to have been unfaithful.

The loose sheets of the transcribed portion were entrusted to Hafsa, one of the prophet's widows. Abú Bekr published the first edition, said to be incomplete and defective. Othmán called in all the copies, and published a new one. Very many other circumstances throw doubt upon the matter. Since, however, the Korán contains few facts, it is of little moment whether the oracular dulness of Muhammad, or of his interpolating scribes, preponderate. After the capture of Mecca, and the appointment of Moáwiyah as secretary, the style of the Korán is, in the main, more intelligible and elegant. The doctrine also varies.

Page 479. The story of Muhammad's epilepsy, or falling sickness, although so indignantly slighted by some writers, is nevertheless to be inferred from Abulfeda. (Gagnier's Abulfeda, p. 9.)

Page 480. The instructive and amusing author of 'Hajji Baba of Ispahan' introduces the hypocritical Imám of Kom, asserting, that if he were willing to expose himself to as many risks and dangers as Muhammad did, he might become as eminent a prophet as the son of Abdallah; for that impudence conquered every difficulty. This assertion hints at the secret of the prophet's success. It proceeded from a bold imposture addressed to a pre-existing state of thought and feeling, aided by some concurring favourable circumstances of time, place, and opportunity.

Page 485. Muhammadanism, as a religion, prevails chiefly in Turkey and Africa. In Persia it can scarcely be said to be held sincerely and *bona fide*. In both cases, however, an accurate knowledge of Muhammadan controversy might be a means of exciting discussion, whether among the zealous or the indifferent; the one permitting it from motives of pride, the other from those of curiosity.

Al Khidr, or *St. George*. (Page 128 and 406.)

The Musalmán notions respecting *Al Khidr* present a curious intermixture of Judaic and Christian tradition. He is the same as our *St. George;* but as the spirit of Elijah re-appeared in St. John the Baptist, so also (say the Muhammadans) did the soul of the zealous *Phinehas* return to the re-animated body of the holy and youthful warrior George. Al Khidr and Elijah are therefore represented as companions, being alike in zeal, and alike partakers of the privilege of transmigration. Al Khidr is moreover said, by some, to have drank of the water of immortality, and to be still living—a fable resembling that of the Wandering Jew. He is mentioned in the Korán, and is said to have convinced Moses of the justice of providential retribution in a very practical manner. The story is the original source of the poem of 'The Hermit,' by Parnell.

The name of Al Khidr, (الخَضِر) "the *Green* One," bears an evident affinity to that of George. Γεώργιος, the adjective of *τὸ γεώργιον* and *ὁ γεωργὸς*, *husbandry* and *the husbandman*, flows from the compound verb which expresses the idea of working the earth, which is clothed with verdure. George is therefore derived from the earth, that produces, and Al Khidr, from the *green* herbage produced. George is a *Christian* name, signifying "the object of God's husbandry;" a beautiful allusion to John xv. 1. and 1 Cor. iii. 9. The Musalmáns always regard the two names as referring to one and the same person, and religiously respect the images and ensigns of St. George, whenever they fall in their way. His martial character is naturally attractive to them; and they pretend that he was a professor of Islám.

It may appear surprising that the very existence of a saint so popular in the time of Muhammad, that he was incorporated into his system of religion, should have been subsequently questioned, and the Greek church accused of venerating an airy phantom, a mere allegory and abstraction; yet, since the Reformation, several writers, among the last of whom is the celebrated Dr. Byrom, have denied that there ever was a St. George, the trophy-bearing martyr, whom, at one time, all Asia and the world respected. A greater number, however, perceiving the absurdity of this hypothesis, have rescued St. George from the limbos of possible existences, and restored him to a rank among actual objects; but they have inflicted a deeper injury upon him than the others, and have confounded the Christian martyr of Lydda with the Arian intruder of Alexandria.

The matter is, however, sufficiently clear, if we consult authorities and records which approximate more nearly in place and time to the scene and date of the event, instead of first examining later traditions. The legend of the Greek church respecting St. George, as published by Simon Metaphrastes, asserts that St. George was born in Cappadocia, of noble parents, who educated him in the Christian religion, which they professed. His father being killed fighting bravely with the enemies of Christ, he removed with his mother to Palestine, where he had great riches. There becoming a soldier, he was soon raised successively by Diocletian to the rank of *tribunus militum* (colonel), and *comes* (count, or member of the war-council). Coming to court at the age of twenty years, he opposed, in open senate, the persecuting decree of the emperor against the Christians.

For this he was tortured and beheaded at Lydda, April 23, A.D. 290. Such is the legend; erroneous, no doubt, in some details, but confirmed by sufficient testimony as to the leading facts.

A book written by St. Ambrose, entitled 'Liber Præfationum,' and not now extant, is quoted by several very ancient writers. The following extract relates to St. George: "Georgius, Christi miles fidelissimus, dum Christianismi professio tegeretur, solus inter Christicolas intrepidus, Dei Filium confessus est; cui tantam constantiam gratia Divina concessit, ut et tyrannicæ potestatis præcepta contemneret, et innumerabilium non formidaret tormenta pœnarum." "George, that most faithful soldier of Christ, who, at a time when the profession of Christianity was kept concealed, was the only one of the adorers of Christ who fearlessly confessed the Son of God; unto whom such constancy did Divine grace grant, that he both scorned the injunctions of the tyrant's power, and also shrunk not from the sufferings of innumerable tortures." *Gelasius*, A. D. 492, (one of the Popes,) complains of some superfluous and unfitting expressions in the lives of saints, and mentions that, among others, the passion of St. George, who, he affirms, is commonly venerated, has also been corrupted. *Childebert*, son of Clovis, who began to reign A. D. 515, founded a monastery in honour of St. Vincent, and deposited there some relics of St. George, by whom, tradition says, St. Vincent had been converted. The Emperor *Justinian* founded a church at Lydda in honour of St. George. *Venantius Fortunatus*, a Christian poet, nearly contemporary with Justinian, wrote an inscription for a shrine of St. George:—

"Martyris egregii pollens micat aula Georgî,
Cujus in hunc mundum spargitur altus honor.

Carcere, cæde, siti, vinclis, fame, frigore, flammis,
Confessus Christum, duxit ad astra caput:
Qui virtute potens, Orientis in arce sepultus.
Ecce sub occiduo cardine præbet opem.
Ergo memento preces et reddere dona, viator.
Obtinet hic meritis, quod petit alma fides.
Condidit antistes Sidonius ista decenter
Proficiant animæ quæ nova templa suæ."

Gregory of Tours, A. D. 596, mentions miracles wrought by St. George:—"Multa de Georgio martyre miracula cognovimus;" meaning, no doubt, that he had *heard* of them. There is a story, of this date, to the effect, that some men, carrying relics of St. George and other saints, came to a place, on the frontiers of Limosin, where a few priests, having a little chantry or oratory of boards, did daily pour out their devotions to the Lord. The men begged for a night's lodging, and were welcomed. Next morning, not being able to lift up their knapsacks when about to depart, they concluded it to be the will of God that they should give some relics to the priests; which having done accordingly, the difficulty was removed. Some miraculous relics of St. George also, about this time, were preserved in a village of La Maine. Theodorus Syceotes died under Heraclius. The legends say that St. George usually appeared to him, taught and directed him during his life. He is, no doubt, the man mentioned in our translation as carrying a communication from the Khalíf Moáwiyah to St. George. Vincentius, bishop of Beauvais, a very learned man, confirms the legend which represents St. George as suffering martyrdom in the Dacian persecution at Diospolis or Lydda. Usuardus, a scholar of Alcuin, A. D. 812, thus writes in his 'Martyrology:'—"The ninth of the kalends of May (April 23rd). This day took place in Diospolis (Lydda), a city of Persia, the passion of the martyr St. George, that glorious champion renowned for miracles; the acts of whose passion, although they be numbered amongst writings apocryphal, yet doth the church of God reverently honour his most illustrious martyrdom amongst the diadems of the martyrs. (We remark, that writers of this period generally consider Palestine as under *Persian* dominion, rather than *Grecian*, which is not far from the truth.) Notgerus, (afterwards canonized,) a monk of St. Gal, in Switzerland, A. D. 912, confirms this legend. The Venerable Bede reports the same. Pope Zacharias, A. D. 742, built a church and monastery to St. George, and enshrined his head,* which had been presented to him by the Venetians. A Saxon MS., in the Library of C. C. College, Cambridge, quoted by Selden, and said to be about the age of St. Dunstan, asserts that St. George was martyred by Datianus the emperor. Nicephorus Callistes, a Greek, A. D. 1305, in the reign of Andronicus the elder, confirms the usual Greek tradition. The Magdeburg Centuriators admit it; in which they are followed by our Fox.

We have passed over an earlier testimony. Adamsianus, A. D. 690, testifies that Arculfus, after his return from the East, "etiam nobis de quodam martyre, Georgio nomine, narrationem contulit."

The scene of the martyrdom of St. George is invariably laid in Lydda or Diospolis, near (it is about three miles from) Ramlah, or Ramula, in Palestine. In addition to the above authorities, Anna Comnena speaks of Ramlah as the place near whereunto the great martyr George suffered; and Johannes Cotonias, in his 'Itinerarium Hierosolymitanum,' observes,—" Mox urbem antiquissimam Diospolim

* See note 1. *infra*.

olim nuncupatam, distantem a Rama (Ramlah) tria millia passuum, eminus conspeximus. Hæc Divi Georgii martyrio et tumulo, et imprimis Petri apostoli prædicatione et miraculis celebris est; nunc solo æquata. Præter pauca Maurorum tuguriola solum superest templum in martyris memoriam, a Ricardo, Angliæ rege, ut aliqui putant, restauratum super fundamenta antiquioris delubri a Cæsare Justiniano erecti." This church of Justinian had been destroyed by the Saracens, who were apprehensive that Godfrey's soldiers would make use of the great blocks of timber belonging to that fabric, in the siege of Jerusalem. Lydda also occupies a place in the traditions and veneration of the Musalmáns; no doubt, from its connexion with the memory of St. George.

This concurring stream of tradition, as to time and place, would seem to establish not only the existence of St. George, but also some distinguishing marks of peculiar personal identity. They, however, who maintain that George the Arian, of Alexandria, is the person referred to, rest mainly upon the following positions:—Jacobus de Voragine, archbishop of Genoa, A. D. 1290, styled by Ludovicus Vives "homo ferrei oris, plumbei cordis," (a man iron-faced and leaden-hearted,) wrote, among other works, the 'Legenda Aurea,' (Golden Legends,) a book teeming with absurdities. In his Legend of St. George, he tells the story of the dragon slain, and the princess rescued, by the military saint (the dragon being supposed to be the symbol of heresy, and the princess of the church). Whence he borrowed this tale, is not known, although a faint tradition exists that *Berytus* in Syro-Phœnicia was the scene of the exploit. Again, in the 'Acts of the Passion of St. George,' there is an account of a conference between George and a certain wizard named Athanasius. This legend is assuredly ancient, and is evidently an Arian version of the contests between George and Athanasius of Alexandria, into the see of which city George intruded himself during the exile of the orthodox archbishop or patriarch. These are the main grounds which have induced some writers to imagine that the Catholic Church has erroneously honoured a corrupt and dissevered member. They are but very weak grounds. If we have some regard to perspective in throwing back our eye upon historical evidence, and do not confound all antiquity in commingled anachronism, we cannot but see where the truth lies. The 'Golden Legend' is of trifling authority even as a record of tradition; and the interpolated Acts were evidently corrupted by the Arians. James de Voragine admitted every tale he met with; and no monuments of antiquity are more liable to corruptions than local Formularies and Lives of Saints. Against this evidence we may confidently urge a successive unbroken tradition, which, in many circumstances of time and place, is wholly inconsistent with the pretensions of the Alexandrian heretic. It is remarkable that St. George was especially honoured in France and Spain,* at the very time when the Arian controversy (especially in the latter country) was in the minds of every one. Is it likely that Catholics should at that season honour so zealous a champion of error as was the Alexandrian George? Is it probable that *Justinian*, so orthodox an emperor, would found a church in honour even of a suspected saint? Modern pride must not presume that there was then no power of discrimination among men. What would be more improbable, than that the East and West, amidst the warmth of the Arian dissensions, should unite in venerating the

* Jacobus de Voragine wrote a history of Lombardy. May not the story of the Dragon and George have been a legend of the Vandal Arians?

implacable enemy of the faithful Athanasius? Why should the tradition end in *Lydda*, and not in Alexandria? Besides, it is justly observable, that George, being a *Christian* name, was probably borne by others before George of Alexandria; for it is not to be imagined that so significant a name, derived from Scripture, was never assumed until the beginning of the fourth century. George the Arian was killed A. D. 361, and St. George suffered A. D. 290. May we not conjecture that the parents of the Alexandrian George gave him the name of a recent and especially illustrious martyr, who perhaps was himself by no means the first who bore the appellation in question?

A curious extract from Epiphanius, although it has been advanced by the advocates of the Arian George, will, on the contrary, distinctly show what were the sentiments of that orthodox and zealous Father respecting the character of the Alexandrian *soi-disant* prelate. And these sentiments were expressed at a time when the real St. George was the object of universal regard and veneration. It can scarcely be thought that Epiphanius was either ignorant of the prevailing feeling, or conceived that the Arian was the object of the honour that George every where received. The passage in question is found in the account of the heresy of the *Anomoioi*,* (Κατὰ Ἀνομοιῶν,) a branch of the Arian sect, which said that the Son was of *like* substance, not of the *same* substance, with the Father. (Epiph. adv. Hæres. Basil. 1540. Græcè, p. 388. Hæres. 76.)—"There are again certain called *Anomoioi* (Ἀνομοιοῖ). These are of recent origin, and their ringleader was one Aëtius, a deacon, so constituted, on account of that same idle talk, by George of Alexandria; (that George) who became bishop of the Arians and Meletians; and who, in the time of Julian (as I have before

* See note 2. *infra.*

shown), was carried in procession about the city, mounted on a camel; having been before that straitly imprisoned, and exposed to many sufferings from the Greeks. He, having been carried about in procession, (as I said,) was beaten with clubs, and dragged along almost the whole of the city. Thus he died; and, after his death, was burnt, and, together with many bones of beasts of burden and other animals, was reduced to ashes, and then scattered to the winds, to be swept away. Since he thus met with his end, one might be inclined to say of one who finished his life in such a manner, Was he not a martyr, since he endured these things from the Greeks? Now, if on his part the contest had been for the truth, and if these things had been inflicted upon him by the Grecians from malice, and on account of his confession of Christ, then assuredly he would have been ranked among the martyrs, and those not the least of martyrs; but the matter objected against him related not to a confession of Christ, but to the extreme violence which, during his so-called episcopate, he all along exercised against the city and the people, in seizing from individuals the property inherited from their parents. And (in saying this) we calumniate not the man; since, in fact, many things were committed by him amongst the Alexandrians. (They report) both how he took possession of all the nitre, and how he designed to assume the management of the marshes of papyrus and reeds, and the salt-pools, in order to convert them to his own advantage; so also his disgraceful means of livelihood. He sought after gain by every expedient; nor was he regardless of the most trifling matters. He had some intention of limiting the *biers* used for the bodies of the departed to a certain number, and that no bodies of deceased persons should be carried forth but by persons appointed by himself. He entertained many strangers, not for the sake of hospitality, but, as they say, for the purpose of revenue; for if any one of them buried a body by himself, he incurred danger; thus some profit accrued unto him from every single body brought out for burial. As to all the instances of luxury and other wrong proceedings, as well as the cruelty with which he conducted himself, I am silent. On account of all this, therefore, the sons of the Alexandrians, but especially the Greeks, no longer masters of their anger, brought him to this end. I have already had occasion to speak of these matters; how that, when news of Constantine's decease was proclaimed, the Alexandrians instantly killed him in the above manner. My present subject has nothing more to do with him, but with Aëtius, who was by him ordained deacon."

This passage would appear nearly decisive. The hesitating query introduced,—"Was he not a martyr?" might bear relation to some superstition respecting the Alexandrian George then creeping into the church, which, probably, soon died away, or is traceable only in the Apocryphal Acts of St. George; but the honour paid to the real Saint was in the time of Epiphanius universal and undisputed, and cannot but have been known to him. Had any undue regard then been offered to the Arian oppressor, Epiphanius would have, no doubt, indignantly exposed and reproved it. The character of George the Arian was also, no doubt, well known to the "concordant numerosity of many bishops" throughout the world, who would have stopped any improper or unauthorised proceedings with respect to him. Moreover, George the Arian was a native ("natus ut ferebatur," Ammian. Marcell.) of Epiphania in Cilicia, not of Cappadocia,* although he dwelt some time in the latter province.

* These provinces were ill reported of:—Τρια καππα κακιστα, Καππαδοκια, Κιλικια, Κρητη.—*Suidas.*

In concluding, therefore, that St. George was a different person from the Alexandrian; that he was a military confessor, and was martyred at Lydda near Ramlah; we shall judge most probably and most rationally. Perhaps, the real cause of the doubts that were ever entertained upon the subject may be found in the dissatisfaction felt at the meagre account, the scanty particulars, recorded of a martyr especially honoured; but this incompleteness is not uncommon in the history of ancient events. The leading particulars are deemed sufficient; and we are scarcely able to judge of the precise degree of merit in a martyr, even under circumstances similar to those with which we *are* acquainted in the case of St. George. That merit may have been understood and appreciated in early ages by those who knew no more of the details than we do. There may have been times and occasions when Christianity was secretly held by many,* and when an instance of the voluntary sacrifice of wealth, rank, and life, from the best motives, may have been of infinite service to the cause. Certain it is, that this Saint was regarded as a profitable example of bold piety; and although pleasing feelings are criminal if they degenerate into superstition, or are imposed as articles of belief, to the injury of important truths; yet that religious application of biography which introduced the examples of good men into the exercises of devotion may originally have been innocent and ennobling, and even effectually disjoined from undue creature-reverence.

St. George was not always represented on horseback. He is described by Theodorus Syceotes (who declared that he frequently conversed with his re-embodied ghost) as a fair young man with yellow hair. Raimondus de Agiles, in the *Gesta Dei per Francos*, speaks of a certain Peter, who saw

* See note 3. *infra*.

our Lord on the Cross, with St. Peter, St. Andrew, and "quendam magnum et spissum brumo colore et subcalvo, et magnis oculis,"—*a certain stout man, of a dark complexion, and great eyes,*—standing by. This turned out to be St. George; but from a curious romantic story it would appear that he was represented as a mounted knight in the thirteenth century. Nicephorus Gregorius, who wrote a history of the Grecian Emperors, from A. D. 1200 to 1344, about which time he is said to have died, has (Book VIII.) a story to the following effect:—Upon the first Saturday in Lent, the eve of the commemoration of the orthodox Emperors and Patriarchs, Theodore, logotheta generalis, (chief chancellor, or registrar,) attended, as usual, the sacred services from eve till midnight. Just at midnight, whilst I was standing by, and listening to the Doxology, some one enters from the emperor (Andronicus the elder), announcing to the chancellor that he had been alarmed by the loud neighing of a horse. Upon examination, it was found to proceed from a wall in the palace, which was in front of a chapel of the victorious Mother of God, whereon Paulus, a celebrated painter, had formerly portrayed the martyr George upon his horse. The chancellor, hastening to the emperor, found him much perplexed with the omen, and, to comfort him, assured him that St. George, by that sign, promised him success in his enterprises. "Not so," replied the emperor; "you know, as well as I, that when Baldwin, the Latin emperor, was beleaguered by my father, and the city taken, the same portent occurred." Baldwin began to reign A. D. 1227.

In the discussion respecting the identity of our Saint, there is some weight in the negative argument, that no instances are recorded or known of the imposition of false or heretical saints as objects of Catholic respect. After much labour, the puritan divines were able to discover two cases only, which they alleged as cases of spurious saintship. *Faustus Rhegiensis* seems to have been regarded with some reverence in certain parts of France, although never honoured universally or widely. He is accused of heresy as a Semi-Pelagian; but antiquity does not support the assertion. In replying to Pelagius, Faustus did not use violent terms; but there is no proof that his mild remonstrances savoured of heresy. It is well known that the appellation of Semi-Pelagian* has been sometimes incorrectly used by over-stating theologians, to discredit those who differ from them.† Another instance of a spurious saint is mentioned by Sulpitius Severus:—St. Martin of Tours‡ met with a little oratory, much frequented by superstitious people as the tomb of some martyr. Suspecting some imposture, St. Martin prayed that the truth might be manifested unto him. Upon this, a certain Shape, or Phantom, passed by, who declared that he was not a martyr, but a thief executed for his crimes. Surely this instance will prove that the intrusion of a saint into the church was not an easy matter; and that whatever might be the easy credulity of the people, their ecclesiastical superiors did not blindly sanction every popular superstition. An organized system of fraud did not at this time (5th and 6th centuries) prevail any where; and in the Eastern church, never. In subsequent ages, an allegory was superadded to the real history of St. George:—he is regarded as the personification of *Holiness*, one of the seven Christian virtues; and

* See note 4. *infra*.

† The *moral* character of several saints has been impugned, not perhaps unjustly. But we here allude to matters of *belief* in primary truths, the approvers of which do not seem to have attained reverence or honour *as saints* in the early ages. Pelagius was respected locally, but never canonized.

‡ See note 5. *infra*.

he is represented as victorious over the dragon-power of temptation. No doubt, this circumstance contributed to spread and confirm his reputation; and he is immortalized in the English language (having long before been adopted by English piety and chivalry) by Spenser, as the Red-Cross Knight, the chief champion of the divine Una, the indivisible church.

St. George is the patron saint of Portugal, Georgia, Genoa, Greece, &c.; but England especially claims him, and connects his Red Cross with her glories. Antonius Macedo, in a work whose strange title is 'De Diis Tutelaribus Orbis Christiani,'* quoted by Fabricius in Bibliograph. Antiquar. p. 264. says, "The general patrons of England are St. Mary and St. Peter; but in military matters, *St. George*." The latter is now, however, regarded as principal patron. The order of St. George of the Garter, at Windsor, instituted by Edward III., is the most noble Order of Europe. Richard I. had some intention of founding this Order. During a tedious siege, it occurred to him (by the suggestion of *St. George, as was the opinion*,) to institute an Order of select knights, who should wear on their legs a leather strap, such as he then held in his hand, in imitation of the Romans, who, by crowns and other marks of distinction, stirred up, and, as it were, caused to leap, the fervid bravery of the heart in their soldiers. The following epigram was written by Callicles, or by Cyrus Theodorus, upon a statue of St. George:—

Παῖς 'Αβραὰμ ὁ μάρτυς οὗτος ἐκ λιθῶν·—
Πλὴν εἰ τὶ σαρκὸς εἶχεν ἠρυθρωμένον,
'Εχιονώθη τοῦτο, λευκὸν εὑρέθη,
Μαρτυρικοῖς δρῶσιν ἐκπεπλομένον.

* See note 6. *infra*.

"Think it not marble, stranger; 'tis a son
Of Abraham's race, a life-blood nourished one,
Whose reddening flesh is blanch'd as white as snow,
Steep'd in the precious drops that from a martyr flow."

The following Iambics are prefixed to the commemoration of St. George, in the Greek Ritual:—

Ἐχθροὺς ὁ τέμνων Γεωργίος ἐν μαχαῖς
Ἑκὼν παρ' ἐχθρῶν τεμνέται διὰ ξίφους.
Ἧρε Γεωργίου εἰκάδι τριτάτῃ αὔχενα χαλκός·

"George, who in battle cut his enemies to pieces, was himself, unresistingly, by his foes cut to pieces by the sword. George was beheaded on the twenty-third."

The following prayers are addressed to St. George, in the Greek Ritual:—Ὡς τῶν αἰχμαλωτῶν ἐλευθερώτης, καὶ τῶν πτωχῶν ὑπεράσπιστης, ἀσθενοῦντων ἰατρὸς, βασιλέων ὑπερμάχε, Τροπαιόφορε, μεγαλόμαρτυς Γεώργιε, πρέσβευε Χριστῷ τῷ Θεῷ σωθῆναι τὰς ψύχας ἡμῶν.—"O mighty martyr George! Trophy-bearer! Thou who art the rescuer of warriors, the guardian of the poor, the physician of the sick, the champion of kings; be our mediator with Christ the God, that our souls may be saved!" In the Collects of the Roman office for April 23:—"Deus, qui nos beati Georgii martyris tui meritis et intercessione lætificas, concede propitius ut qui tua per eum beneficia poscimus, dono tuæ gratiæ consequamur per Dominum nostrum Jesum Christum."—"O God, who, by the merits and intercession of St. George thy blessed martyr, dost rejoice our souls, grant, we beseech thee, that those benefits which by him we crave, we may by the gift of thy grace obtain, through Jesus Christ our Lord." After the offering:—"Munera, Domine, oblata sanctifica, et, intercedente beato Georgio martyre tuo, nos per hoc a peccatorum nostrum maculis emunda, per J. C. D. N."—"Sanctify, O Lord, these gifts of oblation; and, by the intercession of the blessed George the martyr, cleanse us thereby from the contamination of our sins, through Jesus Christ our Lord." At the Post-Communion:—"Supplices te rogamus, omnipotens Deus, ut quos tuis reficis sacramentis, intercedente beato Georgio martyre tuo, tibi etiam placitis moribus dignanter tribuas deservire, per D. N. J. C."—"Almighty God, we humbly beseech thee to grant that we, who are refreshed by thy holy sacraments, may, by the intercession of thy blessed martyr Saint George, worthily serve thee in all ways of living well-pleasing unto thee, through Jesus Christ our Lord." (The Gospel is St. John xv. "Ego sum vitis vera," &c.; the Epistle, 2 Tim. iii. "Thou hast known my doctrine, *manner of life*, purpose," &c.) Collect from Sarum Missal: "Offerimus tibi, Domine, solemne sacrificium pro veneranda S. Georgii martyris tui passione, deprecantes clementiam tuam, ut per hæc S. S. mysteria, antiqui hostis tentamina, te triumphante, vincamus, et æternæ remunerationis te largiente sequamur, per, &c."—"We offer unto thee, O Lord, the solemn sacrifice (of praise and thanksgiving) for the venerated passion of Saint George the martyr; earnestly beseeching thy clemency, that, through these most holy mysteries, we, by thee made to triumph, may subdue the temptations of our old enemy, and of thy gift may obtain the eternal recompense of reward."

Page 537. note 1. Henry VII., in his will, mentions a piece of the true cross, and *a leg of St. George.* They were given to him by the Cardinal d'Amboise, and had been originally brought from Milan. He bequeaths them to his

Chapel in Westminster Abbey. They were probably destroyed at the Reformation.—See Brayley's 'Londiniana.'

Page 540. note 2. Κατὰ Ἀνομοιῶν, κ. τ. λ.

(*Epiph. adv. Hæres.* Græcè, Basil. 1544. Hæres. 76. p. 388.)

Ἀνόμοιοι πάλιν τινὲς εἶσιν καλουμένοι, οὗτοι δὲ πρόσφατοι· ἔσχον δὲ ἀρχηγὸν Ἀετίον, τινὰ διακόνον, πραχθέντα διὰ τὴν αὐτὴν φλυαρίαν ὑπὸ Γεωργίου τοῦ Ἀλεξάνδρεως, τῶν Ἀρειανῶν ἅμα Μελετίανων γεγονότος ἐπίσκοπου, καὶ ἐν χρόνοις Ἰουλίανου, ὡς ἄνω μοὶ προδεδήλωται, τὴν πόλιν πομπεύσαντος ὑπὸ καμήλου· καὶ πρῶτον μὲν πολλὰ ὑπὸ τῶν Ἑλληνῶν συγκλείσθεντος καὶ πεπονθότος. Πομπεύσαντος τε, ὡς ἔφην, καὶ ξυλοῖς παισθέντος, ἔπειτα δὲ συρέντος ὅλην σχέδον τὴν πόλιν· καὶ οὕτως ἀποθανόντος, καὶ μετὰ θανάτου καέντος, καὶ μετὰ πολλῶν ὀστέων κτηνῶν καὶ ζώων εἰς τέφραν συναχθέντος, καὶ μετεπεῖτα τοῖς ἀνεμοῖς ὑπ' αὐτῶν λικμηθέντος· καὶ οὕτως τὸ πέρας ἐσχηκότος, λέξειε δ' ἄν τις περὶ τοῦ οὕτως τε τελευτήσαντος, Οὔκουν ἐμαρτύρησεν, ὑπὸ Ἑλλήνων ταῦτα πέπονθως; Καὶ εἰ μὲν ὑπὲρ ἀληθείας αὐτῷ ἦν ὁ ἀγὼν, καὶ ὑπὸ Ἑλλήνων διὰ φθόνον καὶ τὴν εἰς Χριστὸν ὁμολογίαν τὰ τοιαῦτα αὐτῷ συμβέβηκεν, ὄντως ἐν μάρτυσι, καὶ οὐκ ἐν μικροῖς ἐτέτακτο· οὐκ ἦν δὲ τὸ αἴτιον διὰ τὴν εἰς Χριστὸν ὁμολογίαν, ἀλλὰ δι' ἥν, ἐν τῇ ἑαυτοῦ δηθὲν ἐπισκοπῇ καλουμένῃ, πολλὴν βίαν τὴν πόλιν τε καὶ τὸν δῆμον διέθετο, πῇ μὲν ἁρπάζων ἀπὸ ἀνθρώπους τὰ ὑπὸ τῶν γονέων αὐτῶν κληρονομήματα. Καὶ ἵνα μὴ διαβάλλομεν τὸν ἄνδρα, πολλὰ γὰρ ἐστὶ τὰ ὑπ' ἐκεινοῦ τοῖς Ἀλεξανδρεῦσι γενομένα, — πῶς μὲν τὴν νίτρον ἅπασαν ἐξέλαβε, — πῶς δὲ τὰ ἕλη τὰ τοῦ παπύρου καὶ τοῦ καλάμου, καὶ τὰς λίμνας τοῦ ἁλὸς διοίκειν, καὶ εἰς ἑαυτὸν ἀποφέρεσθαι ἐπενοήσεν. Ὡς πᾶσα αἰσχρότης βίου, κερδοῦς διὰ πολλῆς μηχανῆς ἄχρι, καὶ λεπτῶν πραγμάτων παρ' αὐτῷ οὐκ ἠμέλητο· ὡς τὰς κλίνας ἐπενοήσε τοῖς σώμασι τῶν ἐξοδεύοντων ποιῆσαι ἐν ἀρίθμῳ τινὶ, καὶ, ἄνευ τῶν ὑπ' αὐτοῦ ἐπιτεταγμένων, οὐκ ἐξεκομίζετο τὸ σῶμα τῶν τελευτούντων ἐπιπλεῖστον· δὲ τῶν ξενῶν, οὐ διὰ φιλοξενίαν, ἀλλὰ (καθὼς ἔλεγον) διὰ πορισμὸν βίωθη· εἴ τις γὰρ ἐθάπτε διὰ ἑαυτῶν σῶμα, κίνδυνον ὑφίστατο, οὕτως δὲ ὑφ' ἑκαστοῦ τῶν ἐκφερομένων κέρδος τι αὐτῷ προσεφέρεται. Καὶ σιωπῶ τὰ ἄλλα λέγειν ὅσα ὁ ἀνὴρ ἐν τρυφαῖς καὶ ἄλλοις ἐκομίζετο καὶ ἐν ἀπηνότητι. Διὰ γοῦν ταῦτα πάντα τὴν εἰς αὐτὸν μῆνιν ἠκρατηκότες Ἀλεξανδρεῶν παῖδες, Ἕλληνες δὲ μάλιστα, τουτῷ αὐτὸν διέθεντο τὸ τέλος. Ἐμοὶ δὲ γέγονε πρόφασις περὶ τουτῶν λέγειν, ὡς ἐνηχήθεντες τὴν τοῦ Κωνσταντίου τελευτὴν, εὐθὺς οὕτως αὐτὸν ἀπολέσαν οἱ Ἀλεξαιδρεῖς. Δι' οὐδὲν ἕτερον ἢ περὶ τούτου μοὶ γεγένηται ὑποθέσις, ἀλλὰ διὰ τὸν Ἀετίον, τοῦ ὑπ' αὐτοῦ καταστανθέντα διακόνον, κ.τ.λ.

Page 543. note 3. For some instructive remarks on early Christian martyrdom, see Bishop Kaye's Tertullian, p. 137 et seqq.

Page 545. note 4. Thus, for example, the followers of *Arminius* and *Wesley* have been very incorrectly termed Semi-Pelagians.

Page 545. note 5. The character of St. Martin of Tours has been justly impugned (see 'British Magazine'); but whatever credit we give to his assertion, this instance shows that the apotheosis of saints was not always unquestioned; and if Martin felt some jealousy at the worship paid to others, would not the accusation of heresy, which could be so directly proved, have been a ready expedient for un-canonizing the Arian George? The Arian controversy was still agitated, to a serious extent, in Martin's time. The Arian heretics generally held the dogma of the *similarity* as opposed to the *identity* of substance in the divine Persons of the Trinity. The Anomœi therefore probably professed this general belief with some modifications peculiar to themselves.

Page 546. note 6. Fabricius, in quoting this very curious work, cannot refrain from remarking, "Quis vero non miretur, vel indignetur, hos quoque qui Christianos se et solos ecclesiam esse gloriantur, tam apertè utroque hoc in genere invisa Deo, et improbata antiquis Christianis Ethnicismi vestigia legere, ut Antonius Macedo Lusitamus non dubitaverit, a. 1687. fol. Ulyssipone vulgari ingens volumen, quod inscripsit 'De Diis Tutelaribus Orbis Christiani.'"—It is to be hoped, that Antonius Macedo was rather an exaggerating hagiographist, than an authoritative divine.

For the materials of the above remarks the Translator is chiefly indebted to 'Selden's Titles of Honour,' 'Heylyn on St. George,' 'Pegge on St. George,' in the Archæologia, 'Gesta Dei per Francos,' 'Fabricius Bibl. Ant.' edit. 3rd, 1760, Epiphanius 'adv. Hæres.' &c. &c. and to the authorities referred to by some of the above.

Page 506. In the passage quoted from William of Tyre, the words "Dominicæ dispensationis memoriam" are rendered "memorials of the *stewardship* of the Lord;" but the translator, by a remark in 'Burton's Testimonies of the Anti-Nicene Fathers to the Divinity of Christ,' p. 70. 2nd ed. is led to imagine that the word "dispensatio" coincides with the Greek οἰκονομία, and may therefore mean the *Incarnation*, or, in a lower sense, the *ministry* of the Lord.

THE END.